Gathering the Light

Gathering the Light

Andrew Hain

Published by
Well Within Therapies
17 Acre Road
Kingston upon Thames
KT2 6EF
Telephone 020 8549 1784

British Library Cataloguing-in-Publication Data
A catalogue record for this book is available from the British Library

Disclaimer

The routines, methods, treatments and processes that are set out herein
are a figment of the author's imagination and described for the purposes
of the story only: they should not be practised.
All characters are fictional and any resemblance to anyone living or
dead is purely coincidental.

.

Cover Illustration: "Luss Sunset" by Andrew Hain Copyright © 2010

ISBN 978-0-9545446-3-8

Printed and bound by CPI Group (UK) Ltd, Croydon, CR0 4YY

Contents

Chapter 1: The Meal

It was mid afternoon and Myrta Cranstoun set about preparing the evening meal for herself, husband and son in her usual manner. She was soon to discover that the rest of her day was to be something other than usual. She went downstairs to her husband's small shop to ask what he'd like. Everet was a viander, a craftsman in meats of all kinds. He had a small shop with a preparation area at the rear, and he and his family lived in the three rooms above.

Unusually, Everet was hesitant, his mind seemingly in some far off place. "Everet," said Myrta sternly but gently, "the evening meal. What would you like me to prepare?"

"What?" said Everet, returning to the moment, beckoned by Myrta's voice. "The meal? Tonight? Well, er, um ...." And he fumbled about from one tray of meat to another in total confusion and indecision.

At last he settled on a piece of fresh brisket. "Here, take this," he said, handing the meat to Myrta. "I prepared this only this morning so it should cook very nicely."

"Would you like me to make soup with it too?" she asked.

"Oh, whatever you want to do," said Everet, almost disinterestedly. He seemed preoccupied with other matters so Myrta returned upstairs with the brisket to start her preparations.

"Aonghus," she called out to her son, "here are a few pennies: will you please go to the baker's for some crusty bread? I seem to have run out."

During her cooking Myrta was concerned about Everet's state of mind. It wasn't like him to be so absent minded or undecided. Indeed, she remarked to herself, he seemed totally disinterested in what was a normal daily occurrence about which he would be full of ideas.

Her musings ceased as her soup came to the boil, and she turned her full attention to ensuring that the meal was prepared without any undue carelessness or disaster.

*****

The evening meal in the Cranstoun household was eaten in silence. Everet Cranstoun introduced the practice early in his life, as he came to realise that the world, and all it contains, is as One. Everything that exists is connected, one to another and each to all. The Source is in all things and all things are in the Source.

The evening meal was a meditation in which the food was the focus. Textures and tastes blended together, the diverse becoming the all. Without one part there would be no All.

For his son, Aonghus, the concept was difficult to understand, and it took much practice to pass the meal time without a word being said. An inward journey is like a pilgrimage and is, first of all, the attitude of a mind firmly fixed within the heart. A periodic journey to the heart, particularly on a daily basis, is a good way of developing a mystical habit of mind. And so it was for young Aonghus, practice making perfect.

Words are distractions and detract from the mystical experience of inner silence. It is in the inner silence that self appreciation manifests.

That particular evening, at the due time, Myrta Cranstoun, wife and mother, served the meal as she always did, and all three took their places at the table.

"As we enter the silence," said Everet after they had settled into their places, "let us give thanks for what has been provided, and for the efforts of everyone who has been involved." This was Everet's usual form of Grace, and a signal that the meditation was about to begin. What was about to unfold would shock Myrta and Aonghus, although, Myrta, using hindsight, was aware that there had been signs during the day that everything was not as it should have been.

They were about halfway through the soup course when the silence was shattered by Everet roughly pushing his bowl across the table, slopping some of its remaining contents across the broad beams of dark wood. "I'm sorry," he said, agitated, "but we have to talk. This is too important to put off any longer."

Myrta was in some measure relieved because this afternoon's encounter with her husband had indicated that all wasn't well. Poor Aonghus. He was deeply into his inner silence, letting the fats and the juices of the brisket mingle with the water of the broth, and allowing the textures of the barley, carrots, peas and other vegetables in the soup to flow through his being. He was virtually at one with the soup and the crunch of the crusty bread when he was suddenly and rudely drawn back to the room. Whatever could have upset his father so?

"Today I had a visit from two very unsavoury characters," said Everet. "They came into the shop just after lunchtime, when everything quietens down. Just before you came downstairs, my dear. They said they had a business proposition for me. I told them I wasn't interested, but they insisted that I should hear what they had to say. Well, it wasn't very nice, and I am very concerned for all of us."

"What did they want?" asked Myrta.

"The first one, Ludley, I think he called himself," said Everet, "said he and his confederates had been watching my business over a period of time and were impressed at how successful it seemed to be. I told him that appearances can be deceptive, and if he looked closely he would realise that the shop provides for our basic needs. We do not make huge profits."

"Yes," agreed Myrta, "that's what we wanted. We set out to cover our own necessities, and provide a service and products at a fair price to everyone. That is our ethic."

"Correct," said Everet. "We have no need to charge unnecessarily high prices. We work according to Universal Law. Giving, receiving, sharing, caring. Well, this Ludley says that things will have to change. How so? I asked him. 'Your prices will need to rise,' he told me."

"Why should you raise your prices if there is no need?" asked Aonghus.

"Well, it seems that Ludley and his fellow rogue Boffe had this idea that I would pay them some money: a sort of protection fee. They would ensure that we, our house and the shop would come to no harm in return for a fixed payment each Friday," Everet explained.

"But Everet, we have been here for ten turns, just over, without any incident, or any remote feelings of being in danger." said Myrta.

"I know. I know. But, my dear, times are obviously changing, and not for the better either. You have commented yourself that the Rule of Law is fraying in this town. We have seen much more social disorder than used to be the case, and perpetrators just seem to get away with it. The Marshals appear to be unable or unwilling to do anything to rectify the situation. Sometimes you have to wonder if they are part of some wider conspiracy. In any case, this Ludley said he wanted two crowns each Friday and claims he is being generous by giving us to the end of the month to start to raise our prices. Collection will start on the first Friday of next month."

"That's outrageous!" exclaimed Myrta. "Two crowns is not an insignificant fee. In fact it's getting on for a quarter of our weekly takings. Suppose we do not subscribe to their scheme?"

"Then we can expect repercussions."

"And if we agree, then we shall find ourselves irretrievably caught up in ever increasing demands until we have no customers left and we go out of business."

"Then what will we do?" asked Aonghus

The discussion went on all through the remainder of the meal. By the end of the meal they had fully discussed their situation, and the family had reached a decision: they would approach the Marshals to ask them to investigate.

*****

Two days later there was a knock on Everet's back door. He opened it to find Ludley and Boffe looking somewhat serious and disappointed at the same time.

"Mister Cranstoun," said Ludley, "do you really think the Marshals are going to interfere in our business arrangement? Even if they could find proof of your allegations, and removed me and dear Boffe here," he continued, putting a friendly arm round his accomplice's shoulders, "do you think that would end the matter?"

Everet stood there transfixed. He could not believe what he was hearing. "Have you been spying on me? Watching my every move?"

"No need for that Mister Cranstoun, we have eyes and ears in discreet places. In any case our agreement is just that, an agreement, nothing written down, certainly, but it's a binding contract. A verbal contract agreed between two parties with Boffe here as witness." A look of self satisfaction came over Ludley as he pondered on what he had just said: he wondered where he had suddenly found a way with words. "So let's remind ourselves of the terms and conditions. You pay me or my agent two crowns each week: we undertake to protect you, your family and your business from danger and damage. Simple, and to the point. Failure to make payment on the due day results in the contract being declared null and void, exposing you to danger, for you will be without protection and open to any hostile action."

Despite his daily vows, Everet felt his anger rising. "I haven't agreed anything," he said raising his voice to match.

"Your word against ours, I'm afraid Mister Cranstoun. We'll see you on the first Friday of next month as we agreed. Good day to you."

Everet was left to consider his anger, and was none too pleased with the Marshals. There was at least one amongst their number who was corrupt, and who was to say how far that corruption ran through the force. New plans would need to be laid.

Everet, Myrta and Aonghus sat down after the evening meal to discuss the new information and to formulate a new plan. "Does this mean we have to do their bidding?" asked Aonghus. "It doesn't seem right that these villains can do this to people."

"It isn't right, Aonghus," said Everet, "but it looks like our first and proper step to resolve the matter has been foiled because our Marshals have been caught up in corruption. That really is a shocker. As for having to do their bidding, well, the short answer is 'no', and what we are here to do is to work out an alternative strategy. One that fits in with what we want to do: one that suits our purposes and aims, not someone else's."

They discussed the subject until they could think of no more options or arguments. It was time to come to a decision. "We have been through the situation in great depth," said Myrta, "and now we need to make a decision we are all happy with. I think it's best if each of us takes our time to reach what we think is right for us. So let's not just dive straight in. We have talked long and hard. We have identified things in favour and things against. We are tired. Let's sleep on our thoughts and ask for some guidance."

"Sounds like a good idea to me," agreed Everet. "Are you happy with this arrangement, Aonghus?"

"Yes," said the boy, "though I do find it daunting and complex."

Next morning, after sleeping on their thoughts, they had a final short discussion. The decision was made: they would shut up shop, leave town as soon as was practicable, and move to the far south where, they understood, the quality of life was so much better. They hoped to re-establish themselves in a new environment. Everyone was agreed that a new start was better than the prospect of life getting steadily worse if they remained in Knympton.

They had to act quickly, carefully and decisively, and so started to compile a list of tasks that needed doing. They also began to put together a time plan so that they knew what had to be achieved by what date, and in what order. The plan took shape very swiftly, as it needed to, with each member of the family knowing what was expected from them if their departure from Knympton was to be effected.

Chapter 2: Preparations

The Cranstouns didn't have many possessions, so packing up was never going to be an arduous task. They lived a simple life, following simple but fundamental principles. They were determined that nothing and nobody should interfere with their chosen way of life or intercept them on the spiritual path they were treading. For more than ten years they had lived in Knympton according to their beliefs, and found much reward in what they did. They were good members of the community: caring, helpful and good friends to one and all.

They viewed Ludley's interference as a test set for them by the Universe. Why they were being tested wasn't for them to work out, but they knew that the goals they had set themselves were still achievable, and their aim was to succeed. Ludley was a blockage on the pathway that they had to circumvent: if they allowed him to block their route then they would fail in their quest.

The main problem for the Cranstouns was keeping all of this secret: if Ludley and his gang got wind of this there would be repercussions of a very serious nature, Everet feared. Similarly, if neighbours and friends got to hear of it there would surely be talk and gossip, and that could only end up in one place. No, there was to be no telling of the plans to anyone. So it was with extreme caution that the Cranstouns set about their mission. Myrta made discreet enquiries about taking passage on a boat and was able to reserve places for them: they would set sail on the Monday before Ludley was due to receive his first payment. It was all falling into place.

Everet had calculated that his supplies could be as near as run down by then, and he would make sure that he prepared enough meat to be taken on board with them to share with whomsoever else was making the journey, as well as the crew. He would blame his low stock level on a hiatus in supply should Ludley or anyone else ask.

The property was rented and paid for weekly, so there would be no problems in leaving it empty: it was just a shame that the landlord could not be informed in advance, but they intended to leave a note for him explaining their situation: however, the way that events were to unfold meant that the letter was never written.

Whilst Myrta was down at the docks looking for a ship to take them south she sought out a warehouse where their goods could be kept until required to go on board. After a diligent search she decided that Jared's warehouse offered her everything she was looking for, and agreed to rent some space from the owner who gave her a key to a secure room where they would slowly build up their small collection of possessions. Hopefully, making several visits with small bundles would go more unnoticed than shifting everything at once.

It took several more visits than she first imagined, but she was happy when the last bundle was safely under lock and key on the Friday before embarkation. On the Saturday they would rearrange the small bundles into larger parcels to make it more expedient to get on board quickly. Time and stealth were of the essence.

*****

On the Sunday, the day before departure and just before five o'clock there was a knock on the Cranstoun's door. "Whoever can that be?" wondered Everet as he came downstairs. He was greeted by a young man, fresh faced, small in stature, and it was hard to gauge his age although Everet estimated the youngster was in his late teens.

"Mister Cranstoun?" enquired the lad, removing his cap.

"Yes," replied Everet, "how can I help you?"

"I am Diarmid, junior seaman aboard *The Venturer*. Captain Groves has sent me with this message," whereupon he handed over a note to Everet.

"Come in, come in" said Everet beckoning Diarmid inside and closing over the door.

He read the note: "Dear Mister Cranstoun, due to the nature of tides and the prospect of a fair wind we will be setting sail this evening at nine o'clock. I would be grateful if you and your family could be on board with your goods and chattels by eight o'clock. I look forward to having you sail with us. Signed, Derry Groves, Captain."

"Oh!" exclaimed Everet. "We had better get a move on. Diarmid, tell Captain Groves that we will be there, and ask him to arrange for the porters to meet us at Jared's warehouse in one hour."

"Yes, sir!" said Diarmid as he turned and made off at a fast pace.

Everet peered out into the gathering darkness, but could see nobody save Diarmid receding into the night. He closed the door and hurried upstairs to tell the others of the change in plans. For Myrta this was good news and her hopes and excitement rose in pitch as she anticipated being out of Knympton sooner than planned. This moment of departure had been her focus for a time now, and it was as if she couldn't wait a moment longer. From the moment since the communal decision had been taken to relocate she was certain that she had witnessed the whole moral fibre of the town take another downward turn.

Whilst the Cranstouns were becoming more excited by each passing moment others were becoming more and more perplexed. Ludley or one of his minions had taken to walking past the shop almost on a daily basis. They would have noted that Everet's prices were as fair and reasonable as they always had been. They would have noticed too that the level and variety of produce was decreasing. Indeed, on one occasion Boffe had come into the shop and enquired about the lack of some cuts of meat.

"Yes, Mister Boffe," Everet had replied, "I realise we are low in stock of some cuts, but, you see, at this time of year the supply begins to dry up. The day will dawn soon when we won't have any."

Boffe failed to recognise the irony in Everet's statement, but then brainpower and education weren't his forte: his gifts lay in thieving, extortion and violence.

As Diarmid made his way back to *The Venturer* he was oblivious to the evil eyes watching him from the darkness. Diarmid's route took him down through narrow alleyways from the centre of town to the docks. Evening had now closed in, and the darkness in some alleyways was very deep, the blackness punctuated only sparingly by the dim lights of the buildings on either side. As Diarmid skipped down the last alleyway a pair of hands reached out from an opening, pulled him in, turned him round and a fist crashed into his jaw, sending him sprawling to the ground.

"Get up," said the gruff voice of a shadowy figure, "and don't try anything stupid." Slowly Diarmid rose, taking in what he could of the situation. He wasn't entirely certain, but he could swear the figure was wearing the dark tunic of the Marshals.

"Is this the way the Knympton Marshals go about their business?" asked Diarmid, now standing up and rubbing his jaw.

"There's plenty more of that if you want it," said the Marshal. "Now what business did you have at the Cranstoun house?"

"None that the Marshals would be interested in," said Diarmid, a wave of bravado sweeping over him. Captain Groves' warning to be careful was ringing inside his head, and now he was wishing he had been more circumspect in executing the task given to him.

The Marshal pushed him back against the wall and pinned him there. "Don't get lippy with me, young man. Just answer the question."

"And if I don't?" asked Diarmid, determined to play this out as far as he dared.

The Marshal's right knee thudded into Diarmid's groin: the pain was unbelievable, but somehow passed off quite quickly. "More of this. As much as you want. I can hand this out all night if I have to." The grip on Diarmid's throat tightened.

"OK, OK," gasped Diarmid, "Mister Cranstoun has booked passage with our ship which was due to sail tonight. However, because the winds and tide are not favourable we have been delayed until Tuesday at the earliest. This was the message."

"And what ship might this be, boy?" grunted the Marshal, loosening his grip slightly.

"*The Southern Bell*, sir," replied Diarmid.

"That's it?" asked the Marshal.

"Yes, sir."

The Marshal eased off the pressure again, aimed another punch at Diarmid who saw it coming, and ducked out of it. The Marshal's fist crunched against the rough cold stone of the wall and he let out a loud yell of pain and dismay. In the same movement Diarmid reached down and pulled the Marshal's legs from underneath him, sending him clattering to the ground: Diarmid stamped his boot heel into the Marshal's testicles. "What you give out, you get back in abundance," said the boy. "I can hand this out all night, too," and, with a reinforcing kick squarely to the Marshal's jaw that sent him sprawling to the edge of consciousness, he was off. The Marshal lay in a heap, barely knowing if he was still in this world or was making his way to the next.

Safely back on board *The Venturer*, Diarmid reported his adventure to the Captain, along with Everet's message. "Never mind, Diarmid, you may have a few bruises as trophies of your encounter, but I'll wager the Marshal wishes he had kept his distance. It would have served him better to follow you all the way here than to interfere, but then again, if you don't know all the facts you won't see the bigger picture," he said. "You have done well. Now you must stay on board and keep watch whilst I take some of the others down to the warehouse to oversee what could be a dangerous situation."

Groves then called out the names of a number of crew members, telling them that they were to accompany him to Jared's Warehouse to transport the Cranstouns' goods and chattels back to the ship: he also advised them to be extra vigilant as there could well be trouble from some undesirables.

Chapter 3: The Aftermath

The Cranstouns made their way down to Jared's Warehouse and were busying themselves putting bundles together. Myrta was getting restless. "Where are the porters?" she wondered out loud.

"I'm sure they are on their way, my dear," replied Everet. "Let's just concentrate on getting things together."

There was a noise of people arriving and the sounds grew louder as the entourage approached the small room the Cranstouns had rented. "Ah, Mister Cranstoun," said a voice.

Everet froze as a fear came over him. However, he managed to summon enough courage to look up and see half a dozen men: they looked more like sailors than porters.

"I'm Derry Groves, Captain of *The Venturer*," said the voice. "I know you are expecting porters, but after Diarmid's little adventure, more of which later, I thought it best if I brought some of my men down to do the loading."

"I see," said Everet somewhat worried by this change of plan. "Are you expecting trouble?"

"Perhaps: perhaps not. In any case we are prepared. If we work quickly all will be well," said Groves. His eyes searched the room, looking for a decent sized container. Having located what he was looking for, he went on, "I think the boy should hide himself in this crate until we are on board. And, if you don't mind, I'd prefer you and Mistress Cranstoun to wear these sailors' tunics, just to confuse the issue should anyone be watching us," he said handing over the garments to Everet and Myrta.

The sailors loaded boxes and crates on to trolleys whilst Everet settled his bill with Jared, and the party made their way from the warehouse to the ship. Groves was a little on edge because all was quiet, perhaps a little too quiet. "Just keep going at this relaxed pace," he ordered the crew. "It's very quiet along this wharf and who knows what might happen. Be alert and be ready to take appropriate action. Mistress Cranstoun, it would be better if you walked at the centre of our little entourage." Myrta moved towards the inside where she was more out of sight and would be less visible to prying eyes.

Inside the topmost crate Aonghus was terribly excited by the adventure. He was trying to lie still, but the jarring of the trolley wheels over the cobblestones bounced him about, even although they had wrapped blankets round him in a bid to give him protection and comfort.

As they approached the docks the level of activity increased: some other ships had decided to take advantage of the change in weather conditions and were making ready to sail.

Whilst the sailors oversaw the safe arrival of the Cranstouns and their luggage, the Marshal was slowly returning to his senses, taking several minutes to get his bearings before stumbling off to *The Waggoner's Inn* where he expected to find Ludley.

The Waggoner's Inn was a coaching house situated in the main square of Knympton. As such it was a popular stopping off point for the travellers and traders who regularly passed through the town on the Trade Routes, and much information could be picked up regarding who was shipping what goods where. Ludley and his crowd, the Black Crows they called themselves, were given the use of a back room by George, the Innkeeper, from where they planned their nefarious activities. George, as well as giving the gang the odd nod and wink, demanded a percentage of the ill gotten gains.

Ludley, Boffe and several others were gathered round the table in the room, drinking, laughing and on a rota to work the lounge, keeping eyes and ears open for possibilities amongst the Inn's clientele. The room was at the far side of the bar from the main lounge, and although there was no apparent door between one and the other the gang members could pass via a secreted hallway. Access to the back room was very strictly limited to those who needed to be there.

It was into this little snug that the Marshal eventually stumbled: the time by now was getting on for seven o'clock. The door was thrown open and he all but fell into the room. Boffe looked round. "Ah, Mung, our man in the Marshals," he greeted the newcomer. Then, noticing the distress Mung was suffering, "Goodness, Mung, have you run into a brick wall? What's going on?"

The others picked up on Boffe's words and ceased their activities to look at Mung: a pregnant silence fell over the place. Mung was a sight for sore eyes indeed. His tunic was torn and dirty, his right hand was hanging limp by his side, bleeding from a number of abrasions: he hobbled, almost doubled over, to the table.

"Give him a seat, Vangil," said Ludley, "and whilst you're on your feet get the man a measure of brandy." Vangil evacuated his chair and headed for the bar whilst Mung fell into the chair ungraciously.

"Now, Mung," Ludley went on, "I hope your story is worth hearing."

"I'm sure you'll be interested," replied Mung, wincing through the pain his hand was pulsating through him. "I was out on patrol, nothing specific, just routine, and my route took me past Cranstoun's shop. As we all know you have entered into an arrangement with him about which he is not particularly happy. You'll remember that he came to the Marshals, and it was lucky for us that it was me he saw."

"Yes, Mung, we all know that. So what?" Ludley interrupted.

"Well, I saw someone at the door and he was ushered inside. I waited for several minutes until he emerged, then I followed him."

"Anyone we know?" asked Boffe.

19

"Boffe, shut up and let Mung tell us," said Ludley, his interest and anger rising.

"The visitor turned out to be a seaman. Well, I intercepted him and he wasn't for talking, so I had to, er, persuade him that he should answer my questions. It seems your Mister Cranstoun has made arrangements to leave town on a ship called the *Southern Bell*. Well, fortune is again on our side because the ship was due to sail tonight but the winds and tides are not favourable. The ship won't depart until Tuesday at the earliest."

There was a silence all round the table as the listeners took in the impact of Mung's story.

"He's a crafty one, that Cranstoun," said Ludley. "I think we need to pay him a visit. Maybe he will be unable to travel by the time we have made our views known to him." Everyone laughed. "They say that if men had wings and bore black feathers, few of them would be clever enough to be crows," said Ludley, "but this Cranstoun is one of them. Maybe," he went on, "we should incorporate him into our Society of Black Crows." There was another laugh. "Now, Mung, what's become of your informant?"

"Ah, him, yes. Well, I had to reward him for the valuable information provided and I left him in a heap behind the *Blue Anchor*. If they are looking for him they won't find him in a fit state to say anything for some time to come," said Mung.

"Right," said Ludley. "Drink up everyone, there's work of a serious nature to be done. Vangil, you and Moldin get down to the docks and seek out the *Southern Bell*. Belfort, you and Raddy get to the *Blue Anchor* and find Mung's informant. Bring him back here and keep him quiet and compliant. Flerge, take Mung to the sawbones and get his wounds seen to, then bring him back here. If any of you see anything I should know about get to me quickly, I will be at Cranstoun's place with Boffe. Everyone know what they are doing?"

There were nods all round except for Mung. "There's no need to go to the *Blue Anchor*, Ludley. I know that seaman will not regain consciousness for some time to come. I hit him really hard. How do you think this happened?" he said pointing to his broken hand.

"Maybe so, Mung, but I am taking no chances. Right, get going!" and with that the snug emptied, and the Black Crows set about their business.

*****

The crow is big, black, and beautiful. Its highly polished plumage shows shimmering greens, blues, and purples, glistening like a black raindrop in the light. It dives and rolls like a black thunderbolt out of the sky or speeds along with fluid, gliding strokes. The crow is the archetype of the air, and more. It is assumed to be the brains of the bird world, its deep, sonorous, penetrating voice demanding immediate attention and respect: it is an imposing bird.

The crow is to be treated with care. Along with the raven, the crow is a symbol of conflict and death, an ill-omen associated with the Gods of War. Although the crow is ill-omened, it is also considered to be skilful, cunning, and a bringer of knowledge. It teaches you to learn from the past, but not to hold onto it. It is of most value when trickery is needed. Besides the associations with death, crows were also symbols of the ungodly and of ill repute. If there was a flaw in the Universal Plan, it must be these birds. Indeed, such is the popular view of crows and ravens as malicious messengers that the collective terms applied to these birds are 'a murder of crows' and 'an unkindness of ravens'!

*****

Belfort and Raddy quickly made their way to the *Blue Anchor*. Remembering what Mung had said they went round to the back of the building, but could find nobody. They looked in amongst the waste piles and bins: they even emptied a few, but in vain. "Where can this man be?" asked Raddy. "Didn't Mung claim to have laid him unconscious?"

"That's what I am thinking too, Raddy," replied Belfort, "but look around. Do you see any signs of a struggle here?"

Raddy surveyed the scene: his expression said it all.

"No, nor do I. Looks like Mung has been fabricating stories to boost his image. I'll wager his informant got the better of him and escaped."

"For Mung's sake I hope you are wrong, Belfort, but it's not looking good," said Raddy. "We'd better get up to Cranstoun's house and tell Ludley. I don't think he will be very happy."

Down at the docks Vangil and Moldin ran up and down the quayside looking for *the Southern Bell*. It soon became apparent that no such ship was currently berthed at Knympton, if indeed such a ship existed. "Mung's hearing is letting him down," said Vangil, "for there's no boat of that name here."

"Either that or he's been fed a story, but you'd think a Marshal could tell the difference," said Moldin.

"He'd be daft to tell a story like that to Ludley, so he must think he has vital information. Let's take another look."

They spent another ten minutes searching. No *Southern Bell*. They found various boats, *The Pride of Pender*, *The Venturer*, *The Northern Bull*, *The Swift*, and *The South Wind*. "Ludley's not going to like this," said Moldin, "and if you notice, three of these ships are showing signs of activity that suggest they might be leaving tonight."

"I had noticed that," said Vangil, "but Mung definitely said that conditions were not favourable for a sailing tonight, and wouldn't become favourable until at least Tuesday."

"That's certainly what he said, but he's been hoodwinked. I'm now beginning to think that the Cranstouns are aboard one of these boats and we have missed them. Do you want to tell Ludley?"

Meanwhile, Ludley and Boffe found the Cranstoun property in darkness. Hammering on the door produced no answer. They peered through the downstairs windows, but there was no sign of life. "Could be they are upstairs but not answering," said Boffe.

"More likely they've scarpered," said Ludley, none too pleased at the way things were turning out. "Let's see," he said, kicking in the back door. The door flew open, banging against the inside wall and almost coming off its hinges. Ludley and Boffe went in and upstairs. The place was empty.

"For crying out loud!" shouted Ludley. "That butcher has outsmarted us. Right, down to the docks and see what's doing there."

On their way to the docks they came across Belfort and Raddy. "No sign of Mung's victim at the *Blue Anchor*, Ludley," said Raddy, "and no signs of any fight either."

"I take it the house is empty too," said Belfort.

"Yes," grunted Ludley. "Come with us to the docks, but I fear we are too late."

At the docks they met up with Vangil and Moldin. "Guess what, Ludley," teased Moldin.

"No ship called the *Southern Bell*," Ludley responded.

"Right first time as usual," said Belfort, "although there is one called the *Northern Bull*. Do you think that's the one?"

"Who knows?" said Ludley. "Somehow it doesn't matter anymore. Look, some of these ships are casting off. I thought Mung said the conditions weren't right."

"That's what he said, but looks like he's been spun a yarn by whoever he intercepted," said Boffe.

"Maybe it's time Mung resigned his place in the Black Crows," said Ludley. "Let's head back to *Waggoner's* and hear what he has to say for himself."

*****

Back in the snug at *The Waggoner's* an air of despondency and defeat hung over the gang as they sat morosely drinking their ale. Nobody was saying very much, but everyone was keenly awaiting the return of Flerge and Mung from the physician's.

They didn't have to wait too long. Mung had been patched up as best as the physician could muster. The Marshal looked a sorry sight indeed and was still wincing with pain. "Sit down," ordered Ludley, "and tell us what really happened tonight, Mung."

Mung looked up nervously, hesitating whilst he tried to gather what thoughts were left in his head. "It happened pretty much as I told you earlier," he said.

"Yes, Mung, but pretty much and really are different things," said Ludley. "So this time tell us what really happened. I won't ask again." Ludley slapped the table to indicate his impatience and anger.

"I swear, Ludley, that what I told you was what the lad told me. I gave him such a slap that I was sure he was telling me the truth," said Mung in hushed tones.

"Lad? Lad! You didn't say it was a lad. You indicated that this was some substantial seaman. And this lad outwitted you? What are you coming to Mung? Where is this lad now? He's certainly in no heap behind the *Blue Anchor*, and I'll wager he's in no heap anywhere. Mung, he escaped your clutches."

"He was cunning, he was, Ludley," said Mung, "stronger than his looks suggested. I threw a big punch and he ducked under me. Hit my hand against the wall." Mung squirmed as he relived that painful moment. "Pulled me down, kicked me in the head and ran off."

"Looks like he kicked what little brains you had right out of your head, Mung," said Ludley. "I want you to take a little walk with me and Boffe. It will help you to clear your head, and you can show us where all this happened. The rest of you get back to some real work. I want to know what's going on with the overland traders when I get back."

Boffe and Ludley took hold of Mung by an arm each and escorted him from the premises. They walked him to the Cranstoun residence. "Inside, Mung," said Ludley, shoving the hapless Marshall through the damaged door. "Your days as a double agent are at an end. I don't like failure and I will not tolerate it. Now, if I dismiss you from the Black Crows there's a chance that you might just be tempted to gain revenge by turning us in. I can't allow that either, Mung."

Mung was wide eyed with fear. Ludley could mean only one thing and there was little Mung could do to protect himself. He tried to push past the two crooks, but they stood firm, pushing him back against the wall of the preparation room. "Boffe, this is your department," said Ludley, "excommunicate him."

As Mung made another attempt to push past his erstwhile colleagues Boffe pulled a knife from his belt and plunged the blade into Mung's body once, twice, three times. Mung fell to the floor, blood slowly flowing across the wooden boards. Boffe bent down and wiped his blade on Mung's tunic before resheathing the knife. The gang leaders returned to *The Waggoner's*, leaving Mung to die where he lay.

Chapter 4: Mung

Back in Knympton Ludley and Boffe, satisfied that retribution was theirs, returned to *The Waggoner's* where their colleagues were busy gathering information on the traders who would be leaving town and continued with their drinking, making merry whilst laying plans to plunder the caravans.

"Do you think you will replace Mung, Ludley?" asked Vangil, an evil looking small man about five feet tall.

Ludley slapped Vangil on the back. "Don't know, Vangil, but who cares? What's he really done for us? There's no law man around here big enough or brave enough to come after us," and they all laughed loudly. "Vangil, it's your turn to buy!"

They continued to laugh and drink into the small hours of the night, as they updated Ludley with what they had learned about the security arrangements surrounding the various caravans of goods, until the landlord finally had had enough, and cleared *The Waggoner's* of its clientele.

Meanwhile, back at the former Cranstoun place, Mung was in a serious condition. As he lay somewhere between the two worlds, for the second time in one night he thought, a strange phenomenon began.

Mung felt himself rise from his position on the floor and float towards the ceiling of the room from where he looked down on his body. It seemed no more than a few seconds that Mung spent regarding his lifeless body below, when he felt a strong impulse to turn around. He felt something behind him pulling him towards it, and proceeded to turn his attention from the floor to what should have been the ceiling. There he found a brilliant light, but for some reason it wasn't blinding, hot or in any way uncomfortable. It was love. Mung couldn't find another word, and love, he knew, was an inadequate explanation. All he knew was that he immediately felt a presence that enveloped him with a feeling of total and complete comfort, love, understanding, and so much more that could never be described in words. Even though this started as a dream, he perceived it as though he had died.

Next, he was rising through clouds into a peaceful, loving, delicate, and secure place. Despite not being a terribly religious man he somehow knew that he was in the place where they say God is, and Mung could immediately understand why. No fear, no pain, no hurt, no worry, none of the things holding him down that were with him just a few minutes ago. He felt the deepest peace and love flowing all around and within him. He felt secure beyond measure. A loving presence surrounded Mung, but a brighter image approached him. The entire place was spotless: not a touch of darkness or shadow was around. The light was pure and without a source: it was the Source.

Mung went up through what he could only describe as a tunnel and into the light. His speed of travel was faster than any words he could summon, and found he was with two Beings. They were pure light, energy and peace. They were somehow familiar to him, like family members, but Mung was unable to tell exactly who they were. The first was very tall, taller than anyone Mung had ever encountered. "Who are you?" said Mung.

"I am your Guardian Angel," said the Being. Although Mung believed he was speaking, he realised that the voices were inside his head. "Be not afraid, Yorlan Mung, we are here to help you if that's what you want."

"But if you are my Guardian Angel, why have you let me come so close to death?" asked Mung.

"Ah, well, that's because you have chosen the pathway that you travel. Angels only offer advice and guidance. They do not interfere when people do things for themselves. You have something called free will which allows you to do anything you want," said the Angel.

"Anything I want?" said Mung.

"Yes," the Angel confirmed. "You choose the option, but in doing so you have to accept the responsibility for the outcome too. You can't do anything without it affecting someone or something somewhere."

"Mmm," said Mung, trying to take it all in. "By the way, do you have a name?"

"Of course," said the Angel, "I am called Remliel."

"And can I call on you at any time, for any reason?" asked Mung.

"You certainly can," said Remliel.

"Tell me, Remliel," said Mung, "who is that with you?"

"That, dear Mung, is your Higher Being. Your Soul if you want to put a different name to it," said Remliel.

"Does this mean I am dead?" said Mung.

"Far from it," said Remliel, "although your physical body is in need of urgent attention. The fact that you can see your Soul doesn't mean you have died. You can contact your Soul at any time you want, as well as contacting me. Your Soul will offer you advice and guidance too. It will tell you how things are without the glossing over that your Ego may put on things. Your Soul will never tell you any lies, although what you hear at times may sound brutal and cruel."

"Oh," said Mung, "I need time to try to understand what you are saying, but I fear that time is not something I have a great deal of. I can see myself lying there on the floor, bleeding from knife wounds, my very lifeblood seeping out of me. Can you help me?"

"We can try," said Remliel, "but first you must return to your physical body."

"Yes," said the Soul, "it's not time to die just yet."

When Mung opened his eyes he realised he was back on the floor of Cranstoun's old preparation room: perhaps he had never left it at all. He was drowsy; perhaps he had had a nice dream. Somehow, though, he doubted that, for in the back of his mind there was something, like a little voice, telling him that what he had just been through was real.

*****

In her little cottage in a clearing in Berystede Wood close to where a small streamlet flowed towards the River Kinuli, Brina the Crone sat in meditation. This was the time of the Crescent Moon, when Brina's meditation held an extra sense of reverence. Brina was revered, but feared by the inhabitants of Knympton who knew of her presence, for they perceived her as having occult powers: powers to rake over the past, powers to see the future, powers to curse, powers to heal. The Earth Mother, like all forces of nature, though often wild and untamed, was also kind.

Sometimes she gave advice and magical gifts to visitors who were pure of heart. Some Knymptonians would enter the Crone's domain searching for wisdom, knowledge and truth. There were some in Knympton who realised that she was all-knowing, all seeing and all-revealing, and that she would help those who dared to ask. They knew that she, too, was a powerful healer, gaining success where others had failed. It was said of her that she changed everything she touched, and that everything she touched changed.

She was in communion with Nature, the Universe, and All there is. She was deep in conversation with the Nature Spirits, the Angels, the Archangels and the other Beings of Light. She was in regular consultation with her own Higher Self.

Brina had begun her meditation as she always did, with chanting.

"I am Air, Fire, Water, and Earth

I am Spirit Divine!

I am Brina,

I am the Goddess, I am Woman!

I am the Maiden of the Moon!

I am Brina,

I am Maiden, Mother and Crone!

Water, Fire, Earth, Air

Where the light shines let me be there

Water, Earth, Air, Fire

To the highest pinnacle I aspire

Water, Fire, Air, Earth

Look upon my spiritual birth

Earth, Air, Fire, Water

Sanctify me, a Mother's daughter."

Brina was not old, around thirty five, but her chosen life indicated that she willingly acknowledged her age, wisdom, and power. Through conscious self-definition, she was trying to help to reverse hundreds of years of oppression, degradation, and abuse aimed at older women. Although she preferred to be called elder, mother, or wise woman, she did not dismiss, or disavow terms such as crone, witch, or hag.

Brina was revered by those who beheld her as an older woman who embodied wisdom and knew the truth of cyclic existence. She sometimes cared for the dying, and sometimes acted as a spiritual midwife at the end of life, the link in the cycle of death and rebirth. She was a healer, teacher, shower of the way, bearer of sacred power, knower of mysteries, mediator between the world of spirit and the world of form. For Brina, women's wisdom held healing power, but crone wisdom was the most potent of all.

As she communicated with the spiritual energies she was pleasantly surprised when Archangel Raphael appeared without being summoned.

"Ah, Raphael, come closer, you are most welcome, especially in this time of the crescent moon," said Brina, "but what brings you to my meditation this evening?"

"Thank you, Brina," said the Angel of Healing. "I come on a special mission. I require your assistance."

"I see," said Brina, "and how can I help?"

"The Angel Remliel has asked me to intercede on behalf of the mortal for whom he is Guardian," said Raphael. "The human is called Mung and he lies sorely afflicted, having been set upon by those whose hearts are dark and whose intentions are evil. He is close to death, but the time is not right. You have the skills to help restore this man, for he is awakening to the light."

"He has seen the light?" asked Brina, interestedly.

"Yes, he has had a vision and met Remliel and his own Soul," replied Raphael.

"And where will I find this man?" asked Brina.

"He lies in the house of Cranstoun the Viander, in Moncrat Wynd near the centre of Knympton. Cranstoun and his family have fled although they have no responsibility for this act. Hurry, Brina, for time is of the essence and the opportunity is not to be missed. I will ask Michael to cast his cloak of protection around you," said Raphael. "I wish you well." Then he was gone.

"The protection of Archangel Michael's sword and shield are most welcome, too," replied Brina as she ended her meditation, and closed herself down, ensuring that she was firmly grounded. Then she put on her cloak and set off down the paths to Knympton. First she called at the house of Ardvon Gruvel, one of her regular clients. She explained to Gruvel that she was on an errand of mercy that required secrecy, and she required assistance. She explained that she needed someone to help her lift the body, and who had access to a cart on which to transport it: Gruvel satisfied all these criteria. Indeed Gruvel had one more attribute: he knew exactly where Cranstoun's shop was located and took her there quickly.

Once inside the Cranstoun premises they acted quickly to rescue Mung. First Brina had a quick look at his wounds, and did what she could to try to stem the flow of blood. Then gently, she and Gruvel lifted Mung, carried him outside where they laid him on the cart, on a bed of blankets, covered him up so as to confuse anyone who might see them, and they were off.

"I know of some back streets we can use that will keep us away from lots of prying eyes," said Gruvel.

"Will it add to our journey time?" asked Brina.

"Not by much," said Gruvel.

"Then do it!" said Brina

Chapter 5: The Venturer

Once they were on board and out of sight of any prying eyes that the darkness sometimes hides, Aonghus was released from his confinement in the crate. The family was shown to their cabin deep in the sterncastle of the ship. It was adequate, but sparsely furnished: it had four bunks and minimal storage space. *The Venturer* was a merchant ship, and not particularly designed to carry many passengers. Its owners traded in fine silks, wool and linen in the main, although occasionally it would carry other goods like wine, or exotic foodstuffs, but these were rare occurrences.

The Venturer had brought fine silks from Billington, a town close to Valkanda's border with the Barbarian lands. The silks, in turn had come to Billington, again by ship, from the far eastern lands at the other side of the world. It was easier to ship such goods rather than transport them across the Barbarian lands, although there were land routes that crossed this dangerous place.

Billington was thus a thriving, lively town where, from a Valkandan point of view, west met east. Billington was a colourful, busy trading post where anything could be bought and sold.

The Merchant Company that owned *The Venturer*, The Clerton Mercers, had its headquarters in Billington, and it was from there that the ship plied its trade up and down Valkanda's west and south coasts, calling in at the various ports, Pender, Clyndor, Feluce and Knympton.

Ships were useful when bulk loads needed to be transported, and part loads could be dropped off and picked up wherever required. Smaller goods and loads were carried on pack animals using the trade routes, but these were often plundered by bandits: piracy, although not unknown, was almost nonexistent in Valkandan waters.

Captain Groves gave the order to cast off and the crew set to work, releasing the ship from its constraints and unfurling sails. Slowly *The Venturer* began to move and the helmsman started to swing her round to head westwards down the Kinuli River, out into the Firth of Kinuli and then towards the Western Ocean.

The Cranstouns decided to get their heads down early and get as much sleep as possible: there would be plenty to see during the daylight hours. By the time they woke the next day Knympton would be just a dot on the horizon behind them. Indeed it might even be out of sight, hidden by the twists and turns of the Firth. It was sad to leave, but, they felt, necessary. They had so many cherished memories of the town and their time there that it was quite heartbreaking to leave due to the bad intentions of a few bandits.

For the Cranstouns there was to be no looking back or going back. They had been through the self-enquiry procedure that they had developed to deal with crises and big decisions, and they had each reached the same conclusion. Ludley's intervention in their life had not been coincidental, it had happened for a reason. To the Cranstouns the Universe was telling them to move on, to relocate, to meet new challenges.

Their spiritual quest was to become one with the Universe, with Nature, with All there is. They lived their lives simply, trying to practise abundance, giving and receiving, forgiving and letting go. Their lives were such that they had sufficient means to live comfortably without having to exact the highest price possible for their services.

Living the simple life gave the Cranstouns the satisfaction they needed, and they were happy in their daily actions. Always they had a smile on their faces and a good word for and about everyone.

Aonghus was still in a highly excited state, and was almost speechless when the family was shown to their cabin. Then, somehow, almost as if some hidden hand had removed the blockage, he started to gush. "Oh goodness me, good gracious! Can I have a top bunk, please?" He had been taking it all in, and now it was all coming out. "Did anything happen whilst I was in that box? Did you see anyone suspicious?" Then, when it struck him that his parents were still dressed as sailors he started to laugh. "Shouldn't you two be taking orders from Captain Groves?" he chuckled.

"Oh Aonghus," said Myrta, "I don't think I've ever seen you so excited. How we will get you to sleep I haven't a clue, but we will try." She smiled warmly as she caressed his hair. "Now let's take the first step and get you ready for bed."

"But, mummy, you haven't told me about the journey from the warehouse to the ship," said the youngster.

"No, I have not," said Myrta, "because there is nothing to tell you."

"What?" said Aonghus in disbelief. "No bandits? No heroic rescues?"

"No, Aonghus," said Myrta, "none of that. Indeed, nothing of anything. We walked at a normal pace, in a group, from the warehouse to the ship. Nobody looked at us twice, nobody said anything to us, and here we are. Now stop delaying and climb in to bed. We'll leave the lantern on at a low level so that you will be able to see if you awaken during the night."

Aonghus kissed his mother and hugged his father. "Good night," he said, "I'm looking forward to exploring the ship tomorrow."

"Goodnight, Aonghus," they replied.

Soon afterwards, Everet turned the lantern down to its lowest intensity before he and Myrta pulled back the covers on the lower berths and climbed in. In a matter of seconds, or so it seemed, the parents were asleep, tired out mentally, emotionally and physically by the trials and tribulations of the last two weeks.

However, for Aonghus, all this turmoil and its consequent adventure was far too exciting to put aside, thus he remained awake for an hour or so longer, letting all the ins and outs, the whys and wherefores and the what ifs and what maybes run through his head time and time again, until finally, he too dozed off.

As Aonghus passed into sleep, all the dramas and crises were still swirling round his head and he began to dream ......

Aonghus tried hard to contort his body into as small a ball as possible round his bag of possessions as he hid in the semi dense shrubbery on the edges of Berystede Wood. He had been chased from town by a gang of evil looking men, common thieves and ne'er–do–wells no doubt, and he was in fear for his life. The town of Knympton had deteriorated so much since he had hastily left just over two turns ago: it was almost unrecognisable. Never had he witnessed a place where he could feel evil creeping all around him, pinching at his body with every step he took. He pulled his dark woollen cloak over him, not to ward off the cold, for he was sweating with the effort of running so hard and fast, but to cover as much of his body with it as possible to aid his escape from his pursuers.

He was also trying to still his rapid breathing, brought on by the exertions he had just been through, trying to calm his mind and body, trying to breathe as silently as possible, trying to let the breaths come in an easy rhythm, trying not to gulp and gasp for air. He was also trying to ignore the pricks from the barbs of the greenthorn bush he was hiding under, as they bit into his flesh, raking him through his layers of clothing as he slid as far into the undergrowth as he could.

Behind him the four men were still chasing, following the path they were sure Aonghus had trodden not too long since. Their torches lit the way, but the light did not reach far into the pervading darkness. The night was black and moonless: clouds obscured the stars. The men stopped not far from where Aonghus lay under his cloak, hoping that they would give up the chase and he could relax. Like him, they too were out of breath, their voices betraying their out-of-condition bodies.

"Is there any point in going on?" the tallest of the four gasped. "We have come a fair way from town. I think he has given us the slip, and in any case, we don't want to wander too far into that wood, especially on such a dark night as this."

"I agree, Ludley," panted another in reply. "We have lost him. Our torches aren't that much help. All they are doing is attracting the night midges and the leechmoths. Let the woods have him."

There was a mumbling of agreement as the gang decided to call off the chase and return to town. "Well lads, it's back to the tavern and some more ale. There will be others to pick on tomorrow, I'm quite sure," said Ludley, and the group turned to retrace their footsteps, flapping and swatting at the flying insects of inconvenience which were intent on filling their bellies with some warm human blood. The wind gusted, rattling the leaves on the trees, conducting them in a symphony of scariness and foreboding. In the not too far distance the plaintive yelp of the fearsome Bearwolf pierced the night, warning everyone and everything that it was on the prowl, and it didn't care who or what it would have for supper. The four quickened their steps and made off back to town.

Aonghus continued to huddle under his cloak for some time, hardly daring to breathe. The mention of Ludley's name caused very bad memories to come rushing into his mind. Was this the same Ludley that had precipitated his family's hasty departure from Knympton? Around him he could hear the noises of the wood as it became alive with the sound of nocturnal creatures, and the soughing of the wind through the trees. He had heard what Ludley said, and his mind exaggerated the dangers that had been implied. He pulled his cloak even tighter round him as an unnatural chill crawled over his prone body.

He wondered if these ruffians had chosen him at random, a mere boy of sixteen as their victim. Perhaps they had recognised him as the viander's son. His bag though on the large side did not contain much, just a few changes of clothes and some provisions. Oh, and a few rune stones. Well at least that's what he thought they were ......

As the only passengers aboard, the Cranstouns were invited to breakfast with Captain Groves. As they dined on bread and preserves, washed down with orange juice and coffee – brought from the mountain areas between Valkanda and the Dark Lands – the Captain told them of Diarmid's encounter with the Marshal.

"Well," said Everet gravely, "this maybe explains why Ludley turned up so soon after I had complained to the Marshals about his plan to extort money."

"Very much so," agreed Groves. "It looks like this Ludley has managed to infiltrate the law keepers. Hopefully, the Marshal you complained to and Diarmid's 'friend' is one and the same person. If not, then Knympton has a serious problem indeed."

"Certainly," said Everet, spreading mixed fruit preserve on his bread, "but without more details we cannot be sure. At best we were very unlucky to encounter Ludley's man when we raised the issue." Everet bit into his bread as he mentally relived his encounter. Myrta cut in asking after Diarmid.

"Oh he has a bruise or two to remember the incident by, but he is a strong young man, so he will shake off any effects quickly. It's your Marshal who came out the worse for wear. Punching a stone wall is not to be recommended," replied Groves smiling wryly.

Myrta winced at the thought; Aonghus was wide eyed in disbelief. "Yeeee! Diarmid is a hero!" he said excitedly. "Can I talk to him?"

"Hero is a bit too strong a word for Diarmid," said Groves, "although I will grant you that he's very quick witted and can determine the state of play of situations without much trouble. Add to that his strength and agility and you have a young man who will survive in near enough any circumstances." Groves stopped to drink his coffee before continuing. "I expect you will want to explore the ship, Aonghus, so I will arrange for Diarmid to show you round."

"Thank you," said Aonghus, "that will be excellent."

*****

Diarmid gave Aonghus the grand tour, from stem to stern. He explained that for perhaps twenty years or so the shape of ships in this part of the world had started to change: now they were being built with straighter sternposts instead of curved ends. The new shape had been born from the idea that it would be easier to guide the ships if the steering oar was fixed onto the sternpost and in practice it seemed to work well: the stern rudder made even the heaviest boat easier to manoeuvre. Also, in the new designs were platforms called castles, built high up at the front and the back of the ship, and if necessary, could provide a base for archers and stone-slingers.

Diarmid seemed very knowledgeable about ships it seemed to Aonghus, and he hung on to Diarmid's every word. "More masts and sails were fitted to make the ships sail faster," said the young sailor, "and one of the larger ships that emerged from these new applications was a trading ship called a carrack. In constructing it the planks did not overlap, as they did before, and it has three masts which carry square sails on the two main masts and a triangular sail on the rear mast."

Diarmid explained that *The Venturer* was one such carrack, but at the smaller end of the scale, and it was owned by a Company of Mercers based in the south. Mercers were involved in exporting woollen materials and importing luxury fabrics such as silk, linen and cloth of gold. Knympton, like all the ports, had a Company of Mercers, and they were at the centre of the commercial life of the town and the development of its trade.

"Diarmid," said Aonghus impressed, "you know so much about ships. Do you want to be a Captain one day?"

"That would be nice," said Diarmid, "but there is so much to learn. The Captain uses a device called a compass which tells us where north lies, and he uses other instruments such as astrolabes to measure the height of the sun or the North Star. The results these instruments give us means that we can work out our latitude, or north-south position, so finding our way becomes much easier."

"Is it a tough job being a sailor?" asked Aonghus.

"As you can see," said Diarmid, "life on board ship is very hard. It is crowded, damp and dirty. Sailors often suffer from diseases, like scurvy, which is caused by not eating enough fresh fruit and vegetables, although we on *The Venturer* are lucky because we are making only short haul trips. On ships that travel great distances, like those that travel to the Far East, the main daily foods are salt meat and ship's biscuit."

"I don't think I'd like that very much," said Aonghus.

"Me neither," said Diarmid, "but I think that one day I may have to make one of these long voyages to find out more."

"What's that used for?" said Aonghus, pointing to a small boat strung up above the main deck.

"Ah, that's our row boat," said Diarmid. "We use that sometimes when we have a delivery to one of the smaller villages along the coast. Their docking facilities are not large enough to take a ship like *The Venturer*, so we drop anchor at a point that's close and safe, then lower the row boat and transport the goods."

And so the two continued their trip round the ship, and Aonghus was introduced to members of the crew although he couldn't remember half of their names at the end. After thanking Diarmid for his time and efforts, Aonghus returned to join his parents on the sterncastle. The day was cold but bright, with a gentle breeze pushing them along towards the mouth of the Firth where they would head southwards, or turn left, as Aonghus was wont to put it, to head for the Crellaten Islands and then sail between the Islands and the coast through a strip of calm water known as the Straits.

Chapter 6: Brina's Sanctuary

Whilst Aonghus was having his dream Brina was busy ministering to the maledicted Mung. She thanked Gruvel for his help in retrieving Mung and sent him home. "Please return later this evening, Ardvon," she said, "and bring your drum: it will be much appreciated and most helpful." She was initially shocked when she realised that Mung wore the uniform of a Marshal, and she wondered what he had been involved in to end up in such a sorry, sorry state.

"Brina," she said to herself, "this is none of your business. The Archangel Raphael asked for your help which you freely agreed to give. Trust that there is a Higher Purpose in this."

Before she started her healing process she had to cleanse the room of any negative energies. This she did by using a smudge stick of sage, and using it as a pen to inscribe, in each corner of the room, the power symbols that would help her draw the healing energies to her patient.

She was an adept at drawing the Na-Pra-Chi, the symbol that expressed the power of the Universe being brought to Earth. As she drew it in the air in each corner of the room with the smoke from the smouldering sage she said its name three times. To the uninitiated it looked like a large tailed bird with wings spread, but to those who had been instructed, it helped to direct the necessary energies to where they were required.

Next, Brina went round the four corners of the room a second time, this time drawing and calling on Ku-Ma-Ra, the symbol of balance. It is said that this symbol bears witness to logic and intuition, demonstrating balance and harmony.

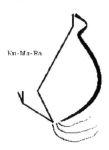

The left side of the pictogram is composed of straight lines, indicative of the left side of the brain where logic and control reside, it is believed. The right side is made up of curves indicating the right side of the brain where intuition and expression reside. When you bring both parts together in equal prominence you get balance and harmony.

Of course, there are sceptics who point out that if this symbol is rotated ninety degrees counter clockwise then it merely portrays another bird. Belief in this system, they argue, is surely for the bird-brained.

For a third, and final, time Brina went round the room drawing out the symbol Om-Nes-Est, the Master symbol, in recognition that everything is All and All is everything.

The room was now cleared of negative vibrations and indeed was energised anew with positive power. Brina was a sensitive, and she could feel the recharged power that her ritual had summoned. She was ready to start the healing processes which would rescue Mung from his desperate situation.

First, Brina attended to Mung's damaged right hand. Gently, she took hold of it and closed her eyes: she was tuning in to Mung's personal vibrations. When she had picked up his signals she could listen in to what Mung's body was trying to tell him. Mung let out a low moan as Brina gently squeezed on the back of his hand. Brina had no idea how Mung had injured his hand, but she was sure that there was bone damage and much pain.

She left Mung on the bed and turned her attention to making a herbal preparation to help ease both problems. From a large jar she extracted an amount of decaying vegetation which she placed in a small bowl: the vegetation was brown and sticky, decaying leaves of the comfrey plant which she harvested every two months from a patch which grew by the stream not far from her door. This would promote the healing of bones and to it she added arnica, which would keep bruising to a minimum, calendula to help with wound healing and fighting inflammation, chickweed to help arrest bleeding, horsetail another ingredient to promote healing of wounds, and white lily which, like the calendula, has anti-inflammatory properties. She stirred the ingredients together before adding a little beeswax in order to produce her balm.

Brina returned to Mung and started to apply the paste to his hand as soothingly as she could. "Well, Mung," she said, "this will help heal the bones and prevent too much bruising. However you damaged this hand I trust you won't try that again in a hurry." Mung moaned. "Don't try to talk, Mung, just sleep, for sleep is the best healer of all." She finished treating his hand by winding a bandage over the paste.

Next, Brina had to cut Mung's shirt in order to remove it without disturbing either him or the wounds, two of which seemed to have stopped bleeding, although the other was still leaking, the staining on the bandage wet. Before she removed the temporary dressings she had applied earlier Brina placed her left hand palm down about four inches above the body over the wounds, and, moving her hand up and down the body started to scan for information.

Two of the punctures were reasonably shallow, but the third gave Brina cause for concern: indications were that the wound penetrated so deeply that it compromised an inner organ. Healing this injury would require all her skills, as well as a great deal of recuperation time.

Going over to her work area Brina opened drawers and cupboards, lifting and replacing items until she found what she was looking for, and returned to her patient with three small clamps. She used one on each of the shallow wounds, carefully ensuring that the edges of each wound would meet in as neat a join as she could manage. Then she applied the same salve as before to induce a quick, infection free healing.

Having attended to Mung's lesser problems she was now able to devote herself to his major injury. How far Boffe's knife had penetrated into Mung's body she had no way of knowing: neither did she have any ability to determine what vessels or organs had been compromised by the blow. However, the first thing to do was to get the wound clamped.

She called on Raphael to help her. "Raphael," she said, calling the Archangel, "my intuition and sensitivities tell me that this wound is very serious, but I cannot determine the exact extent of the damage that has been caused."

Raphael shimmered into Brina's view. "Yes, Brina," said the Angel of Healing, "there is severe damage. This wound on its own would be enough to take Mung's life. To recover Mung from this situation will take all of your skills, but I have every confidence in you, Brina. I will be with you at all times, doing whatever I can to direct the Healing Rays."

"It is a comfort to have you so close, Raphael," said Brina. "Sometimes I feel so alone. Watch over us."

Raphael shimmered out of view, and a sprinkling of Angel Dust fell over and around Mung and his would-be saviour. Brina felt a glow of warmth surge through her, and her flagging reserves of energy received a much needed boost.

"All right, Mister Mung," she said to herself, for Mung was asleep, "let's get this healing started."

With renewed vigour Brina set about her challenge by consulting her Book of Treatments. Since she wasn't exactly sure of what damage she was repairing, she made a list of possibilities. Again she looked up her Book of Treatments and wrote down notes on each item. Her idea was to make a balm and elixir that would cope with what was on her list. That way, she reckoned, by treating all possibilities she would cover all aspects. Even if an item on her list wasn't damaged, giving it healing would only strengthen it. She decided that this indeed was a winning formula and quietly thanked the Universe for the inspiration.

Brina worked assiduously through the small hours preparing ingredients and composing her balm and elixir. From time to time she would revert to her Book of Treatments, either taking further notes, or adding to the wisdom written down therein.

As the sun started to send fingers of light creeping through the trees Brina completed her work. She returned to her patient and unclamped the wound. The bleeding hadn't stopped, but it was much reduced. Carefully she poured some of the elixir into the opening and watched it as it penetrated into Mung's blood vessels. The veins would carry the elixir back towards the heart, and from there be pumped right throughout his body. This way the elixir and its beneficial effects would reach all the internal organs and tissues. She waited a few minutes and poured in some more. She gave Mung a third dose, and, satisfied with the amount she had administered, carefully closed up the wound which she then clamped. Next, she covered it with the balm she had just prepared, bandaged it, and made the Signs of Healing over Mung's body.

"Well, Mung," she said, "that's the first phase complete. Now we have to wait and see. Sleep, Mung, and gather your strength. Tonight we will do more."

Brina was exhausted and took herself off to bed for a well deserved rest, whilst *The Venturer* sailed down the Kinuli.

Chapter 7: Stormy Waters

As the afternoon wore on the brightness of the day began to fade and the gentle breeze began to pick up its pace. Clouds rolled in from the south west, and soon the sky was totally overcast.

"Do you think it will rain, father?" Aonghus asked.

"It certainly has that look to it, my lad," said Everet.

The winds freshened and the sails filled out, the flags atop the masts cracking like fireworks as they flapped in the strengthening breeze.

The water, which had been calm, formed little wavelets which grew on occasion to a size sufficient to cause *The Venturer* to heave slightly.

"Wow!" said Aonghus, staggering slightly as the occasional wave rocking the ship caught him unawares, causing him to reach out for something to grab on to. "Now we really are sailing."

"Hardly, Aonghus," said his father. "I expect the crew treat this as a very mild inconvenience. I'm sure that they encounter much worse than this on a regular basis. It's all part and parcel of being a sailor."

"I suppose you are right, father," said Aonghus. "It would certainly seem to be a tough life aboard ship like Diarmid said."

"Yes, Aonghus," said Everet, "ships do not sail themselves. It takes a whole crew, acting as a well drilled team, to keep a ship afloat and on course. When the going gets tough the tough get going is what they say about sailors, meaning that they do not stop or quit when things get bad."

Aonghus could see a change in the waves by the way a little ship he noted heading for Knympton rolled over the river surface. He watched as the sky darkened, and muttered to himself, "I hope this is as bad as it gets."

However, conditions continued to deteriorate, and the first drops of rain began to hit the decks. Ahead of them a mist had appeared from almost nowhere in a matter of seconds, obliterating the headland that marked the beginnings of the Western Sea that was in plain view only a minute before.

Captain Groves emerged on to the sterncastle deck from his cabin. "Ah Cranstouns," he said, "looks like some rough weather coming our way. I would suggest as a minimum that you put on some waterproof overcoats. This rain is going to get worse before it gets better."

"Wise words, Captain," said Everet: he turned to his family and said, "let's take heed of what the Captain says." The three Cranstouns returned to their cabin to look out the necessary clothing.

Out on the deck Groves called to the man in the Crow's Nest, "What prospects?"

"Heavy mist ahead, Cap'n," came the reply, "and dark clouds everywhere. Could be a big 'un."

Groves called out orders, and the crew jumped to obey so as to bring conditions aboard ship to as amenable a state as possible in order to prepare it as best they could for the imminent bad weather.

The Captain also ordered the helmsman to take *The Venturer* close to the south shore where there might be some respite from the south westerly wind in the lee of the Camberian Hills. This manoeuvre would also have the benefit of guiding them out of the river and into the Western Sea.

Just as the Cranstouns were about to return to the deck there was a knock on their cabin door: it was Diarmid. "Mister Cranstoun, sir," he said, "the Cap'n sends his apologies and wishes to alter the advice he gave you earlier."

"I see," said Everet, "and what might be his advice now?"

"It's more of an order, sir," said Diarmid. "You are to remain here in your cabin until further notice. Seems like the bad weather could last a while and things could get rough. Best if you strap yourselves into your bunks I say."

"A bad storm then," said Everet. "Have you been through many?"

"Oh quite a few, sir, and if you'll forgive me, I have to return to the deck quickly to work the ship with the others."

"Of course, of course," said Everet, "off you go."

The Cranstouns took Diarmid's advice and strapped themselves into their bunks.

"Are we in any danger?" asked Aonghus.

"I would have thought that any storm brings some measure of danger with it," said Everet. "I will not lie to you, Aonghus: just how much danger we are in will depend on the ferocity of the storm and our position at sea. As I don't know the answer to either of these points I cannot say just how bad or good our situation is."

"But we are still in the Kinuli River," said Myrta, "and sheltering behind the hills to an extent. Surely we are safe here?"

"I think Captain Groves is just being cautious, my dear," said Everet, "and I am sure he has a sound experience of conditions in and around the coasts of Valkanda. If we were out on deck we would only get in the way of the sailors trying to cope with the bad weather. We'd be all over the place, and, being unused to the heaving of the ship, we'd only put ourselves in a more perilous position than necessary."

"I am sure you are right, my love," said Myrta, "and now that we are strapped in we should at least remain where we lie despite the waves' best attempts to move us." She tried to smile but her heart wasn't in it.

The waves began a further swell causing the boat to lurch quite violently, and then rock from side to side. The storm was deepening. *The Venturer* had made good progress despite the storm and thanks to the evasive action the crew had taken. The ship rounded Point Clare, the rocky outcrop at the mouth of the Kinuli, and entered the Western Sea.

Out on deck conditions were deteriorating fast. Groves called out orders which saw men scamper into the rigging to furl some of the sails before the full might of the storm caught them. They had no way of knowing how bad it was, but from the speed with which it raced in, Groves guessed that this storm would be bad.

It could not have been more than a couple of hours since they first noticed the mist racing in: now the sky was totally dark, and the wind was whistling ominously through the rigging. The water which had been like a mill pond was now being whipped up into a frenzy of waves. Froth and spray were blown into the faces of the hard working crew. They had passed out of the Kinuli, and could no longer claim any respite from the full force of the weather.

The ship began to heave up and down, as it was buffeted by waves of ever-increasing dimensions. The fore of the ship would disappear under water as the bow tumbled down into each trough, and was almost consumed before rising again to top another giant wave. Everything that the crew had not had time to fasten down securely was slowly but surely being lost overboard.

Groves tied a line around his waist and fastened the other end to the handrail running across the front of the sterncastle. This area afforded him the best protection from the wind and rain, and he could monitor activity below. It was getting nearly impossible for anyone to stay on their feet on the rolling, pitching, windswept decks.

A shiver of horror ran through him when he thought about how much of the water coming over the bow must be seeping into the hold. He had never before experienced a storm like this, a storm that had whipped itself up into such a fury so quickly.

He also thought about the Cranstouns in their cabin, and contemplated the idea that perhaps he had consigned them to death, trapped in the cabin if this carrack decided to roll over, hammered into submission by the winds, or, worse still, rent asunder as it toppled into yet another deep trough. Here, out on deck, he might have the chance to wrap his arms around something that would float. More shivers of horror ran through his body.

He wondered where this storm had come from: at this time of year bad weather came from the north or north east. This one was coming from the diagonally opposite direction, and, even so, a south westerly shouldn't have this force or intensity. The crew battled bravely to try to keep the ship heading in the right direction, but it was a losing battle. The wind and waves conspired to push them in a totally different heading.

Down below Aonghus was plainly petrified with the pitching and tossing, rolling and heaving. "Father, what's happening?" he screamed.

"The storm is unleashing its energy and we are in the wrong place at the wrong time," said Everet trying to restore a calm that had long since taken its leave. "Try not to think about what's happening. I know that's easy to say. Close your eyes and visualise where you'd like to be at this moment in time. Try to breathe slowly and evenly."

"That's a good idea," said Myrta. "We should all do this. I know it looks all doom and gloom, but there will be an end to this bad passage of weather, and I'm sure if you look hard enough there will be a message or other positive aspect to take from this experience."

Aonghus did his best, but there was no quiet moment in which to settle. The ship's timbers creaked: somewhere a door that wasn't properly closed banged open and shut as *The Venturer* rode the waves. Every rock, every roll, every lurch, every toss, every crash flooded through his mind, and was magnified in the process. Aonghus was sure he would never see another day.

Captain Groves made up his mind that this storm had been brewed in the pit of evil, and unleashed upon the world in retribution for no good reason. Lightning flashed, illuminating the dark clouds momentarily: peals of thunder crept across the sky above them, the noise sounding like the sky itself was being torn apart by unseen hands.

The unrelenting wind drove *The Venturer* through the waves as it had never been intended by those who had designed and built her. Its purpose was to navigate the shallower, relatively sheltered coastal waters, not to withstand the fury of a storm such as this on the open ocean. Groves held on to the handrail as if his life depended on it, for indeed it did.

An unnatural, ripping sound caused him to look upwards, his eyes wide open in fear, as, horror stricken, he watched the mainsail part down the middle from top to bottom. It was the beginning of the end thought Groves. Then, as he was trying to work out what to do one half of the sail ripped away and fell to the deck, to be washed overboard by the next crashing wave.

Now the ship was completely unbalanced and out of control. Groves called out to those clinging to the rigging to cut loose the other half of the mainsail, and he watched helplessly as it too disappeared over the side.

Without the mainsail, the ship was totally out of control, not that they had much control of it before. Every wave that smashed into it weakened it. It began to roll and list dangerously. Groves listened to every loud creak and groan as the timbers struggled to maintain integrity, knowing it was now only a matter of time before the ship rolled for a final time and drown everyone aboard. Now and again a creak would be replaced by a crack, and he knew the ship was starting to break up. The ship climbed another huge wave only to plummet into an ever deepening series of troughs as the storm reached its peak. Every time another wave smashed onto the decks Groves' thoughts kept going back to the Cranstouns strapped in their bunks below decks.

Many emotions ran through Groves' mind and body, but, strangely, fear was not amongst them. In a detached sort of way he was able to watch what was going on and remain at peace with himself. There could be only two outcomes: drown or survive, and he was ready for either. As he stood there, master of the ship, Groves could appreciate the beauty of the lightning. It was a strange sort of feeling, hanging on for dear life, but standing there in awe of the beauty and power of nature. He wondered how long this storm had taunted them: he wondered where on the map they might be located.

As these thoughts travelled round his head he was brought back to reality by the sound of the main mast ripping loose from its mountings and heading straight for the sterncastle deck. The end had come, for in being torn out of its mounting, the mast would tear a hole in the bottom of the ship. He dived to one side just as the mast crashed onto the spot where he had been standing, and continued downwards, ripping through the superstructure of the sterncastle, cleaving it apart.

It was every man for himself. Save your life if you could! The ship rolled one more time, and another wave hammered down on it, completing the break up.

Chapter 8: Healing Sanctuary

Brina woke up just as the sun was going down, having slept long and easy after her all night session treating Mung. Before she prepared some food for herself she checked on her patient: he was still asleep. His ordeal and the effects of some of the ingredients Brina had given him had induced his prolonged sleep. She smiled softly to herself. "Brina, looks like your ministrations are having a beneficial effect," she said to herself.

She went to her kitchen and put together a few items that would nourish her. She felt hungry, but did not want to gorge herself. She knew that there was another long healing session starting soon. She had asked Gruvel to return with his drum. He was an accomplished drummer, and his beats and rhythms would add energy to the next phase of the healing.

Brina took her meal outside and sat by the stream, catching the fading light of a day that she had largely missed. As she ate she listened to the bird sounds, the scurrying of animals, and to the gurgle of the water as it passed over the stones in the stream's bed. On a whim she took off her shoes and plunged her feet into the water. It was cold, as you would expect at this time of year, but at the same time it was invigorating. It sent a shock of energy pulsing through her body, bringing her every sense to life.

Her feet were beginning to complain that it was too cold, so she lifted them out of the water. Then, kneeling beside the stream, she cupped her hands and splashed her face with the refreshing water. A glow passed over her, from head to foot and from foot to head. Truly, it was wonderful to be alive, and nature was there to lend a helping hand.

She sat a while longer, her back against a chestnut tree, eyes closed in light meditation: she was at one with the world, and nature was at one with her. She was brought back to reality by the sound of Gruvel's footsteps through the forest path. She heard him knock on her door.

"I'm over here, Ardvon," she called out.

Gruvel couldn't see her, try as he might to locate her. "Where?" he asked

"Behind the house, down by the stream. Come and join me," she said.

Gruvel made his way to the back of the house and saw her propped up against her tree. "Isn't it a bit cold for sitting out?" he asked.

"Only if that's what you think," she said with a laugh in her voice. "Come and sit a while."

As they sat and chatted, Brina told Gruvel about what she had done, and how Mung seemed to be responding to the treatment. She then went on to explain what they were going to do next.

Gruvel knew a little about the ways of the Shaman, Witch, Healer, call her what you will. He knew that it was the oldest form of healing, and had been practised since the beginning of human kind. These practitioners connect with compassionate spirits to elicit their help to heal people. He was given to understand that such practices were common across different cultures in all parts of the world.

He knew what was required of him: Brina had helped him to develop his drumming skills, and now, tonight, she was showing confidence and trust in him to provide the percussive rhythms whilst she journeyed into the world of spirits.

Gruvel had come to accept that Brina was good at what she did, and he was keen to learn as much as he could from her: tonight he would learn more. She was a sympathetic and caring teacher as well as successful healer, and he intended to watch her carefully as she performed her healing on Mung.

They moved inside, and Brina began proceedings by once again going round the four corners of the room, invoking her symbols. She called on the Archangels Michael and Raphael for protection and assistance. Gruvel sat down in one corner of the room and made himself comfortable: it could be the start of a long drumming session.

Brina then went to a cabinet in which she stored her healing crystals. She pondered on them as she made her selection. Sometimes her hand would seem to stray to a deep part of the cabinet and emerge with a bright crystal: intuition played its part in this type of healing. She carefully laid each selected crystal on a tray and, after considering her selection one last time, returned to the couch on which Mung lay, placing the tray of crystals on the floor.

Next, she took a crystal pendulum and began to scan Mung's body, looking for signs of low energy: when she found such a location she selected a crystal from the tray and placed it directly on the spot on Mung's body. When she had finished the scanning, she completed the placement of crystals by surrounding Mung's body with power crystals of quartz which would help to increase the effects.

She looked at the arrangement of crystals, and explained her selection to Gruvel. "Ardvon," she said, "you have already learned about chakras and energy centres."

"Yes," he replied, "you have instructed me about those. I hope I can remember what you told me."

"I am sure you will, Ardvon. Now I am trying to balance the energy centres because the traumas suffered by our friend here have thrown his whole system into complete disarray," she said. "The crystals will help to bring about that balance, and will also help the healing of his wounds by stimulating his inner healing abilities."

"How do you know he has inner abilities?" said Gruvel.

"We all have them, Ardvon," she told him. "Many conditions are set off by imbalances in the body, and so the body can treat them. If people would only take some time to stop to consider their illness and their lifestyle, they might make a connection and be able to do something about it without resorting to pills, potions and powders."

"So why don't they?" he asked.

"Good question. They all seem to be so tied up in their own little world of much haste and little progress to notice," she said. "Never mind, one day they will realise that the real answers come from the inside."

"What crystals are you using, Brina?" Gruvel asked.

"Well, let's see," she said. "I am using Aventurine to help heal the heart and lungs; Emerald is good for physical and emotional healing because it has a tranquilizing effect on the heart and mind, inspiring calm, clear assurance; Jade to strengthen the heart and kidneys; and Lapis Lazuli will strengthen the body's defensive system. I have also used Black Obsidian as a grounding stone; Amethyst will help bring Spiritual Upliftment, whilst Quartz, as you know, removes negative energy and will amplify, focus, store, and transform energies."

"That's a lot to take in," said Gruvel.

"Yes," she agreed, "but with regular practice you will remember what each stone helps with. Sometimes you have to try different things to see what works in what circumstances."

Brina placed her hands on Mung's temples, gently closing her eyes. "Now Ardvon, please start with some steady, but gentle rhythms."

Drumming is a powerful spiritual tool as it helps to induce a Shamanic state of consciousness: the beat of the drum closely approximates the base resonant frequency of the Earth, and so the Healer can become one with the planet. Gruvel began to beat gently on his drum, slowly working into that special rhythm.

The effects of rhythmic percussion take the brain into altered states and so induce trance like effects. On occasions Brina would gather a group of like minded believers together and they would use singing bowls forged from brass, chimes and vocal chanting in addition to the drums, to enter a highly meditative state of consciousness.

Drumming, by getting close to the very beat of the Earth itself, becomes a way to tap into our inner psychic abilities which helps the practitioner to travel over vast distances, effect cures, and know, even affect, the future.

Shamanic drumming gives access to a doorway that can be opened and closed at will: it is most powerful as a prayerful device, as a way to touch your fellow beings at a sacred level in a unique and powerful way. A Shamanic journey, using the drum, is visualized prayer: it is a powerful technology.

Gruvel played on his drum for a very long time, and he was somewhat surprised that he had found the energy to keep up that steady rhythm over such a period. The Angels were surely with him, giving him the strength he needed to play his part in this healing process.

Brina entered a Shamanic state of consciousness through listening to the rhythmic percussion: she journeyed to the world of spirits, and connected with spirit allies for healing work. These spirits are available to help everyone, and her role was often to reconnect clients with their helping spirits, restoring their personal power.

Sometimes the spirits gave further instruction regarding the healing, such as giving herbs, essences, diet changes and touch therapy. Sometimes Brina received prescriptions for poultices, massage, aromatic oils, herbs, and various other things. On many occasions the information she got was new information, so she learned as she healed, and she wrote it down in her Book of Treatments for future use.

Whilst Gruvel kept up his percussive rhythms and Brina travelled the Spirit world, Mung, deeply asleep rather than unconscious, felt himself again rise from his bed to where he could see his body lying there, this time probably a little closer to life than death.

Again he journeyed through the tunnel of light, this time, on the other side, he saw mountains. There were two of them, incredibly tall and smooth, completely covered with snow. He looked down and around himself and discovered that he was on rolling hills covered with perfect green, green grass. Everything was so bright and so clear. Mung looked to the right and saw pine trees, looked down to his left and saw a depression in the land that he identified as a lake.

He began to hear beautiful clear celestial music. It was the most beautiful thing he had ever heard, and it filled him with peace. He looked around and saw people dancing and stretching, moving in fantastic and graceful ways. He moved closer to join them, and saw that they were people he knew, although, again, he could not remember who they were. They made him feel warm, loved and wanted. Mung felt complete, and sighed as he lay down on the perfect grass to feel it, to kind of soak up the pure joy the place seemed to emanate.

Then, as if someone was tugging a rope tied round his waist, Mung was aware of being gently pulled back to the sanctuary, and down into his physical body to continue his sleep. As he travelled back to his physical body he saw Brina administering the healing to it, and he saw Gruvel in the corner, beating the drum in a hypnotic rhythm.

He was aware, too, of Remliel, his Guardian Angel. "Hello, Remliel," he said, "what's happening? Who are these people?"

"Hello again, Yorlan Mung. The last time we spoke you asked me to help you. In turn I asked the Angel of Healing to do whatever was possible to restore your wellbeing. This is what is happening to you. These people are trying to bring your physical body back to full strength."

"Do they know who I am?"

"They know your name and were inspired to find you so that they could take you to a safe place. They know nothing of your circumstances, but that will not affect what they are trying to achieve."

"Am I going to die? These people are not proper physicians," Mung complained.

"Yorlan, you must learn to trust that all will be well. You asked for my help and I have freely given it. By the same token these people have given their help and devotion without wanting to know anything about you, save that you asked for assistance," said Remliel.

"Mmmm," said Mung.

"It is probably best if you return to your body and continue to sleep. Whilst you do so you may want to contact your Higher Self, and have a conversation about your situation," said Remliel. "It's up to you. I am not forcing the issue. No doubt we shall speak again. I wish you well, Yorlan Mung." With that Remliel was gone and Mung was safely back in his physical body.

Gruvel played his drum like he had never done before: he had kept up the rhythms, he felt himself become part of the whole healing experience: it was as if he had entered a new and higher plane of sensitivity. He and his drum were as one: each part of the other. Together they were transcending consciousness, entering new levels of being.

Brina had entered the highest states of being with the help of the drumming. She was sure that the healing energies that were flowing through her as a channel and into Mung were the purest she had ever felt: she gave thanks to everyone who had played a part in this wonderful healing session.

She then broke her connection to the Higher Realms, gave Gruvel a signal that he should wind down his rhythms and drew the healing signs over Mung. "You are in the hands of the Universe, Mister Mung, as we all are. From what I have experienced I am certain that it has plans for you. Sleep well, sleep long."

She and Gruvel retired to Brina's kitchen where she made them a fortifying beverage which they drunk mostly in silence. "Ardvon, I want to thank you for your part in this healing session tonight. Your drumming reached new levels of intensity and sensitivity," she said.

"Yes, Brina," he said, "I felt that too. I was being watched over and guided as well as being given the energy and stamina. It was a most wonderful feeling. One I'd like to experience again."

"There's no doubt about that, Ardvon," said Brina. "Now, if you don't mind my brusqueness, I need to sleep too so that I can be here for our guest when he awakens."

"Of course, of course," said Gruvel. "Thank you for a wonderful experience and I am sure that your healing is working fast and well. I will bid you, 'Good night'." With that Gruvel left Brina's and made his way back down the forest path towards Knympton. He floated more than walked and he enjoyed the feeling of elation.

*****

Sefira Mung was beginning to get worried. Yorlan had not been home for two nights now: he had said nothing about a prolonged absence when he left to go on duty on Sunday. She understood that a Marshal's work had an element of secrecy attached to it, and she knew also that danger lurked round every corner.

Yorlan had been absent for longer periods than this before, but, always, he had told her in advance. She went over the events of Sunday in her mind one more time. Try as she might, she could not recall him telling her of some time-consuming mission or lengthy tour of duty that would necessitate such an absence. She would give him until morning to return: if he hadn't shown up by breakfast she would take action.

Chapter 9: New Horizons

As the main mast cleaved its way through the sterncastle all hell was let loose aboard *The Venturer*. The crew, knowing that everything was lost, desperately searched for something that would float to hold on to: it was their only chance of survival in this beast of a storm. If they found something could they cling onto it for the length of time they would need in order to ride out the ferocious wind and the gargantuan waves it was creating? Where would the tides take them?

The questions weren't exactly uppermost in their minds: they were desperate men fighting for their lives. In moments of such desperation you acted purely on instinct as the body sought a way, any way, to survive against the odds. Like the boat, the crew dispersed in all directions.

Down below, or what had been below, the Cranstouns were still strapped to their bunks. They heard the crashing of the mast onto the deck, and then could only assume that further damage had been wrought. Aonghus was struggling to free himself, but Everet called out to him to stay where he was. "I can't remain here any longer, Father. I am so scared, and not knowing what's going on is only making me worse," said Aonghus.

"I know this is really difficult, Aonghus, but we must stay together. If we remain strapped into our bunks then we will all head in the same direction, wherever that may be," said Everet. "It sounds like the storm has beaten the boat into submission and who knows what will happen to us or where we might find ourselves."

"Oh!" said Myrta. "To be honest I do not care where we might find ourselves, for at least we will be alive. I fear we are heading for the bottom of the sea." And with that she started to cry, gently at first, but it soon became a wail of foreboding.

"Mother!" cried Aonghus. "Can I come in beside you? I too cannot see a way out of our situation, and I would like to hug you one last time if our fate is to be drowned in some unknown drop of the ocean." He too started to cry.

Before she could reply Everet intervened. "Aonghus," he said, "we are all fearful, but you cannot leave your bunk: it would be too dangerous even to contemplate such an action. By the sounds of crashing timber *The Venturer* is breaking up and fate sometimes has a strange way of playing its hand in that if you were to undo your strap and make the effort to climb down, then this cabin will split asunder, and we will go in different directions. It is possible that this could happen anyway, but let's not invite temptation." Aonghus started to cry even louder. "Aonghus, do you understand what I am saying?" asked Everet.

"Yes, father," sobbed the boy.

"We will have to trust that we will come out of this bruised, but otherwise unscathed," said Everet.

The tossing, the pitching, the rolling and the heaving continued for what seemed an age and then, almost too suddenly, it seemed to stop. As they lay in their bunks the Cranstouns realised that the fury of the waves had indeed subsided, but there was still a considerable swell propelling them to an unknown destination.

After a time Myrta and Aonghus stopped crying, although the boy would let out a series of sobs every now and again. "Hush, Aonghus," said Myrta gently, "we're still alive and we're still together. Count your blessings."

"What blessings?" asked Aonghus rather shortly. "We are battered by a storm so severe that it seems to have been the worst one known to the crew, and you ask me to count my blessings!"

"Aonghus, darling," said his mother, trying to maintain an air of calm, "we do not know how severe this storm is compared to others. We have only experienced storms whilst on the land, and bad as some have been I agree that this one at sea was quite in a class of its own for ferocity. We have had no input to our decision making from the crew so we are making a judgment on very few facts and that, as I try to teach you, is not the best way to arrive at a decision. There are blessings: I have mentioned two. There are others, and it would help to calm you down if you concentrated on looking for what else of goodness has come out of this."

Aonghus tried to settle back in his bunk, but he found it hard to relax. Still the sobs came at a regular rate, and his mind was filled with doom and foreboding.

The up and down movement still continued, although not with the same severity, and it concentrated Aonghus' mind on his predicament. Where were they? How far away from Knympton has the storm taken them? Would they ever set foot on land again?

Strangely, too, the rising and falling had a hypnotic effect, and before he realised it, Aonghus was fast asleep: his body had taken over and shut down.

It took a little while for the parents to realise that Aonghus was asleep, for their minds, too, were full of anxious thoughts.

"Everet," said Myrta quietly, "I think Aonghus has fallen asleep."

"Good thing too," said Everet. "It will do him nothing but good to sleep through as much of this as possible."

"What are our chances of getting out of this situation?" asked Myrta.

"Hard to say, my dear," said Everet. "I feared the ship was breaking up, but, so far, our little bit has remained intact. OK, there has been some water penetration, but not so much as to cause any danger."

"Yes," said Myrta, "you are right. We will need to trust that the Universe has a solution in mind for us. The fact that we are still alive and together suggests that the Beings of Light have been working for us."

"Our Guardian Angels have certainly had to work hard," said Everet, a wry smile creeping across his face. "However, we are far from safe. I can't hear any voices outside, and that's not a good sign."

They both fell silent, and, almost holding their breaths strained to listen for the sounds emanating from outside.

"Listen," said Myrta, "there are no sounds other than those of the waves. No voices, no wind even. Oh, and the timber is creaking, not splintering."

"Could the storm be abating?" asked Everet. "Maybe it has blown itself out. I can't imagine where we are though."

"Nor I," said his wife, "but in some respects I don't really care so long as we are together. Wherever we may land, and I expect the way the winds and the tides work, we will eventually land somewhere, I am sure that we can survive."

The Venturer had indeed broken up, as Everet had feared, but somehow the Cranstouns' cabin and several others around it had remained together as a unit. By some quirk or fluke of design this area of The Venturer was a reasonably watertight section, and had sufficient buoyancy to ride the waves.

Like Aonghus, Myrta and Everet fell asleep, worn out by the excitement of danger, and, rocked by the up and down motion, they found it hard to resist closing their eyes.

As the Cranstouns drifted into sleep, so their little unit drifted on the high seas, steadily moving in a north eastwardly direction: they were headed for the Langerhans Islands which lay off Valkanda's northern shore.

According to those who had visited them, the Islands were rocky, barren and too remote from the rest of the Valkandan population to provide a viable location for a settlement. The Islands were located in the Cold Sea, where the weather was harsh for most of the year. Beyond the Islands, far to the north, lay the Dark Lands, which, according to myth and legend, was a place to be avoided at all costs. Occasionally some adventurers would sail to the Langerhans, but always they returned disappointed.

Aonghus, Myrta and Everet had their deep slumbers rudely awakened by a very loud crashing and the sound of splintering wood. They opened their eyes wide in terror, and sat as bold upright as their binding straps would allow.

"Are you alright?" asked Everet, looking across at his wife.

"Yes, yes, I'm ok," she said. "Aonghus, what about you?"

"I'm ok," said Aonghus, back in control of his emotions. "What happened?"

"Don't know," said Everet, "but we have stopped moving up and down," he continued, as he started to undo his restraining strap. He eased himself gingerly out of the bunk and straightened up very slowly. Every fibre of his body was aching with the treatment that had been meted out by the elements. He rubbed his arms and legs, he gently flexed his joints, and he examined his midriff where the strap had chafed so badly that some weals were bleeding. Finally, he stretched his arms upwards. "Oh!" he exclaimed, "that's better. I think you two can release yourselves from your bindings, but move very slowly for you will ache from head to foot."

They released themselves, and amid groans and moans finally stood straight on the floor of the cabin. The ship, or what part of it they were in, had indeed ceased its up and down movement: they could still hear and feel the waves crashing against their sanctuary.

"We have stopped moving," Everet repeated, "stopped moving in any direction at all. I don't think that the waves we can feel hitting us are of the same magnitude as before. The storm is over. Listen."

They all fell silent.

"Can you hear that?" Everet asked.

"You mean that jingly, swishing, scraping sound?" said Myrta.

"Yes," Everet replied.

"What is it, father?" said Aonghus, baffled.

"I do believe that's the sound of waves against a shore," he said, a big smile spreading across his face. "Let's take a look outside."

As they headed for the cabin door a big wave hit the ship, and it fell onto its side. The Cranstouns were sent sprawling. The contents of drawers and cupboards spilled out over them. One drawer hit Aonghus on the leg causing a sharp pain and resulting in a large bruise. Another had landed on top of Myrta, but she escaped injury. Everet was momentarily trapped by a tumbling cupboard which left him with raw looking scrapes down his forearms where he tried to fend off his wooden assailant.

Kicking the cupboard away, Everet enquired of the others and took comfort in their affirmative replies. "Let's try again to get outside," he said. However, words were easier than actions, for the cabin door was now above them and the handle out of reach. "Aargh," screamed Everet in frustration. "Everything happens for a reason," he went on, "and that cupboard fell from its mountings so that I could use it as a stepping stone towards the door." He roughly positioned the offending cabinet then climbed on to it.

"Careful, dear," said Myrta, "the cabin door will open downwards, if you get my meaning."

"What?" said Everet sliding back the locking bolt. "Oh yes, yes," he said as Myrta's wisdom penetrated his brain. As he reached to undo the latch another big wave struck the ship, and Everet rocked unsteadily on his perch. However, he quickly regained his balance, and opened the door. He tried to pull himself up through the door, but was unable to gain any purchase or leverage: he climbed down.

"I need to find something else to put on top of the cupboard to give more height. Here, Aonghus, help me shove this set of drawers into position."

The two of them cleared an area below the door then shoved the chest into place. Everet climbed up, soon disappearing through the gaping doorway. "Wait here," he called down. "I'll take a look at our situation and see what's what. Back soon."

"Take care, my love," said Myrta.

He had to half crawl, half walk along the corridor now that it was lying at a strange angle, and made slow progress. He stumbled along, trying to remember directions. He was about to open the door of the next cabin, but stopped when he realised it would fall away from him and leave a hole which would be difficult to traverse. It was best to get his family off the ship first if this was possible: they could search these other rooms later.

Everet finally reached the doorway that led out onto the sterncastle deck. It had been bolted from the outside, and so it took him a little while and considerable effort to get it to open.

He scrambled up into the doorway to find the deck gone. He looked round this little section of the ship, and was utterly amazed that they had survived. Several cabins and a couple of store rooms had maintained their integrity against all the odds, and somehow this part of the ship had survived a storm of horrendous magnitude.

"Thank you, thank you, thank you," he said, tears streaming down his cheeks. "The Universe indeed works in strange, mystical and bountiful ways."

He looked out: the boat had beached in a bay, and they appeared to be in a safe position. The shore was three to four feet from his vantage point, and the water was shallow enough even for Aonghus to wade ashore. He hoped they could find a place to shelter.

Chapter 10: Sefira makes Enquiries

When Sefira Mung awoke next morning, she was greeted with sunshine, a rare commodity at that time of year. Its cool rays filtered through the glass and brought a dainty light to the room. She was alone in bed: Yorlan still had not returned. She arose, got dressed and made her way to the kitchen.

As she cooked her breakfast she pondered on what to do about her husband's absence: it was so unlike him to go off without saying anything. Then some dark thoughts crossed her mind, and she tried to push them back out: nevertheless, they persisted, and it brought her mood down.

She ate her meal at the table, wondering what had happened to Yorlan, and where he might be. She knew that he sometimes mixed with the crowd at *The Waggoner's*, and she knew also that they were a pretty rum bunch of people. She could not really understand why he kept their company, but he always told her that he gathered information from them which was useful in his role as a Marshal.

Sefira didn't pry too much, but she couldn't get to grips with Yorlan consorting with petty thieves and criminals, especially when they seemed to know that he was a Marshal, a law keeper. Time passed by, and Sefira knew that she had to take action. She washed up her dishes and utensils, tidied the house a little, and then prepared to go out.

Sefira walked down through the town until she reached the Marshals' Station. It was a substantial stone built edifice, designed to contain and detain: a building that engendered a dread just to look at. Disregarding the shiver of coldness that ran down her spine, Sefira turned the handle on the door and entered.

A gruff looking man was standing behind a counter, writing into a journal of sorts. He paused, pen in mid air, as Sefira approached and looked up at her. "Yes, missy?" he said. "How can we help you?"

Sefira recognised the markings on the man's tunic: "Good morning, Sergeant," she said, "my husband has gone missing."

"Is that a good or a bad thing?" said the Sergeant mischievously, but changed to a more serious tone when he saw that his little joke had misfired. "When did you last see him?"

"Sunday morning, when he left to come on duty," said Sefira, shortly.

"Come on duty?" said the Sergeant. "Where? Here?"

"Yes!" said Sefira almost shouting in her exasperation. "My husband is Constable Mung, and he's been missing since Sunday morning. Do you know where he is?"

"Missus Mung!" said the Sergeant in some disbelief. "Pardon me for not recognising you. No, I haven't seen Yorlan, not yesterday, and not today. Please wait here, and I will ask the Captain."

After a short time the Sergeant returned with the Captain in tow. "Mistress Mung," said the Captain, "please come with me," and he led her to his office. "Please," he said, "take a seat."

"Have you any news?" Sefira asked.

"I'm afraid not," said the Captain. "I remember him arriving here on Sunday morning for his tour of duty, and he was assigned a beat to patrol. He should have signed off by five o'clock, but there's no record of him having done so." Sefira sucked in her breath. "I wondered if he had been overcome with an illness during the course of his watch, and that was why he had not shown up," he continued.

"Oh good grief!" said Sefira, now fearing the worst. "Have you sent anyone out to look for him?"

"No, not yet," replied the Captain. "Now that we know he is missing I suppose we have to organise a proper search."

Sefira could not believe what she was hearing. How could they treat this so lightly? "Are you saying that the beat Yorlan was supposed to be patrolling has remained unmanned since some time on Sunday?" she asked angrily.

"It would seem that way," said the Captain sheepishly.

"And this is what we pay taxes for? Negligence and incompetence? Really, Captain, the community deserves better than this, I deserve better, and so does Yorlan. After all he is one of your men." Sefira rose from her seat, and headed for the door. "I expect you to right this matter straight away, and I also expect to be kept informed. Yorlan could be lying in some filthy alley more dead than alive and you are sitting in your comfortable chair doing nothing!" She stormed out, slamming the door behind her.

Sefira headed back for home to await news from the Captain. She hoped her outburst would reinforce the urgency required from him to find her husband. On the way she came across a Constable patrolling the market place and took the opportunity to ask if he knew anything: she took no comfort in the man's obvious ignorance.

"Sometimes I wonder what you Marshals get up to," she said to the unfortunate Constable, "but if you do hear anything please tell your Captain as soon as possible."

On a whim she decided to pay a visit to *The Waggoner's Inn* and make enquiries of her own. It wasn't quite on her way home, but she thought it was worth asking there: after all, Yorlan told her he often went into *The Waggoner's* to uncover information. At this time of day it was not particularly lively, although there were a number of people about, coming and going to meet the demands of trade. "Landlord!" she called out as she entered the entrance hall. There was no reply so she called out louder: still no reply. Then she noticed a bell on a desk, stomped over to it, lifted it up and gave it an almighty shake: the sound would have raised the dead.

George came rushing through from the back room. "What's all the noise about, lady?" he asked.

"Well, either you didn't hear me call out, or chose to ignore me. The bell obviously gets your attention." Sefira was at the height of her anger by this time.

"Calm down, lady, please, before you do yourself an injury," said George, "and please, put the bell down too before you do anyone else an injury."

"Have you seen Constable Mung?" she asked, her voice ablaze with menace.

"One of the Marshals, you mean?" said George, still eyeing the hand bell in Sefira's hand.

"Of course I do, you stupid man," she retorted. "What other Constable Mungs do you get in here?"

"I don't know any of the Marshals by name, lady," he said, "besides, they rarely visit this establishment. We have no trouble in here, unlike some of the other Inns I could name."

"When was the last time a Marshal came round then?" she continued.

"Dunno. At least a sevenday or more ago. Anyways, as I said, I wouldn't know them by name," said George beginning to get agitated.

"Mung is slightly taller than you, dark hair, losing his physique a bit, but then that's middle age for you. Recognise him?" she said.

"Describes about three quarters of the people who come in here, my dear," said George with a smile. "Anyways, lady, who, exactly, are you, and why are you looking for Mung?"

"Ho, ho," said Sefira, unamused. "Who I am does not concern you, and I'm not looking for Mung, I'm looking for Constable Mung. I know he comes in here, but I can see I'm not going to get anything out of this conversation so I will bid you, 'Good Day'," she said turning to leave. She had taken three steps when she stopped and turned round abruptly. "Here's your bell," she said, slamming it into George's hand with a clatter, and then she left.

"Ludley will be pleased to hear that someone is missing Mung, and is actively looking for him," he thought to himself. "I suppose I'd better tell him when he arrives tonight."

Chapter 11: A Chorus of Bird Song

Brina awoke to a chorus of birdsong. She lay in her bed for some time just listening to the calls and songs of the various birds: their music filled her with life and vitality. She loved the sounds of nature, and birdsong was a particular favourite of hers. She knew if she looked out of her window she would be able to see the birds that were singing: she even knew which birds were present, identifying each by its song.

As she lay there her thoughts centred on the fact that the birds are always singing, and always it is a happy sound. "It uplifts us," she mused, knowing that most people do not realise this: they treat birdsong as just another noise. From morning until night the birds never stop, even although they have their lives to lead. They, like people, have to eat: they, like people, may have other mouths to feed also. They have to watch out for predators, and they have to build their nests at appropriate times of the year. They go about their business, their life, singing the joys of being alive. Theirs is a celebration of life, adapting and improvising without a second thought.

"But what about people?" she thought. When things go wrong or are delayed they grumble, grumble, and grumble. More often than not it will be someone else's fault: never is it their own. They allow themselves to become disappointed, letting their spirits fall. Anger takes over, and people find it difficult to modify their plans.

Brina knew that if everyone were to allow their spiritual nature to come to the fore they would make better progress: this was a message she was striving to teach, but there were too many deaf ears. If only everyone would see the big picture, they would not be rushing to judgment; they would not be dishing out blame to all and sundry. Then, when delays hit, they would take that step back, looking for the message or the lesson to learn, adapting and moving on.

Always there is something to sing about, for the Universe is bountiful and takes care of us, Brina knew. The answer is always there. It's just that too often Ego hides it from us, she explained to herself. The birds seem to know that all will be well, and sing about it from the treetops. "Oh when will people realise that it is time they learned that lesson too?" Brina asked herself in a mild frustration as she got out of bed, and prepared herself for another day.

Brina looked in on Mung: he was still sleeping; his breathing was easy and regular. He seemed to be at peace, and she left him to get on with her other matters. She made herself some breakfast, and went outside to eat it. She sat by her favourite tree, but resisted the urge to immerse her feet in the water. She ate her small breakfast accompanied by the birdsong, the singing of the stream as it made its way to join the Kinuli, and by scrapings and callings of squirrels as they chased one another around and among the many branches.

When she had finished eating she put her cup and plate down on the grass, and lay gently back against the tree trunk. Then closing her eyes she allowed herself to merge consciousness with the tree. Since early times trees have been considered special by humans. Apart from being the home of animals and birds, trees were also thought to embody a spirit, and people would leave offerings to the spiritual presence that resided in the tree.

In Brina's mind a silvery glow surrounded the area, and she saw the auras of other trees and plants. In this state Brina knew that the tree would absorb negative energy from her body, without it doing the tree any harm. She asked the chestnut tree for permission to give it the negative energy that she had accumulated in her body.

Trees can transform and use this energy for their own enhancement. When she received permission she stood up and hugged the tree, visualising all her negative energy from her physical, mental, emotional and spiritual self, running down her arms and into the tree via her palms. She stood there for some minutes letting her negative energies drain from her, to be transformed by the tree into something useful it could benefit from.

When she was finished she thanked the tree for its participation, and moved away from its energy field. She then brought her consciousness up through her body and into her head, taking deep breaths: she stamped her feet on the ground to bring herself back to full conscious awareness.

Brina returned to her cottage to find Mung awake and looking round his surroundings. "Good morning, Mister Mung," she said, "how are you feeling?"

Mung looked her over with the eye of an inquisitor: "I am rather groggy and I hurt all over. I have seen you before, who are you?" he said rather brusquely.

"Well, that's just what I expected to hear," she said ignoring his gruffness, "You have been seriously wounded, and the battering you took doesn't come without pain. My name is Brina, but I have no recollection that we have met before."

"Maybe I have seen you around the town," suggested Mung. "When I was out on patrol," he went on, still trying to put their previous encounter into perspective. He tried to sit up, but the pain defeated him.

"No, no," cautioned Brina, "be patient, and keep still. You have a way to go yet before you can sit up unaided." Mung lay back, and tried to relax. "I doubt if you have seen me around town for I tend not go there very often. I usually find that I can get what I want from round here."

"Where's 'round here'?" said Mung.

"Berystede Wood, close to the stream. This is my cottage," said Brina.

"How did I get here?" asked the Marshal. "My last recollection is being with Ludley and Boffe at Cranstoun's place."

"I can confirm that I found you at the Cranstoun premises," said Brina, "but you were quite alone, and, can I say, so close to death's door you had almost stepped through. A friend helped me bring you here"

Mung closed his eyes, and thought hard. His patrol on Sunday had all gone wrong when he spied that young sailor lad at Cranstoun's door. He had underestimated the boy, consequently taking a beating. Then he had compounded it all by trying to lie to Ludley. He remembered that last encounter in Cranstoun's preparation room, and his eyes opened wide in fear as he remembered Boffe stabbing him three times.

Then he seemed to relax again as he remembered his encounter with the Angel: no he had had two meetings with him: Remliel, he had called himself.

"Are you all right, Mister Mung?" said Brina, a little concerned.

"Yes, yes," he said, "just bad memories, but I have strange memories of other things too. Oh, please call me Yorlan," he said, beginning to lose his abruptness.

"All in good time, Yorlan," she said. "Do you think you could manage a little light food and a warm drink?"

"I could try, if it's no trouble," Yorlan replied.

"No problem at all," said Brina as she headed for her kitchen.

She returned with some bread and a herbal infusion. "This ought to do for starters," she said as she propped him up on pillows and cushions. "We don't want to rush things, and risk upsetting all the things we have achieved."

"We?" said Yorlan. "You mean you and me? Or do you mean you and someone else?"

"Well now," said Brina, "let me see." An expression of concentration came over her face.

"It wasn't a hard question, or even a trick question, Brina," he said.

"Oh I know that," she said. "I'm just making sure I account for everyone who has helped. Let me see, now. Well there's you, and there's me, and there's Ardvon Gruvel who helped me to find you and bring you here. Oh, and he helped in your healing too. So there were three of us humans. Then there is the Archangel Raphael who requested my help on your behalf. Well that's not strictly correct; he requested it on behalf of your Guardian Angel. So far that's five. Is there anyone else I don't know about?"

"How did you know about my Guardian Angel?" asked Mung.

"I just told you," she replied. "The Archangel Raphael told me. He also told me where to find your body. How do you know about your Guardian Angel?"

It was Mung's turn to take on the expression of concentration as he tried to remember details of his astral travel. He related his story of his strange voyage as he lay on Cranstoun's floor. Brina listened with great interest. Stories like the one Mung was telling were rare, but nevertheless significant. "I felt as if I was in the presence of God," said Mung, "although I have little time for the priest or his incantations. If only the priest could tell us about scenes I have witnessed he might fill his church. Instead he tries to put the fear of God into us, and uses a language nobody really understands. If my experience is anything to go by then God is not about fear and damnation, but about love and beauty."

"That's quite an experience, Yorlan Mung. "You have been blessed," said Brina. "Does your Guardian have a name?"

"Yes," said Mung, "his name is Remliel. He said I could do whatever I want. He also told me that it was not my time to die: twice he has told me this."

"Ah, Remliel, the Angel of Awakening," said Brina.

"Awakening to what?" asked Mung.

"That's for you to explore, Yorlan," said Brina. "Think about what happened, why it happened, and what became of it all. Besides you have just uttered some very wise words about God."

"You know," said Mung, "when you were healing me I had another of those strange experiences and I saw you carrying out your practices. There was a man playing a drum, too."

"Yes, that was Ardvon," she said, "and that experience gave him an infusion of creativity that took his drumming to unbelievable levels, so in some measure you have contributed to his development."

"I haven't seen you in town, then," he said. "I saw you in my strange experience. I must be going mad."

"Not mad, Yorlan, awakening," she replied "and you ask me what you are awakening to." She laughed as she said it. "Maybe you can teach me. You are doing well, but you must remain lying down for some time yet. Try to sleep some more, you are quite safe here. I will return later, and we will talk some more," she finished, removing the pillows and cushions she had used to prop him up.

Chapter 12: Lost

Everet made his way back to the cabin with the good news, and explained their situation to the others. "I do not know where we have landed, but there is dry land," he said. "I am sure we will survive, but it may well be a hard road to travel."

"But we have no food or water," said Aonghus. "How can we survive if we don't eat or drink?"

"You may be right, son," said Everet, "but in our situation we need to take one step at a time. There will be some source of water, even if it means capturing rain water. I saw some trees, so perhaps there will be fruits or berries. I know it's not a great prospect, but at least it's something. We have to adopt a positive attitude."

"Yes," said Aonghus, "but we don't know where we are." Then he remembered his dream with the howling of the Bearwolf and the activities of the Leechmoth and the Night Midges. "Who knows what wild animals may prowl round this place," he added.

"Aonghus!" Myrta reprimanded. "Your father has asked you to adopt a positive attitude, and, hard as that may be to put into practice, I think you should at least try to cast yours fears aside before you know the real extent of what is facing us."

"Yes, mother," said the boy, bowing his head.

"Aonghus," she said more gently, "I know it's very hard. I know you are frightened. We are all afraid of what we may find, or of what may happen to us, but if we try our best today we will be satisfied with what we have done when we look back tomorrow. This sorry situation is forcing us to look at each day as it dawns. We have no way of knowing what it will bring. However, we must try to make sure that not only are we prepared for it, but that we welcome the challenge. We will find out an awful lot about ourselves in the coming days. Your father and I are here for you, and you shouldn't feel ashamed to tell us of your fears and doubts."

"Thank you," said Aonghus. "What like is this place we have landed in, father?"

"You will see for yourself soon enough, my lad," said Everet. "Now let's put together a few items to take with us to help us set up some sort of base."

Laying out their waterproof coats on a bunk, they placed various items of clothing and some blankets on them: then they wrapped the coats round the items and made manageable parcels. "We'll take just enough to give us some comfort and shelter," said Everet. "We can always come back for more stuff if we need it."

He asked Myrta to climb up onto the cabinet, and then he climbed up after her. "Now, Myrta," he said, "I want you to reach up, grab hold of the door frame, and when I give the word try to pull yourself up. I will help by pushing you from below."

"That would be good," she said. "I will need some help, but don't push too hard!" They laughed a bit at that, and then laughed again as they struggled to get Myrta into the void. After some exertions she was up.

"Right," said Everet, "now I will hand you up the parcels." Myrta took possession of them and placed them further along the corridor.

"OK, Aonghus, you next," said Everet. Aonghus clambered up, and with relative ease Everet assisted him through the door then climbed up himself. He squeezed past the other two, to lead the way to the exit he had found.

They looked out at where the ocean had taken them: "There are hills, trees, grass. It's rugged and it's beautiful in its way," said Myrta. "All we need now is trust, patience, and a lot of hard work," she added with a laugh. She was relieved it seemed a welcoming place, but no doubt there would be trials and tribulations to be navigated on the way to survival.

"It's not too far down, Myrta," said Everet. "Can you clamber down?"

"Clamber down?" said Myrta in mock horror. "I'll descend like the lady I am!" she giggled. "Wouldn't it be best if we took our shoes off first?" she asked. "It will take a long time for them to dry out otherwise."

"Oh, such wisdom!" exclaimed Everet joining in the lightness of the atmosphere.

Aonghus was helped down into the water by Everet who then passed parcels to them before climbing down and collecting his own from just inside the doorway. Together they waded knee deep towards the shoreline. "I'm going back aboard," said Everet. "I think we should use our mattresses as well. I will bring them one by one to the doorway there and hand them to you."

Soon they had gathered a good little of pile of items they thought would be useful, and set off up the shore to look for a place of shelter. They climbed off the stony beach and headed for a copse of trees. "I think the trees may help provide shelter from wind and rain," said Everet. "I'm no expert and any ideas you may have will be welcome."

"How long do you think we will be here?" said Myrta.

"Who knows?" replied her husband.

"In that case I suggest we need something that is fairly robust. Remember we do not know where we are or what the weather will be like in this place. It may be calm at the moment, but it could change for the worse at any time," said Myrta.

"We also need to consider if we have the right materials for the job, so to speak," said Everet. "At the moment all we have are some blankets and our waterproof coats."

"What about on the ship?" said Aonghus. His parents looked at him questioningly. "Maybe there are things in the other cabins that we could use, maybe other waterproof coats."

"Good idea, Aonghus," said Everet, "but let's find a suitable spot first then reassess our needs."

"Look at the way some of these trees are bent over," said Myrta. "That shows the predominant wind. I guess we need to protect ourselves from that by having our entrance away from that direction."

They reached the copse, and dropped their bundles. They wandered round, in and about the trees, seeking a place of maximum shelter. They came across a small clearing which seemed bright and dry.

"Maybe we could build a shelter somewhere here," suggested Everet. "There are young trees that could perhaps be bent over to form a frame, and more mature trees to give some sort of protection."

"That's all very well and good, Everet," said Myrta, "but we have no rope to tie things down. You will have to return to the ship to see if you can find any. You may also want to take a look round and see if there are any beams or planks of wood that we could easily salvage to give a bit of rigidity to whatever we build here. Whilst you do that Aonghus and I will search around here for dry leaves and such to give us some warmth. We will also need some method of lighting a fire so please see what you can find on the boat."

"Have you done this sort of thing before?" said Everet with a smile. "I am glad someone is organised and knows what they are doing."

Myrta reached down and picked up a small twig which she threw at her husband in mock disdain. "Get on with you," she said.

Everet made his way back to the shore, and just as he was about to descend onto the shingle something caught his eye out at sea, between the wreck and the horizon. He stopped and looked: it was a boat. It was covered by a tarpaulin, and so he couldn't see who was on board, if anyone. Certainly there was nobody steering it, and certainly, nobody was propelling it. "How strange," he thought. He decided that perhaps he should not try to reach the wreck, but instead alert the others. He ran back to where they had decided to make camp.

"That was quick," said Myrta, "but you have returned empty handed."

"There's a boat headed this way," he said. "It's a smallish boat, but I can't see if anyone is on board because it's all wrapped up in tarpaulin. We should keep together. Let's go and see what transpires."

They reached the edge of the wooded area where they found some bushes to crouch down behind, and still get a good view of the bay. They watched as the tide pushed the boat slowly towards them. Finally, after what seemed an eternity, the boat hit the shingle and tilted to one side, obscuring their view.

There was a movement underneath the tarpaulin: from their vantage point they could just about make out a head emerging from the tarpaulin, peering over the stern of the boat; then it disappeared back under the cover, only to be replaced by a pair of legs, followed by the rest of whoever they belonged to. Whoever it was slipped over the stern and into the sea. The person pushed the boat further onto the shingle, waiting for the slightly larger waves before each push to help move the craft.

When the boat had been beached satisfactorily the sailor walked round to the bow, grabbed a rope which he buried under some rocks on the shore above the high watermark, and, satisfied that the rope would hold fast, he stood up to survey the landscape.

Aonghus was first to react, breaking cover and heading for the beach. "Diarmid!" he shouted, "Diarmid, it's so good to see you!"

Chapter 13: Investigations

With Sefira Mung's words still buzzing round his head Captain Norton Folgate instructed Sergeant Trine to instigate a complete search of Mung's last known patrol beat. "Call in Constable Litton to help you," he said, "and be quick, but be very thorough. I don't want that woman back here screeching in my ears. How Mung puts up with that I don't know."

"Maybe that's why he's gone absent, Captain," said Trine, remembering Sefira's short temper. "Right, sir, I'm off. I will collect Litton on the way."

Trine walked at a brisk pace to Litton's house and knocked on the door: he was relieved to find his colleague at home. "What brings you here, Sergeant?" asked the Constable.

"Mung's gone missing, so we have to walk his last patrol to see if we can unearth any clues as to why," said Trine.

"Oh!" said Litton. "That's not good news at all. I know I don't often have much to do with the man, but he's a fellow Marshal. Although it's my day off, I am more than happy to join the search for him," said Litton.

"That's very good of you, Litton," said Trine. "Get yourself into uniform and we'll be on our way."

The two of them set off round Mung's last tour: they went down every alley, they searched in dark and smelly places, and they asked people they passed on their way. Every initiative drew a blank, and they were dumbfounded. As their search became more fruitless, so their pace and enthusiasm dropped. "This is hopeless," said Litton. "He could be anywhere."

"I know," agreed Trine, "but he's somewhere: we have to find that place otherwise we'll have the Captain to deal with. C'mon, let's keep going."

"He could have been kidnapped and taken anywhere, even on board a ship. A number of them set sail on Monday. Maybe Mung is in the hold of one of them," said Litton.

"Now you're sounding like a daft man, Litton," said Trine. "Who would want to kidnap Mung? I mean what's he got that's worth a ransom? And why take him on board a ship?"

"Who knows?" said Litton, "How well do you know Mung, or any of us for that matter?" he continued. "Maybe someone with Mung's attributes is required by some slave master in Billington."

"Now I know you've gone mad," said Trine. "Less talk and more action," he said as he quickened the pace.

They walked up the lane that backed on to the Cranstoun premises, checking in amongst the bins for signs of Mung's whereabouts. "Look, Sarge, over there," said Litton pointing to the Cranstoun's back door.

"What are you on about?" said Trine. "Cranstoun's back door is usually open during business hours: he works in that little room preparing his meats."

"But there's no life around the place," said Litton. "Listen, it's very quiet."

"Let's take a closer look," said the Sergeant.

Carefully they stepped up the path leading to the back door which was still ajar. As they reached it they stopped and listened: there were no sounds from within. Gingerly Trine pushed the door further open: both men froze slightly when the hinges creaked.

With a heightened awareness Trine and Litton entered the doorway, and cautiously made their way into the room.

"Hello," Trine called out. "Sergeant Trine here, hello," he called out again. Taking some courage from there being no reply he headed for the front of the shop with Litton in tow. The place was empty. No meats, no produce, no display. "Let's try upstairs," said Trine and they made their way up the flight of steps. There were no signs of the Cranstouns' presence here either, although there were signs that they had left in a rush. "This is very odd, Litton," said the Sergeant. "Looks like the Cranstouns have left in some haste, but at the same time they haven't left too much behind."

"Maybe it was a planned departure which required speed at the last minute," suggested Litton. "Maybe everything was in place then something unexpected came to light right at the end."

"That's a possibility," said Trine. "If that is the case we need to try to find out where they were going and what went wrong to cause a rushed exit. But that doesn't explain Mung's absence. There's nothing up here that connects Mung to this place so let's take another look downstairs."

Back in the preparation room the two Marshals had a good look round. "There's a big blood stain on the floor here," said Litton, "but then again this is a butcher's shop, so you expect that."

"Yes, Litton," said Trine, "but take another look. I would say that there has been a body on this floor which caused the stain. There," he went on, pointing to an edge of the stain, "can you see that a body has been removed from here. Look at the way the blood trail has been dragged out of shape."

"You're right, Sarge," said Litton, "but whose body? And where is it now?" Litton squatted down beside the tell tale marks eyeing them intently, trying to make sense of what he was seeing, when something caught his eye under a workbench. He reached under and pulled out the object: it was a Marshal's badge.

Chapter 14: Mung and Brina Chat

Brina called in to see how her patient was faring: Mung was awake and taking in his surroundings. "Hello," she said, "remember me?"

"Oh yes," he replied. "I haven't gone completely mad yet."

"Would you like a drink?" she asked, certain that she knew the answer.

"Some cool water would be very welcome," he said. "I feel so parched."

"I'll get some from the stream; it will be lovely and cool. Don't wander off whilst I'm gone," she said with a laugh in her voice, disappearing out the room. She was back before Mung knew it, and he accepted the water gratefully. "Take it easy, Yorlan," she said, "just little sips, not great gulps."

She propped him up again with pillows and cushions. "Ready for some more chat?" she asked. He nodded. "Good," she said. "Now you don't have to tell if you don't want to or don't feel ready to, but I'd like to hear your story."

A pained expression came over Mung's face as he engaged his conscience in silent conversation. "Not ready?" asked Brina.

"It's not that," he said. "It's just that, erm, I don't know you all that well. You're a bit of a stranger to me, and I'm not sure what the consequences might be." Brina could see Mung was squirming as he fought an internal battle with himself.

"That's alright," said Brina. "I can understand that. Would you like me to tell you about myself first?"

"That would be very helpful, said Mung, "so long as I'm not prying."

"You won't be," assured Brina, "and feel free to ask questions. I came to Knympton many years ago from Feluce where I was born. I have always felt at one with nature, and found that nature provided everything I needed. I learned my healing skills at the Mission of the Celestial Sisterhood, located on the larger of the Crellaten Islands, which lie off the coast opposite Feluce. I became inspired to take my skills further afield, with a view to coming to Knympton as a place where I thought my skills might be welcome. I arrived in Knympton to find a big bustling unfriendly place where people seemed more intent on material matters than spiritual ones."

"That's very true," said Mung, nodding to reinforce his agreement. "This town is not particularly welcoming, unless you have money to spend. So what did you do?"

"I was tempted to get on the next ship and return to Feluce," said Brina, "but there was a voice inside me telling me that I should stay to see my vision through. I did make some friends, and helped people, but there were still too many people with what I would call closed minds who regarded me as evil incarnate. It got to the stage where I knew I would have to move to a safer location."

"You mean here?" said Mung.

"Yes," said Brina. "One of my friends told me about this place. At that time this was a derelict building in need of care and attention. As soon as I saw this place I knew it was perfect," she went on, "for the Universe had brought me here and had provided what I needed. My friends also helped me to renovate the cottage and make it habitable again."

"And you still use your skills and talents to help people," Mung said more in statement than in question. "How does that work?"

"Those that I have helped in the past tell their friends and family, and word spreads around those who are sympathetic to my skills," said Brina. "I will always give help and healing when someone requests it, without question. It's not for me to judge who is deserving and who is not: I accept others as I find them."

"And that's what you did in my case," said Mung. "You have come to my assistance. Indeed I really owe you my life. I'm quite sure I would be dead by now if you hadn't intervened, and given of your time and talents."

"Ah," she said, "in your case it was the Angels who made the request on your behalf, but no matter, you asked, I gave." She laughed as she said this.

"Even although you knew nothing about me?" Mung said. "I could have been anyone, from saint to sinner."

"Yorlan," she said gently, "I am responsible for my actions. Indeed I am responsible for my words and thoughts as well. I act according to what I believe. You are responsible for your actions. I will help to heal your wounds, to make your body whole, but I am not here to try to alter your personality, although I will help you to do that if that's what you decide you want to do. As you now know the Angels will help anyone who asks with no questions asked, no judgments made: that's what's called unconditional love. This world could do with a whole lot more of it."

"How very true," said Mung, somewhat contritely. "Everything you have told me is true. You have been very open with me, so I will tell you more about me. However, I would like this to go no further than these walls."

"Agreed," said Brina, and she drew up a chair and made herself comfortable: this could take a while, and it could be very interesting. "Tell me more about you, Yorlan Mung," she said. "You have told me a little of how you were beaten up, but you haven't told me much about yourself."

Mung began to tell Brina of his unremarkable and unsuccessful life. He had never had a great ambition to be anyone special, or achieve great things. "I just sort of bumble along from one thing to the next," he said. "Sometimes I am lucky and things go really well, but usually I have to struggle a bit just to get the ends to meet. That's how I got involved with Ludley. I knew of him in my work with the Marshals, and an opportunity came up that I regarded as being in the best interests of us both, so I became an associate of his Black Crows." And so Mung continued, rambling through his tale of who he was, and how the world had not been very kind to him. Everything bad that ever happened to him was, in Mung's eyes, someone else's fault.

The Marshal sat there starry eyed as the details of his astral travel kept filling his memory, and he broke down completely as he described the beauty and grace he experienced for the first time in his life. "Everything was just wonderful, Brina," he said wiping tears from his eyes. "Truly wonderful, and to be given another chance at life was just, well, it was just amazing."

"Yes," agreed Brina, "experiences like that come to teach us something. Can you begin to understand what message was there for you?"

"I have been thinking about my extraordinary adventures," said Mung, "and they are certainly telling me something, that's for sure. But were they just dreams, vivid dreams, powerful dreams that have made an impression in my head?"

"No, Yorlan," said Brina, "that was a very real experience. Perhaps when you are a little stronger I will explain what happened to you in greater detail. But for now accept that what you saw happened: any conversations you had actually occurred. If they hadn't, if these were dreams, then you and I wouldn't be having this conversation today."

"Maybe I am dead after all," said Mung.

"Anything but," said Brina.

"I am beginning to realise that I am being given the chance to mend my ways," said Mung. "I haven't been a terribly good husband, Marshal or scoundrel even."

"You're a bad husband, are you?" asked Brina, her interest picking up more.

"I guess I am. I haven't exactly been honest with my wife at times, although I would say I have provided for her," said Mung.

"She doesn't know about your activities with Ludley?" asked Brina.

"Oh no," said Mung. "That wouldn't be good for her to hear."

"And where is she now?" said Brina

"Well," said Mung, "I believe she's at home, but she will be wondering why I haven't returned for days on end."

"What actions do you think she will have taken?" said Brina.

"Well, when I have been absent for several nights before I always told her in advance, so, having disappeared without any warning, I would say she will be very worried. What action she has taken I can only guess at," said Mung.

"Right," said Brina, "first thing we must do is get a message to her. Will she have gone to the Marshals' Station to ask after you?"

"I really don't know, but my gut feeling says she would have, she's a very thorough woman." said Mung. A look of horror came over him as he said it.

"What's wrong?" said Brina.

"I'm wondering if she has gone to *The Waggoner's* as well," Mung confided.

"And what's wrong with that?" said Brina.

"That's where Ludley and the Black Crows meet to discuss their business," replied Mung. "If word gets back to him then he might go after Sefira as well."

"That's a chance we will have to take," said Brina. "However, I have a trick or two up my sleeve."

"What do you mean?" asked Mung.

"Let's put it this way," said Brina, "we know that your body has not been found by anyone. This Ludley character left you for dead, yet your body has disappeared. He may consider this to be a good thing, for it completely removes him from suspicion. Now if your wife starts to make enquiries he may be interested in seeing what becomes of them. Tell me, Yorlan, why did he take you to the Cranstoun premises in the first place?"

Mung told Brina about Ludley's plans to extort money from the Cranstouns whose business seemed to be producing a nice profit, and how this "easy" money looked like disappearing because the Cranstouns were of a mind not to pay up. He told her that Everet had arrived at the Marshals' Station to report the goings on and how fortunate, or so it seemed at the time, that he, Mung, was on desk duty that day: he promised the Cranstouns that action would be taken. "Well," said Mung to Brina in his own defence, "action was taken -- I reported it to Ludley, and he reinforced his intentions to Cranstoun. Trouble was, Cranstoun still wasn't going to pay up, preferring to up sticks and run off, so that's what happened."

"Right," said Brina, seeing the pieces of Mung's jigsaw drop into place, "and when you saw the young sailor at Cranstoun's door you decided to get to the bottom of it so that you could alert Ludley."

"Oh yes," said Mung, "and that's when it all came apart."

"And once it emerged that his easy money had indeed disappeared, and Ludley realised that you were fancifying the story he decided you were no longer of any use to him, so he took you to the Cranstoun's place to murder you, hoping to pin the blame on them, seeing as they had fled the scene," said Brina.

"I hadn't thought of it like that," said Mung. "But then again I had other things on my mind. He's more devious than I ever gave him credit for."

"Yorlan," said Brina, "I think you are only beginning to realise that Ludley is indeed a very dangerous man. If he perceives himself as a crow then know that the crow is a very intelligent bird. Crows can eat just about anything, and will wait for an opportunity to steal food rather than go hunting for it. Crows work together to warn off predators, and will join forces to drive them away. They build their nests high up in trees so that they can watch what is going on around them, taking action as they see fit. Crows are masters of change and movement; mystery and illusion. They are fearless and have a trickster quality about them. They know when to reveal themselves, and when to stay hidden. They are most devious and cunning."

"You've never met Ludley," said Mung, "and yet you have described him perfectly."

"He's certainly a man that's capable of anything, so we mustn't underestimate him," said Brina. "Leave it to me, Yorlan, I will get a message to your wife, and your old friend Ludley will not know a thing about it. Does your wife like cats?"

"She doesn't mind them, why?" said Mung.

"It helps me in my preparations," said Brina

*****

George had decided that he couldn't wait for nightfall to await Ludley's arrival, and sent a messenger to seek out Ludley requesting his urgent attention. Ludley gave the lad delivering the message a few shekels, and set off for *The Waggoner's* wondering what all the urgency was about.

He arrived in the back room to find George waiting for him. "This better be good, George," he said, "for I have lots of other business to attend to."

"Judge for yourself," said George, trying to remain in control of his emotions. "There was a woman in here earlier asking after Mung by name, and by her demeanour I think she will not take 'no' for an answer. I thought she was going to clout me with the hand bell in reception."

"Mung's wife most likely," said Ludley. "Sounds just like her: feisty, fiery and hell to cross according to Mung. What did you tell her?"

"Told her I didn't know any Marshals by name, and anyways they're not in here very often," said the Inn keeper.

"You let on you knew Mung was a Marshal?" said Ludley, his anger threatening to overflow.

"No, no. Of course not," said George, a cold sweat beginning to break out across his forehead. "She asked after a Marshal called Mung. She won't know he's one of the Black Crows, well was one of the Black Crows."

"Let's hope not," said the chief scoundrel, "but she'll need watching. Leave it with me, George. You did well to let me know quickly."

Ludley left, and George let out a huge sigh of relief as he returned his attention to more mundane matters.

Chapter 15: Making Plans

Diarmid and the Cranstouns hugged each other in celebration. "How did you get here?" said Diarmid, puzzled. "You were supposed to be strapped into your bunks below decks."

"We were," said Everet, "and that's what has possibly saved us. But let's leave our stories until later. We have not long landed here ourselves, and we are trying to find a suitable place to set up a shelter. Indeed I was on my way back to what's left of *The Venturer* to look for suitable materials," Everet went on, pointing to the wreck.

"Well, there's only the tarpaulin on the row boat," said Diarmid. "I haven't any food or water."

"The tarpaulin will be very handy, for we only have our waterproof overcoats as protection against any rain," said Everet. "I was hoping to find something better on board."

"Mmmm," said Diarmid, thinking. "If I'm not mistaken there is a storage cupboard of sorts close by your cabin which should contain dried meat and some fresh vegetables and fruit, although who knows what, if anything, remains of them."

"Is the row boat secure enough like that?" asked Everet.

"Yes," replied Diarmid. "That should be sufficient to hold her for the time being. The tide is receding at this point. Let me help you find what we can."

As Diarmid and Everet turned to head for the wreck Aonghus asked if he could accompany them. "Well," said Everet, "I suppose that will be alright so long as you are careful. We do not need any accidents."

"I'll be very careful," said Aonghus, and the three males set off for *The Venturer*, whilst Myrta headed back to the clearing in the copse.

Diarmid was finding it difficult to believe that the Cranstouns had survived, and that this section of the ship could remain in one piece. "It's a miracle," he said as they clambered on board and helped Aonghus up. They made their way cautiously along the corridor, picking their way carefully over the beams and wall supports that were now serving as the floor. Progress was moderate and finally they came to the gaping hole that was the open door of the Cranstouns' cabin. Diarmid stood still and closed his eyes as he tried to visualise this part of the ship.

"What are you doing, Diarmid?" said Aonghus. "Why have you closed your eyes?"

"I am trying to remember the layout of this part of the ship," he said. "I'm trying to get a picture of it in my mind. I wasn't often in this section so I am not as familiar with where things are here as I would be in the forecastle." After a few minutes Diarmid got his bearings. "Right," he said, "it's all coming back to me now. If we continue along this corridor we will find that store room: it's next to Captain Groves' cabin. Let's hope we are lucky."

"I didn't know we were in such esteemed company as the Captain," said Everet. "I thought his quarters would have been far more salubrious, perhaps in a corridor by themselves."

They made their way along the corridor, and Diarmid stopped at a door: "This is the Captain's cabin," he said, "so the store cupboard should be this door here," he continued as he pulled open the door. Various items fell out towards him and he took evasive action.

When all seemed to have settled down he looked into the cupboard. "Just as I thought," he said, "there are a number of items here that will be useful to us in our situation."

They sifted through the contents of the cupboard and made a pile of those items they deemed most useful: the salted beef, vegetables, two cooking pots, rope, an axe, a flint, candles. Then they searched the Captain's cabin and found a spyglass and some maps. "This is all good stuff, Diarmid," said Everet, "but it would be useful if we could find a pitcher or some bottles to hold water."

Aonghus found the Captain's anteroom and disappeared into it: he reappeared almost as quickly. "There is a crate of wine in there," he said, "and somehow it has remained unbroken."

"The Captain's little luxury," said Diarmid. "'Tis a shame he's not here to enjoy it with us," he went on as he headed for the anteroom.

"I think we have found enough to keep us going for a little while," said Everet. "This beef will feed us for a day or so, and I'm sure Myrta will be able to put something together that makes the most of what we have. Let's get this stuff ashore."

The three of them waded back to the shore, carrying their booty up into the woods, then along the faint pathway to the clearing where they dumped them at the foot of a large tree. "I'll go back to the row boat and get the tarpaulin," said Diarmid. "Perhaps Aonghus can help me." Everet agreed and the two lads made off.

Everet and Myrta discussed the construction of a shelter, and soon settled on what they regarded as the best place to set it up. Everet used the axe to trim a few branches from some pliable young trees as they began to shape the supports over which the tarpaulin could be laid. Everet went to the shore to pick up a reasonable sized rock to use as a hammer which they used to peg their supports down. There was plenty rope to tie things together: they were pleased with the skeleton of the shelter they had constructed, and were also confident that it would hold fast.

The boys returned with the tarpaulin, and helped Everet to cover the frame: they finished off the front of the shelter with a couple of the waterproof raincoats they had salvaged from the ship. The four of them stood in admiration of what their efforts had achieved.

Next, Myrta asked the boys to take a cooking pot and look for water, but cautioned them not to travel too far from the clearing. "There must be a small stream somewhere close by," she said. "I can't believe there's a sweeping bay here and no fresh water running into it. Everet, can you construct a fire?"

"That should not be too big a problem so long as we have dry tinder. However, I need to go back to the shore for some stones to enclose the fire: we don't want to set this whole wood aflame. If I can find some flat stones that will help us for cooking too," he replied.

Everet returned and set about constructing his fire. He laid the stones in a rough circle: in one section he arranged three larger stones as support for the flat stone he had found, and in the centre he arranged further stones to support the cooking pot. Next he set about lighting a fire with the dry leaves and twigs that Myrta had gathered, using the flint they found on the ship. It took several attempts but finally Everet managed to produce a spark and some smoke, which he carefully managed until the flames began to rise. "If nothing else this will keep us warm, and deter any wild animals from coming too close," said Everet.

"What we need now," said Myrta, "is to construct a spit so that we can roast this meat. Do you think we can manage that?"

"You are terribly organised and full of ideas," said Everet, "but I will see what I can do. Do you have an image in mind for this spit?"

"Yes, of course," said Myrta. "My vision is of two supporting sticks, perhaps there should be a forked bit at the top, with a rod strong enough to hold the meat to lie between them, but it must be long enough for us to be able to turn it to ensure an even cooking."

"Nothing complex then," said Everet, laughing. He picked up the axe and went off to find his raw materials. "How does that look?" he asked when he had finished.

"That's just what I was looking for," said Myrta. "Now I can push this piece through the meat and start cooking."

The boys walked along the outline of the bay and found what they were looking for at the far end from where they had camped: a little stream flowed outward into the bay. They followed it backwards into the woods and up a rise till they came to a little waterfall and pool. They filled the pot and gingerly transported it back.

Myrta and Everet congratulated them on finding the water then Everet opened two of the wine bottles and promptly emptied the contents into the bushes. The boys looked at him in surprise. He explained that the wine would have been fine in an emergency, but since there was a source of water then that's what he preferred to drink. He asked the boys to return to their source and wash out the bottles, then refill them with water that they could all drink.

Myrta emptied some of the water into the other cooking pot, and asked Everet to settle it on the fire. As the water rose to boiling she peeled and prepared some of the vegetables, cut them up into small pieces and threw them into the water. "Actually," she said to Everet, "can you cut enough of the meat to fit the pot so that we can make a stew come soup. That way everything will cook together, and will probably last us longer than doing it conventionally." Everet cut the meat as requested and placed it in the pot. "I'm sorry we won't be using your spit tonight, Everet," said Myrta.

"That's not a problem. We'll probably use it another time. Anyway, you are maximising our resources," he replied. The boys returned with the bottles of water. "Great work," said Everet. "Would you like another task whilst the food cooks?"

"Sure," said Aonghus, happy to be busy.

"We have no bowls or cutlery: neither do we have any cups. Do you think you could go back to the ship and find some? There are cups in the cabins, but where you might find the other things I don't know."

"I have an idea," said Diarmid. "Let's go!"

It wasn't long before the boys returned with everything they had been asked to find. "The Captain's cabin," said Diarmid in response to Everet's questioning look. They all laughed.

They sat round the fire as the darkness started to creep in, preparing to eat heartily. Everet explained to Diarmid that it was a Cranstoun practice to eat the meal in silence and concentrate on the food. "I don't think you will find it too hard to do, Diarmid," he said when the lad questioned him. "We should also thank the Angels for ensuring our safety," said Everet.

"Angels?" said Diarmid. "Are you telling me that Angels are real?"

"Yes," said Myrta, "I believe they are. Don't you?"

"Not really. Well, I have never really thought about it to be honest," said the sailor. "I thought that maybe they were just a part of children's stories."

"That's alright," said Myrta. "Many people believe that, but who looks after the world and everything in it, do you think?"

Diarmid looked puzzled and confused: "I suppose that would be God," he said.

"Good," said Myrta, "and do you think that perhaps he has helpers and messengers to see that the world gets along the way it needs to?"

"I can see that having helpers would allow God to do what he has to do," said Diarmid.

"Well," said Myrta, "that's where the Angels come in. God knows all our wants, and satisfies all our needs. What we want and what we need are often two different things, and so God uses the Angels to provide the necessities and pass on messages," she said.

Everet could see the lad was getting out of his depth and broke in. "This is neither the time nor the place to explain something so deep. Let's just leave it that you can thank whoever you think you need to for your deliverance from the wreckage," he said. "If you are interested we can discuss this when times are better."

"That's a good idea," said Myrta. "Let's just eat our meal in silence and thankfulness."

The meal though frugal tasted like the finest banquet. "Tomorrow," said Everet when everyone had finished, "we will try to work out where we are, and then see what we can do about finding our way out of it. For now we should all try to sleep as soundly as we can. We'll stoke up the fire so that it burns right through the night."

Everet lay in his makeshift bed watching the flickering of the flames. Although he was tired he couldn't drop off to sleep, instead sending out his thoughts of gratitude for their survival thus far to anyone and everyone who was listening to the silence. As the flickering of the flames and the gentle crackling of the dry twigs lulled Everet into a light hypnotic trance his head began to fill with a strange, yet encouraging voice. It was as if someone was trying to reach out to him, trying to offer words of comfort, words of wisdom. It was as if someone was trying to save him.

"This isn't the first time people have been shipwrecked and survived," the voice said. *"Man has been able to survive many alterations in the environment throughout his time on Earth, and that ability to adapt to such changes has kept him alive while other species have gradually died out."*

Everet pondered this, not questioning where the voice came from or to whom it belonged: in his trance like state all he could do was listen and take note.

"The same survival instincts that kept those others alive can help keep you alive as well," the voice continued. *"However, these instincts can also work against survival if you don't understand their presence,"* the voice cautioned.

Everet thought about his fear, the emotional response to those unknown dangerous circumstances that have the potential to cause death, injury, or illness.

"Ah, fear," said the voice, picking up on Everet's thought. *"For the person trying to survive, fear can have a positive function if it encourages caution in situations where recklessness could result in injury. Unfortunately, fear can also immobilize you. It can cause you to become so frightened that you fail to perform activities essential for survival. Just about everyone will have some degree of fear when placed in unfamiliar surroundings under adverse*

conditions: there is no shame in this, but you need to increase your confidence and thereby manage your fears."

The voice was calming, reassuring, and confident: Everet hung on to its every word.

"It is natural for you to be afraid, and it is also natural for you to experience anxiety. When used in a healthy way, anxiety urges you to act to end, or at least master the dangers that threaten your existence. If you were never anxious, there would be little motivation to make changes in your life."

Everet understood what was being said: in this shipwreck setting it would be necessary to reduce his anxiety by performing tasks that would ensure survival. But then there is frustration and anger. These are never far away when there is stress. Although he was calm and relaxed, Everet could imagine the situation only too well.

"There are many events in a situation such as you now find yourself in that can cause frustration or anger," said the voice soothingly. *"Getting lost, poor weather, inhospitable conditions, and physical limitations are just a few sources of frustration and anger. Be careful, for frustration and anger encourage impulsive reactions, irrational behaviour, and poorly thought-out decisions."*

"If I do not properly focus my angry feelings, I will waste much energy in activities that do little to further either my chances of survival or those of the others with me,' Everet said to himself, 'and where would that lead us?"

"It would be a rare person indeed who would not get sad, at least momentarily, when faced with the lack of everyday items as happens in a situation like yours. Again, beware, because if this sadness deepens, it can turn into depression. If you allow your frustration in failing to achieve to get the better of you, you will find yourself becoming angrier and angrier. That anger will not help you to succeed, in fact the opposite is true, and then the frustration level goes even higher: it becomes a vicious circle of self destruction.

"This destructive cycle of anger and frustration continues until you become worn down physically, emotionally, mentally and spiritually. When you reach this point, you will start to give up, and your focus will shift from, 'What can I do?' to 'There is nothing I can do.' Depression is an expression of this hopeless, helpless feeling. There is nothing wrong with being sad as you temporarily remember what life was like back in Knympton. Such thoughts, in fact, can give you the desire to try harder and live one more day. On the other hand, if you allow yourself to sink into a depressed state, then it can sap all your energy and, more importantly, your will to survive."

"It is imperative that I resist succumbing to such a depression," Everet told himself. He was comforted by the wisdom of the voice. Maybe it was the nature of the voice, maybe it was something else, but Everet found himself being very rational in his thinking. "I have told Aonghus that we will discover a lot about ourselves in the coming days and weeks: who knows what we can expect to find?"

"The loneliness of this predicament may bring to the surface qualities you don't know you have," the voice told him. "You may discover some hidden talents and abilities. You may even tap into a reservoir of inner strength and fortitude that has been lying dormant all these years."

"All of us here will find out a whole lot more about who we are and what we are capable of. Adversity comes to teach us, not destroy us." Everet was feeling much more positive already.

"One last thing," said the voice. "The circumstances leading to your being in a survival setting were dramatic and tragic. Your group may be the only survivors. While naturally relieved to be alive, you simultaneously may be mourning the deaths of others who were less fortunate. It is not uncommon to feel guilty about being spared from death while others were not. This feeling, if used in a positive way, will encourage you to try harder to survive with the belief you were allowed to live for some greater purpose in life. Whatever reasons you give yourself, do not let guilt feelings prevent you from living. The living who abandon their chance to survive accomplish nothing: to do so would be the greatest tragedy."

Everet considered these last words very carefully. He could see now that the whole episode from Ludley demanding money, to being here, was fraught with meaning. There was a lesson to be learned, a message to be understood. It may take a while to unravel, but Everet determined that unravel it he would. He would take heart from the voice's last words: he would survive, and he would make something of the rest of his life.

He thanked the voice for its intrusion, for its wisdom and encouragement. "Whoever you are you have spoken wisely and you have spoken well. You have given me much hope, and the will to carry on regardless." Then he fell asleep.

Chapter 16: Hunt for the Marshal

Trine and Litton left the Cranstoun residence, closing the door as best they could: the lock had been broken to gain entry by whoever had last used the place. They made their way back to the Marshals' Station to report their findings to Captain Folgate.

"The number on this badge indicates that it belongs to Mung," said Folgate, "but it doesn't make us any the wiser as to his current whereabouts, and neither does it give us any clue as to whether Mung is dead or alive. And as for the Cranstouns, well, there's another mystery."

The three Marshals sat in discussion of their findings, listing out the all the knowns and unknowns: the latter was by far the larger list. "Litton," said Folgate, "I want you to go back to the Cranstouns' place and ask around about their disappearance. Have another look round their shop as well, there may yet be further clues. Check both inside and out." Litton got up and headed off, none too pleased that his day off had been replaced with detailed investigative work.

"Trine," Folgate continued, "you need to go and have a word with Mistress Mung: there's more to this than meets the eye. She may be able to tell you things that will give us an insight into this sorry mess. I don't have to remind you to go cautiously in your questioning."

"No, Captain, you don't. I know she's a real handful when she doesn't get the answers she is looking for, however, I'll be as tactful as I can," said Trine as he got up from his chair, and proceeded towards the door.

"That's what I was afraid of," said Folgate with a smile.

*****

Ludley had instructed Moldin, Raddy and Flerge to form a rota to watch Sefira's every movement. He wanted to know where she went, who she talked to and who visited her at home. He was somewhat angry at having to divert attention and resources away from more lucrative projects, but if Mistress Mung was asking awkward questions, then he needed to be one step ahead so that he could fix any required alibis. Why nobody had found Mung's body puzzled him: someone must have noticed that the Cranstouns had gone. Where was the Cranstoun's landlord? Why hadn't he been to collect his rent and make the discovery. Ludley was getting anxious that his plan to blame the Cranstouns was beginning to come apart, and that wouldn't do.

*****

Litton took another good look round the Cranstoun premises, taking his time as he sought out further clues. He had asked the shopkeepers on either side what they knew about the Cranstouns' seemingly sudden departure. All that he could glean was that Cranstoun had been visited a few times by a couple of men who didn't seem to be buying or selling meat: there had been raised voices. He also learned that a sailor lad had visited them shortly before they disappeared. There was no mention of a visit by Mung or any Marshal.

As Litton continued his search of the workroom a large, well dressed man threw open the door and barged in. "Who are you, sir?" asked Litton, turning to face the newcomer. "And what is your business here?"

"I could ask you much the same question, Constable," said the man gruffly. "I am Druh Winstor, and I own these premises. Word has come to me that my tenants have fled."

"If you mean the Cranstouns, then, yes, they are not here. They would seem to have left quickly, but in an organised fashion. Do you know of any reason why this has happened?" the Marshal enquired.

"It's a big surprise to me," said Winstor, dropping the gruffness as the seriousness of the situation began to take hold. "They were model tenants. Always paid their rent on time, never a quibble, and very nice people too. Not the type to do this without good and valid reason. But why should this interest the Marshals?"

"Well, sir, one of our Marshals has also gone missing, and his badge of office was found under this very workbench," said Litton, indicating with his left hand. "As you will also notice there is a large bloodstain on the floor that we suspect is human. Our investigations so far indicate that our missing Marshal may have been injured here: we think his body has been taken elsewhere. The Cranstouns' absence is not good news for them either."

"Are you saying a murder took place here, Constable?" asked Winstor.

"Without a body that is hard to say. Basically we don't know what happened here, but we will get to the bottom of whatever it was," said Litton. "Until we do, I am afraid that these premises will be off limits to all and sundry."

"But that's preposterous!" objected Winstor. "How is a man to make an honest living when his assets are sequestered?"

"How indeed, sir," said Litton, "but I would venture that you have other assets that will see you through until we are finished here. Besides, I need you to accompany me down to the Marshals' Station where Captain Folgate will wish to speak to you."

Shrugging his shoulders and sighing in frustration Winstor gave in and headed for a meeting with the Captain.

*****

Trine approached the Mung house in some measure of trepidation: the woman was feisty, had a tongue as sharp as any barber's razor, having previously demonstrated that she was not averse to using it freely and indiscriminately when she believed the situation merited it.

In his concern for staying on the right side of Sefira Mung, Trine failed to notice that the front of the house was already being watched by Raddy who noted Trine's arrival.

Trine knocked on the door and was ushered in by Sefira. "I hope you are bringing good news, Sergeant," she said closing the door behind him. She showed Trine into the sitting room. "Take a seat, Sergeant; what do you have to tell me? Have you found Yorlan? Is he still alive?"

"Missus Mung, please, please," said Trine as he sat down. "One thing at a time."

"Of course, Sergeant," she said, "It's just I'm a bit on edge, what with all this not knowing anything."

"I understand that, Missus Mung," said Trine. "Unfortunately we are not much further forward ourselves. We have found Yorlan's badge of office, but as yet there is no sign of the man himself."

"Where did you find it?" said Sefira.

"It was discovered in Cranstoun's back shop, under a workbench. Do you know why Yorlan might have been there?" said Trine.

"You mean the butcher's shop down towards the market?" said Sefira.

"Yes," said Trine, "that's the one."

"I have shopped there a few times. Nice meat and good prices when you consider what's gone into its preparation," said Sefira. "However, I have no idea why Yorlan would go there, except on Marshal's business. What do the Cranstouns have to say about his visit?"

"Well, that's just it," said Trine a little uncomfortably, "there is no sign of them either. They have vanished, taking most of their belongings with them. It's a most unusual situation."

"And you have no idea where they have gone, or why?" Trine shook his head. "Maybe Yorlan has taken them somewhere, or maybe they have abducted him for some reason, perhaps to gain safe passage somewhere," said Sefira, alarmed. They both sat silent for a minute or so then Sefira continued. "I wouldn't have thought the Cranstoun man capable of that sort of behaviour, though."

"How do you mean?" said the Marshal.

"Well, all the times I have been there he has treated me, and others, very well. Nice man, always smiling, always with a good word and a certain pleasantness about him. I can't believe he would have resorted to any sort of physical violence with anyone," said Sefira as she visited the shop in her mind. "I know he must be proficient with a knife, but I would never take him for someone who would use one on a fellow man."

"We're not certain at this point in time," said Trine, "but it looks like someone was badly injured and the body removed: who that person is we cannot say. There are four people unaccounted for, but on the evidence that

82

Yorlan's badge was found under a workbench close to the bloodstains the suggestion is that it's your dear husband who has been injured," the Sergeant went on.

Sefira's jaw dropped open, her hands rising to cover the gap automatically. "Oh no! Surely not my Yorlan," she said, the shock evident in her expression.

"I'm sorry if what I said has upset you, Missus Mung, but you did want to be kept informed," said Trine softly. "Are you alright?"

"It's not your fault, Sergeant," she said. "It's just the shock. I suppose in some respects I have been expecting the worst, but it still doesn't adequately prepare you for the reality."

"Of course not," said Trine as gently as he could. He was seeing an entirely different Missus Mung to the one who had taken the Marshals' Station by storm. "Is there any information about Yorlan you can give me that may help us find him?"

"Not really, although he did spend a lot of time in *The Waggoner's*," she said.

It was Trine's turn to look surprised. "I wouldn't have taken Yorlan as a serious drinking man," he said.

"No, he's not," agreed Sefira, "but he did spend a lot of time there. He told me he was on Marshal's business when I asked him about it." Trine raised an eyebrow. "Said he was able to gather information that helped in his duties."

"I see," said Trine. "Do you know what sort of information?"

"No, he wouldn't discuss that with me. Said it was confidential, related to keeping the law. I went down to *The Waggoner's* to ask after him, but the silly man who runs the place told me he hadn't a clue who Yorlan was," said Sefira, her anger beginning to rise again at the thought of George the landlord.

"And you don't believe him?" said Trine.

"Hardly," said Sefira shortly. "Yorlan was spending such an amount of time there that he must have known who he was. Maybe you should go ask him."

Trine thanked Sefira for her information, again apologising for any bad tidings he had brought. He promised that she would be kept informed, asking her to get in touch with him if she should remember anything else that might help to locate her husband. He pondered on a few matters as he made his way back to the Station.

*****

Back at the Station Trine discovered that Folgate was in conversation with Druh Winstor: Litton told him that Winstor had arrived at Cranstoun's claiming to be the owner of the premises. Trine didn't know the man personally, but knew that he owned a few properties around Knympton as well as in other towns.

However, Winstor could not add anything that would help clear up the mystery that surrounded Mung and the Cranstouns. "The Cranstouns were model tenants, Captain," said Winstor. "I have already told your Constable everything I know. I can't believe they would do this. Business was going well too, from what I hear, so something must have scared them off."

"Yes," replied Folgate, "or someone. What you tell me about them only reinforces the picture we get from other sources. Nobody can understand why they have departed. Gone in a rush in the end, but obviously well planned in advance." There was a silence between the two men. "Alright, sir," Folgate went on, "you are free to go, but keep us posted if you are planning to leave town. There may be further questions that arise from our findings."

"Thank you," said Winstor getting up from his chair, "always happy to help the Marshals. Can I repair the door at the Cranstoun premises, or is it off limits?"

"You can fix it, but please do not touch anything inside," said Folgate, "and, it would be handy if we had a key for the time being: further investigations and all that."

*****

Trine paid a visit to *The Waggoner's*, but George continued his litany of denial regarding Mung, claiming he kept a civilised establishment. Clearly, according to George, his well run Inn had been confused with one of the other, not so well run, alehouses. "These other places are dreadfully managed," he assured Trine, "unlike this one. Surely you ought to know a simple fact like that from the amount of trouble that the Marshals have to deal with?"

The Sergeant reported this back to Folgate who made a note in the case file.

Chapter 17: Brina Sends a Message

Brina once again checked on Mung's condition, and, happy that he was comfortable and with no immediate needs, she told him that she was going into the woods to send a message to Sefira.

"How do you propose to do that?" asked Mung.

"I have my special ways and use messengers that can bypass the most stringent of guards," she replied. "Just lie back, relax and send out a mental picture of your wife and your house."

Mung looked quizzically at Brina: "What?" he said. "Just imagining my wife and house will enable you to find them? Couldn't you explain a bit more just what it is you are going to do?"

"I suppose I should," said Brina, "but stop me if you don't understand, because it can seem very strange indeed. Do you remember I asked if your wife liked cats?"

"Yes," said Mung, "I do and I thought that that was a strange thing to ask me."

"The reason I asked was to identify which kind of animal I should use as a messenger," said Brina, "and the cat is, for me, an obvious choice."

"I see," said Mung. "Do you have a cat?"

"No, Yorlan, I do not have a cat, "said Brina, "but one of my little talents lies in being able to make contact with them at a spiritual level. I can merge my thoughts with those of a cat, or other animals, if I need to."

"You can turn yourself into a cat?" said Mung in disbelief. "What kind of evil magic is that?"

"No, Yorlan, I am not going to change physically into a cat, so you can drop that idea straight away. What I am about to do is called visualisation, which allows me to use the power and abilities of an animal with me during this excursion. My visualisation is a special one, called a Shamanic journey, when I will visit the astral plane." said Brina. Mung was still not convinced. "You have visited the astral plane, Yorlan Mung, when you met the angels and conversed with them," she told him.

A look of bliss came over Mung as he remembered these journeys. "Yes," he said, "beautiful they were too."

"Exactly," she replied, "and there was a message for you in these journeys. My journey will have a reason also, namely to get a message to your poor wife." Mung nodded in agreement: "So there will be no evil magic, Yorlan, because I only operate for the best outcome for everyone."

The look on Mung's face told Brina that he was still a little perplexed, but would nevertheless do as he was asked. "It all helps the process to go smoothly," she assured him. "Before I go," she continued, "I need you to give me directions to your house."

"I can't give you directions from here, because I don't know where I am exactly," said Mung. "How about I give you directions from, say, *The Waggoner's*?"

"Yes, that will do," said Brina. "I can work with that." So Mung gave her the directions she would need to follow to arrive at his house. Brina then gathered up the few objects, stones, jewels and ingredients she would require for her ceremony before leaving her cottage.

She walked quite a distance, into the deeper part of Berystede Wood, to an area where the townsfolk would never dream of going: the woods had an aura of mystery and foreboding that kept all but the knowledgeable from straying too far from the beaten paths. At last she found her place of solace, a little clearing which she blessed with her symbols and delimited with a circle and pentagram.

She again blessed the sacred space before entering into the circle. She sat down and emptied the contents of her bag: a white candle, a mirror, some incense and her flint tool. She lit the incense, placed it at each point of the pentagram then returned to the centre of the circle, sat down and calmed herself: now she was ready for her special meditation.

She called on Archangel Michael to cast his cloak of protection around her and Sefira Mung, and to be on guard against any dark forces with his mighty sword: she felt Michael's cloak swathe round her, also sensing his shield and sword were not far off either; protection was hers. Next she called on Ariel and Sofiel, the Angels of Nature to oversee the needs of the animal with whom she was about to enter into communication; next, she called on Ambriel, the Angel of Communication to ensure that the message to be delivered was clear and understandable. There were shimmerings of light as the angels came to assist Brina.

Brina was about to embark on a journey that only experienced Shamans could make. The training had been rigorous and lengthy, the practice long and difficult: the skills of shapeshifting could not be developed overnight. Brina was about to merge her spirit with that of a chosen animal, in this case a cat. From an early age Brina had recognised that she was a spiritual shape shifter, had seen aspects of animals in her personality and actions, aspects which had helped to shape her into whom she had developed. She had worked with cats before, finding them to be the perfect vehicle for what she had in mind: cats are very spiritual and psychic beings.

*****

Cats are held in such reverence by some societies that the penalty for killing one could be death. In other cultures when a household cat died, all the members of the family were obliged to wear a floral tribute as a token of mourning. Some cultures even associate the phases of the moon with cats' eyes.

86

As a sacred animal, cats were believed to give fertility to the ground so were often buried under fruit trees, and some were even sacrificed in corn fields for this very purpose. In less enlightened cultures, cats were the animal most associated with witches, demons and evil, and many a poor feline had suffered as a result.

It may be that cats owe this association with witches to their undoubted psychic nature which gives them the ability to see unseen things. A cat that left the home of a sick person was a sad sign, as it indicated the coming death of the afflicted, and many have noticed how responsive pets in general are to the realms of the unseen.

*****

Brina's talent lay in being able to merge her light body in the astral plane with that of a power animal. She did this by inwardly uniting with the animal. Her sense of smell or sight became heightened; there was increased dexterity in her limbs, and a feeling of the power that the animal represented.

When Brina merged into those elements of the natural world, she entered their being, stepped into their essence, becoming one with them. Each aspect of that element became an aspect of her.

Brina's shapeshifting meditation was one of the relationship between humankind and nature, in this case animals. It was based on assuming certain characteristics of an animal. Traits and talents were included in these characteristics: these were assumed for a limited time and for a particular purpose.

Brina discovered that the most important requirements of shapeshifting were psyche and endurance. Psyche determined the maximum rate at which changes could be safely made, while endurance determined both how long one could keep shapeshifting, and also how long a form could be maintained once achieved.

Shapeshifting is a merging, sometimes called the 'thirteenth factor', the point where there is no division between body, mind, and spirit. Everything becomes Oneness, a place of being where all knowledge and wisdom are readily accessible, dependent on intentions and desire. Merging is the mystic state where the practitioner becomes one with all things.

For Brina, the two main components of the merging process were breath and intention. First, Brina set her intention: she ensured that it was specific, simple and directed, for she would focus on it before, during and after merging. Next, she paid attention to how she was breathing.

Propping up her mirror, she placed the white candle in front of it before lighting it. She closed her eyes, and breathing deeply, allowed herself to relax, and mentally drift to her favourite place of relaxation.

When she felt herself beginning to slip away, she opened her eyes and stared into the mirror. She softly called out to the spirit of the cat that she wanted to use.

"Oh spirits of the natural world, I ask that you appear as I accept you into my life. Guide me as you have so guided those before me."

She closed her eyes again, and after a few minutes she was aware of the cat's spirit there with her in the circle. She felt the energy coursing throughout its body, its breathing escaping into the sounds of silence around them. The cat, somewhere in Knympton, felt a similar awareness of Brina's spirit.

She felt the transformation beginning to occur. Slowly, she opened her eyes, gazing past the shadows of the mirror and saw herself fully immersed into the cat. She welcomed it and allowed it to speak its messages to her. She asked the cat if it would take a message to Sefira Mung: the cat agreed.

Brina conversed with the cat which was in town, and from their combined knowledge of Knympton was able to direct it to *The Waggoner's*. "This is our starting point," Brina told her animal counterpart, "from here we will find Sefira Mung." The cat walked round the streets and alleys according to the directions Mung had given Brina. As it made its way down an alleyway a dog barked and gave chase, but the cat was far too agile, easily evading the poor creature, leaving it barking in frustration. In Brina's mind she could hear the cat laughing: "What a silly dog you are," said the cat. "I can't believe you thought you could catch me!"

The cat reached what ought to be Mung's house and stopped opposite: Brina compared what the cat was seeing with Mung's mental projection, which though faint, was nevertheless strong enough to indicate that this indeed was his home. The cat looked up and down the street, and saw Flerge trying his best not to be noticed whilst watching the Mung residence.

The cat bounded across the road, into the neighbouring garden, then made its way round to the rear before jumping over the fence into Mung's yard. The kitchen window was slightly ajar so the cat took another leap, landing on the sill before stepping through onto a small table then jumping to the floor. "Miaow," called the cat. Sefira came running through to see what the noise was. "I thought I heard a cat," she said. "Now where did you come from?" Noticing the open window she said, "Oh it's my fault is it?"

"Miaow," said the cat again.

"Would you like some milk?" said Sefira reaching for a bowl and a jug: she poured some out, and put the bowl down beside the cat. The cat took several licks then paraded into the sitting room where it jumped up onto a chair and sat down.

"Like your comforts do you?" Sefira asked her visitor. "You are a very pretty cat."

"Miaow," said the cat once more.

Sefira sat down opposite the cat, somehow absorbed by it. She looked the cat over several times. "What a beautiful cat you are," she said. "Such gorgeous eyes you have!"

Far away, in her sacred circle in the woods, Brina was conscious of what was going on. *"Yes, Sefira, look into the cat's eyes. The cat's eyes will enchant you, take a look, step in."*

Quite before she knew it, Sefira was indeed entranced, caught up in the cat's eyes, and sat back in total relaxation. It was as if she had drifted off into a light sleep: she thought she was dreaming, for the cat was speaking to her.

"I have a message for you, Sefira Mung."

"Really?" said Sefira disbelieving. "Since when did a cat speak?"

"I am no ordinary cat, Sefira, so please listen carefully."

"If you insist," said Sefira, drifting further into her trancelike state.

"Your husband, Yorlan, has been grievously injured and lay at death's door. He almost slipped through, but the Angels came to his rescue: he is now being cared for by a friend of the Angels. He is recovering, but the process will be long. Although he is not out of danger he is making progress."

"Oh no!" said Sefira, alarmed. "Where is he? I must see him."

"Where he is must be kept secret for the time being, Sefira. There are those who wish to harm him, and will do anything to discover his location. You too must be careful, for they are watching your every move. There is one outside right now."

"I must see Yorlan to know that he is alright," said Sefira.

"All in good time, Sefira. I will return to you with news of his progress, and when the time is right I will lead you to him. For now you must be brave and have patience. Be very careful who you speak to, and be very aware of who is around you. Those responsible for Yorlan's injuries are watching you, but do not be afraid, you will come to no harm."

Sefira sat quietly in the chair, her eyes still closed, and so was unaware of the cat's departure, as Brina had directed it back into the kitchen and out through the window into the garden. Slowly she drifted back into reality and sat mesmerised.

"Did I really have a conversation with a cat," she asked herself. "I must have fallen asleep and dreamed the whole thing up, but the message was comforting."

"I have one more request if I may," said Brina to her animal alter ego.

The cat listened to what she had to say and gave its agreement to carry out her instructions. It made its way up the road to where Flerge was doing his best to be inconspicuous. The cat approached him. "Miaow," it said.

"Go away, pussy," said Flerge trying not to break his concentration.

"Miaow," said the cat insistently, rubbing itself against his leg.

"Oh alright," he said. "You want me to stroke you?" He bent down to stroke the cat. Brina watched through the cat's eyes as Flerge stroked the cat a couple of times. "That's it pussy, now get lost," he said pushing the cat roughly from him. The animal jumped quickly away from him, uttering a "raorrr" as it scampered away.

Brina asked the cat if it knew how to return to its own area from this location and, getting an affirmative, thanked the cat for its help and expressed a wish that they could merge again. Leaving the cat to return home, Brina began to withdraw her consciousness from it, and slowly returned to her own physical form.

Still breathing very slowly she opened her eyes, and made herself aware of her surroundings. She thanked everyone for their part in a successful venture before completing her grounding technique to ensure that she was truly back in her own reality. She gathered up her accoutrements, blessed the circle and closed it down.

Gently she stepped outside the circle, and made her way back to the cottage. "You can stop projecting those images now, Yorlan," she said as she entered. There was no reply. Concerned, she looked in on Mung: he was sound asleep, a look of serenity adorned his face.

"Sleep well, Yorlan Mung," said Brina softly, "may your dreams be pleasant."

Chapter 18: Getting the Bearings

Next morning Everet was first to awaken: he looked over at the others who were sleeping peacefully. As silently as he could he got up, went outside and found that the fire was still smouldering. He gathered up some dry leaves, carefully placing them amongst the embers before adding more twigs, and, finally, stouter pieces of wood. Soon the fire roared back into life, crackling and sending sparks high into the air.

He then looked for the bottles containing the water, and, finding them just inside their accommodation, emptied one into a cooking pot which he put on the fire to boil. A cup of tea would start the day off nicely.

Everet crept back into the tent, and soon located the map that they had found in the Captain's cabin: hopefully he might get some idea of where they might be, but he would really need Diarmid's input.

The water in the pot came to the boil: Everet quickly found the ornate tea box which belonged to Captain Groves, opened the lid, added a small amount of tea leaves to the pot, turning the water a deep shade of red, much to Everet's liking. "Lovely," he thought to himself, "what a nice way to start the day." He closed the box securely and replaced it back inside the tent.

He wakened the others, apologising for having to do so, but explaining that much had to be done. They sat with mugs of tea discussing the day's agenda.

"I see you have been studying the map, Mister Cranstoun," said Diarmid. "Can you make anything of it?"

"Yes, Diarmid," said Everet "I have taken a look, but I need your input too. Please call me Everet, no need for formalities here. We were just about out of the Kinuli when that storm hit us."

"That's right," said Diarmid, "we were almost out of the estuary. We tried to sail close to the shore at Camber Point, but as soon as we hit the Western Sea the full force of the storm hit us."

"If my memory serves me correctly," said Everet, "the Captain seemed surprised at the direction of the wind."

"Yes," Diarmid replied, "the wind was from the south west, which is very unusual, especially so at this time of year."

"So that would drive us north east, up the coast this way," said Everet, drawing his finger over the map. "But the question is, 'how far up the coast?'"

"To be honest, Everet," said Diarmid, "I wasn't counting the hours or measuring the ferocity of the wind: I was trying to survive, so I have no idea either how long the storm lasted or how long I drifted in the row boat. I was petrified."

"Of course," said Everet, "we were all fearful: it was not an experience I would ever want to repeat so long as I live. The intensity was quite amazing, so I guess that would drive us even further than we might think."

Diarmid studied the map with great concentration. "I'm not sure," he said, "but we might even have blown as far as here," he went on pointing to a little group of unnamed islands just off Far Cape.

"What makes you say that?" asked Myrta as she looked on.

"Just the ferocity of the storm, and the length of time we seem to have been at its mercy," he replied.

"Well, we can't just blithely jump into the row boat, and head off in what we think is the right direction for us if we really don't have any idea where we are starting from," said Myrta.

"As always, my dear," said Everet, "your practical nature comes to the fore. Of course you are right, but establishing direction is not going to be easy. Look at the sky, it's not telling us very much."

"What do you mean, father?" asked Aonghus peering through the canopy of trees.

"Today, the sky is very bland. There are no colours in it save for the dull grey of the clouds. No matter where you look it's the same dreary colour," said Everet.

"I still don't understand what you are saying," said the boy.

"Well, can you see the sun?" asked Everet.

"No," said Aonghus, "it's hidden behind the clouds."

"Exactly," said Everet, "so we cannot really say in which part of the sky it is shining. If we could see the sun then we would have an idea of which direction east is, because the sun rises there, and as far as we know it's early in the day, probably mid morning."

"So how will we find out if the cloud cover doesn't change?" asked Aonghus.

"We will need to watch for darkness approaching," said Everet. "It follows the sun, so whatever part of the sky starts to darken first will be towards the east."

"Or whatever part remains lightest for longest will be west," Diarmid added. "Then we will know north and south, and at least have an idea of where we should be headed."

"You are a smart lad, Diarmid," said Myrta. "I am glad you are with us."

They finished their tea and what fruit was still edible as they planned their activities for the day. "We have enough meat and vegetables for today," said Myrta, "but after that we are on sticky ground, so we need to find a source of food quite urgently."

"The stream where we got the water may have some fish," said Diarmid.

"That would be exciting!" said Aonghus. "We could go fishing."

"Yes, Aonghus," said Everet, "but what equipment do you have?"

Aonghus' excitement quickly abated when he realised that there was no means to capture his quarry: "So what will we do?"

"Where there is a need," said Myrta softly, "creativity is never far away. If you find the fish I'm sure you will find a means to catch them." Aonghus brightened.

"You boys can go fill up our water bottles whilst looking for fish, but don't wander too far. Keep a lookout for berries and fruits too," said Everet. "We'll head for the ship and see if we can find anything else useful."

*****

Aonghus and Diarmid picked up the empty bottles and set off towards the stream they had discovered the day before. They found their way quite easily, arriving soon at the little waterfall where they had filled the bottles. They decided to follow the stream backwards towards its source on the hill: they filled one bottle for use on their journey.

They trailed the stream onwards and upwards, climbing steadily. There were outcrops of rocks to get round as they followed the watercourse through various clumps of trees. It was in one of these coppices that they found some nut trees: Diarmid thought they were called filberts. They also found a few berry laden trees. However, Diarmid had no idea what they were or if they were edible.

They soon reached the source of the stream which was in a small rocky crevice midway up the hill: the water bubbled out of the ground with a gurgle, forming a little pool, before slipping down the side of the hill, growing wider as it went, until it reached the shore.

From their viewpoint the boys realised they were on a small island, and that there were other, bigger islands not too far away it seemed. They knew that they had to get back to base quickly with the news. They gathered as many nuts as they could on their way back to the waterfall, filled both bottles and sped back to camp.

*****

Everet and Myrta reached the remains of the ship, climbed aboard, picking their way cautiously along the corridor. From the furthest end they began to open the cabin doors, looking in to see if there were any goods that could be put into service: all they found were a few more potatoes in the store cupboard that Diarmid and Everet had already plundered. They returned to base quite disappointed.

Myrta busied herself in preparing the last of the food, trying as best she could to make the most of her ingredients. Everet scrounged around for more wood for the fire. "I hope Aonghus finds his fish," said Myrta, "because after tonight we will have nothing."

Everet said, "I will help the boys to look for alternatives. This will be our priority."

Their gloominess was rudely interrupted by the arrival of the boys who were obviously excited about something. "Maybe they have found the fish," said Myrta.

"They certainly have found something, and I expect we will learn just what very shortly," Everet replied. The boys came gasping back to the tent. "Slow down, slow down," said Everet, "get your breath back then tell us your news."

"We are on an island," said Diarmid, "just as we supposed we were. But there are other bigger islands not too far away. We can't see them from here. But if you go up the hill you can."

"Do you think you could relate what you saw to the maps we have?" asked Everet.

"I could try," said Diarmid, full of excitement.

They rushed to their tent, looked out the maps, and began to look in earnest for their location. Diarmid looked hither and thither, his gaze tracing the line of the north coast. "These unnamed islands," he said, "don't have the correct arrangement for what I have just seen. However these islands here," he went on pointing out the Langerhans Islands, "pretty much fit the view from the hill."

"Then we were blown a tremendous way off course!" said Everet.

"Heaven help us!" said Myrta. "So far? That was one potent storm. However will we find a way back to anywhere, let alone Knympton?"

"Look," said Aonghus pointing to the map, "the Qaf Mountains are not so very far away, and they say that these mountains are at the edge of the world."

"That's what they say," agreed Everet, "and only the Dark Lands lie beyond. We don't want to go there. Let's all take a walk up this hill and use the spyglass. Perhaps it will help us establish if Diarmid's thinking is right."

*****

They gathered up the maps and spyglass and set off. "Did you find any food, boys" asked Myrta.

"Yes," said Diarmid, "there are a few filbert trees and some others with berries, but I can't tell you what they are."

"Fine," said Myrta, "we'll gather what filberts we can on the way back and look at your other trees too."

Soon they reached the vantage point on the hill where the islands of the group sprang into view. "Such a pretty view," said Myrta admiring the scenery, "if you are not lost!"

They spread the maps out on the grass and aligned them to match what they were seeing. "I think you have identified our position very well, Diarmid," said Everet. "It looks like we are on the north shore of this island here," he went on, pointing out the assumed location. "Now we know which direction is which at least, if our reading of the situation is correct."

Diarmid was looking through the spyglass. "From what I can see, you are exactly right, Everet," he said. "Now we need a plan to get us off this island and onto land. The sea route home is not a viable option."

"It's not an option at all," said Everet, "I have had enough of sea journeys for a while."

They studied the map again, more for reassurance than anything else. "Look," said Aonghus, again pointing to the map, "there seems to be some sort of settlement marked on the map just here on the slopes of the Hills of Cuhullin. What do you think that might be?"

"Let me see," said Everet picking up the map for closer inspection. "Well done, Aonghus, you are right. There does seem to be evidence of a settlement, but it is unnamed on this map."

"Could we reach it?" asked Myrta. Everet nodded. "Easily?" she enquired.

"With good conditions and favourable factors I would say we could perhaps get there in a couple of days," said Everet. "What do you think, Diarmid?"

Diarmid studied the map intently, trying to work out distances. "I don't know," he said. "Possibly longer than that, but my feeling is that we should make this journey in small steps. We should get ourselves off this island and onto the next one."

"Sounds like good advice, Diarmid," said Myrta. "Perhaps we should make our way back, and start packing up what we think we will need. The sooner we start the sooner we will reach the mainland."

They headed back, collecting as many nuts as they could on the way. Once back at camp they opened out the maps again and proceeded to lay out a plan of travel: they would follow the coast as much as possible, traversing the deeper water only when absolutely necessary.

With their spirits uplifted they set about breaking camp with a new found energy, knowing that there was indeed hope. They finished off by eating some of the nuts they had gathered, washing them down with strong, warm tea. They extinguished the fire, and set off along the little path to the shore where the boat bobbed gently up and down on the waves.

Myrta and Aonghus got into the row boat then Diarmid and Everet pushed it from its mooring before clambering aboard. Everet and Diarmid took an oar each, Myrta was stationed up front to guide them and watch for any signs. Aonghus was asked to take control of the rudder and steer them according to Myrta's instructions: the next part of their journey had begun.

Chapter 19: Sefira and Folgate

Sefira had another visit from Brina in her feline form early the next day, telling her to get ready to leave the house and visit Captain Folgate at the Marshals' Station. She explained that the Captain was to be informed that Yorlan was alive and making progress from his wounds. She would know when to leave because there would be an almighty noise of cats squabbling with whoever was posted to watch her, and the spy would be distracted from his concentration.

The promised fracas did not take too long to materialise, giving Sefira barely enough time to get herself prepared. However, on peering out the front window she saw the hapless Raddy, who had taken over watch duty, being harassed by at least half a dozen cats that were driving him to distraction. With Raddy's attention elsewhere, Sefira slipped out the front door and down the road towards town.

Quickly and briskly she stepped along the cobbles, soon disappearing out of sight as she headed for the Marshals' Station. By this time the cats had retreated from their successful mission, leaving Raddy almost literally licking his wounds, and trying his best to straighten out his trousers which had suffered severe damage from the cats.

Sefira marched boldly into the Marshals' building, almost throwing the doors open as she progressed. "Hello, Sergeant Trine," she greeted the burly Marshal, "I am here to have words with Captain Folgate."

"Oh, er, hello, Missus Mung," replied the Sergeant. "Just wait here and I will tell him you have arrived," he added as he got down from his stool, and headed for the Captain's office. Trine knew it would have been useless to ask if an appointment existed, as he did not want to raise her hackles unnecessarily: the Captain would not have thanked him for doing that.

He reappeared quickly. "Through you come, Missus Mung," he said as he ushered her towards Folgate's office.

"Mistress Mung, how nice to see you," said Folgate. "Please sit down."

"Thank you, Captain," said Sefira, "but let's dispense with the niceties. Time is of the essence and I am looking for results."

"Of course you are," said Folgate. "We all are. Do you have any new information for me?" he asked.

"Perhaps," said Sefira, "but tell me your story first."

"Well," said Folgate: then he told her what the Marshals' investigation had produced. "So there you have it, Mistress Mung," he said. "We are unable to tell you where your poor husband is, or what condition he is in. Neither do we know what has become of the Cranstouns, although we have more than enough character references to indicate that they shouldn't be part of your husband's disappearance. However, until we find everyone, we have no way of being certain about anything."

The Captain's disappointment clearly showed in his tone of voice. "Oh," he added, "it looks like a cart may have been used to remove a body from the Cranstoun's premises." Sefira looked at him questioningly. "There are wheel marks in the back yard, but we lose track of them very quickly," he said. There was a pause then, "Did you have something to tell me?"

"Well, I suppose I have," said Sefira, "but you will think that I have lost my sanity when I tell you."

"Go on," encouraged the Marshal.

"Well, yesterday a cat, one I haven't seen before, came into the house through my kitchen window. I offered it some milk, but it didn't really want that. It proceeded to the sitting room and made itself comfortable on my good chair," she said somewhat indignantly.

"Mistress Mung," said Folgate, "has this anything to do with Yorlan?"

"Yes," she said, "of course it has, otherwise I wouldn't be wasting my breath telling you about it. Anyways, I sat down in the chair opposite, and I swear that cat entranced me with its eyes: it was as if I was daydreaming. The cat told me that Yorlan had indeed been injured, but had been rescued and saved."

"Really?" said Folgate. "A cat told you this? Mistress Mung, are you serious?"

"See, I told you that you would question my sanity. I questioned it as well. At least the message is encouraging and positive."

"Mistress Mung, I think you are deluding yourself into thinking this way," said Folgate. "I don't suppose the cat told you who did the injuring, or who did the rescuing or even where we might find your husband."

"That information was withheld," agreed Sefira.

"How convenient," said Folgate. "Mistress Mung, this is a serious enquiry which makes no sense at the moment, and information like yours is unlikely to help us. Where is this cat now?"

"I haven't a clue. I told you I had never seen it before. I did see it again this morning though," said Sefira.

"And did it speak volumes to you?" Folgate was unimpressed and his attitude had changed.

"Well, actually it did," said Sefira. "Captain Folgate, I am no rambling old wife who has lost her mental capacity. This cat told me that my house was being watched by those responsible for all this trouble. It also told me that it would create a diversion so that I could come here unseen by those watching me."

"Good Lord!" Folgate shouted. "What next?"

"More information will be forthcoming in good time. I am to be careful about where I go, and to keep my wits about me," said Sefira. "Send a Marshal up our street, and let him tell you if anyone is watching me. I will return when I can tell you more, Captain."

Sefira maintained her dignity as she got up from her chair quietly. "I bid you good day, Captain," she said as she departed.

The Captain sat in his chair, head in his hands: he was at his wit's end. He wondered what else could happen. "Trine!" he called out: the Sergeant appeared. "Send a man up past Mung's house to see if anyone is hanging around suspiciously."

*****

Raddy was maintaining his watching brief when he noticed Sefira strolling up the road, her shopping basket filled with various items. "Oh oh," said Raddy to himself, "when did she get out and where has she been apart from the shops?" He sat there musing on how she could have escaped his gaze. Realisation hit him hard. "Those cats," he told himself. "She got out when those cats attacked me. Oh Lord help me, Ludley will not like this: however, I daren't not tell him in case someone else has seen her around town."

The scoundrel was in a huge self torment, and his concentration again lapsed. He failed to notice the Marshal approaching him. "Hello, sir," said the Marshal, "care to tell me why you are here?" The look of surprise on Raddy's face barely concealed a look of guilt: he started to stammer.

"Looking for a property to rob, are we sir?" said the Marshal.

The thief recovered his composure just in time. "Certainly not, Marshal," he said. "This may sound strange in an odd sort of a way, but I was set upon by a number of wild cats. Look at me. I am scratched beyond belief, and my trousers will have to be thrown away once I get home. I was merely resting here trying to recover not only some strength, but dignity as well."

"You certainly are in a bit of a state, sir," agreed the Marshal. "But you can't rest here; you are unsettling the good burghers. I would suggest you return home, wherever that may be, right now, as quickly as you can muster. Now be off."

Raddy seized the opportunity with both hands and took himself off as fast as he was able. He looked a sight for sore eyes bumbling down the road, his trousers ruined, the tatters flying like little flags in the breeze.

Chapter 20: On the Move

In the row boat the group set themselves as they had previously decided, with Myrta up front to direct and guide, like a Guardian Angel figurehead on an ocean going rigger, Aonghus at the stern manipulating the tiller, and Diarmid and Everet in the middle, one on either side, manning the oars.

Diarmid had rowed before, indeed when the row boat had been required on *The Venturer*'s voyages Diarmid was always assigned an oar. He had no problems with the mechanics of rowing, slipping into the role with effortless ease.

He would lean forward as he manoeuvred the blade of the oar bow-wards to start the stroke, rotate his wrists so that the blade entered the water perpendicular to its surface: he would brace his feet against the boards and use his powerful thigh muscles as he pulled on the oar; at the end of the stroke he would again roll his wrists so that the blade was parallel with the water's surface, feathering they called it, and then he would start all over again.

Diarmid's rowing was rhythmical, powerful and efficient. Not so Everet's, but that was understandable as he had never rowed before. It was no real surprise that he experienced trouble on all fronts, despite Diarmid's best efforts to explain. Sometimes his blade would not be immersed deeply enough, and when he pulled the oar it would skim through the water, and poor Everet would fall backwards, the blade slapping the surface of the water.

At other times he would immerse the blade too deeply, making it difficult to pull on it: this had a tendency to destabilise the boat and more than once its occupants thought they were going to capsize. Diarmid smiled ruefully when this happened, telling Everet that he had caught another crab.

Everet, try as he might, couldn't get the rhythm of the activity, and as for feathering, well that was a complexity too far.

With the haphazard propulsion from the oars, Aonghus tried to compensate with the rudder, but, he too, didn't quite understand the technique so his efforts resulted in the boat zigzagging its way forward.

For the first hour or so the row boat slalomed across the bay, with a lot of effort being transformed into not a lot of gain. Realising that effort was being wasted, Myrta called a halt to the rowing, but cautioned Aonghus to keep focussed on holding the tiller still: that way they would at least drift in a straight line.

"Everet, my dear," she said, "I know you are trying your best and working really hard, but a lot of what you are doing is going to waste."

"Yes, I realise that too, my love," he said, "and it's wearing me out physically as well."

"Maybe if Diarmid sat beside you, and guided you through a few strokes you might get a better idea of what's needed to get the stroke just right," said Myrta.

"We could give that a try," said Diarmid. "Rowing is not an easy activity to pursue and it takes time to learn properly. Everet's doing a good job considering this is his first attempt."

Diarmid pulled in his oar and stowed it safely before moving across to join Everet. "Alright, Everet," he said, "let me show you how to roll your wrists." Diarmid gave Everet a demonstration, and then Everet tried a few times, but found it difficult. "Maybe we should abandon this feathering movement and concentrate on the mechanics of the rowing stroke," said Diarmid, and once again he gave Everet a demonstration of the action. "Before you try, Everet, we'll get Aonghus to straighten us up."

Aonghus adjusted the tiller slowly until the boat was again heading in the desired direction. Everet took control of the oar and tried a few strokes. "That's better," said Diarmid. "The idea is to dip the blade in just so far as to cover its upper edge then pull: that way you'll get the most from the stroke, and you won't have to fight to get the blade out of the water at the end of the stroke."

"Perhaps we should try rowing at a slower rate, Diarmid," said Myrta. "That would give Everet a better chance to make a proper stroke. We might even make better progress by slowing down, if you get my meaning."

"Yes, we could try that," said Diarmid. "Also, you have probably noticed that this boat is designed for two rowers on each side, so I will sit closer to the bow on my side, so that I can keep an eye on Everet's stroke rate. That way I will be better able to coordinate my stroke."

That said, Diarmid moved his position and after some readjustments the rowers declared themselves ready to try again.

"On a count of three, Everet," said Diarmid.

"When you are ready," Everet replied.

"One. Two. Three," said Diarmid. Everet acted on cue, and began his stroke, with the younger sailor pulling in unison. Slowly the row boat moved forward. Everet concentrated on the mechanics, taking time to make the strokes: Diarmid watched and reacted accordingly, giving words of instruction and encouragement, almost alternately.

The boat made a slow, yet steady, but nevertheless welcome progress, with Aonghus having quickly mastered the art of steering, keeping them on a straight line. There was a gentle current helping to pull them along too, and that, together with a very calm and flat sea, helped them forge towards their target.

Gradually they made their way eastwards, following the line of the coast, never venturing too far from the shallows. It was tiring work for Everet, both physically, as he pitted his strength against the resistance of the water, and mentally, as he concentrated on his every movement and placement of the oar.

By late morning they had reached the point where they had to change direction and travel south, heading for a small intermediate island not far, or so it seemed, from the island on which they had been washed ashore.

"Big effort now, Everet," said Diarmid, "we'll be crossing deeper water. You have done very well so far, just keep going as you have been."

"I'll try," said Everet his muscles throbbing from unfamiliar use.

"We can take a rest when we reach the small island," said Diarmid, "and rethink our strategy, although it would be good if we could row on as far as the big island."

"Yes, yes," puffed Everet, "but let's reach the little one first."

There was a noticeable difference in the effort required to make the crossing as the current and tide kicked in, trying to take them off course. Diarmid and Everet dug deeper into their reserves of strength, and Aonghus too found he required more muscle power to fight against the current's onward surge.

Myrta offered words of comfort and encouragement as she kept a lookout, giving instructions to Aonghus when required to keep them as close to their desired bearing as possible.

After what seemed like forever, they reached the shallow waters off the small island. Everet and Diarmid pulled in their oars in order to take a well earned rest. The current here was gentle, allowing them to drift on it, although Aonghus maintained a vigilant attitude at the helm.

Some minutes later a little bay came into view and Myrta suggested they beach the boat to recuperate from their efforts: they could lie down or take a walk to stretch their legs, and anyways, a cup of tea would be most welcome.

Once ashore the rowers quickly found a spot where they could lie down and stretch out, whilst Myrta and Aonghus set about preparing a fire to make tea. She returned to the row boat to look for the remains of the fruit that had been recovered from *The Venturer*, along with the nuts they had gathered before they hurriedly left their first camp. She brought with her also the maps to study their progress whilst the water came to the boil.

Everet had fallen asleep and was doubtless dreaming of better times, either in the past or yet to come: whatever it was, Myrta was certain it didn't involve row boats and oars. Soon the water was at boiling point, and tea was made: she gently roused Everet from his slumbers, telling him to have something to eat and drink.

The four of them sat round the small fire, quietly musing and playing with their thoughts. The warmth from the fire was welcome: the weather had held up for them, but there was a chill in the air which was bound to become more pronounced as the afternoon wore on and turned to evening.

"I have been looking at the map," said Myrta, "and we have come a fair distance. Is it possible we could make it as far as the next island today?"

"My arms ache," said Everet. "I don't know if I could survive another session in the boat today."

"That's understandable," said Myrta, "but if we could make it, then I do believe that we could reach the settlement by the end of tomorrow."

"Let me see the map again, please," said Everet. Myrta handed it to him, and they studied it together.

"I'm pretty sure we are here," said Myrta pointing to a spot on the map. "If we could get to here then I am sure we can go all the way tomorrow, that is, if the weather holds up for us."

"What say you, Diarmid?" said Everet.

"It would be good to take as much advantage of the good conditions we have today, if that's at all possible. However, you shouldn't wear yourself out, and if you need time to recover then we'll stop here," said Diarmid.

"Tired I may be, aching I most certainly am, but let's give it a try. We should get as far as we can whilst there is light and fair weather, for who knows what tomorrow will bring," said Everet.

With that they once again broke camp, and loaded their goods into the row boat. Diarmid pushed them off gently, jumped in, and he and Everet prepared their oars. "Right, Everet on a count of three......"

*****

By late afternoon a very tired and weary Everet was glad to be helping to set up a temporary shelter on the larger island. He wanted nothing more than some hot food and a good night's sleep. The others, too, were tired by the seeming monotony of the journey, and being cramped up in the row boat for such long periods.

Whilst Everet and Diarmid did their best to make a tent, Aonghus looked for a source of water, and Myrta set about cooking the last of the meat: it was now urgent that a new source of food be found.

Aonghus returned from his water finding mission with the bottles successfully replenished. He was also excited as he told the others of a pool where he could see fish swimming. "That's good, Aonghus," said Myrta, "we will eat what we have then rest. I'm sure the fish will still be there in the morning."

"Can't we go get them now?" the boy asked, somewhat disappointed.

"No, Aonghus," said Myrta, "we need to rest. Besides, how are you going to catch them?"

"Well, I don't know," said Aonghus. "There must be some way."

"There is," said Everet, "and we'll discover what it is tomorrow."

Chapter 21: Foul Moods

The Marshal returned to the station to report to Trine. "There was a man hiding in the bushes up past Mung's house, Sarge," he said, "but it was no big event."

"What do you mean, Harvens?" queried Trine.

"Well, this man was in a state of distress. His clothes were ripped to shreds and his face and arms were covered in scratches," said the Constable.

"And that's not a big event?" asked the Sergeant.

"He said he had been attacked by a posse of wild cats which had taken a sudden dislike to him for no reason he could think of," said Harvens. "I told him the good people in the houses round about were a bit suspicious of his being there, and advised him to get home immediately."

The Sergeant looked at Harvens in astonishment. "He left in a hurry," added the Constable.

"Did you get his name or where he purported to live?" asked Trine.

"No, Sarge, I didn't see any need. The man was in some discomfort and embarrassment, so I sent him on his way," replied Harvens. "I did what I believed was necessary to settle the matter quickly and efficiently."

"Oh, I don't think the Captain is going to like this, Harvens. Be prepared for some stern words when he finds out," said Trine as he headed for Folgate's office.

"What kind of police force are we?" asked Folgate, dismayed. "Does nobody have any intelligence?"

"I can't believe it either, Captain," said Trine. "He was sent to investigate a complaint, and he makes a mess of it. I can only hope he has learned a lesson."

"Send him in here, Sergeant," said the Captain. "I will put him right on this one, and hopefully future investigations as well. No wonder we are the laughing stock of the town at times."

Harvens emerged from the Captain's office some time later a wiser man. Folgate had spared no rod in berating the man for his incompetence. When the Captain was in such a mood it was best to say nothing, just let him rant. "Let him get it off his chest," said Harvens to himself, doing his best to look culpable.

"OK, my lad," said Trine to the Constable, "get back on the beat and use that head of yours in a proper fashion."

"Yes, Sarge," said Harvens as he left the station.

Trine went into the Captain's office to offer him some tea. Folgate was a picture of misery, sitting with his elbows on his desk, his hands cradling his head. "What am I supposed to do or believe, Trine?"

"How do you mean, sir?" asked Trine.

"Well, the Mung woman tells me she has had conversations with a cat, and now a gang of the self same creatures seemingly attack a man who was allegedly keeping an eye out for the dear woman," explained Folgate. "Something tells me that there are strange goings on taking place in our manor, and I don't think we have heard the last of it, by a long chalk."

*****

A sense of déjà vu hung over the back room of *The Waggoner's* when Raddy entered, clothes in shreds, and his face and arms a mass of scratches. There were a few deep ones which were still bleeding. Indeed he was a sight for sore eyes, with trails of fresh blood streaming down his face and disappearing into his shirt collar. Thoughts crept back in time to when Mung had arrived the worse for wear with a tale of sorrow that was not believed by Ludley, and look what had happened. A stillness, almost a deathly hush, quickly fell on the room.

"What's the trouble, Raddy?" said Ludley looking him up and down: Raddy stood there bewildered, not knowing where or how to begin. "Raddy," said Ludley, the irritation in voice beginning to increase, "I asked you a question. Has the cat got your tongue?" The silence was deafening. The Black Crows were cowed, hardly daring to breathe.

"Wh.. wh what do you know about the cat?" asked Raddy, scarcely able to summon the words.

"Oh, for any sake, Raddy," said Ludley shortly, "it's only an expression. What are you on about? Just tell me. Now!"

The gang members winced as Ludley slammed his pint pot against the table to emphasise the urgency he required. "I was on watch duty at Mung's place, nothing going on, then this cat appeared from nowhere, started to rub itself against me. I pushed it away, but it wouldn't take that as an answer, so I aimed a boot at it," said Raddy trying to recall as much detail as possible.

"And?" prompted Ludley.

"Oh, it disappeared with a scream," said Raddy. The others started to smile. "Then, before I knew what was going on, there was a dozen or more of the beasts all around me, scratching and biting. I fell over trying to lash out, and the cats swarmed all over me like some piece of meat. I was fearing for my life when they stopped, and disappeared as fast as they had come."

"Really?" said Ludley. "A big tough man like you beaten by a dozen cats?"

"Yes, yes," said Raddy, fear beginning to show in his voice. "They were everywhere. As fast as I got to grips with one, another would take its place. Have you ever tried fighting a posse of cats?"

"Anything else to report?" asked Ludley.

"Oh yes, but you won't like it," said Raddy.

"Raddy, I will be the judge of that, not you," said Ludley, "You tell me what it is, and I will decide."

"As I was gathering myself together a Marshall appeared," said Raddy.

"What?" said the gang leader, "Out of nowhere, like the cats?"

"C'mon, Ludley," said Raddy, "give me a chance. I was wiping myself down and checking my wounds when he arrived. Came up from behind me. Luckily he wasn't very inquisitive, just sent me on my way saying the people in the houses were getting edgy about some dodgy characters lurking about."

"Raddy," said Ludley, "there is something not right about this. Cats just don't appear out of nowhere. Are you sure of your facts?"

"Yes, yes," protested Raddy. "Why would I tell you anything different? I'm not as stupid as Mung."

"I don't know if it helps or not," interrupted Flerge, "but last time I was on watching brief I had a similar experience with a mangy cat rubbing itself against me. However, it went after I gave it a kick."

"You're right," said Ludley, "I don't know if that helps or not either. Trouble is, our plans have been interfered with, and the Marshals, however inept they might be, are aware of us now."

"What are we going to do?" asked Boffe.

"Boffe, you are the one who got us into this mess. You failed to carry out a job properly, and look at the consequences. We've lost Mung's body, and now we daren't get any closer to his wife to find out what she knows," said the head villain. "You go away and think about it. Come back tomorrow with a plan that will work. Got me?"

Chapter 22: Mung Recovering

In Mung's periods of wakefulness Brina had kept him up to date with what was happening. She told him of her visits to Sefira, and described the first man who, not so carefully, had been watching the Mung house.

"That's Flerge!" said Mung in amazement. "So Ludley is watching what Sefira gets up to. He must be troubled to divert what I know he considers are 'valuable resources' to a watching brief."

"Yes," said Brina, "your disappearance has ruined his plans. You can bet he now believes you are not as dead as he wanted you to be as well. That man has a big problem, and doesn't know how to solve it." Brina then described the second watcher, telling Mung how a posse of cats had caused trouble for him, causing him to miss Sefira's departure."

"That sounds like Raddy you have described," said Mung. "Was he badly scratched?"

"A few big scratches but nothing too serious, and his trousers in tatters," she laughed. "Will he have the guts to tell Ludley he missed Sefira's coming and going?"

"He'd be a fool not to," said Mung, "especially considering the treatment that was handed out to me for withholding information."

Mung was now remaining awake for longer periods, a sure sign that his strength was returning. Brina was pleased with his progress, although Mung's wounds still needed careful management. "Yorlan," she said, "your injuries are on the mend, but I'd like to ask Ardvon Gruvel to come over to participate in another healing session. Would you be agreeable to that?"

"You mean the man with the drum?" asked Mung.

"Yes," said Brina, "that's the man. He's very good."

"The sound of his drum was entrancing," said Mung. "I was totally captivated by it. Yes, I think I'd like to hear that again. Perhaps, being a little more aware of what's going on, I will enjoy it even more."

"Maybe so," said Brina, "but you mustn't put any expectation on a healing session, Yorlan. What happens or doesn't happen does so for a reason: whatever the reason, it may well be beyond our understanding or comprehension. By all means listen to the rhythms of the drum: by all means enjoy Ardvon's talent, but please, try to detach yourself from the outcome."

"But isn't the healing you are asking for supposed to help me?" said Mung. "Surely, I am supposed to feel better afterwards?"

"Yorlan," said Brina softly, "when I conduct a healing session I ask for help from my spirit guides, Angels and Higher Beings of Light. I also ask that whatever help is given, that it is for the greater good of all concerned. Healing is not usually instantly administered, although sometimes what we call miracles occur when it happens that way. Sometimes the person seeking

106

healing needs to learn a lesson, or receive a message, thus the healing influences may be delayed until that happens. Therefore what you must do is try to disconnect yourself from what I am doing whilst keeping an open mind. As you have already discovered strange experiences can occur during a healing session. Do you understand what I am trying to say to you?"

"Sort of," said Mung, "but I do want to get better soon."

"Of course you do, Yorlan," said Brina, "but everything takes its time. When the time is right your injuries will clear, but there is nothing you can do to bring forward that moment. We can apply creams and balms to promote healing, but time itself is the ultimate agent."

Mung still looked perplexed so Brina tried a different approach. "Yorlan," she said, "do you ever pray?"

"Not with any great meaning or devotion," said the Marshal.

Brina told him that many people pray only when they are at rock bottom and in a crisis: their prayers are therefore filled with demands and requests which they hope God will instantly answer. People forget that they have to play a part, expecting an instant change to take place. When nothing seems to change some of these people give up, saying there is no God or that God doesn't care about them.

She explained that praying in desperation was not the best way in which to pray. It would be better if everyone was aware of all their thoughts and actions then they could ask if they have God-like qualities. "People rarely go into the silence and listen for answers," she told him. "You can't hear the answer if you don't pay attention. Ask for what is going to assist your spiritual progress. Do not ask for lessons to be taken away, but ask for guidance as to how to deal with them."

"Also," she continued, "as you pray remember to include thanks for all that you have. This focuses and uplifts the mind, reminding you of your blessings. This frame of mind will be the right one for handling whatever comes your way."

"But what about the priest who prays for a living, or so it seems," said Mung. "He exhorts me to pray so often that I would never get any work done."

"Ah," said Brina, "those type of prayers are carried out in a ritualistic manner, with a form and structure that is human invention and theological practice. People usually regard prayer as part of an act of worship. It's as if God demands it, or that prayer is the only way to communicate with the Divine. It needn't be like that, for prayer is a channel to the Universe: it's how you 'talk' to Creation, to All that is. It can be used at any time, in any situation. You don't have to be in church, and you don't have to be on your knees in front of any icons or candles, although you can use these if you wish, if it helps you in what you are doing."

"So church prayers are useless," said Mung.

"Not at all," said Brina. "All I am saying is that you can pray at any time in any place. You should use prayer as you would engage another human: as a means of communication."

"How can you have a normal conversation with God?" asked Mung

"Because," said Brina, "you are always connected to God, and God is always connected to you. Also, you get back what you give out, so if you keep making demands of God, so, in some way there will be even greater demands made of you. There are so many things that have been provided for you by Creation, yet you are blind to this. You take so many things for granted you scarcely acknowledge how they came to be."

Mung had a look of bewildered puzzlement.

"Have you ever tried listing things you are given without your intervention, like sunshine, flowers, or rain?" said Brina. "Have you ever said, 'thank you' for air to breathe or water to drink?"

"No, I haven't," said Mung. "You are right. We all take so much for granted. We seem too busy with other things to realise what has been given to us freely."

"Look around you," said Brina. "List what you have, list what you really need. You are abundant without realising it. Take time to consider your existence and when you have truly and honestly investigated it, realise that you do not have to make demands of God because God has already done more than well to provide you with what you need."

Mung was struck speechless as his mind raced round all those things that were there, already provided: the basics of life, the basics for life. "I will contact Ardvon," said Brina, "and you can consider how you can participate in the healing."

*****

After the evening meal Ardvon Gruvel arrived at Brina's, drum in hand. "Come in, Ardvon," said Brina, "our patient is awake. Go right through and say 'hello'."

"Hello, Yorlan," said Ardvon, "I trust that you are making progress."

"Hello, Ardvon," replied Mung, "I feel I am getting stronger each day and that my body is indeed recovering. I owe my life, such as it is at present, to you and Brina, and for that I thank you deeply."

"I am here to be of service," said the drummer. "It's a pleasure to help."

Brina arrived in the room carrying various crystals which she set down on a small table. "First, I must prepare the room," she said lighting a clump of sage. Brina blew on the sage to encourage it to smoulder, then went to each corner of the room in turn, tracing out her healing symbols. In each corner she invoked the necessary elements, the Na Pra Chi, the Ku Ma Ra, the Om Nes Est, and asked for the appropriate healing energies to flow.

Next, she arranged her crystals in a grid around Mung, finishing by placing particular sensitive crystals at vital points on his body. Meantime, Gruvel seated himself in what Mung realised was the southern corner of the room to prepare his drum for the healing.

"Are you ready, Ardvon?" Brina asked.

"Yes, whenever you want to begin," he replied.

"Excellent," said Brina. "Now, Yorlan, I would like you close your eyes, and just think of a nice quiet place where you won't be disturbed. A place that is your's alone: a place of special significance where you can relax, and just be. Please remember the conversation we had earlier, and make no expectations on the healing energies that may flow. Indeed it would be good if you were just to be, and go with the flow, no matter where it may take you. You are in a safe and loving environment with the support of Ardvon and myself, as well as the healing entities of the Higher Realms. No harm will become you."

"I will do my best, Brina," said Mung, "and I'm sure that Ardvon's drumming will take me somewhere extra special." With that he closed his eyes, and began his inward journey.

"Right, Ardvon," said Brina, "let's hear your drum. Slow and gentle to begin with, then just allow yourself to be guided by the energies." Ardvon began as instructed, and Brina waited for a few minutes to allow the energies she had summoned to be amplified by Ardvon's drumming vibrations. When she felt ready, she stood beside Mung, and, lightly placing her hands, palm downwards, on Mung's chest, she began to invoke the Archangels.

"I call upon Archangel Michael to protect us with his cloak of deepest blue, and to deflect anything not in our best interests with his mighty shield. I call upon Archangel Raphael to send healing and your helper Angels to administer to this man. I call upon Archangel Chamuel to bring peace, to enable us to find what it is we are searching for."

She too closed her eyes, allowing the rhythm of the drum to guide her and the energies to where they would be of greatest benefit, and was soon lost in the vibrations as she opened up as a channel for the healing energies.

Mung soon drifted off, ably assisted by Ardvon's delicate, yet persuasive playing. The beating was steady, was rhythmical, was compelling, and Mung drifted off to that safe and secure place only he knew existed.

He was by a stream, in a clearing in a wood. The sun's rays lanced through the canopy of the trees creating a magical, mystical refuge of beauty, peace and solace. He sat down, his back against a welcoming chestnut tree. Lazily, he kicked off his shoes, rolled up his trousers, letting his feet dangle in the water. He felt at one with nature, with the world. Here was peace and tranquillity. There was nobody to bother him, nobody to tell him what to do, nobody making demands or expectations of him. How wonderful he felt.

Around him, in the room a mist of a deep blue hue began to form in one corner. Ardvon saw it, and marvelled at it. The Archangel Michael had indeed blessed them with his presence. Slowly, the mist spread out, stealing across the ceiling, before sliding down the walls, then flooding across the floor. Ardvon watched as Michael's protection engulfed them in its completeness.

He continued with his delicate, yet hauntingly complex rhythms, raising the level of the vibrations. He could visualise the sound waves he was making mixing with Michael's protection, enhancing it, ensuring that only good could reach through to them.

Then, as he looked around the room he saw little twinklings of light, some pale green, others a deeper green, and he knew from Brina's teachings that the Archangels Chamuel and Raphael had also responded to the Shaman's calling: they were thrice blessed, he thought. Never before had he been present in the company of three Archangels all at once. This was indeed a glory night, and only good could come of it.

Mung, by this time, had moved on from his dalliance by the stream, and was walking alongside it: he could hear the water gurgling, and he was heading for the source of the noise. He came by a little waterfall and stopped, watching in delight as the water poured over the upper level, splashing against the stones and rocks of the lower level. The water formed a small pool where it seemed as if it was taking a rest after the trauma of falling from the upper level. Then, having rested, the water would continue on its journey to wherever that might be.

As he stood there admiring the beauty of nature he became aware of a presence with him, yet he had heard nothing of this person's arrival. He turned to find what looked like a monk, not far from him, but it was hard to make out any features as the cavernous hood of the silver grey habit was drawn completely over the face.

Mung had no idea who this could be, and could not begin to guess why this meeting was taking place. The monk threw back the cowl revealing his features, and shook his head to free his shoulder length brown hair from the constraints of the hood. With hair this length, Mung decided that this was no monk. "Hello," said the stranger, "I am Jeremel. I am an Angel Guide and have come to let you know that I have been assigned to help you through your difficult period."

Mung stared incredulously at the Guide. "But you have no wings that I can see," he said. "How can you possibly be an Angel?"

"Ah," said Jeremel, "not all Angels have wings. We take different forms at different times. We reveal ourselves to people in many ways." As Jeremel spoke Mung was aware of shimmers of green, purple, blue and yellow. "We in the Angelic Realms are here to help you, and we are particularly happy when you humans make contact with us. We will always respond to your requests for contact. You have been blessed, Yorlan Mung, and there are greater things awaiting you."

"What things?" asked Mung.

"Do not be so hasty, Yorlan. These will unfold in the fullness of time when conditions are right. You have lessons to learn first, and every situation that arises does so to bring you insight."

Mung was dumbstruck and his jaw dropped in astonishment. As he gathered his wits about him, and was getting ready to ask the next question, Jeremel faded out of view: as Mung looked around him he realised that he was quite alone. "Maybe I should make that walk back to where I started," he thought, and he set off to retrace his footsteps.

As he did so, he was aware that this was not the pathway he had previously trodden, and, instead, he was being led through a field of long grass. Again Mung was aware of splashings of green and purple and then he saw what looked like a small boy with wings come into his line of sight.

Suddenly, or so it seemed to Mung, this boy was skipping around in front of him, skimming along the top of the grass, leading Mung in a particular direction. The boy had a wand in his right hand which he was waving all around. There was a cascade of glittery material being dispensed from the tip of the wand, and the boy was a picture of joy as he danced around, sprinkling his angel dust everywhere he went.

The whole mood was uplifting, and Mung felt the happiness in the atmosphere that was being generated. "I will take you upwards," said the boy to Mung. "You are definitely on the right pathway." Mung happily followed for what seemed a long time, feeling so happy that all his cares had disappeared.

"Thank you, Ardvon," said Brina, "I think it's best if we leave Yorlan to slumber on. I will watch over him. Can you find your own way out?" Ardvon gathered up his drum and hugged Brina. "What a wonderful evening, Brina," he said. "It seems as if it gets better every time. I will leave you to watch over your patient, and we can talk further tomorrow."

As the door closed, Mung's awareness drew him back to his surroundings. Gently he opened his eyes, doing his best to take in his whereabouts. "Gently, Yorlan Mung," said Brina softly, "don't rush back."

"I was by a stream, then by a waterfall where I met an Angel guide ….." and so Mung related his adventure to Brina.

Chapter 23: Fishy Business

Next morning Myrta was first to awaken: she looked out of the tent, and saw that there was a thin mist hanging over the island. On stepping out of the tent, she felt the fine wetness of the drizzle which clung to her in little beads of water. "What a poor start to the day," she said to herself. "Perhaps it will brighten up later so that we can continue our journey."

She started to stoke up the fire, which thankfully had not been doused by the wetness of the night, with some wood they had fortunately kept dry by storing it in the tent: the mist clung to the trees like teardrops, and was, in its own way, a pretty sight to behold. There was a large spider's web spun out between some tree branches just above where they had made their tent: it looked like a necklace encrusted with diamonds. As the wood on the fire began to crack into flames, she filled the cooking pot with water from the bottles Aonghus had filled the previous evening.

The smell of the smoke and the crackling of the fire soon stirred the others and they too were disappointed to note the change in the weather. Myrta saw the expressions on their faces.

"I know," she said, "it's very unsatisfactory, but we have to make the best of what we get. We can use the time to find fresh food. We have nothing left to eat."

"Great!" said Aonghus. "We can go fishing in that pool I found yesterday."

"Yes, Aonghus," said Everet, "that's right, but first we need to devise something to fish with. What do you suggest?"

With that Aonghus was dumbstruck. "I don't really know," he said. "Have you any ideas, Diarmid?"

Diarmid suggested finding a branch stout enough and long enough with a fork at the end. "We can attach a piece of cloth or similar to the fork, and we will have a net of sorts."

"That sounds like a feasible proposition, Diarmid," said Everet. "Let's have some tea then we can get to work. After drinking their tea in an almost indecent haste the boys went off in search of a suitable branch, whilst Everet searched their belongings for a suitable piece of cloth with which to form the net. It wasn't long before the boys were back, and they watched as Everet did his best to fasten a small sack to the forks of the branch. "There," he said holding up the completed article, "will that do?"

"Looks good to me," said Diarmid taking charge of the fishing net. "Right, Aonghus, lead the way, and let's see what we can catch." The boys sped off, heading for the pool where Aonghus had claimed to have seen fish.

Whilst the boys went off on their mission Everet and Myrta searched nearby for fruits or berries to add to whatever the boys could manage to catch.

"I hope they will find some measure of success," said Myrta. "It would be such a boost to their self confidence."

"Yes," Everet agreed, "that it would do. Aonghus is so excited by the prospect and I just hope he does not despair if things should not work out just the way he has set his expectations."

"Everet, look, over there," said Myrta, "bramberries."

"Wonderful. Just what we need, and so many ripe ones," said Everet. "We need to go back and find something to hold them. We must gather as many as we can. They will be useful to have on board as we row."

"You go back, and I'll start picking," said Myrta.

Everet soon returned with one of the cooking pots, and they began to harvest the bramberries. As they moved along the bushes they found some apple trees, and were able to gather some of these as well. The apples were small and slightly bitter, but Myrta said that the sweetness of the bramberries would eliminate the sourness.

They returned from their venture very pleased with themselves. The mist had lifted, but the day was still cold and damp. "Hopefully, we will be able to make further progress," said Everet, "and, who knows, we may even reach our intended destination."

*****

Aonghus and Diarmid reached the pool: it was fairly large and looked quite deep. There were indeed fish swimming around. "There are no huge fish that I can see, Aonghus," said Diarmid, "but that's probably in our best interests." The pool was at the edge of the beach, where the shore met the land. It had been formed by the river tumbling over the rocky outcrop and forming a waterfall: as the water hit the shore it gouged out the pool, before continuing for another forty or fifty yards to meet the sea.

"How so?" asked Aonghus.

"Well, our mighty net here is untested and may break if we have too heavy a load," he smiled. "Besides, the water will add to the weight of the sack so it is indeed best if we go after the smaller ones."

"Have you done this before then?" asked the younger lad.

"I have fished before, but using proper equipment," said Diarmid. "This will be a new experience for me." He took the branch and gently dipped it into the pool. Slowly he manoeuvred the net until it was a little way from the bank. He let it rest there, the bottom of the sack resting on the floor of the pool.

"What are you doing?" asked Aonghus. "Why aren't you chasing the fish?"

"Because that would be lot of effort for little or no reward," said Diarmid. "This way, when a fish swims over the sack I can raise it quickly and make the capture." Almost as he said this a fish came across the centre of the sack: Diarmid struck, raising his net as quickly as he could. He hauled it to the bank and they both peered in: the fish had eluded them.

"Are you sure this is the best way?" said Aonghus, disappointed.

"Trust me," said Diarmid. "This is better than chasing the fish. I will try again, then you can try whatever you think will bring results." Diarmid reset his trap, and waited patiently for another opportunity. They waited quietly and, sure enough, another fish, or maybe it was the same one, crossed the edge of the sack. Diarmid was surprisingly quick to make his move, and as he swung the net back towards the bank they could see that a fish was thrashing about inside the sack.

"Yes!" Aonghus was ecstatic. "You are so good, Diarmid, you got one."

Diarmid laid the net down a little way from the edge of the pool: he grabbed hold of the struggling fish with one hand, carefully feeling inside with the other to take possession of his trophy. He pulled it out, and had some difficulty in keeping hold of it: quickly he returned it to the sack and held it shut. "Aonghus, go down onto the shore and bring me a couple of decent sized flat stones."

When Aonghus returned, they placed the larger stone on the ground then Diarmid reached into the sack and retrieved the fish. Holding onto it with both hands, he positioned its head over the stone. "Right, Aonghus," he said, "take the other stone to its head."

Aonghus was reticent. He looked aghast at Diarmid and hesitated. Diarmid took one hand off the fish, grabbing the stone from Aonghus. He crashed it down: Aonghus paled and turned away in horror, feeling physically sick as the fish's head caved in, and became a horrible mixture of water, blood and squashed brains. Diarmid was too engrossed, and only noticed Aonghus' discomfort when he had finished dealing with the fish.

"What's wrong?" asked Diarmid, but Aonghus was still too traumatised to speak. "Sit there and recover your wits. I'll try to get us another." Indeed Diarmid was more successful than even he imagined, and they finally set off back to camp with four fish.

Everet and Myrta were delighted with the boys' efforts, but Aonghus still hadn't cheered up. "It was horrible to watch the poor fish get its brains smashed out," he said. "What a shocking way to die."

"Yes, Aonghus," Myrta agreed, "but we need to eat, and the fish will give us sustenance and allow us to travel onwards. I will make you some tea: hopefully that will help you to calm down."

*****

The weather had not improved during the course of the morning, but they decided to continue their journey towards the mainland. Myrta had cooked the fish along with some roots she and Everet discovered whilst picking the bramberries and apples. To have fresh food again was so delicious, and Myrta had made them a meal to savour.

114

With renewed vigour, they set about striking camp and packing their goods back into the boat. Over the meal they had read the map once again, and reconsidered their strategy. There was a really large island just to the east of where they currently were, and they decided to head straight for it: from there they would follow its coastline south, before heading eastwards again. If they could get to the point where the coastline changed direction they would have made good progress, and could stop for the night, knowing that their destination was achievable the day after.

Everet soon discovered that his aching limbs had not fully recovered, and was struggling somewhat with the rowing action. Progress was very slow, and the weather had not at all brightened up, so spirits were very low.

"I'm sorry, everyone," Everet said, "but I am really aching from head to foot, and it may be that we will need to stop more frequently than I imagined."

"That's alright," said Myrta. "Take whatever time you need. However, my concern is that we have no other food than these sour apples and the remainder of the bramberries, and I don't want to upset Aonghus by sending him fishing."

"Agreed," said Everet, "but I don't want to reach the point of total exhaustion either."

"You say when you have had enough, Everet," said Diarmid. "Perhaps I can take both oars for a while."

They continued, eventually coming close to the larger island. They began to follow its coastline southwards, never straying too far from the shallows. They had the benefit of a friendly current, so their journey was helped, much to Everet's relief.

Then bellies began to hurt, and feelings of nausea began to creep over them. Something was wrong. Myrta suggested they head for shore, but the coastline was rocky with nowhere to land. Aonghus let the tiller fall from his hand as he turned and retched overboard. Diarmid quickly pulled in his blade and made a grab for the youngster, fearing he might fall overboard.

Then one by one the others wanted to throw up as well. It was not a pretty sight as each occupant struggled to hold onto the contents of their stomach. "Oh," moaned Myrta, "what have we eaten that's done this?"

"The apples, maybe," said Everet, "they were a bit sour. Maybe too bitter."

"No," said Aonghus, "it was the fish. From the moment Diarmid stoned the poor creature I have felt unwell. Now we have eaten it, and it is taking its revenge."

"I don't think it's quite like that, Aonghus" said Everet, "although you have a point about the fish being the cause of our unease. I certainly did not recognise the species, but then again I am no expert on fish."

"Whatever it was, we need to get to shore and recover," said Diarmid.

As he uttered the words the weather began to creep in on them again, and Myrta looked ahead, seeking a place of refuge where they could get under cover before any deluge began. Again, almost as an answer to an unspoken prayer, a small bay came into view: Diarmid grabbed both oars and began pulling on the blades. "Steer us for the bay, Aonghus," he shouted.

Being relatively experienced in the art by now, they set up camp as quickly as their poorliness would allow them, and had the fire going in no time. Aonghus and Diarmid rested for a while, then went for a walk to explore the immediate surroundings, and returned quite excited. "There are the remains of an old cottage not far from here. It has no roof, and looks to have been abandoned a long time ago," said Diarmid. "I think you should take a look."

All four made their way to the cottage remains. "It's been some time since anyone lived here," said Everet, "but they obviously took time and effort to build a substantial dwelling."

"It's said that the islands were inhabited at one point, but that must be a long time ago," said Myrta. "They say it was too cold and harsh in the winters, eventually causing the youngsters to drift off, looking for warmer locations. When those that remained behind died, so too did any community."

They looked around and discovered what might have been a kitchen garden at one time. "Look," said Myrta, "that looks like potato plants over there, and I'd say that these are cabbages still going strong in the climes."

"Well, at least we don't have to take a rock to them before we eat them," said Aonghus.

They strolled round, gathering up quite a few vegetables which had continued to grow and reseed over the years, acclimatising to the conditions. It would be a stew of vegetables for anyone who felt like eating.

"I can understand us gathering these vegetables, mother," said Aonghus, "but I don't think I am ready to eat just yet." The others murmured in agreement.

"Fine," said Myrta, "but I will boil some cabbage leaves in water, and we can drink that as a medication to help clear our insides."

Chapter 24: Friends in Need

The castaways decided that one more night at their refuge would be beneficial. They had fresh food to eat, and water to drink. Myrta used the last of the bramberries to make a warming infusion which they sipped slowly, savouring the taste and feeling its warming effects spread through their bodies: it was a comforting feeling.

As they drank they once again pored over the map, trying to work out, as best they could, where they were, give or take a few miles. They pondered over it, and finally came to a consensus.

"If we are here," said Diarmid, "then I would say that we may have to make the rest of the journey in two phases."

"Really?" said Everet a little disappointed. "What makes you say that?"

"Take a look at the coastline, Everet," said the sailor. "It's very rocky and jagged. If we stick to the shallows we may find there are too many rocks close to the surface so we would have to slow down and navigate very carefully indeed."

"I see," said the older man, "and if we head out into deeper water?"

"Then we put ourselves at risk from strong currents. Also, if the weather were to quickly turn for the worse we would be in serious trouble trying to find shelter," said Diarmid.

"These are wise words indeed, Diarmid," said Myrta. "What do you propose?"

"Well, we won't be sure of conditions until we set off, but I would suggest we keep as close to the coast as is possible," said the lad. "It will mean that you, Myrta, will have the responsibility for guiding us safely by keeping a vigilant watch from the bow, and you, Aonghus, will have an equally important task of responding quickly and accurately to your mother's calls." He waited for the impact of his words to sink in, then asked, "Are you ready for such a mission?"

There was some hesitancy from mother and son, and Everet spoke up. "I agree that with such a rocky coastline there may be dangers lurking in the shallows. However, can't we ply a course just a little further out than we have done so far?"

"I am concerned about this coastline, Everet," said Diarmid, "and I wouldn't like to say how far out we would have to travel to find clear water. As I said, in the deeper water the current may be so strong that we wouldn't be able to battle against it, and it would take us off course."

"But the current helped us to get here," said Everet, perplexed.

"It certainly did," said Diarmid, "and it may be that I am overestimating the dangers. However, our sickness incident should have taught us to stay as close to dry land as we possibly can. What would happen if something befell me,

Everet, not that I'm trying to belittle your efforts, I'm not, without them none of us would be here, but to be honest about it, your rowing skills are not the finest."

Despite Diarmid's reassurance Everet did feel belittled. "I have put a lot of effort into getting us this far. I have tried hard with every fibre of my being, and by the Saints, it hurts every muscle I have. Are you saying I would not be able to cope?"

"Everet," Myrta scolded, "you know that's not what Diarmid is saying. He's just told you that he appreciates everything you are doing. He is merely pointing out risks we have to face, and to lose Diarmid would put the rest of us in serious jeopardy."

"Yes, yes, yes," said Everet. "Diarmid, I am sorry for the outburst. Let's all get some sleep and we'll see what the morrow brings.

*****

Aonghus fell asleep almost instantly: the effects of the food poisoning had hit him hardest, and, although showing outward signs of having recovered, his inner body was telling him otherwise. This night he was sleeping the sleep of the dead, and as his slumber reached its greatest depth his subconscious mind started to come alive.

In the blackness of his deep sleep, a dull grey mist began to form. Slowly it increased in volume, and appeared to be solidifying. Gradually it took shape, bursting alive as a fish, of the same variety that he and Diarmid had harvested at that little pool. It flapped its willowy tail, flicked its fins, and began to swim around inside Aonghus' head. Three plopping sounds followed immediately, and, lo and behold, there were now four fish swimming in a circle, head to tail, round and round. Their iridescent colours glittered against the blackness of the back ground.

"Hello, Aonghus Cranstoun," said the fish in unison, *"do you remember us?"*

Aonghus' inert body began to twitch as recognition penetrated his logical brain. *"That's right, Aonghus,"* said the quadrotoned voice, *"we are the fish whose heads were smashed by your rock."*

"I didn't kill you," said Aonghus wordlessly.

"You didn't strike the blows," agreed the fish still circling in his mind, *"but you found the rock that was used. You're as good as a killer, Aonghus Cranstoun."*

"Why are you here?" said Aonghus, his body still twitching restlessly. "You have already exacted your revenge with your poison."

"Ah!" said the voice, *"so you think some mild discomfort is worth taking our lives? You are still alive. We don't have that privilege. You took it from us."*

118

The fish stopped circling and flicked themselves upright, using their tails like feet: their gill fins looked like arms encased in flouncy sleeves. The fish extended their fins as if holding hands with their two neighbours. Aonghus watched in disbelief as his uninvited guests began a piscean danse macabre. They stepped one way, then the other. They pirouetted, they came together to the centre then retreated. They somersaulted, they cartwheeled. It was a beautiful dance.

"*Fish can do anything,*" they said. "*Fish know everything,*" they intoned.

"Why are you telling me this?" asked the boy beginning to perspire with terror.

"*Would you like to hear us sing?*" they asked, and, without waiting for an answer, began to warble.

"*We are the fish from the cold Cold Sea,*
We come to the shallows for fun.
We like to swim, we like being free
We do not answer to anyone.
We've been created to swim and roam
We travel far and wide
But always, we'll return to our home
When we find a welcoming tide.
We like to swim in the coastal pools
When the tide has left them filled
We never thought we'd meet some fools
And end up getting killed."

The last word was said with such malice that it reverberated round and round Aonghus' skull.

"*Aonghus Cranstoun,*" said the fish, "*we know who you are. We know what you've done. We have mildly chastised you for your evil act. We will know if you kill another of Creation's little friends, and we won't be so lenient again.*"

"I won't, I won't," screamed Aonghus, body aquiver.

"*You'd better not, my lad,*" said the fish. "*We're inside your head. You ate us, and now we are part of you. We will know.*"

Aonghus was trembling in his bed, eyes wide open, screaming, and sobbing. His mother was cradling him, trying her best to calm him down, but it was taking a big effort.

"Aonghus," she whispered, "what's wrong? What's causing your distress?"

"The fish," said Aonghus between sobs. "The fish are in my head. They're going to kill me." He was still shaking uncontrollably.

"Aonghus," said Myrta, "you've been dreaming. It's only a dream. A bad dream, yes, but you are alright now. There's a good lad," she went on, stroking his head, comforting him.

Gradually, Aonghus stopped shaking, but was still subject to sobs and sighs. "That's it," said Myrta, "calm down. We're all here with you. We'll help you. Just try to let it all pass."

"Maybe you'd like to come and sit by the fire for a while," said Everet. "Just sit and watch the flames. Watch them flicker and bring warmth. Come, I'll sit with you."

*****

Next morning the sky was bright enough although it was raining steadily, the drops sounding out a soothing rhythm, but it did little to erase the memory of Aonghus' nightmare. He looked pale and withdrawn, and he just sat there, staring emptily ahead of himself.

"Aonghus," said his mother softly, "Aonghus, it's alright. You're quite safe." The boy didn't react: it was as if he was still in that other world. Myrta placed a cup of hot tea in his hands. "Drink this, Aonghus, it will help you." Aonghus took the cup, but held it with such little conviction that his mother feared he would spill it. "Aonghus, pay attention or you will have an unpleasant accident."

This seemed to get through to the boy and his grip on the cup tightened. "That's a good lad," said Myrta. "Now start to drink it before it cools down." At last Aonghus began to look as if he was part of the same world as the rest of them, although his bright nature was nowhere to be evidenced.

Slowly, he sipped his tea, staring darkly into the liquid between mouthfuls. Then he spoke. "Will this rain prevent us from travelling?"

"It needn't," said Diarmid. "Look at the sky, it is bright so I imagine that the rain will go off quite soon."

"That's good," said Aonghus, "because I don't want to spend another night in this place."

"That's understandable, Aonghus," said Everet, "but we have to do what's necessary for our survival. I am sure we will be able to strike camp soon, and make our way round the south end of this island."

Aonghus' mood wasn't uplifted by his father's words. The prospect of another night here filled him with dread. Were the fish really part of him now? What about all the other animals and birds he had eaten throughout his life? Were they, too, part of him. How strange people must be if all the animals they ate were part of them. The fish said they would know what he did, and would punish him if he ever killed another creature. Did that mean he would not eat meat or fish ever again? Surely not. It just meant that he couldn't be involved in the actual killing.

*****

As Diarmid had predicted, the rain stopped, and the sun tried to pick its way through the clouds. Everet made the decision to strike camp, and the group sprung into action like a well rehearsed ensemble. There was a method in their actions, born out of experience, and they each had particular jobs to do, which they set about with gusto, despite their weakened condition.

Soon everything was packed into its allotted place on the rowboat and the group started to push the boat back into the water from its beached position. As the water began to lap around the hull and give the boat some buoyancy, Myrta clambered in and took up her position in the bow: she was followed on board by Aonghus who took hold of the tiller.

Everet and Diarmid eased the boat a little further into the water before they, too, climbed in. They got themselves into their accustomed position, laying their oars into the rowlocks.

"Right, Everet," said Diarmid, "on my count we'll take five strokes then stop."

"I'm ready," said the older man.

"And pull," Diarmid gave the command and they were off.

After five strokes they stopped rowing and pulled in their oars, letting themselves drift.

"As you know," said Diarmid, "I'm not too sure what we'll encounter on this leg of our journey, so we will go carefully. Myrta, you are totally responsible for our safety: we are depending on you not only to spot the dangers, but to call out the correct instructions for Aonghus to steer by. Aonghus you must remain alert at all times, and respond immediately and accurately to whatever call your mother makes. Is that understood?"

"Perfectly," said Myrta.

"I will do my best," said Aonghus.

"Good," said Diarmid. "Now, Everet, you and I will row gently and slowly until we find out more about the conditions that await us. Are you ready?"

"Yes," said Everet, "start anytime you want."

Progress was necessarily slow, as the conditions were as unfavourable as Diarmid had suggested they might be. However, they did not want to venture too far from the shore at this time, so that slowed them down as well.

Myrta kept a vigilant outlook at the bow, calling out dangers several times to which Aonghus was alert, and reacting promptly. A sombre mood hung over everyone, but at least they were making some advances.

The sun still hadn't managed to penetrate the cloud cover, but the day had brightened, with little wind to ruffle the surface of the sea. Everet's rowing skills had certainly improved, Diarmid noted, and the boat's progress through the water was certainly smoother, more noticeably so.

"You're doing well, Everet," said the sailor breaking the silence, "and we're all benefiting from your work."

"Thank you," said Everet appreciatively, "this gentle pace certainly makes a difference to my coordination. If only it had been at this pace from the beginning."

"We have to react according to needs and conditions, Everet," said Diarmid, "and we have had testing events along our journey from which we have all learned."

"Besides," said Myrta, not averting her gaze from in front of the boat, "there's no good pondering on what might have been. What has happened, has happened. We can never alter that; only learn from what it brought us."

The silence descended on them once more as they contemplated Myrta's words. They were rounding a headland when she called out for the rowing to stop, and for Aonghus to head them outwards.

"Diarmid," she said, "you need to take a look at what confronts us."

Diarmid and Everet stopped rowing and pulled in their blades. Diarmid shuffled round in his seat, then stood up to get a better view. What he saw filled him with dread. It looked as if there had been a recent landslide, a major erosion of the cliff face. However it happened he had no idea, but the result was that the channel was strewn with rocks and boulders that carried quite a distance out to sea.

"How are we to pass this?" asked Myrta.

Everet, by this time, had also turned to face ahead and he, too, was as dismayed as his rowing partner.

"Who knows?" Diarmid said, almost at a loss for words. "To try to steer a course through the rocks looks like a recipe for disaster, and to head that far out to sea brings the risk of very strong and dangerous currents."

"We would seem to be," said Everet, "somewhere between the rocks and a hard place."

The group discussed their situation for some time before coming to the conclusion that they would have to head out to sea in order to get round their current difficulty. They had to manoeuvre so slowly round some rocks that at times their progress became unnoticeable. However, they were indeed moving further from the shore towards the deeper water.

The rocks seemed to go on forever, and Myrta's concentration was totally focussed on avoiding them: Aonghus was at fever pitch awaiting the next call from his mother; all his troubles seemed far behind him now as he strove to carry out whatever instruction would steer the boat away from trouble.

Diarmid and Everet rowed ever so gently, almost afraid to take large strokes in case they propelled the boat too close to an as yet unseen danger.

"I think we're almost clear of the rocks, Diarmid," said Myrta. "Perhaps you should take a look."

The men stopped rowing and Diarmid again swivelled round before carefully standing up. "You're right, Myrta," said the lad, scanning the way ahead. "I can see from the way the water looks that there is a clear channel. The bad news is that the current is against us."

"How strong do you think the current is?" asked Everet.

"It's hard to judge from here, but I would say that we have some very hard rowing ahead of us, Everet," replied the sailor.

Everet's spirits fell a little at Diarmid's reply: the thought of hard rowing was already flooding his mind with memories of aches and pains, and he began to wonder if he was really up to it.

Perhaps they should go back to where they found the shell of a dwelling and the remains of a kitchen garden. Life would be harsh there, but, with a big effort, they could make a go of it. Out here in the wide expanse of the sea their future was less certain. It would take just one small mistake, by any of them, and disaster would strike hard.

Everet was so wrapped up in his feeling of self doubt that he didn't notice that Diarmid had returned to his rowing position and was waiting for him.

"Wake up, Everet," said Diarmid, "it's time to work hard. Just take it slowly and rhythmically, and don't try too hard. Just do it without thinking about it."

Everet turned to look at Diarmid. "What do you mean, 'don't think about it'?" he asked.

"You're doing very well for someone new to rowing," said Diarmid, "and I can see that you understand the mechanics of it. All I'm asking you to do is to keep with the rhythm and technique you have developed. By all means count yourself through your stroke, but don't get caught up in trying to deliver the perfect stroke every time. Just let it happen."

"You make it sound easy, Diarmid," said Everet, "but I will try."

"Good man," said Diarmid, "I'm here to watch and help. Call out if you're not happy, and we'll try to deal with it. Are you ready to row?"

"Yes," said Everet, now roused from his self doubt.

"Aonghus, are you ready?" asked Diarmid.

"Yes," said the boy, nodding.

"Myrta, you still need to keep a sharp look out, even although it looks like we are heading for clear water."

"I'm watching, Diarmid," she assured them.

They began to row harder, and soon reached the point where they needed to turn into the channel. As Aonghus steered the boat into the open water the current hit them with a heavy bump, rocking the boat and grabbing at the rudder as if with a strong, unseen hand, pulling the tiller from Aonghus' grip.

There was a brief spell of panic aboard as everyone came to terms with the harsher conditions. Aonghus scrambled to regain his hold on the tiller, and get the boat back on course. Everet only just managed to get his blade out of the water, but quickly readjusted by pulling as hard as he could. Diarmid was also taken by surprise, but took confidence from Everet's recovery, and soon was back in sequence with his co-rower.

It was very tough fighting against the current: both rowers were straining every sinew each time they pulled on their oars. Progress was painfully slow.

"We're in the middle of the channel, Diarmid," said Myrta. "Should we steer for the edge to minimise the strength of the current?"

"Yes," panted Diarmid, "but watch for dangers where the current may swirl."

Myrta directed Aonghus, and they steered as close to the edge of the channel as they dared. However, the rowers did not notice a great deal of abatement in the current's strength.

Advancement was indeed slow, and Everet was feeling the strain on his muscles. He was aware that a lot of effort was producing very little forward momentum. "How far have we travelled, Myrta?" he called out, trying not to break the rhythm of his rowing.

"We are making good progress, considering the strength of the current," she replied.

"How much farther until we clear these rocky parts, and get back to the shallows?" he added

"That's still a long way off, my love," she said. "I can't really estimate how far."

"Diarmid," said Everet, "I don't know how much more of this I can give. I am aching throughout my entire body."

"I am too, Everet," Diarmid said. "This current is fast and strong: much more so than I expected."

"Is there some place we could stop for a while to gain some respite?" asked Everet.

"Where?" said Diarmid. "We're quite far out. If we stop rowing we'll be taken backwards faster than we could ever hope to make up."

"Perhaps," Myrta cut in, "I could guide us in between the rocks, and we could find some solace there."

"Are there any opportunities ahead?" asked Diarmid. "We could try, but we need to be very careful."

"I'm looking," said Myrta, "but I can't see anything immediate. Can you keep going for a little while longer?"

"We'll give it a try," said Everet, his voice displaying the strain he was putting his body through.

They fell into silence again, each one concentrating on their particular job. The rowers were finding reserves of strength they didn't realise they had. Myrta was amazed at the efforts the rowers were making, for she knew how much effort was being put into every stroke. She mused that it seemed strange that, in times of greatest crisis, resources always seemed to be made available. It was as if some unseen universal force was lending a helping hand, in answer to unspoken prayers.

"There's something in the water a little way ahead," Myrta said, "but I can't be sure of what it is."

"What do you mean?" said Everet.

"Well, one moment there are black shapes just above the surface, then the next they are gone," she said by way of explanation. "Oh! They've just reappeared, but not where I first saw them," she added with surprise.

"Sounds like some sea creatures," said Diarmid, "maybe whales, dolphins or porpoises."

"I thought whales were huge creatures that were pretty unmistakable," said Myrta still watching intently.

"Some are like that," said Diarmid, "but others are smaller. I take it these aren't huge then, Myrta."

"No, not huge," said Myrta, "but they are heading straight this way, whatever they are."

"How far?" said Everet.

"Still a good way off, but getting closer each time they resurface," she replied. "Are we in danger from these creatures, Diarmid?"

"It is unlikely," he replied. "There are many stories of friendly encounters, but very very few of dangerous ones."

"What do they look like," asked Aonghus, excited by the prospect.

"Let's just wait and see," said his father. "We need to concentrate on what we are doing."

A short time later Myrta announced that the creatures were getting really close, and she could count seven of them. Not long after that the creatures were with them, swimming all round the rowboat.

"Dolphins," said Diarmid. "We shouldn't be in any danger from them."

"Not being in any danger is good, Diarmid," said Everet, "but can they help us out of our difficulty?"

"How, Everet?" asked the lad. "They don't speak, although they do make some clicking noises, and dolphins don't have any ears to hear us. Anyway, let's not be distracted by them. We have to find somewhere we can take refuge. Myrta, is there anywhere we can pull in to?"

It was a few minutes before Myrta answered. "Yes, there is a gap just ahead, maybe five more minutes if you can keep going."

"Let's aim for it!" said Everet, pulling hard. "Aonghus, listen very carefully to your mother's instructions."

With some difficulty they managed to steer the rowboat into a kind of respite area, and found that they could actually tie a rope round one of the protruding rocks: they wouldn't lose any gains they had made, and they could all relax. The dolphins continued to swim close to them, arcing out of and into the water. The group admired the dolphins' grace and beauty.

"Mother," said Aonghus, "I have had a thought. You know that these fish from my bad nightmare told me they were now part of me."

"Yes, Aonghus," said Myrta, "but please try to dismiss that from your mind."

"No, let me continue," said the boy. "Well, if that was true then maybe I can talk to these fish, and ask for help."

"That's a very strange notion indeed, Aonghus," said Myrta, "but if it helps you to release these bad memories, then please do what you think is best."

Aonghus closed his eyes, and tried to conjure up his memories of the four iridescent fish that had haunted him with horrific brilliance not many days before. Slowly his mind began to settle, and he let whatever thoughts pass through until at last the four fish appeared.

"Hello, Aonghus Cranstoun," they said as one. "You have called us to you, have you been a naughty boy again?"

"No, I haven't!" said Aonghus, somewhat indignant. "You know I haven't done anything naughty. Well, you told me that you would know if I had been and would return unsummoned."

"That's right, Aonghus Cranstoun," said the fish, "but you have summoned us for a reason: we thought maybe you had been just a little bit naughty, and were feeling guilty and wanted to confess."

"I'm sorry to disappoint you," said Aonghus mentally. "However, I do need your help, if that is at all possible."

"Depends on what it is, Aonghus Cranstoun," said the fish. "Pray, continue."

"We need help to get past this current in order to get over to the mainland where there may be other people who can help us to return home. We are extremely tired, and unable to battle against the current for very much longer," he explained.

"And?" said the fish.

"I was wondering if you could talk to these dolphin fish to see if they could help us in some way," he said.

"Mmmmm," said the fish, "we could try, but these dolphins aren't actually fish."

"Of course they are!" said Aonghus in disbelief. "What else could they be?"

"Let's not argue, young man, because a great number of different types of creature inhabit the oceans, and not all of them are fish. We'll see what we can do," said the fish, as they disappeared with a popping sound.

Almost immediately they reappeared, forming a little circle and swimming round and round. *"Well, Aonghus Cranstoun, it seems these dolphins are indeed here to help you, and it is fortunate that you were blessed with this idea to use us as a means of making communication. The dolphins tell us that you can talk directly to them, and you should contact the one who leads the group, his name is Morfan."* With that the fish again disappeared.

"How do I do that?" asked Aonghus. The fish showed no signs of coming back, so Aonghus sat a while longer, calling out mentally to them, almost begging them to return to answer his question: his plea went unanswered.

Chapter 25: Soul Loss

In Brina's belief system, and that of her fellow Shamans, when a person suffers from a physical or psychological trauma their soul splits, with one or more parts no longer contributing to the person's being. Instead, those parts remain fixed in the event, but in an extraordinary reality which Brina calls soul loss. This often results in loss of memory, or a feeling of incompleteness, although the body finds it easier to survive the traumas through this disengagement of part of the soul.

Once the traumatic event is over, complete healing can occur when the parts of the soul that are missing return. As a Shaman, Brina knew the techniques to be able to facilitate this, by journeying into the extraordinary reality with the help of spirit allies, to find the missing soul parts and bring them back. This would be followed by a period of integration, where the sufferer gets to know the returned soul parts again, and together they work to heal the old wounds. This often takes several months although it can also occur more quickly.

Brina also used the technique called power animal retrieval because everyone can enjoy the power, strength and comfort of an alliance with a spiritual power animal. The spirits of wild animals work with Shamans, guiding them through their journeys, giving advice and performing healings. Now that Mung was making progress, and was out of imminent danger, Brina felt that it was time to explain this procedure to him.

She realised, too, that she would have to introduce Mung to the techniques of meditation. Still, she was hopeful, because Mung had met and conversed with his Guardian Angel during Astral Travel, which had truly awakened his awareness of the spiritual world in and around him.

She would talk to Mung over the coming days and explain, little by little, what she believed were the required next steps in his healing. She would tell Mung that the procedure of soul loss and retrieval could involve anguish and psychological pain, but she was sure also of the benefits to be reaped. All this required Mung's approval and agreement.

Mung was truly awakening to the light, and bore the scars, both physical and mental, to prove that the dark side did not always provide what was necessary. Mung was almost like a captive pupil: unable to go anywhere, he was keen to learn more. "Please," he said to Brina, "can you explain it all again. I find it difficult to come to terms with what you have already told me, although I can hear a little voice inside me telling me that what you say rings true. I want to be sure of what it is you are trying to tell me."

"Of course I can, Yorlan," said Brina. "It's not an easy thing to grasp hold of or understand. I will go over this as many times as you want me to until you are satisfied that you know what it is I am saying. The bottom line is that I believe that this will strengthen you in more ways than you perhaps realise at this time."

Brina explained that the body responds to traumas and incidents in a way that tries to minimise the damage, be it physical or other. Loss of soul parts is just one such self-protective response to trauma. When a person's consciousness feels it cannot survive a particular situation such as abuse, addiction, or danger, part of the vital essence that makes a person whole seems to split off in order to survive the experience by escaping the full impact of the pain. This loss creates damage to the energy body and the spirit.

"This condition is normally called shock," said Brina, "which is something you may have heard of."

"Yes, I have in a sort of a way," said Mung, "but tell me more about these energy bodies. As far as I know I am composed of flesh and blood, although the priest tries to tell me about my soul, but I don't get that bit."

"Well, then, Yorlan," said Brina, "I will try my very best to explain what these are, at least as I understand them. Please interrupt me when I have said something that doesn't make sense, and we will try to sort it out as we go along."

"I will stop you if you say something I don't understand," said Mung.

"You are right, Yorlan," Brina started. "You are flesh and blood. This is your physical body, which works well on the physical plane, as we call it. This is the world that you interact with on a daily basis, the 'real' world if you like. There are other planes where your other bodies operate."

Mung threw her a questioning look. "For example," she said, "when you had your beautiful encounters with the Angels, you were operating on what's called the Astral Plane." Mung's look hadn't changed. "Let me try another approach," said the Shaman. "We hear different sounds, some are 'higher' and some are 'lower', and that's because of how the vibrations are felt. The more vibrations there are, the higher the sound. Well, these Planes have vibrations too, and in our physical reality we are aligned to all the vibrations of the physical plane. The Physical Plane is one of the low Planes. If we were to readjust our vibration sensing to a higher setting we would 'see' a different Plane, like has happened to you when you were able not just to see, but to hear and interact with the Beings who inhabit the Astral Plane. It is a higher vibrational area."

Mung's demeanour told Brina that he was beginning to understand. "All these Planes can interact with each other as you are aware from your experiences, and it means that everything that exists, in whatever Plane, is connected. Everything is indeed One. This means that whatever we do on this level has an effect throughout every level. Are you still with me?" asked Brina.

Mung indicated that he was, so Brina went on to explain that no matter how strange we may consider the Universe to be, we are part of it, and it is part of us. This means that each person is a reflection of the Universe. "As above, so below," said Brina to reinforce her words. She further explained that in addition to our physical body we had an etheric body, made of life energy, an astral body which is shaped by thoughts and feelings, a mental body which is shaped by awareness and which can transcend time and space. Finally, we have a spiritual body which is where our Soul resides.

"This is indeed complex, Brina," said Mung. "How on earth did you find this out?"

"Ah," said Brina, "that's another story altogether, but personal experiences have a lot to do with learning lessons."

She explained that each body had its own nature and function which had a role to play in a person's overall development. "For instance," she said, "the physical body allows the Soul to act and react in the material realms. And so it goes on. I think I have said enough at this point in time to have given you lots to think about. We can continue this another time, if you wish," she said.

Over the next few days Brina and Mung had many long chats about soul loss and retrieval, but did not return to the subject of the different planes of existence. She explained what she would do, and Mung considered if he indeed wanted her to go through with it, not sure whether he wanted to relive the trauma that had almost cost him his life.

Brina was very patient so as not to push Mung in any particular direction, but was always on hand to explain things, answer any questions, and chat through any concerns.

After a few days Mung decided that he wanted Brina to carry out this Soul Retrieval: his life was pretty meaningless at this point in time. His job as a trusted member of the community was now surely over: indeed he may even face charges for the dishonest acts he had committed and been involved in. Neither had he been completely honest with Sefira, who had stood by him, caring for him all these years. What would she say if they were ever to meet again? Where could he go? He couldn't remain at Brina's forever although she had never indicated that, but her life was one of a reclusive person so he would only get in the way. What was there to lose by reliving the trauma? Some more pain, some anxiety, perhaps, but he would come out of it a better, wiser man. At least that's what he told himself. After all, he had experienced these strange journeys since the night Boffe knifed him, and they only indicated that there was much to live for.

"Brina," he said softly, "do whatever you have to do. You have caused me no harm so far. Indeed you have saved me and shown me nothing but kindness. I have nothing to fear on that side of things."

"Really, Yorlan?" she replied. "Are you sure? Are you certain?"

"I am," he said. "What's a little mental anguish if it means I gain so much in other ways? Tell me more of how you will do this act."

"I will explain as best I can, as I have done several times for you. I don't really know how much you will understand, but stop me when I take you into the complete unknown," she said.

"I will," said the patient.

"What you see all around you, what you call 'real' life, is what I call ordinary reality. It's a reflection of what's going on inside our heads in some respects," she started.

"You're starting to lose me already," said Mung.

"Alright," said the Shaman. "Our outer health and wholeness is an expression of our inner health and holiness. Each of us is here to bring spirit into matter, and matter to spirit. My work is to help people connect their inner and outer worlds, to heal old wounds within, to become able to bring dreams from the world of spirit into the world of matter, thus enabling them to enjoy an imaginative and abundant life, dancing their dreams awake," she added, "Do you understand that?"

"Sort of," he said, "but please continue."

"To be able to do this I need to travel in what is called extraordinary reality to pursue your lost soul parts. You remember we talked about the other Planes of existence?"

Mung nodded his head. "Well, I will be travelling in and through them," said Brina. "It is like entering the spirit world itself, where I will find signs regarding your well-being, your emotional states, mental attitudes and past lives. That is where lost soul parts go," said Brina, "and I will find them and bring them back to you."

"That sounds like a dangerous venture to undertake," said Mung. "However will you keep yourself safe?"

"Indeed it is a journey fraught with threats and menaces," she told him, "but I will have spirit helpers and guides who will help to bring me into contact with your soul parts. Then, when I bring them back, I can restore them to your body," she said.

"When will you do this retrieval?" asked Mung.

"When we are all ready and prepared," said Brina. "I have to be sure that you, too, will be safe during my journey, so to help with that I need to teach you the rudiments of something called meditation."

"Meditation?" said the Marshal. "What's that?"

"It's practice that involves sitting quietly and stilling the mind," said Brina trying to keep her explanations simple yet effective.

"For how long?" asked her patient.

"For however long it takes," she replied, "and it's a practice that needs to be carried out on a daily basis."

"I hate to repeat myself," said Mung, "but for how long?"

"The simple answer is, forever," said the Earth Mother. Mung looked surprised. "Once you get the hang of it, you will want to do it every day, Yorlan," she assured him. "Now let's get you out of bed and into a chair, then we can take the first steps."

Mung carefully hauled himself up into a sitting position, then swung his legs over the side of the bed. He sat there for a moment gathering his strength before easing himself forward gingerly until his feet came into contact with the floor. Steadying himself with his hands, he slowly stood up. Brina was at his side helping and encouraging him. Mung was pleasantly surprised to find that his short walk across the room to the big chair was carried out without too much distress: a twinge here, and a stiffness there. Brina made sure he was comfortable and warm.

"Now we are ready for the first steps into meditation, Yorlan," she said, "but do say if you feel tired or otherwise unable to continue."

She explained that meditation is how a person reunites their soul with the Oneness. The soul, created by the Oneness manifests its consciousness and life force through seven centres of light, located in the spinal axis. Sheathed in a bodily prison, the soul awareness and life energies become merged with the physical body and its worldly pleasures and pains. Meditation awakens the soul awareness in the seven light centres. The soul remembers its Universal nature and origin. By awakening the soul, a person can access inner peace and joy. The more the person meditates, and the deeper the meditation becomes, she explained, soul and the Universal Spirit become reunited in a state of utter bliss: devoted exponents called this state of being 'samadhi'.

Mung sat there in deep consideration of Brina's explanation, then finally said, "That seems like a lot of work and concentration to me."

"Indeed," said Brina, "it requires devotion, but the reward is well worth the effort. When you meditate you are able to connect the little joy of the soul with the indescribably vast joy of All there is, and what better outcome could you ask for?"

"Are we going to start now?" asked Mung almost in resignation.

"Not just at this moment. We need to make sure that your posture is correct. It's very important to be sitting in the right position," said Brina. "Your backbone needs to be as straight as possible: this will aid your comfort, and you will be able to sit in meditation for long periods once you have mastered the correct position."

Mung shuffled around in his chair trying to get his back as straight as he could in the circumstances, without causing too much stress and strain on his wounds. "That's good," said Brina, "just let your feet rest flat against the floor. Later, when you are properly recovered from your injuries you can try sitting cross legged on the floor." Mung gave her a look and said that his legs were not that flexible.

"You are doing well, Yorlan," she said. "Now abdomen in, chest out, shoulders back, chin parallel to the ground, with your hands, palms upwards, resting on your legs at the top of the thighs where they meet the belly."

Again Mung persuaded the various parts of his body to respond to Brina's words.

"Right, Yorlan, the next step is to become aware of your breathing. Here are the steps. Listen carefully, and then I will demonstrate for you," she said. "Inhale slowly through your nostrils to a count of 3: hold the breath to a count of 3; exhale slowly through the mouth to a count of 3."

Mung watched, fascinated. Brina did it so effortlessly, but then again she did this every day, and had been doing so for who knows how long.

"Now it's your turn." Her words roused him from his musing. "In through the nose for 3, hold for 3, out through the mouth for 3."

Mung tried it. It wasn't as easy as Brina made it look. "Good," she said. "Again." It was a little easier the second time. "You are a good pupil, Yorlan. You will soon get the hang of this. Now I'd like you to practise this six to ten times. We will use the count of 3 until such times you can exert full control of your breath in this way, and then we will use progressively longer counts."

Mung looked at her as if she was speaking in some unknown language. "This is quite difficult enough, Brina," he said.

"I know," she replied, "but as you gain mastery of your breath you gain mastery of your mind."

She then took Mung through other exercises designed to completely relax his body, and relayed to him a technique whereby he could concentrate on using what she called his third eye, the body's centre of consciousness. "Has your priest never quoted to you from the Gospels, Yorlan?" she asked.

"Yes," he said somewhat perplexed. "What have the Gospels to do with this practice?"

"Has the priest ever told you that *'The light of the body is the eye: if therefore thine eye be single, thy whole body shall be full of light'.*"

"Can't say I have heard that before," said Mung. "Is that in the Gospels?"

"Yes, it is," said Brina, "but it is often misunderstood. Perhaps you can see its relevance to what we are trying to achieve? But later, Yorlan, consider that later. We have much to be getting on with."

"Brina," he said, "I am trying to carry out your instructions, but other thoughts are entering my head. What do I do with them?"

"When a thought comes uncalled, just watch it like you would a bubble disturb the surface of a pond," she said. "Become aware of the gap between your thoughts. When one thought ends, and just before another one begins, there is a very brief but discernible emptiness that is your true nature. When you find it, hold it for as long as you can. That is the thoughtless state we are trying to reach. I am going off to prepare some food, but I want you to keep practising what we've just been through."

Brina left Mung and headed for the kitchen. Mung continued with his practice, perhaps trying a little too hard to master his breathing. With time, and guidance from Brina, he would relax more, and, in doing so, find it easier to reach the stillness. In the stillness he would find nothing, and in the nothingness he would find everything.

Chapter 26: Friends Indeed

Aonghus opened his eyes, returning to the awareness of where he was. He wore a look of bemused frustration as he looked around, becoming fully alert. The others gazed at him in anticipation.

"Well?" said his mother. "What have you discovered?"

"I spoke to the fish from my nightmare," he said, "but they weren't nasty this time."

"Oh!" said Myrta. "And what did they have to say to you?"

"They were most helpful," said Aonghus, and he related the story of his encounter.

"I see," said his mother, "and were you also able to speak to the dolphins?"

"No," said the boy, "that's the frustrating thing. The fish just disappeared without telling me how to."

"Perhaps," said Myrta, "you should try again. If the dolphins are indeed here to help us then there must be some way of communicating with them. Look," she went on, "they are still swimming close by."

"But how?" asked Aonghus.

"The same way you contacted the fish," said Myrta. "We'll all help you by surrounding you with peace and love as you try to contact the dolphins."

Aonghus was thus persuaded to enter the quiet again, to try to communicate with the dolphins. He closed his eyes and began to travel inwards. The sound of the waves lapping against the rowboat helped to take him into his own inner space where he felt comfortable. More importantly he knew he was safe here.

He tried to picture what the dolphins looked like from the brief glimpses he had had. A hazy image appeared in his consciousness and he silently called out Morfan's name. At first there was no response, nothing, just blankness, and the gentle rhythm of the waves against the boat.

He continued with his efforts, knowing how important this contact was and continued to call out mentally to Morfan. Then he heard it, faint at first, but growing louder: a series of clicks that he knew was inside his head. He was not hearing these sounds via his ears.

"Hello," he said, "my name is Aonghus."

"Greetings, Aonghus Cranstoun," said Morfan. *"We have come to help you in whatever way we can."*

"Thank you," said the boy, "but however did you know about us?"

"Your thoughts," said the dolphin.

"My thoughts?" said Aonghus somewhat perplexed.

"Yes, yours, and those of the others with you," said Morfan. *"Your thoughts have been troubled, and are a cry for help."*

"But my thoughts never leave my head," said Aonghus.

"Oh, but they do, Aonghus," said Morfan. "Even if you don't say a word your thoughts travel far: very far indeed."

"Oh!" said Aonghus.

"Yes," said Morfan, "you humans have yet to learn much about thoughts, and how they affect everything."

"Really?" said the boy. "I thought that what is in my head is private, and known only to me."

"There you go again, Aonghus Cranstoun," said the dolphin, "thinking without realising. You have much to learn, but at least this encounter is a start. No matter, the urgent thing is to help you. What can we do?"

"We are in deep trouble," Aonghus began. "We are trying to reach a settlement on the mainland somewhere beyond this channel between the islands. However, my father and Diarmid are extremely tired, and cannot row hard against this strong current for much longer. We will then be at the mercy of the ocean, and who knows what will happen to us."

"I see," said Morfan, "then we can most certainly help you."

"That would be good, but I can't see how," said Aonghus.

"The rope that ties you to the rock at present," said Morfan.

"Yes," said the boy, "what about it?"

"Do you have another piece similar?" asked Morfan.

Aonghus tried to visualise what they carried with them in the boat. His head moved as if he was actively looking although his eyes remained closed. He pondered the question for some time, and finally said, "Yes, I can see a similar piece."

"Good," said the dolphin. "Here's what I want you to do."

Aonghus received instructions from the dolphin after which Morfan broke contact. The boy slowly let his awareness return to his situation, and gently opened his eyes. The others were staring at him in great anticipation: a sense of expectancy pervaded the group.

"Well?" said Myrta. "Did you make contact?"

Aonghus was still not fully returned to the present, and sat there, unmoving, staring into the distance.

"Aonghus," said Myrta, "bring your focus back to the boat. We are here with you, you are quite safe."

Hearing his mother's reassuring words helped to restore Anoghus' sense of being. He looked at the faces staring at him in anticipation, each with bated breath. He stared back, not quite sure what they were waiting for.

"Aonghus," said Myrta, "do you have something to tell us?"

Realisation fell into place, and Aonghus smiled. "Yes," he said, "I most certainly have."

"Don't keep us in suspense any longer, my child," said Myrta. "We have much to consider, and time marches ever onwards."

Aonghus told them of his encounter with Morfan, and how the dolphins had responded to all of their thoughts. The others sat in rapt astonishment as the boy's tale unfolded.

"They want us to tie another piece of rope to the bow of the boat then two dolphins will take the other ends of the ropes and pull us through the current."

"Let me get this right," said Everet. "We are to have two ropes available?"

"Yes," said Aonghus.

"And do we have to row the boat as well?" asked Everet.

"No," said Aonghus, "the dolphins are strong enough to pull without any help. You will only get in the way if you try to row."

"I see," said Everet, "that's really good. When are we to get underway?"

"As soon as we want, but we're not to delay too long," said Aonghus. "Oh!" he added, "we need to get the boat clear of the rocks, and the dolphins will take over."

"Then let's get on our way," said Everet.

They made their preparations, looked out the other piece of rope, and tied it securely to the bow. Diarmid and Everet took up their rowing positions, then Myrta untied the rope holding them to the rock.

Diarmid and Everet paddled carefully whilst Myrta guided Aonghus in his steering. Finally, they were clear of the rocks and back in the channel. They felt the current kick in violently, necessitating the two rowers to use what strength they had to propel the boat forwards.

"Quick, mother," shouted Aonghus, "throw the ropes into the water."

"Yes, yes, Aonghus," she said, "everything in its own time." She threw the ends of the ropes into the fast flowing water, one on either side of the boat. The dolphins swam round the boat, and two picked up the rope ends between their teeth. There was a violent shudder as the dolphins took over, and the boat's occupants were thrown sternwards, such was the strength of the force.

Recovering, Diarmid and Everet hauled in their oars, and then the sailor scrambled towards Aonghus: together the boys managed to pull the rudder free from the water. The boat was now firmly under the control of the dolphins.

Diarmid and the Cranstouns relaxed as far as they dared, and began to enjoy the journey. The dolphins swam all around them while the group of seven took it in turns to pull the boat.

Progress was greater under the dolphins' control, and they made good headway. After all their bad experiences since leaving Knympton this was a welcome upturn in their fortunes: they would enjoy the experience whilst it lasted.

As the light began to fade, Morfan instigated another conversation with Aonghus. The boy heard a series of clicks in his head, signifying that the dolphin was calling.

"Hello, Morfan," said Aonghus, "you have helped us enormously. Without you we would have struggled, and would not have made a fraction of the distance you have brought us."

"That's why we came, Aonghus Cranstoun," said the mammal. "We have brought you a good distance, but we too are tired."

"I can understand that," said Aonghus. "Do you need to rest?"

"Yes," said Morfan, "we'd like you to go ashore for the night, and we will come back to finish the journey when the light returns."

"I will tell the others, and Diarmid and my father can row us to the shore," said the boy.

"That would be good," said Morfan. "Now I must depart. We will speak again soon."

Aonghus informed the others of the dolphins' plans, and Everet fumbled around, restoring his oar to the rowlock, whilst Diarmid helped Aonghus replace the rudder mechanism before taking up his rowing position.

The dolphins sensed when the boat's occupants were ready, dropped the ropes before swimming off to rest and recuperate. The current kicked as hard as ever, almost taking Diarmid and Everet by surprise. They reacted automatically, once again bringing the boat under their control.

"Take us in, Aonghus," said Diarmid, "but listen to your mother's instructions."

Under Myrta's guidance they were soon in calmer waters where the rowing was easier, heading for the shore and a good night's sleep.

*****

Diarmid was asleep as soon as his head hit his makeshift pillow. He was so relieved by the dolphins' intervention and knew, but for their help, all would surely have been lost that very day.

As it was, they had made such good progress that they were within a short journey of their goal on the mainland. Hopefully, the dolphins would return as promised to take them across to the other side.

However, that was a worry for tomorrow: tonight he would sleep soundly. Diarmid crept so far inside his own consciousness that he had no recollection of sleeping at all. He was safe despite the blackness that enfolded him: he just knew this was so, and did not stir or move the whole night through.

It took Aonghus a little while to drop off to sleep despite his tiredness. The excitement of the day was still coursing through his veins like a river in spate after the winter snows had melted, although he tried very hard to remain still, and not disturb the others.

His encounters with the dolphins puzzled him. How did they know the group was in deep trouble, and how did the dolphins find them?

Morfan, the dolphins' leader, had told him that everyone's thoughts had been the signal for help. But, Aonghus told himself, there had been no visible signal, and nobody had cried out: thoughts were silent and personal.

Weren't thoughts just little ideas that popped into your head? Weren't thoughts the silent beginning of an outward expression like words or actions? Aonghus could not understand how anyone else, never mind these fishy creatures, could know what was going on in his head. The thought frightened him in a strange way. If it was possible to pick up someone else's thoughts, why hadn't he been able to do it? His brain was beginning to race with possibilities, but these were surely stupid ideas.

It was then he heard a voice in his head. *"Calm down, Aonghus,"* it said, *"or you will never get to sleep."*

"Who are you?" asked the boy, eyes wide open in dismay as he looked all around.

An image materialised before his eyes: it was one of the fish. *"Surprised?"* it said, as it flicked its wispy tail.

"Where are the others?" asked Aonghus, beginning to settle.

"Around," said the fish, *"it doesn't need four of us to relay this message."*

"What message?" said Aonghus.

"That what the dolphins told you is true. Your thoughts brought them to help," said the fish.

"How?" said Aonghus. "My thoughts are silent."

"They are indeed, young man," the fish agreed, as it swam back and forth in front of him, its colours glittering as it moved. *"But believe me, they travel, and travel far."*

"How?" said the boy again.

"Later, when you are ready, this can be discussed further. Not now. What you need to do is sleep: rest and recover, and when you have reached the other side of the water you can begin to learn more."

Aonghus pondered these words for several minutes. "I suppose you are right," he said.

"I am," said the fish, *"and by the way, dolphins are not fish, they are mammals."*

"They live in the water," protested the boy.

"I know," said the fish, *"but please believe me they are not fish. We have been through this before. Now close your eyes, and slow down your breathing, it's time to sleep."*

*****

Myrta was awakened by the sound of birds singing high in the trees that surrounded them. She lay there for some time, just listening to them. For the first time since they had set out on this fateful journey she felt able to relax, and she took advantage of the situation to enjoy the inner calmness that was spreading through her body.

Everet was next to waken, and, as he opened his eyes, he, too, became aware of the peace that had descended on the group. He glanced across at Myrta, and was pleased to see her calm demeanour. She had worked so hard, and been so supportive throughout this ordeal. He wasn't for disturbing her from this well earned rest: besides he could also benefit from doing nothing for a while longer. He was sure the boys would sleep on until wakened.

They didn't have too long to wait for the boys to stir: Aonghus was awakened by the clicking of Morfan in his head. *"It's time to waken up, Aonghus: time to travel on whilst conditions are favourable."*

The party scrambled around, grabbing what they could for a quick breakfast, and then set about packing everything into the rowboat. The final leg of this dangerous journey was about to begin, and they could hardly contain their excitement at the prospect of reaching the mainland.

Chapter 27: Soul Retrieval

Mung had been diligent in his meditation practices, and was now good enough, and strong enough, for Brina to be able to tell him that she would perform the Soul Retrieval.

"When?" he asked. "Today? Now?"

"Calm down, Yorlan," she replied, "it takes time to set up."

"Yes, I understand that, but you have everything you need, do you not?" he said.

"Well, yes and no," she said. "I have to prepare you, me, and the room for the journey. I also need help from some others, because retrieval is not something that should be attempted on one's own."

"Others?" said Mung suddenly suspicious.

"Oh Yorlan," said Brina, "do you think I'd bring anyone I couldn't trust? I'm not going to turn you over to anyone, friend or foe." A look of relief and childish guilt came over Mung's face. "I need the help of Ardvon, whom you've already met, and I need a few others, too, to help with various aspects of the journey."

"I see," said Mung. "I take it Ardvon will be drumming."

"Yes, and another drummer as well: a man called Bruno. Collette and Shamira will help me prepare, and will watch over the whole process, keeping us all as safe as possible. However," she continued, "this event will not take place until the full moon two days hence."

"Is there some significance to this?" asked Mung.

"Again, Yorlan, my answer is yes and no," said Brina. "The full moon is the peak of the cycle, when the moon shines brightest and fairest of all. This full moon is somewhat significant because the moon will also appear very large indeed. The power of the Goddess is at its maximum when the moon is fullest."

"I think I see," said Mung, although he was clearly still perplexed.

"Oh, and another reason for waiting is that where I am going I will need all the light I can muster," said Brina.

"Then why not go at midday when the sun is bright?" asked the patient.

"Because those I need to seek out are nowhere to be found in the pure light of day, Yorlan. We are dealing with the dark side, and that means dark in all respects. Now you must keep up with your meditations, and I must begin my preparations," said Brina.

The two intervening days seemed endless to Mung as he waited for the moment to arrive. He had kept going with his practice, and was indeed finding it easier to still his mind and concentrate on the inner self. His mentor was pleased with his progress, both physical and spiritual.

Brina, as a practitioner of these ancient arts, knew that there was only this vast, almost indescribable, overwhelming, ever-moving great moment of now: now is where there is no division into past, present, and future. She had made such journeys before, and knew it was possible for her to operate outwith the constraints of time and space, to travel to that place where the traumatic event is still occurring for her patient, so as to find, and bring back, that person's life force and the missing soul parts held in that event. She also knew that Mung's therapeutic healing of the event, and its consequences, would only truly begin when she had been successful in her quest.

*****

With everyone now gathered Brina finalised her preparations, carefully laying out her accoutrements in order to create a sacred space for Mung, one where he would be held in a container of love, and one that would protect him from any interferences from the outside world.

When she finished creating the sacred space she sat Mung in its centre and asked him to enter his meditative state: she then began her journey. Ardvon and Bruno began their drumming sequences: Colette and Shamira slipped into a trance like state where they would act as watchers and gatekeepers, protecting everyone involved.

Slowly Brina entered into the quiet, and stilled her mind. Her concentration was focussed inwards, reaching for her Higher Self, and from there up through her etheric bodies until, at last, she reached the spiritual plane.

She called on her power animal, a large brown bear, to take her into the Inner Worlds, to help her negotiate, barter and deal with the entities holding the fragment of Mung's soul. Her intention drove them forward, and the bear's knowing led them to where the missing soul portion could be located.

Brina knew from past experience that she would undoubtedly meet some very gruesome characters in this inner World, obnoxious creatures who would not give up the split soul easily, because it gave them life essence, the one thing humans can accumulate and take with them from lifetime to lifetime. These horrible creatures had no way of becoming human, despite their deepest wishes.

These creatures have such a great longing for human form that they will do almost anything to get a human to give up part of their soul. They offer humans riches, love, success, material wealth, and fame: anything for a soul. Human morals may be lacking at times, but these creatures do not have any at all, so they will not hesitate to lie, cheat or steal as a human often does.

With such horror and evil to confront, it would take all Brina's concerted efforts and strength to remain focussed on her intent. There are many such beings in the inner World trying to confuse and divert attention. Brown Bear was there to guard Brina: he would prevent any attack on her, for her soul, too, was at risk.

The Shaman straddled the bear's back and they set off on their journey. Down, down they went into the Under World. They came out in a dark and damp place that reminded her of a dungeon cell she once had the misfortune to have been cast into. There were dark thorny bramberry vines growing everywhere, and the ground was soft and swampy, covered in moss: the sky was obscured by the thick, dark green foliage of the tall trees and climbing ivy: creatures were scurrying on the ground, hiding under the rocks, and slithering into dark, dank, and slimy places.

Brina and the bear travelled onwards, almost unaware of their surroundings, the bear knowing exactly where it was headed, until they came upon a tumbledown squarish dwelling made from boulders, logs and foul smelling slimy mud. There were no signs of windows, just an occasional hole in a wall, and a small opening on the side facing them acted as a doorway.

Brina could hear the squeals and cackles coming from inside: the closer she and the bear approached, the more devilish and hellish the sounds became. Brina told herself that these were distractions to lower her guard, and she resolved to remain focussed on her intent. The retrieval of Mung's soul was uppermost in her mind, and nothing, not these noises or anything else was going to deflect her from that.

She dismounted, and approached the opening with much caution. She had to get down on all fours to be able to peer inside: the smell of the whole place was gut wrenching, and she fought hard not to retch. There was little light, and the fire, or what remained of it, was almost out. She kept her gaze on the inside, and as her eyes adjusted to the reduced light, she could just about make out three short creatures, who, although appearing humanlike, were of an ugliness she would have found hard to imagine. They had long hair, gathered in plaits, streaked with the same slimy mud that held their dwelling together. Their clothes barely concealed their bodies: the stench inside the building was horrific, and again she fought back the reflex to throw up.

The creatures were holding the portion of Mung's soul between them, admiring it, and stroking it lovingly as they uttered their hellish whistles, whilst shrieking in delight. They didn't notice Brina at first as she watched, strangely captivated by their behaviour, treating Mung's soul like some much loved pet animal.

Brina turned from the door, and reaching into her satchel, brought out a candle and lit it, shielding its light with her cape. She returned to the opening, knelt down where she had been, and, in a move of graceful swiftness, drew back her cloak. She placed the candle in the opening and its flame lit up the room. The joyful shrieks turned to cries of horror as the light hit the creatures. They screwed up their eyes, trying to shield themselves with outstretched hands. They tried to get out the door, but Brina blocked their passage by extending her arms, her hands holding her cape open wide.

143

"What do you want?" cried one as a fearful shudder rippled through its body.

"I want that soul portion," said Brina in her most authoritative voice.

"Never!" they cried in unison, trying again to get past Brina and escape out into the cold damp forest, but she was alert and again prevented them.

"What will you take in return for the soul?" she asked them.

"We will never give it up," said the first one, "it's ours now and we are keeping it."

Brina raised her voice: "You must relinquish the soul!"

"Never!" they retorted.

Brina pushed the candle even further into the room as the bright light seemed to hurt their eyes, causing them to turn away from it to protect themselves from the flame.

"How did you get this soul?" she demanded.

"None of your business!" cried the creatures.

Brina reached into her satchel, pulled out a mirror fragment, and showed it to the creatures. As they edged closer to have a look at it Brina noticed that many other creatures were being attracted to her, making it more and more dangerous for her to be there. She realised that she had to end this event quickly before she was attacked by other beings who were attracted to her own soul.

She continued to tempt the creature who was holding Mung's soul portion to reach out for the mirror with both hands. As it loosened its grip on the portion, the bear broke through from a side wall and grabbed the soul in his mouth. At the same time Brina threw the mirror into a far corner of the room: as the entities scrambled to catch it, she grabbed hold of the bear's tail and was dragged away from the dwelling. Quickly, she remounted as they raced out of the woods and up into the night sky. As soon as they reached the opening from which they had entered this place they quickly disappeared through it, back to the Outer World. Only then did the bear gently place the piece of soul into Brina's hands from his mouth, and she thanked him once again for his protection and help.

Back in her room Brina was aware of Mung sitting on the chair, deep in meditative trance. She placed the piece of soul in her mouth and then covered Mung's mouth with hers. She breathed in deeply through her nose, and with one big out breath she blew the piece of soul into Mung's body. The patient gave a tremor as the soul piece passed down his throat into his innards. He began to splutter for breath and tried to stand up. Collette helped Brina to deal with Mung's discomfort, whilst Shamira brought some water for him to sip on. The three of them barely managed to restore Mung's posture.

"Yorlan Mung," said Brina softly, "how do you feel?"

144

Mung sat there for a few minutes, trying to take in what had gone on, but not fully understanding. "Whole," he said.

"This is excellent news, Yorlan," said Brina, "and now the healing process truly begins."

"I thought it had begun," said Mung, beginning to recover. "Am I not in a better condition that when you found me?"

"Yes, Yorlan," said the Shaman, "you most certainly are, but from here on I am certain that you will experience other benefits, too."

"Such as?" said Mung, not quite understanding.

"Listen, Yorlan," said Brina gently, "an individual's reactions after going through soul retrieval are as varied as the number people who go through the process. Each person, though part of the whole, is unique, and so is your returning soul."

Mung looked at Brina questioningly.

"Alright," said the healer, "what I am trying to tell you is that soul retrieval means different things to different people: it is important not to have any fixed ideas about what you may be expected to feel. Let me say, for instance, that some people feel great joy, some people sadness, some people feel fuller, some people feel lighter, some people feel nothing at all. I could go on for the rest of the night telling you what people have claimed to feel. However, we are not entirely finished with this process yet."

"Will you discuss this with me tomorrow, then?" asked Mung.

"Of course I will," said Brina. "When have I not been willing to share with you?"

"I'm sorry," said Mung. "I didn't mean to cause upset. I can wait. As far as I am aware I am not going anywhere." He laughed as he said this.

"No harm done," said Brina. "Let's close down the energies, and thank those who have helped make this a successful retrieval."

The group formed a circle around Mung, and went through their processes, closing down the energies that had been brought to the fore for protection and guidance. They thanked the Lords of the Light, the Archangels, the Angels, their personal guides and helpers, finishing by closing down their own chakras, their energy centres. Brina then sealed the room with Love and Light before drawing out her power symbols, the Na-Pra-Chi, the Ku-Ma-Ra and the Om-Nes-Est, at each Cardinal point: the room was now clear.

"Thank you, everyone," said Brina to her helpers, "this could not have been done without each and every one of you."

"Thank you from me, too," said Mung. "I do appreciate what you have done for me. I'm not known to you, but yet you gave up your time to share your skills for my benefit."

"Perhaps you would like to know what those skills are, Yorlan?" asked Brina.

"Yes please," said Mung, amused and perplexed at the same time. "I know Ardvon is a very talented drummer, and I am thinking that Bruno, too, must be very skilled with the drum."

"Yes," said Brina, "indeed they are skilled. Bruno, please tell Mung of your part in tonight's event. I will go and get us a drink, I think we need one."

"Well," said Bruno, "I follow Ardvon's lead. You are aware of his massive talent, and it's a pleasure to play alongside him. His sense of rhythm is outstanding, and together we began slowly and gently, counterbalancing each other with our different drums. The drum I play is called a Jimbay, and as you can see it is carved in one single piece from a hollowed out piece from a hardwood tree. The wood for this drum is called Kaddi and these trees grow only in a region far beyond the Qaf Mountains. You can imagine that it is expensive to buy." He paused to laugh as he remembered just how much the wood had cost, before continuing.

"As you can see the Jimbay is shaped like a drinking goblet, and that's what makes it so different from other drums. Also, Jimbays are not smooth inside, but have a spiral channel that adds to its sound qualities. The drum head, or covering is made from goatskin which is a really tough leather that will last a lifetime."

"I suppose it takes time to learn to play," said Mung.

"Like everything else," said Bruno, "it takes dedication and application. The proper sound is achieved with as little effort as possible, to give the best possible effect. The idea is to either concentrate or disperse the hand's energy, and position the hand in the correct place." Bruno demonstrated by striking the drum with fingers firmly together, and this produced a sharp, bass tone. Then he demonstrated what he called a slap which is executed with the fingers relaxed: the difference in sound was quite remarkable to Mung.

"Oh," exclaimed Mung, "and I thought a drum was a drum." He laughed to cover his embarrassment.

"That's not all, Yorlan," said Brina arriving with mugs of a hot herbal infusion, "the Jimbay is special in another way."

"Yes," agreed Bruno, "it is said that the Jimbay contains three spirits: the spirit of the tree, the spirit of the goat, and the spirit of the instrument maker. A properly made Jimbay is made from one piece of wood so that the spirit of the tree is fully present. I have seen Jimbays that are inferior, as they are constructed from many slats of wood: there is no tree spirit in those drums at all."

"And dare I ask who is the maker of this Jimbay?" queried Mung.

"I am," said Bruno. "I travelled far to study the proper making of these drums and spent a long time in apprenticeship to an old Soul Warrior in the far east, close to the borderlands. This drum is my pride and joy."

"Anything to report on the events of this evening, Ardvon?" asked Brina.

146

"Nothing exceptional," said Ardvon. "We were able to build up the tempo at a nice even pace. However, once we got going there were times when we encountered some difficulties in gauging what it was you needed. Hopefully, we were able to produce what you required."

Brina gave Ardvon a look that told him he needed to explain further. "We were watching you closely, but there were times when I wasn't sure. I looked to the Angels of Protection for guidance, and took my lead from them."

"Ah, the Angels of Protection," said Brina. "Who did we have with us tonight, Collette?"

"We called on Michael, naturally," said Collette. "His primary role is to protect with his sword and shield. Also, we asked Michael to cast his cloak of deepest blue around you to give you added protection as you travelled the Inner Worlds."

"Thank you," said Brina, "I certainly felt his presence with me. Who else did you ask for help?"

"We called on Gabriel, Uriel and Ariel too," said Collette.

"Good choices," agreed Brina. "For Yorlan's benefit can you explain your actions?"

"Well," began Collette, "Gabriel serves on the white ray of purity which assists light workers in working with the true light to bring about qualities of purity, order, hope, joy, and discipline. The Seraphim who serve with Gabriel placed their presence over us, and that allowed us to absorb that light and energy into our bodies much the same as a sponge absorbs water. When we desire to unite with divine consciousness through purity of body, mind and soul, these angels can help us to achieve that goal. Archangel Gabriel offers the strength of Divine Mind to overcome fear, and also carries the energy of protection and power."

"Yes," said Shamira, "Gabriel was very much with us tonight. The energies that the Seraphim overlaid us with were quite outstanding and powerful."

"I am impressed, Collette," said Brina. "You are fast becoming an adept in calling on the Angels. Please, continue."

"Thank you," said Collette, a girl of around eighteen years who came to Brina for lessons in spiritual matters. "Archangel Uriel is the Angel of the Earth and the keeper of the mysteries which are deep within the planet. I called on him because he also supervises the Nature Spirits, those fascinating little sprites who inhabit the elements of earth, air, fire and water, and who lend so much to the beauty of nature. In your journey I believed you would need help and support from as many sources as possible."

"Excellent, my child," said Brina, "and Uriel will vigorously dispel darkness with light at those times when we are in greatest danger, thus offering support on the spiritual journey. Truly, an inspired choice."

Collette flushed at Brina's words, but her mentor only encouraged her further. "Now tell us about Ariel, my dear."

"Archangel Ariel is the caretaker and protector of the Earth," said Collette, "She watches over all beings whether human, animal, or spirit, her mission being to ensure their survival. Ariel's name means 'Lioness of God', and she is associated not just with lions, but all animals. Archangel Ariel is there to support us when we need the qualities of bravery, courage, focus, confidence and grace."

"Again, a magnificent choice," said the Shaman. "In addition Ariel can be called when control of demons is required, and, believe me my child, there were many of those around me tonight, so thank you for your care and attention."

Brina looked at Mung who was wearing a look of total bewilderment, as he seemed to be struggling to take it all in. "Are you with us, Yorlan, or have we left you some way behind?" They all smiled, remembering their own early steps along their individual pathways.

"I can hardly take it all in," he said, "but then again everything that Collette has said makes perfect sense with what I was experiencing."

Brina sat upright in her chair at Mung's words. "Really?" she said. "Care to tell us some more? I am sure everyone will be very interested to hear what you have to say. It's not every day we get the chance to be involved in a Soul Retrieval."

"I don't mind sharing at all," said the patient. "I'd be glad to help all those who have helped me. Well, Brina," he continued, "as you know I have been practising this meditation process for a little while at your behest. Each time I have entered the quiet I have found it easier to settle into the whole event."

"Yes, Yorlan," said the healer, "you have been a very good pupil and seem keen to learn. Do go on, please."

"Tonight you asked me to go through my preparations as normal, which I tried to do. However, it was a little more difficult, knowing that there was a greater purpose to it tonight, and also, with the extra people present, I felt somewhat self conscious. Nevertheless, I realised the importance, and was determined not to let anyone down, especially you, as I was very aware of the dangers you were possibly exposing yourself to."

"Understandable," said Brina. "Were you able to put these concerns to one side and slip into the quiet?"

Mung continued with his story. He told them that he found the sound of the drums very soothing and gentle: it was this more than any effort from him that had finally banished his unease, and, before he knew it, he was in his safe place in the quiet. He thanked the drummers for their influences.

"I sat there in my beautiful spot, doing my best to reach outwards and upwards. I was aware of various colours of light appearing all around me. It was as if I was enclosed in some sort of giant bubble. Particularly prevalent was a pure white light, so bright it lit up the whole room, filling it with a powerful energy. I take it this was the Archangel Gabriel?"

"Yes, Yorlan," Brina confirmed, "any other sensations?"

Mung replied in the affirmative, telling them that just inside his perceived bubble he could see a deep shade of blue all round the outer edge of the bubble. He was now making a connection to Archangel Michael protecting him. He said that all around him, within his bubble of protection he was enclosed in an emerald green. "I felt so warm and comfortable in that green light," he said, "and I knew that everything would work out for the best."

"As it did," said Brina. "That was the presence of the Archangel Raphael, and you must have called on him, Yorlan, for nobody else did."

Mung looked at her, puzzled. "I didn't call on anyone," he said. "I wouldn't know how to."

"Then, your Guardian must have acted on your behalf," said Brina. "No matter, Raphael was obviously here with his Angels of Healing. Is there anything else?"

Mung told them that he wasn't aware of the room as such, wasn't aware of any other colours, although he had this overwhelming feeling of peace and love which brought an inner calmness and the knowledge that he was indeed safe and could come to no harm. "I know I coughed and spluttered at the end, and awoke to find you ladies ministering to me," he said. "I thought I was choking at first, but the feeling rapidly subsided as I began to realise that my entire being was somehow filling up with a golden white light. I just feel as if I am in a dream world."

"You have done very well, Yorlan," said Brina. "Let me assure you that you are in the real world, and your experiences all related to the Soul Retrieval. You must be somewhat surprised yourself to find that you have such abilities."

"I would not have believed it if you had told me say a month ago," he agreed. "Now, Brina, what about your journey? Will you tell us?"

Brina told them of her journey through to the Inner Worlds on the back of her Bear, and of the encounter with the horrible creatures who were playing with Mung's soul part. She told them how she had demanded the return of the soul part, and how the creatures refused to give it up. She told them of the gathering accumulation of other entities who had come to see what the row was about. She looked at Mung saying, "These three entities who were playing with your Soul fragment were so ugly that they defy description. However, I sensed that they are manifestations of the three knife blows you suffered."

"Didn't you fear for your own Soul?" asked Shamira.

"I sensed the danger, Shamira, but knew I was well protected. Had I felt fear I would have sent out the wrong energies and these would have

149

multiplied, defeating my purpose," said Brina. "It was at this point I used the mirror as a lure, as a decoy, hoping they would take their attention from the Soul fragment. I waited, and sensed that the situation was reaching its climax. I saw the creatures let go of Mung's Soul part, so I signalled for Bear to come crashing through the wall of the dwelling to rescue the fragment, and take me with him as he departed. Mission accomplished, and we are safe and sound."

The others burst into a spontaneous round of applause for Brina. It was now her turn to blush with embarrassment.

"Excellent work," said Mung, "but please tell me, why a mirror? What is so special about a mirror?"

"Lots of things, Yorlan, lots of things," said Brina. "However, I think we have done enough discussing tonight. I am certainly tired, and I am sure the others are too. I would like to share with everyone about the mirrors, for there are lessons for us all, but not tonight. Now we sleep and restore our bodies."

"But when will you tell us?" Mung persisted.

Brina asked the others if they could return the following evening, and, getting a positive answer said, "Then that's settled. Tomorrow evening. We will meet again."

Chapter 28: Fellowship

The rowboat was within easy reach of the mainland, the dolphins having pulled it across the wild raging current of the deep channel. The boat's occupants again realised that what had been achieved would have been beyond their capabilities. Without the dolphins they could not have survived.

Morfan signalled to Aonghus that their help was coming to an end, and wished the party well.

"Morfan," said Aonghus, "I know I speak for all of us when I say that we cannot thank you enough for what you have done. Without you we were doomed. Your intervention has given us a chance of survival, and I am sure that we will grasp it tightly."

"Our purpose in life is to help where and when we can. We are here to be of service, and it is through service that we find spiritual progress. When you are of service to another you are serving the entire Universe."

"Ooh," said Aonghus not quite comprehending.

"I have perhaps said too much, but one day you will surely realise that there is truth in what I am telling you now. You are young and have much to learn, but you have ability, and you have potential. How else could you communicate with me?"

"Mmm," said Aonghus, still not understanding.

"Remember, Aonghus Cranstoun, to be there for others is a wonderful opportunity, but you must wait to be asked for your help, and when you are, give it wholeheartedly, without judgment and always with love. Good luck."

Aonghus sat in the boat totally immersed within himself. There was so much to learn as Morfan and the fish had indicated. Who would teach him? How would he find those who could develop his potential?

"Are you alright, Aonghus?" said Myrta. Her voice burst the bubble of the daydream.

"Yes, yes," said the boy recovering, "the dolphins are telling me their work is finished, and we need to take over control again."

"Please thank them with all our hearts," said Myrta, "for without them I hate to think what may have become of us."

"I have, mother," said the boy, "I have."

"Goodbye, Morfan," he said to the dolphin, "and thank you, for everything."

The dolphins swam round the boat one last time then swam off towards the open waters of the Cold Sea, no doubt to join others of their species, and with certainty to help anyone else in danger.

*****

The party reached the shore, and set about hauling the rowboat as far up the beach as possible. Hopefully, this would be the last time they would use the boat.

Everet was certainly of the mind that if he never saw another oar, let alone have to use one, it would be too soon. "What do you think, Diarmid," he asked, "will we have to row again?"

"Who knows?" said Diarmid. "Look on it as a new skill gained, and not as an evil you have endured."

"My word!" said Myrta. "Such deep words from one so young." They all laughed.

"Let's look out the map," said Everet, "and see where we have to go."

They laid out the parchment on the shingle, weighing its corners down with stones to stop it from blowing away.

"Diarmid, you are more used to reading these things. What say you?" said Everet.

The sailor studied the map then surveyed the landscape, looking for tell tale signs or landmarks. After several moments of looking around, Diarmid peered back at the map, finally coming to the conclusion that the signs of habitation they were looking for were not too far away. "I think we are here," he said, pointing to a location on the map, "and this indication of a settlement is here," he went on, his finger moving to a new location. "Not far, and we can reach it today."

Everet studied the map noting Diarmid's estimation of where they were and looked round, as Diarmid had, at the landscape. "I'm no expert," said Everet, "but I do think you are right, my lad. Let's set a course and we'll be off."

"Of course," said Diarmid, "but not so quickly. We need to be sure of where we are going. Reading the map tells me we are heading into the hills. The lack of fine details indicates that nobody has actually been ashore to find any paths. It could be that our intended destination is just a ghost town, like that little cottage we found on the island. Because there is an indication of a settlement is no guarantee that there is one. Besides, we could be interpreting the map wrongly, and that mark may be something else entirely."

"Oh!" exclaimed Everet taken aback a little. "Yes, you are right. We must not build up expectations only to be disappointed when they don't work out. Let's proceed with caution. Where, then, would you suggest we head for?"

"Let's stick to the edge of the shore, and head that way towards the end of the bay," said Diarmid pointing out his chosen route. "Then we can see what lies beyond, and maybe pick out a route that will lead us into the hills."

"Excellent," said Everet. "Let's be on our way," he went on as he carefully folded the map and stowed it into his jacket.

"Don't we need to take anything from the boat?" asked Myrta.

"We should reach where we are going later today," said Everet. "Is there any need?"

"And if our destination is not the one we hope it is?" asked Myrta

"We'll trust that it will provide some kind of shelter and return here tomorrow," said Everet. "We don't want to weigh ourselves down unnecessarily."

They set off along the edge of the shore where the ground was quite flat and the going was very easy: soon they had reached the other end of the bay. They again consulted the map and agreed on the next leg of their journey. The land began to rise up quite noticeably, and progress slowed down because of the roughness of the terrain. Still, they were happy with the distance they had covered.

Their climb became tougher still as outcrops of rock seemed determined to bar their way: undaunted they climbed and scrambled over the rocks, equally determined that the end of their quest was close at hand.

They rounded the spur that was the foot of a towering mountain, and as they drew themselves up, they could see a little plateau not too far above them: atop this levelling of the mountain was an impressive stone building. Joy filled their hearts, and the release of emotions brought tears to their eyes. There were plumes of smoke reaching skywards from behind the walls. With renewed vigour they set off on the final climb.

*****

The building was indeed impressive, with high walls which looked like they had been there forever. The huge doors in the middle of the wall facing into the valley were of sturdy oak, held in place by huge metal hinges. The doors showed signs of wear and tear, probably damage from arrows, battering rams and other weapons of war. The fact that they still stood indicated that this building was something of a stronghold.

On one door was an iron grill which had been blocked up. Close by, a rope dangled: Everet pulled on it, and they heard a bell toll within a cavernous hall. He pulled on it once more such was his joy.

Eventually they heard the sound of footsteps approaching from within, then the undoing of a bolt. A face appeared in a grill: it was that of a young girl. "Hello," said Everet, but before he could say anything else the face was replaced with the wooden shutter, and the bolt was securely fastened.

The group looked at each other wondering what was going on. Then they heard larger bolts being drawn, and the door slowly opened. The young girl held it to, blocking any entrance as she eyed the party in concentrated examination.

She then turned inside, and began to shout loudly, "Sorella Anastasie Gyere gyorsan, itt van. Megérkeztél ide. Ez nekünk, most." She danced and skipped

153

as she shouted her words. "Sorella Anastasie, Sorella Anastasie. Gyorsan gyorsan! Hol vagytok? Hol vagytok? "

An older lady came running from within the hall. "Mi a hiba?" she said. "Aki jön?" She looked at the girl. "Novicia Gelsen, Aki jön?"

The girl pointed at Myrta "Thomson az Alban Eiler."

Now everyone looked at Myrta who seemed much surprised and taken aback. What was this girl saying? Who did she think she was? She certainly did not recognise her from anywhere. What was she implying or accusing her of?

The older lady surveyed Myrta, then the others in turn. "I'm sorry," she said, "the Novicia thinks you are someone else. Please, do come in, you look as if you need some rest and tender loving care."

"Novicia Gelsen," said Anastasie, "Téved. Nem az Alban Eiler. Kérlek nyugodj meg és beszélj, úgy, hogy mindenki számára érthető legyen. Most már nyomon követése és zár minket a nagyteremben."

"Yes, Sorella," said the girl suitably chastened.

The Sorella led the group along a dim corridor: the low level of light was provided by an occasional torch mounted on the wall; their footfalls echoed round the cavernous passageway. Everet could just about pick out the frieze that ran the full length of the walls. From what little he could see he knew that a great deal of painstaking work had gone into the decorative feature.

They passed several doors on the side walls along the way: beautifully panelled they were, again adding to Everet's mounting admiration of the work that had been done in the design and construction of this building. The corridor ended in a junction that saw passages lead off to the left and right: there was a door in the wall immediately in front of them. The Sorella turned the handle and the door opened effortlessly on well oiled hinges: she bade them enter into the Great Hall.

In the middle of the floor there was a huge table with benches on either side: at the far end there was a dais on which stood three magnificent thrones, all upholstered in deepest violet, with the middle throne larger than its companions. The windows high up the walls on either side of the hall let the daylight flood in, giving the hall a light, warm and comfortable feel. Heavy drapes of the same deep violet colour as the thrones hung from the windows adding to the warmth of the room which was heated by a open log fire midway along each side wall.

"Please," said the Sorella, "sit down at the fire and make yourselves comfortable whilst I arrange for some food to be prepared for you." With that she left via an unobtrusive door at the far end of the room, close to the dais.

"What place is this, father?" asked Aonghus, pulling off his boots.

"Who knows?" said Everet, "but it all seems friendly and welcoming."

"Apart from the strange tongue we were greeted in!" laughed Diarmid.

"Yes," said Everet, "I have never heard any other tongue save our own. I know there are many ways to speak our language, but that wasn't one of them I'll wager."

"Is this some kind of a sanctuary do you think?" said Myrta. "The lady who brought us in here would seem to be in some position of authority."

"That's what I was thinking," said her husband, "and according to where we think we are, we are far from any large town. Perhaps this is some kind of remote convent."

The group sat in silence for a while, each reflecting inwardly on those matters that were most important to them. However, tempted by the heat from the burning logs and the great physical efforts of their journey, they each drifted off into slumber.

They didn't hear the Sorella return, accompanied by two other ladies carrying trays of hot soup and warm bread. The cooks laid the trays down on the table, and set out places for the guests.

"Ahem," said the Sorella softly, "sorry to rouse you from your slumber, but the food is here and is hot."

"Thank you," said Everet rising, encouraging the others to follow. "We greatly appreciate your hospitality."

"We do not get many visitors here, only the occasional pilgrim and soul seeker," said Anastasie. "Please sit and eat," she continued. "You can tell me your story later."

She and the ladies retreated, leaving the group to get on with their soup and bread. "This is nice," said Myrta, "and it makes such a difference having properly prepared food."

"But you always prepare our food properly," said Aonghus.

"Yes, yes, Aonghus," said Myrta, "but since our shipwrecking I have had to improvise with what was available. Mostly we hadn't a clue what we would eat, or indeed if we would ever eat again."

"Mmm yes," said the boy, "it has been very difficult, and it's amazing just how well we have all coped with the situation."

"Exactly," said Everet, spoon halfway to his mouth. "It just goes to show that even in all the bad times there has been something good to take forward."

They soon finished their soup and began idly chatting, musing about the place they had come upon. They didn't notice the door behind the dais open or the two ladies approaching, each with a tray on which were more bowls of steaming hot food. The group was startled by the clink of the bowls as the trays were put down on the table.

One of the ladies cleared away the empty soup bowls whilst the other served up the next course. Aonghus peered into his bowl. "What is this, please?" he asked the lady.

"Bean stew," she replied, her voice almost a whisper.

"Lovely!" said the boy. He looked at his mother and went on, "I don't think I could face fish," he said, a smile creeping across his face.

His mother returned his look. "Whatever is in your bowl is fine, Aonghus," she said, "so please eat."

The ladies again withdrew, leaving the group alone.

*****

After some time the Sorella reappeared, and suggested that the group return to the comfort of the fire. She threw on a few logs, and they watched the sparks from edges of the old glowing embers climb into the air and perform a little dance before disappearing to who knows where.

"Now," she said, "how do you feel?"

"Relieved," said Myrta. The Sorella's look told Myrta that she needed to explain further. "We are so glad that the map we followed had accurate information. We have been trying for many days to reach here, always in the hope that there would be a settlement where we could find help."

"Indeed," said the Sorella, "I need to hear your whole story, but first let me introduce myself, and tell you a little bit about our community."

"That would be nice," said Myrta, and introduced the group to the Sorella.

"Thank you, Myrta" said the Sorella, "my name is Anastasie and I am the Sorella or Head Sister of this community. We are known as the Fellowship of the Violet Flame, and I will explain more about our activities later. We are small in number, currently twenty three of whom seven are men and the remainder women."

"Small, but no doubt a very good team," said Myrta.

"Yes, that's exactly right, Myrta," said Anastasie. "People come, people go. There's no pressure to stay or leave. Those who are here are so for a reason, and will leave for a reason. Everything happens when the time is right."

"Oh!" said Everet, "so much wisdom in such few words. You too have a story to tell," he went on with a grin. They all laughed.

"Oh yes," said Anastasie, "everyone has a tale to tell. Perhaps you can tell me how you got here, Everet."

"Well," said Everet, "I'll certainly try." He looked at the other members of the group as he continued. "If I get anything wrong or forget to mention anything please speak up."

So the castaways related their story from leaving Knympton through the storm and shipwreck, the meeting up again with Diarmid, and ending with their arrival at the sanctuary.

Time seemed to stand still as the itinerary of the adventure unfolded. At various points in the tale the others would help Everet out with details and insights. They discussed the good fortune, for that's what it seemed to be, that they had been blessed with, finding it came their way mostly at the lowest points of their ongoing ill-fated journey. They seemed not to notice the night drawing in or the Sorella feeding logs to the fire at regular intervals.

"… and so it was with a great sense of relief as Myrta has already expressed," said Everet, "to see this place really existed, and the wisp of smoke, probably from this very fire, climbing from the chimney confirmed that it was occupied."

"Ooh," said Anastasie, "that is one big story. I also get a feeling that you can tell me more."

Everet was puzzled. "More?" he said. "I think that from all of us we have included everything about the past, who knows how many, weeks."

"Maybe," said Diarmid, "we haven't included everything."

"What have we missed, Diarmid?" asked Everet.

"Our welcome!" said the sailor smiling. "We wondered what we had come to when we heard the girl shouting." Again they all laughed.

"Ah," said the Sorella, "Novicia Gelsen. Yes, that must have sent an awful dread through you." It was her turn to laugh. "Gelsen arrived here from the far north, in the Dark Lands."

"That's how they speak there?" asked Myrta.

"Yes," said Anastasie.

"And how are you able to communicate with her?" asked Myrta.

"I too was born in the Dark Lands so there is a stroke of fortune," said the Sister. "Gelsen reverts to her native tongue when she gets excited, and just lets it all out."

"Yes," said Everet, "she was pretty excited about something."

"Not something, Everet," said Anastasie, "someone." She looked at Myrta. "My dear," she said to her, "she saw you and thought you were the Alban Eiler."

"Yes, that's the term she used," agreed Everet, "so who is this person?"

"Later, Everet," said the Sister. "But that's not what I meant when I said you can tell me more, but I won't press you here and now."

"That's a relief," said Everet, "for I don't know what you are getting at."

"No matter, Everet," said Anastasie, "It is almost time for what we call Abendessen or evening meal, and I must oversee some procedures. After the meal we will again sit here and I will tell you more about us." She got up and started to leave, turning towards them. "I will send Frater Krem who will show you to your rooms where you can prepare for dinner. He can also arrange for some fresh clothes. You also need to know that when a bell rings to call you to eat, we eat in here, in the Main Hall. However, we eat in total silence."

"Thank you," said Myrta, "fresh clothes would be a welcome blessing."

The Sister left the room, and a short time later a man came to collect them. "Good evening," he said, "I am Krem. Please follow me."

Krem took them out of the hall along a corridor. He showed Everet and Myrta into a small bedroom. "This room is for you. Next door the lads can sleep. There is hot water in the pitcher on the chest of drawers. I will arrange for fresh clothing to be brought to you."

"Thank you, Frater," said Myrta, "you are most kind."

"The pleasure is all mine," said Krem. "Now are you sure you can find your own way back to the Hall?"

"Yes, Krem," said Everet, "thank you for your concern. We will see you at dinner."

The Frater withdrew, and made his way back to where he needed to be to complete his duties. The boys took themselves off to their room to wait for the sound of the dinner bell.

"Hot water to wash in," said Myrta. "How nice that will be. It's amazing what you take for granted and think nothing of it. Then, when you do not have access to it, you realise how unthankful you really are." With that she poured some into the basin, and began to splash her face with the warm fluid. "Oh for a bath in which to soak!" she said. "I wonder what the chances of that might be."

"Perhaps a word with Krem or the Sister will sort that out: the community here seems very keen to share what it has," replied Everet.

A short time later there was a knock at the door: it was Gelsen with a pile of fresh clothing. "Some fresh clothing for all of you," she said. "We have tried our best to pick out what might fit you all. If anything is not right please tell me, and I'll try again."

"Thank you," said Myrta taking hold of the garments. "I'm sure we'll get by with these." The girl turned and quickly disappeared down the corridor.

There was barely time for everyone to wash and put on the fresh clothes before the bell summoned the community to Abendessen. The Cranstouns and Diarmid made their way down the corridors and into the main the Hall. The table was set out with bowls of bread, cheese and eggs. There were also bowls of fresh, raw root vegetables and bowls of fruit. At each place setting there was a goblet of fruit juice. The community had gathered to share a meal.

There were six unclaimed places set out at the end of the table closest to the dais to which they were ushered by Krem. Silently he bade them sit down and took his place beside them.

Anastasie then entered the Hall from the door beyond the thrones: she stood in front of the largest throne, and threw her arms wide, her hands outstretched. At this sign the entire gathering stood up and bowed their heads. The visitors hastily joined in.

"For what we are about to consume," said the Sorella, "let us truly give thanks. Let us remember everyone and everything involved in getting this food to our table, and acknowledge our appreciation of their efforts. Whilst we eat

158

this humble food let us remember all those who are less fortunate than ourselves, those who struggle to find food, those who have no shelter, those who have no family to turn to in times of trouble and distress. Let us give thanks for our abundance. So be it."

There was a short silence ended by the Sorella clapping her hands once: the gathering sat down, almost as one, and the meal commenced. The Sorella took the last remaining place at the table.

Chapter 29: Reactions and Mirrors

Next day Mung was surprised to find that he felt so energised on awakening. His aches and pains seemed to have diminished, and he felt a whole lot better within himself than he had for many a long day. He greeted Brina with a huge smile: "Good morning, Brina," he said, "how are you this fine day?"

"My, my, someone is definitely feeling better. See what a good night's sleep can do?" she said with a smile almost as large.

"I do believe that sleep is only part of the reason," said Mung.

"Yes," Brina agreed, "and once we have had a little breakfast we can discuss this aspect of your healing. Perhaps, if you are feeling up to it, you can get out of bed and sit in the comfortable chair."

"I feel that I could do much more than that," said Mung as he began to throw back the covers.

"Let me help you," said the Shaman. "You are nowhere near as strong and capable as you feel just yet."

She gently supported him as he stood up, and she assisted him to cover the short distance to the chair, now positioned by the bedroom window. Then she went off to her kitchen to prepare a light breakfast of sliced fruits mixed with some cereal grains.

She returned with two bowls of the meal, gave one to Mung along with a spoon, and sat on another chair close by. "It's a very nice day out there," she said following Mung's gaze through the window into the forest. Some of the trees were already beginning to produce buds, and on the ground Mung could see the early signs of nature awakening after the winter hibernation.

"I dare say it is," he said, "but I guess it's not for me just yet, even although I feel I could happily wander around out there."

"That's exactly right, Yorlan," she agreed, "but soon, soon."

They ate their cereal and fruit, finishing off with some bread and herbal tea, silently contemplating the view from the window. "I will wash up these bowls and mugs, Yorlan," Brina said, "and then we will have that chat we postponed from last night." It took her some ten minutes or so to finish her chores, before returning to find Mung lost in a gaze beyond the trees.

"Yorlan," she said softly, "are you here with me or somewhere else?" Mung stirred, almost reluctant to return to the present. "Somewhere nice?" enquired Brina.

"Yes, very pleasant," Mung replied. "Are we ready for that chat?"

"Of course," said Brina. "You were asking about what to expect from the soul retrieval."

"Yes," said Mung, "and you partly explained that you couldn't tell me the whole story."

"That's right, Yorlan," said the Earth Mother, "because every experience is a personal one. What you will experience will be different to others, but will, nevertheless, add to the greater understanding. Let me tell you what others have felt after their retrieval, and perhaps, over the days that follow, you can compare such experiences to your own."

"It will be interesting to hear what you have to say," said Mung. "Please continue."

"Well," went on Brina, "most people report a feeling of wholeness or completeness, as you too have reported. This is the main benefit from such a technique which is why I, and others like me, are prepared to face the dangers in travelling to these Nether Worlds. You may find that some memories which have been blocked out return, helping you to understand more about that event, and also about how you feel now."

"I see," said Mung, "but I honestly can't say that is happening to me."

"Time, Yorlan," said the Shaman, "time alone will tell. The Soul Retrieval is not yet complete, only the first stage. However, more of that later."

Brina went on to tell Mung that other benefits that had been reported included a feeling of regaining or achieving a "personal power", a greater ability to make decisions about their life, a sense of being more "alive", a feeling that a new growth or healing process was beginning. She told him that each person is unique, with each experience bringing different results from their soul retrieval.

"This is why I could not, and would not tell you in advance what to expect from what we were about to undertake," she said. "Do you understand what I am telling you, Yorlan?"

"Yes," said the patient, "I do. Now, perhaps the return of my soul fragment is allowing me that understanding."

"Exactly so," she replied. "Now that your soul has been restored to its completeness you must be open, not only to allow yourself to fully receive what is being returned, but also to allow you to notice any signs of new needs in your life."

"How so?" asked Mung, intrigued.

"Well," replied his mentor, "perhaps you need to celebrate the return of the lost parts of your self, perhaps you need to go outside more, and by that I mean get involved in activities like walking in nature, just admiring this wonderful world we inhabit. Then again it may be that you need to give yourself a period of introspection to consider just exactly what has happened on the inside."

"Mmmm," said Mung, "you are making sense to me, Brina. I already know that I have changed, and that the retrieval has added to whatever is going on within me."

161

"You are certainly beginning to sound like a wise man, Yorlan," she said laughing. "In saying that I am not saying you were an idiot before. I think you know what I mean."

"Yes," he replied, joining in the laughter. "I do feel that the retrieval has started a new stage in my healing process, and not just the wounds on my body."

"Now we are getting somewhere!" said Brina. "Bringing the fragmented parts of your soul together is, perhaps, like finding the key to completing your healing process. It is important that you listen to yourself, for that will allow the retrieval to be as effective as possible. It's as if you are a new born child, so you must care for yourself with love and compassion: you have been given a precious gift, and now you have the responsibility to look after it with love and understanding."

Mung looked at Brina in amazement and wonder as her words reverberated round his head, resonating deep inside him. "Wow," he said as he came to terms with this new found truth.

Brina continued by explaining that in the second stage of the retrieval she would assist him in making his own journeys for insight, telling him that she would be with him in the initial stages for guidance and support. The work she would undertake with Mung would help him to understand the nature of the gift of himself, and how to welcome it back.

She told Mung that she would also encourage him to strengthen his connection with nature, because a relationship with nature is essential to being able to connect to Spirit, or the Sacred, which is the source of our well-being. Here she explained about oneness, and how everything on the planet is connected, whether we could see that connection or not. Nothing exists in isolation, all is one, and one is all. "We are in everything, Yorlan," she said, "and everything is in us."

"Let me take that thought away for consideration," said Mung. "I'm not sure that I fully understand what you are saying here just yet."

"By all means," said Brina, "think about it. See if you can look at things differently. Maybe you will be able to find some events or incidents in your life that, when you look at them from a different angle, you will see are very much connected."

Brina then explained that Mung's introduction to meditation had not just been for the purposes of helping with the soul retrieval. This practice also had a place in the post retrieval scenario, for it introduced Mung to a form of ritual. She explained that the use of rituals and ceremonies helped to eliminate negative patterns, allowing more positive patterns to be established. "You may find that ritual will help you to uncover your own truths, Yorlan," she said. "It will help you to transform that which needs to be altered. What the first stage of the retrieval has done is to build a bridge from your old self to a new self: ritual and ceremony will help you cross that bridge."

She looked at Mung who was quietly taking in what she had said. "How do you feel about all this?" she asked him.

"It's not so much that I am confused, it's more that you are giving me new ideas and insights," he replied. "I have been through a great deal with much trauma. Lots of things have happened to me that I could never ever have imagined. After last night I now know that I am changing in many ways. I need time, as you said, to ask myself questions, and answer them as honestly as I can." He sat there thinking about what he had just said. "See!" he exclaimed, "I am changing. I am considering giving an honest answer!" he laughed long and loud.

"Oh Yorlan" said Brina, joining in. "Let's leave it there. You have much to think about, and I don't want to give you too much too soon. You think about what we have said this morning, and I will tell more this evening when the others return."

"Ah, yes," said Mung, "the mirrors."

*****

Brina left Mung to his contemplations whilst she brought herself up to date with various tasks and chores. Also, she wanted to make a journey into Knympton, more to avail herself of what, if anything, was going on in the town. Reports from her group of acolytes was one thing, first hand experience was another. Besides, it was a fine day for this time of year, and the walk would do her good.

Before she left she made sure that Mung was comfortable, and assured him that he would come to no harm in her absence. She asked Archangel Michael to protect the house by standing guard, and set off down the pathway. At the point where the pathway took a sharp turn she looked back, and could see the sparkles of the golden white light surrounding the cottage: Michael and his Angels of Protection were ever watchful.

She returned sometime later to find Mung in buoyant mood, seemingly energised as a result of his wholeness returning. She laid her purchases down in the kitchen, before wandering through to Mung's bedroom.

"Ah Brina," he said, "did you have a successful trip?"

"Yes, Yorlan, I did," she replied. "The town is quite bustling today, and all the traders seem to be doing good business. It was very difficult to haggle down their prices, but fortune favours the brave, and I did really well with my purchases."

"Good news," Mung said. "I have a question for you."

"Ask," said Brina.

"Earlier you said I need to celebrate the return of my Soul fragments, and the restoration of my wholeness," he said. She looked at him, inviting him to go on. "I have given that matter considerable thought whilst you were on your errands, and I am wondering if it will be possible for Sefira to visit, to see the new me. That indeed would be a celebration in itself."

"That is an excellent idea, Yorlan Mung," said Brina. "As you know I have kept in contact with Sefira without actually having met her face to face, woman to woman. Let me deal with that, for we still need to take care. Eyes are still prying, but from further away. Your ex-colleagues think they are being clever, but then again they have never dealt with me before." She laughed loudly as she remembered some of the escapades with Ludley's hapless watchers. Now let's have a little something to eat before the others start to arrive."

*****

Mung was more than ready when the others arrived to hear Brina's tale of the mirrors and learn from her. For the first time since his arrival at Brina's Mung was able to leave the bedroom, and was propped up comfortably in an armchair next to the big open fire in the lounge. Brina sat in the matching chair on the opposite side of the hearth, with the others seated in an arc between Mung and the Shaman.

Brina began by telling them that the use of mirrors was indeed a very ancient practice, to which there were many aspects. Beyond the mists of time someone realised that, if they looked in a still pool, the creature staring back up at them, was indeed, themselves. Over the years a true realisation came into being: by using a reflective surface such as still water, glass or highly polished stone they could see the future, the past, and those who had died, if they stared hard enough and long enough. Brina explained that this procedure was called scrying, and mirrors used for this purpose were kept covered when not in use.

"It is said that the image you see is your actual Soul, and so out of this belief grew the fear that very bad luck would befall those who caused a mirror to break when they were looking into it," she told them. She also said that some people believed that demons, and the illness and bad luck they caused, could be frightened away by staring at themselves in the mirror.

"However," she went on, "mirrors can be used for much more than just scrying, as they are gateways and vehicles for all sorts of entities, particularly negative creatures who prowl in the nether regions. This is why scrying mirrors need to be kept covered; otherwise they provide the entrance for these demons into our world." She looked round the group to judge their reaction to this information.

"So are you saying that mirrors should not be used as simple looking glasses?" asked Shamira, a little horrified at the prospect of inviting in unwanted entities.

"Not at all," said Brina. "Looking glass mirrors have not been magically charged for any purpose, so they are quite safe to use as you describe. Mirrors

164

that are to be used in ritual or magic are the ones that need to be kept covered when not required." Brina told them how she empowered mirrors, and outlined a procedure for being able to foresee the future or unravel the past.

"How far back into the past or forward into the future can you go, Brina?" said Bruno, intrigued.

"Ask yourself what you believe is possible," said Brina. "If you can go back one week to see who committed a certain act, why could you not go back one year? Ten years? What about 50 years? What about seeing events that took place before you were born? Now I put the thought before you... if you have the talent to pick up an event which occurred only a short time ago, why could you not go back to events that happened years ago? Or hundreds of years?"

"So it's down to the person's own power or belief, then?" said Bruno.

"Basically, yes. That is the answer," said Brina, "but a lot of practice is also required. This is why I taught each one of you how to meditate. Meditation gives you the discipline required to reach out with your mind as far as you can take it. The true meditator can reach out to forever with his mind."

"I assume that the same thing applies to the future?" said Bruno.

"Exactly," said Brina, "although the future, because it hasn't happed yet, is not defined as the past is: what you are doing is looking at possibilities. How far into the future is it possible to foresee? Is there a limit that you think you can see, and if so why that limit?"

"Let me see if I am picking this up correctly," said Ardvon. "You are telling us that there are no limits save for those we put on ourselves."

"Yes," said Brina delighted that her teaching was being understood. "If you think you can't then you won't. If you have even the slightest doubt in the world then you will have already lost the attempt before it was done. You must remain positive at all times."

"I am sure this is all fascinating stuff for the others here, Brina" said Mung, "but I am a newcomer to all this way of being, and I am somewhat muddled. I cannot see how what you have just told us fits in with your visit to the Under Worlds to fetch my missing soul part."

"Oh Yorlan," said Brina, "I am sorry. What I have been outlining is only one facet of mirror magic. This is the main use of mirror magic, but you are right, this attribute of the mirrors is not what I used with those horrible, horrible creatures."

"Oh," said Mung, "pardon me for interrupting. Please continue."

"Perhaps it would be best if I left that aspect of mirror magic at this point," said Brina. "You can then go away, think about it, and if you want me to pursue it please come back, and we will take it further. Let me tell you about the mirror that I gave in exchange for Yorlan's soul part."

Brina explained that the little mirror piece she took with her had been fully prepared for the purpose required. Brina had spent days empowering it with a magical spell. This spell she called the "mirror cage", an invasive spell which has the effect of sucking the target into the mirror. The target is then like a prisoner in a strongly guarded cell, unable to escape by any means: there is also no possibility of communicating with those trapped inside. Only the person who cast the spell can dispel the mirror cage, thus freeing whoever is trapped. She explained that although the mirror she used was as tough as she could find, those trapped inside it would die if it was broken.

"Now that is very clever," said Mung. "So these creatures cannot steal anyone else's soul."

"Yes," said Brina, "they have been removed out of harm's way. They will trouble nobody ever again."

"So why can't that be done to all the nasty demons in the Nether Worlds?" asked Collette.

"It would take forever, my dear," replied the teacher. "Do you know how many of such creatures exist?" Collette shook her head. "No, nor do I, my child. What we must do is work for the light in our own world where there are just as many demons to contend with. Journeys like the one I made last night are special events requiring the talents of many light workers to be successful. They are also far more dangerous than any work we do in this realm. Be proud to have been involved my dear, for without you, without you all, I could not have done it."

They continued to discuss mirrors and their usages for some time, until at last they finally realised that time had simply vanished. The group broke up, and the four acolytes bade their farewells to Brina and Mung. The Shaman helped her patient back to bed. "Tomorrow, Yorlan," she said to him, "I will contact Sefira, and we'll begin to make the arrangements for your celebration. Sleep peacefully, sleep well."

"Thank you so much, Brina," said Mung, "I wish you pleasant dreams."

It did not take much time, or effort, for Mung to fall asleep. His dreams were pleasant, as Brina had wished, and largely featured fond memories of himself and Sefira in the days of their courting. Mung smiled in his sleep as these recollections were relived with enormous amounts of joy.

Chapter 30: The Violet Flame

Abendessen came to an end: Anastasie got up from the table, and stepped onto the dais in front of the large throne. Again she stretched out her arms in a signal for the others to rise. "My friends, as you can see, we have some guests who have stumbled across our Sanctuary as they search for help from a series of calamities. We welcome them with open arms, and will do all we can to offer whatever we are able. Our guests are Everet, Myrta, their son Aonghus, and a friend, Diarmid: please take time to make them welcome in your own way. I will explain to them now the nature of our work here, and you can each tell them where you fit in when you speak to them in the course of their stay with us. Thank you, my friends."

The Sorella returned to the table to usher the guests over to the more comfortable chairs by the fire. Once everyone had settled, she began to tell them about the work of the Fellowship of the Violet Flame.

"You may be totally unaware of this, but across Valkanda there are another six places just like this one," said Anastasie. "Each one is in a reasonably remote area, and each one is close to the outside edge of the territory."

The group looked at each other quizzically. "None of us is aware of anything like that," said Everet. "Should we be?"

"Ordinarily, no," said Anastasie, "but there are some people who have an awareness of one or more centres. As I said earlier we get people who come here to learn, we get pilgrims and soul seekers, people who need our help in some way."

"You mean spiritual seekers?" said Myrta beginning to understand.

"Yes," said the Sorella, "that's right. You are, if you'll pardon my expression, a rarer commodity. Your needs, as you currently see them, are not spiritual, they are more physical and materially based. Anyway, let me return to the seven sanctuaries. Each one works on a particular ray."

"Sorry," Everet interrupted, "I can safely say that you have lost us already. We are not spiritual seekers, and we don't understand what you mean by ray."

"Ah," said the Sorella, "what do you know about light?"

"Not very much," said Everet, "save for that the sun brings it to us."

"And the dark?" asked the Sorella.

"It defines the night, after the sun sets," replied Everet.

"Right," said Anastasie, "then I will try to make this as simple as I can." She thought about her next words very carefully. "You are right in what you say regarding the sun and the light it brings. When the day is bright we can see very clearly, and get on with things. When the sun sets we struggle to see what is front of us. There is also another aspect to the light: it gives us life and growth."

"Yes," said Everet, "I can follow that explanation, but your manner indicates there is even more to come."

"Oh yes," said Anastasie, beaming knowingly. "You will be aware that in the darkness lie all our fears and horrors. It is in the darkness we have our nightmares, where our worst expectations materialise." Aonghus shuddered when he heard these words, his thoughts going back to his own recently suffered traumas. The others nodded in agreement, and Myrta put a comforting arm round her son.

"There are those who would try to banish these creatures of the dark, and aim to always be in the light. These are the spiritual seekers," the Sorella went on, "and we, the members of this Fellowship, are such, as are the groups who live in the other sanctuaries. Through the collected experiences of those who have gone before us we have come to realise that what we call the light is in fact made up of seven separate components, each of a different colour."

"Why don't we see these individual colours?" asked Everet.

"Most of the time they work in harmony with each other to bring us what we call white light," said the Sorella, "but sometimes, on wet days especially, we get a chance to see these individual rays." The group looked at her in some disbelief. Picking up on their wonderment the Sorella said, "Rainbows!"

"Of course!" said Myrta with a laugh, "So that's what they are? But I thought there were only 6 colours in a rainbow, red... yellow... blue... green... orange, and purple."

"That's the way a great very many see the rainbow," agreed Anastasie, "but what you call purple is, in fact, two colours, indigo, which is a very deep blue, and violet, which is a rich purple."

"Well, well," said Myrta, "fancy that."

"Well, each of the seven rays differs from the others, not just in colour, but in the attributes that it brings. Suffice it to say that we here work with the Violet, or Seventh Ray, hence our name. Our sanctuary is called the Abbestery of Saint Germain."

"Are you saying that you worship this Violet Flame here?" asked Everet.

"No, not at all," said Anastasie, "we work with the Violet Flame. We do our best to redirect its energy and attributes across Valkanda. The other sanctuaries carry out similar work with their chosen Ray. When all the Rays come together we are flooding Valkanda with a spiritual white light."

"And what does that do?" asked Everet.

"Well, for one thing, it helps to keep the darkness at bay, although at present it doesn't prevent it from establishing itself in some places," said the Sorella. "We are trying our best, along with the other sanctuaries, to keep acts of evil to a minimum, allowing the population to live a more satisfying life. What we also need," she continued, "is for the population to join us in our efforts. When that day dawns then evil will be banished forever."

"Is it ever likely to dawn?" said Everet. "There will always be those who profit from what you call the darkness and will not wish to relinquish their easy pickings."

"How true," said the Sorella, "but if we all adopted such a negative outlook then the darkness would close in quicker than you could blink, Everet, and then where would we be? As it is, we are finding that there is a growing awareness of what spiritual white light can achieve, and indeed we are gaining ever increasing numbers of supporters and helpers from the population at large. So in answer to your question, yes, I do think that day will dawn when the darkness will have been banished."

Aonghus, who had been listening intently, spoke up. "Can you tell us more about this seventh ray and what it does? It sounds very exciting."

"Most certainly, I will be delighted to tell you about the Seventh Ray, young man," said Anastasie, "but first let me tell you some details about the Violet Flame."

The Sorella went on to explain that the Violet Flame was a gift to the planet from the Beings of Light who dwelt in the spiritual realms, as a means to help us wipe out our past mistakes. She explained that whilst it wasn't possible to go backwards in time the violet flame has the power to erase, or transmute the cause, the effect, and even the memory of our past mistakes.

"What does transmute mean?" asked Aonghus. "I have never heard that word before."

"Transmute means to change something," said the Sorella, "whether that change is to its form, appearance or nature. The Violet Flame changes negative energy into positive energy, darkness into light, or misfortunes into opportunities if that helps you understand better."

She explained that everyone's past actions, both good and bad, come back to us. "This is the Law of Karma," Anastasie said, although she could see that the group did not fully comprehend the idea. "We are each responsible for all our actions," she explained, "and whatever energy we give out into the Universe will travel round, and come back to us at some future point. So if we have given out some negative energy, and realise that we have to balance it in some way, then the Violet Flame can help us do so."

"Are you saying that if we have bad thoughts about someone, then these bad energies will come back to affect us in some way?" said Everet.

"Yes, Everet," said Anastasie, "that's exactly what I am saying."

"But that's impossible!" he said. "How?"

"That's something you will have to take in faith, Everet," said the Sister, "for I am unable to explain how it works, I only know that it does."

"But how come I, we, have been smitten by a whole series of disasters and traumas when we have led upstanding lives?" Everet persisted.

169

"Have you never thought ill of anyone, Everet?" asked the Sister. "Not even a tiny little bad thought?"

"Of course I have," replied Everet beginning to sound grumpy. "Haven't we all when someone has done something to us? I have never wished anything so horribly bad on anyone to have attracted everything we have just been through."

"Perhaps, Everet, you need some time to ponder the answer to that question and see what you come up with," said Anastasie. "We can continue to help you find the answer tomorrow. I have to go soon to join in our Evening Services, but before I go I'd like to tell you how the Violet Flame works."

Anastasie explained that the Violet Flame works by changing what she called "vibrations". As they studied the Violet Flame and received teachings from the Beings of Light, the Fellowship was coming to realise that energy was a largely unseen force which moved, somewhat like the sea, in waves. Everything we are, she explained is actually in motion, moving up and down in its own vibration. Even those things which seemed to be solid and unmoving were in motion. "I know you are finding this hard to believe or conceive," she said, "but trust me, please, and go along with what I have to say for the present."

Our bodies vibrated similarly, according to Anastasie, and she went further to suggest that the human body was in fact made up of an uncountable number of smaller parts, each of which vibrated at a particular rate. When negative energy is given out our bodies could sense that energy, and become a home for it. When this happened our vibrations became slower, causing us to lose our spiritual connection. Bad energy was a force that aided the darkness.

The Violet Flame, when invoked, changed this negative energy by surrounding it and transforming it into white light. "It literally enlightens us," she said, "and we feel so much better!"

There was a short pregnant pause as the Sorella's words filtered through into the minds of her guests.

"You may have heard of people called Alchemists," said the Sorella. "These are men who are looking for the magic formula to turn everyday metals into gold, and so make their fortunes."

"Only in a vague sort of way," Everet replied. "Do they use the Violet Flame to do so?"

"No," said Anastasie, "it doesn't work like that. Let me try to explain." She went on to say that whilst they sought to create wealth by changing the structure of common metals, the Violet Flame was a process of transmutation symbolic of a higher and nobler alchemy - the alchemy of self-transformation.

Spiritual Alchemists were not looking for material wealth, but spiritual wealth. They were looking to transform themselves into more spiritual beings, by becoming more loving, wise and compassionate. The capacity of the Violet

170

Flame has the power to bring this about by transforming negative attitudes and feelings within ourselves. It has the unique ability to transform fear into courage, anxiety into peace, and hatred into love.

The secret of the Violet Flame is that it is a self-transforming fire that leads souls upward, by drawing up to the highest spiritual levels all those qualities which weighed heavily and opposed the spiritual virtues. In the process, the hard and heavy materials in their bodies would be transmuted into a rare, and more luminous material. Transmutation, then, was a spiritual process which raised the soul into a state of unity with the Divine.

"As I said, it enlightens us," Anastasie beamed. "It fills us with light."

Everet looked at the Sister and thanked her for her explanation. "I cannot begin to say that I understand any of it, but then again, I cannot say that you are not right. It is, as you say, something to ponder over, and you have given us much information to dwell upon. It is getting late: you have duties to perform, we are tired. Perhaps we can resume this conversation tomorrow when everyone is fresh."

"Of course," said Anastasie. "The Matins bell will ring to awaken the community, and that will be followed a short time later by the call to breakfast. I am sorry, Aonghus, that I cannot explain about the Seventh Ray tonight; perhaps we can do that tomorrow also. I will see you all then. Sleep peacefully."

Chapter 31: Sefira gets a Visit

Brina gathered together what she needed, and placed the items in her basket. She made sure Mung was comfortable and, as was her practice, called on the Angels to protect the cottage whilst she was gone.

She gently closed the door behind her, and made her way down an obscure pathway which, she knew, would take her to that special place where she would not be disturbed.

The morning was bright, albeit cold, and the sun was doing its best to break through the cloud cover. As Brina laid out her blanket she could hear the birds singing merrily in the trees. "They're always singing," she thought, "always so happy. Humans need to take a lesson from the birds. Indeed, humans need to take a lesson from all of nature."

She had gone through these preparations many, many times before, but she still took great care when setting out her space. Every item was placed just so, each one given the necessary deference and respect. Her final act was to light the candles, after which she sat cross legged in the middle of the blanket. She began her ceremony. "Om," she intoned, slowly letting the Holy sound reverberate through her body. "Om," she again said, sending the sound out to the Universe. She repeated the mantra until she was satisfied with her connection to the All-that-is. Now she was ready.

She expanded her consciousness out into the ether: it was almost as if Brina herself was flying through the air. She was searching for her friend, Felina the cat, to ask for help once more.

Round the alleyways of Knympton Brina sent her consciousness until at last she saw the cat curled up, sleeping under a bush in a garden.

Gently, she made contact with Felina's consciousness. "Hello, my friend," said Brina. The cat's eyes opened wide. "Sorry," said the Shaman, "didn't mean to frighten you."

"Can't a cat get a decent sleep after a hard night's work prowling?" asked Felina, smiling. "How can I help you this time, my dear?"

"I need to pay another visit to the lady," said Brina.

"Now?" said Felina.

"If you wouldn't mind," said the Crone.

"Well, all right, but let me have a good stretch first," said the cat, as she began to uncurl from her sleeping position.

"You remember the way?" asked Brina.

"I'm a cat," said Felina faking annoyance. "Let's go."

With that their consciousnesses merged, and Brina was again one with the cat, experiencing what Felina thought, felt and did. They cut this way and that, under fences, over walls, avoiding the busier places until they arrived at the Mung house.

"Don't stop here, there may be someone keeping watch," said Brina. "Go a few doors further on." The cat obeyed, and at Brina's further request cut round the side of a house.

"Now where?" asked Felina.

"Through the gardens and back yards," answered her passenger.

The cat soon arrived at Mung's back door: it was closed, as was the window Felina had used on previous occasions.

"Scrape the door," suggested Brina: the cat complied. They waited for several minutes. "Scrape it again," said Brina, "and howl as well." They again waited, and after a few minutes there was the sound of the lock being turned. Slowly the door opened, just a crack, and they could see Sefira peering out.

Felina let out another Miaow, and Sefira opened the door a little more to poke her head out. The gap was wide enough now, so Felina made her move, gaining entry before Sefira could react.

Realising what had happened, Sefira closed the door, and turned to face the cat which was now sitting on the kitchen table.

"It's you again," said Sefira, recognising the cat. "Do you have another message for me?"

Felina jumped down from the table, and strutted into the sitting room where she took up a position on one of the fireside chairs.

Sefira followed and sat in the other chair: she knew the drill, and just relaxed as far as she could; she knew she would hear Brina's voice resounding in her head.

"That's good, Sefira. Just relax. and look deeply into the cat's eyes. We've done this several times before, so you know you are safe and will come to no harm."

"Hello, Brina," said Sefira. "How is Yorlan?"

"The good news, Sefira, is that he is very much improved. Indeed he has made significant progress in the last two days."

"That is good news," agreed Sefira.

"There is even better news."

Sefira sat more upright in her chair.

"It's time for you to see him!"

"These are excellent tidings," said Sefira, "but I am thinking there's more to this than meets the eye."

"Shrewd woman, Sefira, but first tell me what the Marshals are doing to find him."

Sefira told Brina of her several visits to see Captain Folgate. "The Marshals would appear to have all but given up hope of finding Yorlan," Sefira said. "They agree that there are signs of a violent act at the Cranstouns' place, but there are no other clues save for Yorlan's badge."

"Any news of the Cranstouns?"

"No," said Sefira. "They have seemingly just disappeared completely. There are some among the Marshals who blame the Cranstouns for Yorlan's disappearance. I have found it difficult to contain myself when such a suggestion has been made, but bitten my tongue I have, and said nothing."

"Yes, Sefira, it must be hard to say nothing whilst knowing that, whatever has happened to the Cranstouns, they are not responsible for Yorlan's situation."

Sefira sat for several minutes staring into the cat's eyes. There was a calming silence during which she relaxed completely, settling right into the chair. Sefira was deep in trance when Brina's voice again resonated in her head. Sefira received her instructions for her trip to see Yorlan.

"Do you understand what I want you to do, Sefira?"

"Yes, my dear," said the Marshal's wife, "I know what to do, thank you."

"See you tomorrow, Sefira."

The cat jumped down from the chair.

"Please open the back door for us."

Sefira rose, and walked through to the kitchen: she peered out the window to make sure nobody was watching then opened the door just wide enough to let the cat out, then closing and bolting the door. An excitement pervaded her very being, and it was almost as if she floated across the floor. She needed a drink of hot tea to ponder over her instructions. She filled the kettle, and put it on the fire: she sang softly to herself as she waited for the water to boil.

Felina made her way back to the garden where she had been rudely awakened from her slumber. "Thank you, my friend," said Brina, "I hope you will forgive my intrusion."

"In a strange way," said Felina, "I rather enjoy these covert sessions. People don't give us cats the credit we deserve. They think we're just awkward, selfish creatures who can turn on the aggression at the drop of a hat. Our spiritual attributes and psychic abilities are very rarely appreciated."

"I understand," said Brina, "but more fool anyone who underestimates a cat. As a token of my appreciation I will arrange for some food to be left outside Sefira's house for you."

"Most kind," said the cat.

"You're welcome," said the Shaman. "Now I must break our mind connection, and return to my own reality. I wish you well. Until next time"... and the connection was gone.

Brina pulled her consciousness back into her own body in a slow process: to rush this was asking for all kinds of troubles. Gradually, Brina returned her awareness to the clearing in the wood where she sat in her sacred circle. Slowly, she opened her eyes, and took a deep breath. She placed her hands palm to palm in front of her sternum and gave thanks. "Namaste, Felina," said Brina. "The Divine Light in me salutes the Divine Light in you."

She completed her ritual by blowing out the candles, sending love, light and understanding out to the world as she did so. She gathered her accoutrements together, carefully placing them in her basket. She then folded her blanket and headed back to the cottage.

Chapter 32: Sefira goes on a Visit

Next morning Sefira rose early as usual, dressed simply before going downstairs to have her breakfast of oats and barley soaked in milk. As she ate she wondered what the day would bring. Where was Yorlan? How was he? She knew he had suffered terribly, so badly wounded was he that he would have died had it not been for Brina's intervention.

Indeed, she could not work out how Brina knew about Yorlan's plight or where to find him. However, she was glad that her husband had been found and had been, was still being, cared for.

She loved the man dearly even although he had let himself go over the last number of years: his physical appearance had deteriorated, and his physique, which was attractively muscular in his younger days, had gone soft, a dreadful paunch having taken hold of his midriff.

He had become sloppy and lazy in his activities, and this had contributed to his changing appearance. All the time he spent at *The Waggoner's* had only added to his troubles, and who knows what sort of company he kept there. Certainly Sefira hadn't been impressed by the place, especially when she had confronted the Innkeeper regarding Yorlan's visits there and he had claimed to know nothing about her man. She didn't like that at all, and would have words with Yorlan about it.

These words, Sefira decided, could wait until a more appropriate moment: she was very much looking forward to seeing him again. With that thought in mind she got up from the table, and washed her dishes.

With all her chores completed, Sefira put on her coat, covered her head with a black shawl, as instructed by Brina, picked up her basket, and went out the front door. Without as much as a glance in any direction she strode off boldly towards the market in the centre of town.

She stopped occasionally to window shop or browse amongst some of the open stalls, but always she was progressing towards Bruno's furniture shop. Soon enough she arrived outside and perused the goods in the window display. Seemingly interested in the display she entered the premises, and began browsing round the various chairs, stools and tables set out in the shop. Every item was a beautiful creation, but, in reality, each a little too expensive for Sefira to buy. "Perhaps one day," she told herself.

Her browsing had taken her towards the back of the store, faraway from the prying eyes of Vangil who was on watch duty for the Black Crows: Ludley was still being careful about the whole Mung and Cranstoun business, although he had more or less given up on the latter. They had escaped his clutches, and had apparently run off to some unknown location no doubt to start all over again.

Mung was a worry: Boffe had knifed him good and proper, of that he was as certain as he could be. They had it all planned to perfection. The Cranstouns had run off, and they had left Mung to take his last breath at the Cranstoun's abandoned premises. Even the stupid Marshals could relate the facts, couldn't they? However, the disappearance of Mung's body had ruined everything, and now he had to devote good resources to watching Mung's wife to try to find clues to the whereabouts of the hapless double agent.

Vangil pretended to busy himself in this and that as he watched from a safe distance for Sefira's emergence from the furniture shop.

Inside, Sefira was directed by Bruno to a small office at the back of the showroom. As she stepped into the room she was greeted by Colette. "Hello, Sefira, I am one of Brina's students. My name is Colette, and this is Shamira who will take you to Brina's cottage."

"Hello," said Sefira. "Brina told me you would be here. She has picked well, for you are of similar stature to me."

"Exactly so," said Colette. "Now let's exchange coats and shawl so that we can execute the next part of the plan."

Colette helped Sefira out of her coat and put it on, whilst Shamira held up Colette's blue coat for Sefira. "Quickly now, for your watcher may grow impatient. My, the bonnet suits you really well," Colette laughed.

"This looks rather fetching," said Sefira, catching a glimpse of herself in a mirror.

"Right, Sefira, back to the showroom, but please wait at this end until I have lured your watcher away," said Colette.

They watched as Bruno escorted Colette to the door, opened it for her, and bade her goodbye. Colette stepped out into the street and walked off. Watching from deep inside the shop Sefira's sharp eyes picked out a man in the not too far distance who, when realising what was going on, abruptly replaced the item he was perusing, and made off in Colette's direction.

They gave Vangil a few moments to pursue Colette then Shamira and Sefira exited the store, and headed in the opposite direction, quickly disappearing down some back alleys and side streets, gradually making their way out of Knympton, towards Berystede Wood.

Once out of town they slowed down their pace. "So far, so good," said Shamira. "In just a short while we'll be there."

As she spoke, Shamira cut off from the beaten pathway onto a much lesser used one. "Mind how you go, Sefira," she said, "the bramberry bushes can easily snag your coat, or, worse still, scratch your arms and legs to shreds."

"Ow!" yelled Sefira as a tendril of thorns scraped across her foot. "Is there much more of this?"

"No, not really," said Shamira. "Perhaps another mile or so, but the going gets easier."

"Hallelujah to that," said Sefira taking great care with every step.

The path wended this way and that, until they rounded a huge clump of rhoddi bushes, and came across a small clearing. "We are here," proclaimed Shamira.

"Where?" said Sefira looking all around.

"Brina's cottage is located just through the clearing, down a little path," said Shamira. Sefira looked at her quizzically. "Trust me, Sefira," said the girl. "It's as I have told you, but my instructions are to leave you here and Brina will come for you."

"You are not going to abandon me to this fearsome forest are you?" asked Sefira, a little tremor in her voice.

"You are not being abandoned: I am following instructions. As I said, Sefira, trust is the key word. Now I must go to inform Brina that you are here, and I want you to promise me that you will not follow me."

Reluctantly, Sefira agreed and stood where she was, senses on full alert whilst Shamira proceeded through the clearing and out of sight. Sefira's fears started to play on her mind, and she was sure that she could hear unfamiliar sounds emanating from all around her. "Think positively," she told herself. "You have been brought this far without harm."

"Indeed you have," a voice said in Sefira's head. "You are protected, there is no harm that can befall you."

The voice was warm and rich, its tone soothing and gentle, yet communicating strength. "Who are you?" asked Sefira.

"I am Michael, Archangel of Strength and Protection, and I have cast my cloak around you so that you remain safe," came the reply. As if to emphasise his words Sefira became aware of a twinkling canopy all around her, and amazement spread across her face.

Still wrapped up in wonder Sefira was jolted back to the present by Shamira's voice. "Brina knows you are here, and will come to meet you very shortly. Now I must return to Knympton. I will see you again soon. Good luck!"

"Thank you, Shamira, for your part in this adventure. I look forward to seeing you again," Sefira called out, waving goodbye to the girl who was now rounding the rhoddi bushes and disappearing from view.

Feeling quite safe now, Sefira studied her surroundings in a more relaxed manner as she waited for Brina's arrival: she did not have to wait long. "Ah, Sefira," said Brina, her voice as gentle as a rippling stream, "How nice to meet you face to face, human to human!" They both laughed and embraced.

"Oh Brina," said Sefira, "I am so excited about this visit. I do hope poor Yorlan is able to cope with my arrival."

"He is very much looking forward to it," said the Shaman, "and he is very much dreading it too. There is much to talk about and much to explain. We cannot expect to achieve everything in one short visit, but we can lay solid foundations."

"I will be relieved just seeing he is on the road to recovery," said the wife, "and we can wait for all the explanations until he is fully recovered."

"Yes, yes," said Brina, "small steps will get you there at your own pace. Anyway, I see you have called on Michael's protection."

"You can see that too?" asked Sefira. "I thought I must be going strangely mad when it happened, but I didn't call on Michael, he just appeared."

"You can tell me all about it later," said Brina, "but believe me, you called on Michael. Let's go." With that she led Brina through the clearance, and down the little obscure pathway to the cottage.

Meanwhile, back in Knympton Collette led Vangil on a mystery tour round the market. She led him one way then another, stopping where the moment took her, and admiring goods on display.

Sometimes she would engage the stallholder in conversation over an item before purchasing it, and putting it safely into her basket. At other times she would browse the shop windows in order to check that Vangil was still maintaining his discreet distance. When she picked up his image in the glass she would smile to herself, adjusting her shawl before moving on.

She was enjoying this adventure and wished she could carry it on for longer, but she knew that Shamira and Sefira had had enough time to make their way to Brina's and now she must disappoint her watcher.

She made her way to Ardvon's stall: again she browsed round without raising any suspicion. Ardvon gave her a signal that he had spotted Vangil. Collette left the stall and took several steps in the direction of Vangil who did his best to blend in to the shadows and look disinterested. As she approached closer she allowed the shawl covering her head to slip down, revealing her features.

Panic overcame Vangil in that horrifying moment: this was not Mung's wife, but a slip of a girl. How could he have been so stupid to be have been hoodwinked by so simple a switch? Worse still what would Ludley think about this latest disaster? In total disarray Vangil broke cover and started to run back up the street. First, he stopped and turned, then came the other way, racing past Collette, head turning from side to side as if he expected Sefira to appear at any second.

Collette returned to Ardvon's stall where they shared a good laugh at the success of Brina's plan. Now she must return quickly to Bruno's shop, tell him of the good news, and help him to place a protection spell over the premises.

Chapter 33: More Revelations

The Matins bell was gentle, but persistent, rousing the members of the Community of the Abbeystery from their slumbers. Slowly Everet and Myrta shook themselves into alertness: not so Aonghus and Diarmid who were still asleep when Everet called in on them.

Gently shaking them, he said that they must get up to prepare themselves for breakfast. He reminded them that there was much work to be done. Somewhat reluctantly, the boys got out of bed and organised themselves for the travails of the coming day.

They had barely got themselves ready when the gong sounded for breakfast, and the family made its way to the Hall, joining the other members of the community for the meal. It was a simple meal of cereal and bread, washed down with strong, hot tea.

The community was well organised, with each member knowing what his or her role was within the organisation, and so, when the meal was over, they all set about their given duties to ensure that the Abbeystery functioned efficiently.

The family remained at the table, unsure of what to do or where to go. The Sorella joined them, and began to converse with them. "I have duties to attend to right now, but will be free later this morning. We can continue last night's discussion then, if you wish," she said.

"That would be interesting," said Everet, although his manner suggested he was a bit out of his depth with the subject matter.

"We can discuss other matters that may be closer to your needs, if that would serve you better," said the Sister. "Think about it."

"Maybe," said Myrta, "there are some tasks we could undertake to help out until you are ready to speak to us."

"How kind," said Anastasie. "I will ask Krem to assign you some gentler duties: you have had quite a torrid time of late and your reserves of strength must be running low." The group smiled wryly.

"Yes," said Myrta, breaking into a laugh, "I know two young lads who could barely open their eyes this morning."

"Oh mother!" said Aonghus, reddening.

Anastasie had hardly left the hall when Krem came back to greet them. "I have just the tasks for you," he said with a smile. "Nothing too onerous, but nonetheless helpful. Follow me, please," he continued as he led them to their place of duty.

*****

Later they again met up with Anastasie in a smaller room where they were served some hot tea and cake. "Thank you for your efforts this morning," she said. "We appreciate all the help we can get."

"We like to be of service," said Everet, "and it gave us an insight into some of the work you do here."

They engaged in small talk for a short time then Anastasie said that despite her offer to explain the seventh ray, she had sensed that there was a more demanding topic that required discussion.

"What might that be?" asked Everet.

"You may remember, Everet, that when you told me about your story I suggested there may be more to tell," said the Sister.

"Yes, I remember that," said Everet, nodding, "but I also remember saying that the details were as complete as we could make them."

"You did," said the Sorella, "but there is more to tell Everet. Not only that, but you and Myrta have most to tell."

Husband and wife looked at each other in astonishment and puzzlement, wondering what the Sorella was meaning. "As you can see," said Myrta, "we are a little puzzled by what you say. We have told you everything about our arriving here."

"Yes, I know you have told me details of your journey from Knympton to here, and very interesting encounters you have had," said the Sorella, "but you haven't told me why you decided to leave Knympton."

"Ah," said Everet, "that's another sad episode in our recent history, but I will try to explain." Everet, with some help from Myrta, related their encounter with Ludley and his gang, and, rather than submit to the demands laid upon them they took the decision to leave as soon as was possible with a view to making a fresh start elsewhere.

Anastasie listened with interest, sometimes interrupting Everet to gain a deeper understanding of the situation that they found themselves in. "Well, Everet, that is really quite a story, and I can't believe that a Marshal would act so underhandedly."

"Yes," said Myrta, "the Marshals are supposed to protect us from the rogues, and here was one who acted like he was one of them. It really is quite shocking." Myrta shuddered as she remembered the whole sorry tale.

"And this is what you do is it, Everet?" Anastasie said. Seeing a puzzled look coming over Everet's face she added "When bad times confront you?"

The viander was beginning to get angry by this accusation, "What do you mean by that, Anastasie?" he asked, his voice rising.

"Gently, Everet," said the Sister, "I only want to help you, not rouse your anger. Packing up and leaving is your way of dealing with situations, is it not?" Everet looked her straight in the eye. "Am I right or not?" asked the Sister. "This is not the first time you have taken this course of action."

Everet sat quietly for some minutes then slowly agreed. "You are right, Anastasie, it is not. We have taken this action several times over the years. Myrta and I have no liking for confrontation, so when a situation has arisen

181

that we do not agree with we have taken a decision to leave, to move on, to start again as you say."

"And have you been happy to do that?" asked the Sorella.

"There was no other option for us," said Everet.

"And the outcome?" Anastasie probed.

"We have always been able to begin again," said Everet. "I am blessed with good skills in cutting and preparing meat, always being able to source good quality animals."

"I have no doubts as to your skills as a viander," said Anastasie, "but what have you gained by your actions?"

Everet cradled his head in his hands: realisation was hitting hard. Myrta put an arm round him and said, "We have each other and we have Aonghus. We have our health and so far we have been able to survive."

"All true," said Anastasie, "but, may I ask, where are you bound this time? You are a long way off your chosen destination; all your possessions are at the bottom of the Cold Sea."

"You are right, Anastasie," Everet whispered. "This time we have lost everything, and we even came alarmingly close to losing our lives. We have been very lucky."

"I am sorry to have caused you to look at your circumstances and what has gone on before," said Anastasie. "I am trying to help you, and I do believe that we are making some progress here." The group looked at the Sorella encouraging her to say more. "It's not all as black as you imagine it to be. The bottom line, as I know you have now realised, is that sometimes, to avoid confrontation you have to stand and fight. I know that sounds like contradiction, but believe me, it is not."

"So it's back to Knympton for us, is it?" said Everet. "Who will protect us?"

"It's back to Knympton if that's what you choose, Everet," said Anastasie. "You see, in everything you do there is always a choice for everyone. Your every action is your own choice, not someone else's, unless you give away your free will to choose." She looked round at the group. "Am I talking in riddles again?" she asked seeing their puzzled looks.

"I don't think we quite see what you are trying tell us," said Myrta. "Perhaps you could simplify it for us."

Anastasie said she would do her best to do that. She explained that, from her perspective, everyone contained a spark of the Divine deep within them: everyone was part of Creation. She explained that the spark was sometimes called "soul" and that "soul" never died: "soul" used the physical body to gain experiences in order that it could evolve and develop. When the physical body died, "soul" lived on.

To help "soul" grow, Creation, sometimes called the Universe or God, provided circumstances so that "soul" could learn from them. Anastasie explained that creation was trying to help Everet and Myrta to experience what standing up for one's beliefs really meant by putting them into confrontational situations.

Often, the Sorella told them, "soul" did not recognise what was happening or failed to understand what message was being given, so Creation repeated the lesson, not immediately, but in due time, so that "soul" may have another opportunity to develop.

"So it's not really our fault that we have been the victims of circumstance?" said Everet.

"I wouldn't put it quite like that," said Anastasie. "It's more like you weren't ready to learn the lesson, so you were given another chance. When you walked away in the past you have been blessed with being able to set up again from scratch without too much trouble. This has led you to believe that your actions were correct."

"Ah," said Myrta as comprehension took root, "but this time one disaster has followed another, and you have invited us to look deeper into our circumstances. At last we see that confrontation is necessary for our souls to develop."

"Yes," said the Sorella. "Creation has nevertheless kept you alive during your traumatic time. Indeed, Creation has provided you with the help of young Diarmid. Creation wants you to survive in order for your souls to move forward."

"I need some time to think about what you have said, Anastasie," said Everet. "Your words make sense of what has been happening to us over the years, but I am still not sure that Knympton is the place for us."

"Of course you need time, Everet," said the Sister. "Please take however long you need to consider what I have said to you. Your group is welcome here for as long as it takes you to decide on your next steps."

"Are you saying that Diarmid is a gift from God?" asked Aonghus.

The Sorella smiled, "Yes, Aonghus, everyone and everything are gifts from God. All are sent to help us in some way."

Chapter 34: Mung and Sefira

Mung sat in the big chair by his bedside in a state of excited trepidation. How would he react? How would Sefira react? All the details of his double life over the last few years began to tumble into his mind, one on top of the other. Remembrances of all the lies and not quite truths rose from the backwaters of his brain into full prominence.

Brina seemed to have been gone for an awful long time, giving Mung all the time he didn't need to anguish over his past deeds. A film of perspiration covered his brow, and he was in the process of wiping it dry when the Shaman appeared in the doorway. "Well, Yorlan," she said, "your request can now be granted. Are you ready?"

"As I'll ever be," said Mung. "Where is Sefira?"

"I'm here, Yorlan Mung," said a very familiar voice, "and not a moment too soon either from what I hear." Sefira strode into the room then stopped dead after a few steps. Her face revealed her shock at what her eyes were telling her.

Mung saw her reaction: "Yes, my love, it's really me. It's me as I am now."

"Good Heavens, Yorlan," she said, now running over to him, and hugging him closely to her. "Oh Yorlan, what have they done to you?" Sefira asked, pulling him even tighter to her.

"Careful, woman," said Yorlan, "my wounds still hurt."

"Oh sorry! Sorry my sweet," Sefira said loosening her grip somewhat. "Are you alright?"

"I'm as fine as I can be at this point," said Mung, "and a darn sight finer than I would have been had this fine lady not rescued me from my hellish situation," he continued, smiling at Brina.

"Now, now, Yorlan, said Brina, "you know that is just partly true. Let me leave you two in peace for a while. I have some work to do."

"Thank you so much," said Sefira.

"Not too long though, Sefira, his strength is not all that he thinks it is. He will tire easily, and remember what I said to you," said Brina as she left them.

"How much do you know?" asked Mung.

"Very little," said Sefira. "Brina has told me only that you were very close to death when she found you."

"I see," said Yorlan, "and you would like more details now?"

"Only what you want to tell me, "said Sefira, "but however little that might be I'd appreciate it more if it were the complete truth."

Mung was stunned: he looked his wife in they eye, as if to challenge her.

"Yorlan," she said in response, "you must think me completely stupid with some of the stories you have told me these past few years. You are like an open book, and I can read very well."

"But why didn't you say anything at the time?" asked the Marshal. "You just accepted what I had to say. At times you expressed your disapproval quite plainly, but you never actually accused me of lying to you."

"Yes, Yorlan, that is true," said his wife, "but I know you so well that had I done so then the situation would have deteriorated even further. Indeed there were times when I do believe you might have turned violent."

Mung sat there, eyes looking down, chastened to the point of embarrassment. Sefira pressed home her advantage. "There was many a night when you came home in such a foul temper that saying nothing was my best guarantee of safety."

Mung was appalled at his past behaviour. All these memories told him Sefira was telling the truth. "Sefira, my dear," he said softly, "please forgive me for these transgressions. I have had plenty of time recently to relive all these events, and I am ashamed of what I have done. I have betrayed everyone's trust, especially yours, and I am so, so sorry."

"In some respects, Yorlan," said Sefira, "you have been a pretty nasty individual intent on getting what you want no matter what the cost to anyone else. I do believe you would have sold your grandmother for a shekel had the opportunity arisen."

Mung looked at her, his eyes welling up with tears. "I plead guilty as accused," he said, "but I also plead for clemency and leniency in the sentence."

"Yorlan," said Sefira, "deep down I know you have a heart of gold. Somewhere along the line you have fallen from the pathway. Now you have a chance to climb back onto it, but only you can make that decision."

"Sefira, my dear," he replied, "your words are as wise as Brina's, and perhaps I should have listened to you in the past. I have certainly fallen from grace. I have fallen a long way, and now it is plain that my way was the wrong way. I would like to find my way back to the straight and narrow, but from where I am it's a long climb. Please believe me when I say that I am determined to get there. However, it would my task easier if I knew you were with me."

"There you go, Yorlan Mung," said Sefira, a smile creeping across her face, "always looking for the easy way out!" She laughed, "Of course I'll be at your side as I have been through the dark times. For your transgressions I forgive you." She reached over to kiss him long and hard on the lips, throwing her arms round him: he responded in kind.

They held their embrace for some time in the silence. He ran his fingers through her hair, and whispered his gratitude in her ear. Eventually he gently broke the embrace. "Thank you, my dear, for your understanding, patience and tolerance, but mostly I want to thank you for your love. You know, despite my past actions which might lead you to a contrary view, I love you with all my heart."

"Oh Yorlan," said Sefira, "now you are being soft." She paused for a moment, reflecting. "It's so nice to hear you say such words, what a welcome difference."

Just then Brina came back into the room. "Everything all right?"

"Yes," said her patient, "everything is just fine right now, and will get better as my health improves. My wonderful wife has lifted a huge weight from my shoulders."

"You are a very fortunate man indeed, Yorlan," said Brina. "Make sure you can keep any promises you make."

"Brina," said Mung, "from where I have been, from the depths to which I plummeted, there is only one direction for me to travel. I have Sefira to help me, and I have you to guide me. Where can I possibly go wrong?"

They all laughed. "Yes, Yorlan," said Brina, "where?"

"I am glad that you have come back at this point, Brina," said Mung.

"Why so?" asked the Shaman.

"Because Sefira has yet to hear the tale of how I arrived here," he said, "and she wants to hear only the truth."

"So what's stopping you?" asked Brina.

"Well," said Mung, "some of the details may sound a little far fetched, and I know that you can vouchsafe what I am about to relate."

"Yorlan," said Brina, "you don't need me here to verify anything you say. Tell your tale, and let Sefira be the sole judge of what you say. Then, after she's heard what you relate, she can come to me if she feels the need for verification."

Mung looked at Brina almost pleading with her to stay. "Yorlan you must not prejudge," she told him. "If you tell from your heart then Sefira's heart will hear it."

Mung's shoulders fell in disappointment: he was not convinced Sefira would appreciate his story.

"Just open your heart, Yorlan, but please, only the briefest of details at this point. You are tiring, and we don't want to set back your progress," said Brina. "I will return presently."

"Well?" said Sefira, impatient to hear.

"Sometime around a turn and a half or two turns ago," he began, "I was approached by a man called Ludley who offered me money to help him out. It was no big thing he said; just to turn a blind eye here and there whilst keeping my ears open for any wayward gossip...."

Mung continued, telling Sefira that he couldn't see any harm in what was being suggested, and Ludley was as good as his word when it came to payment. He told her that, looking back, he could see he was gradually stepping into deeper and deeper water, and by the time he realised what was really going on he was out of his depth.

"I was ensnared," he said. "Ludley had me on the end of a hook, and there was nothing I could do to get myself out of it."

"Who is this Ludley?" said Sefira.

"Turns out he is a thief and a thug with a gang of ne'er do wells in tow," said Mung. "The crime wave that crashes down on Knympton is largely down to this gang: they call themselves the Black Crows."

"Don't tell me," said Sefira, "they hang out at *The Waggoner's*."

Yorlan indicated that Sefira was astutely correct, with the Black Crows meeting in a little back room that only they had access to. He told her that they used their discreet room to eavesdrop on the clients in the lounge, and organised their activities from there.

"Did you ever get involved in these activities?" Sefira demanded.

"Never!" said her husband. "I was never involved in the action. My use to them was in other ways, and it was my failure to deliver that led to this," he said, pointing to his bandages.

He explained that Ludley was putting pressure on the Cranstouns to pay a regular protection fee or face having their premises vandalised or business interrupted by some other means. The Cranstouns had gone to the Marshals to make a report when he was on duty, so their complaint never got any further. He told her of his encounter with Diarmid, and his false account of the matter to Ludley. When the thug realised that the Cranstouns had fled he, Ludley, and his henchman, Boffe, took Mung to the Cranstoun's house. There Boffe had knifed him, and he was left to die.

He told Sefira of his spiritual experience as his life ebbed away, slipping into a state of unconsciousness in the Cranstouns' place, and waking up in Brina's. "From what I can gather from Brina," he said, "Angels were involved and they are responsible in part for my life being saved."

Sefira sat there silent, wide eyed and open mouthed as Mung told her briefly of his further spiritual encounters. "Well I never," she said eventually. "That's an amazing story, and, considering what I could tell you about my experiences lately, I honestly believe every word you have spoken."

"Really?" said Mung, his visage brightening.

"Yes, yes," said Sefira, "with no doubts. I can appreciate why you wanted Brina here, but I have no doubts about what you have outlined about your recent experience. Maybe, when your health returns more fully, you can go into more detail."

"Of course," said Mung, "and you can tell me about your experiences."

"Agreed," said Sefira, "but I must register my disapproval of your past behaviour although I am beginning to see that there might be something positive to emerge from all the bad deeds you have been involved in."

Just then Brina again appeared in the doorway: it was as if she had never been too far away and knew when to intervene. "I'm sorry," she said, "but we must bring this meeting to an end."

"When can Sefira return?" asked Mung.

"In a few days or so," said the carer. "There are details to sort, plans to make. Your ex-friend Ludley still watches Sefira's movements." Turning to Sefira she said, "In two days time please return to Bruno's furniture shop, and he will pass on a message. In the meantime you may want to inform the Marshals that you are being followed. That will help us to persuade Ludley to call off his watch."

"Are you aware of being followed, my dear?" said Mung. "Do you feel threatened?"

"Actually, I'm not," said Sefira. "I couldn't tell anyone was following me. It was Brina who made me aware, but it does not bother me."

"We'll discuss this further another time," said Brina.

"Yes," said Sefira rising from her chair and going over to Mung. "Until then I will bid you goodbye, and hope to notice an improvement in your wellbeing." She kissed him: "Take care, Yorlan Mung," she said smiling.

*****

Vangil was somewhat distraught to discover he had been duped. A cold sweat passed across his face as blind panic set in. He stood there, frozen with fear, staring in disbelief at the girl he had followed believing her to be Sefira Mung.

He watched Mung's wife go into the furniture shop, didn't take his eyes off the place whilst she browsed inside, and he was immediately back on her tail when she emerged.

As far as he was able to make out there were no other customers in the shop when she entered, and none visited whilst she was there. But yet here was the evidence of a different set of events. When the girl lowered her shawl revealing her golden tresses and youthful looks he was taken completely aback.

His panic discharged, he looked all around: no sign of anyone else remotely dressed like the girl. He turned round and retraced his steps, eyes wide open, looking for Sefira.

He reached the furniture shop and peered in the window: there was no sign of Sefira, not that he really expected to find her. Frustrated, he opened the door and marched in.

"Good day, fine sir," said Bruno approaching him. "How may I be of service today?"

"There was a woman in here earlier," said Vangil, "short, black coat and shawl. She was carrying a basket."

"Woman?" said Bruno, "You mean young lady, sir."

"No, no," protested Vangil, "I mean what I say. There was a woman aged about 40 turns in here earlier today. She was dressed as I have already described."

"Pardon me, sir," said Bruno remaining calm, "but the only person in here as you have described was a slip of a girl. Nice looking: lovely fair hair too." He paused before going on, "Mistress Collette. She was here looking at some chairs on behalf of her grandmother. In fact these are they," he continued, pointing out some expensive looking upright chairs.

Frustration getting the better of him, Vangil turned on his heels and stomped out of the shop, slamming the door behind him. If what the shopkeeper told him was true then he had lost track of Sefira Mung earlier. He wracked his brain, replaying the whole sorry adventure over and over again: he could not see where else the switch could have occurred but in the shop.

His next problem was how to explain this disaster to Ludley.

*****

Brina led Sefira back down the pathway, and out to the place where Shamira had brought her earlier. "Please wait here by the roddi bushes: Shamira will be here quite soon," said Brina. "I have asked Archangel Michael to watch over you and protect you: you will be safe in his hands."

"Thank you for everything, Brina," said Sefira. "Since I last saw Yorlan I can see positive changes in his appearance even although he has been sorely stricken. I greatly appreciate the attention you have given him."

"It has been very interesting for me to have been involved in his rescue and recuperation," said the healer. "We still have a way to go, but the worst is over. You will see further improvement next time."

"I'm sure I will," said Sefira. "Thanks again, and I hope to see you soon."

"You will," said Brina. "Goodbye for now."

Chapter 35: Insights and Decisions

The Cranstouns continued to carry out whatever duties could be assigned to them, but always on their minds were the words of the Sorella. Her summing up of their lives had been accurate. They had moved on whenever confrontation raised its head. Certainly, they realised that they had made only a token gesture at resolving the issue: however, when the situation threatened to deteriorate they had neither the resources nor the will to stand their ground and face it squarely.

Now that the Sister had enlightened them, they realised that a very big decision was required. Over the past three nights they had discussed their circumstances, and what they had learned: they also took Anastasie's wise counsel into consideration. They had reached a judgment: it was time to return to Knympton to confront those who had threatened them. With or without the assistance of the Marshals they resolved to bring the issue to a conclusion that would enable them to live their lives according to their own wishes.

Everet left the others, and sought out Anastasie to ask for a meeting to determine how they might take the first steps: they were far from Knympton, in very unfamiliar territory.

"I'm very pleased that you have given this serious thought, and have come up with an answer," said Anastasie, who had agreed to meet them in the Main Hall. "Can I ask if everyone is of the same opinion?" she enquired. Each of the Cranstouns confirmed that this was what they wanted. "And what of you, Diarmid?" asked the Sister.

"I am happy to go back to Knympton, and do whatever is necessary to help Everet, Myrta and Aonghus," he said. "I also would like to report the details of our shipwreck to the owners of the vessel, and perhaps see if there is work for me aboard another ship."

"Excellent!" said the Sorella. "Now we must plan how to get you to Knympton."

"We have some charts," said Diarmid, "but the detail on them for these parts is very scant. We do not wish to return by the same route that brought us to the Abbeystery."

"Fetch them," said Anastasie, "and I will ask Krem to join us: his knowledge of the surrounding area is quite remarkable."

They spread the charts from *The Venturer* on the huge table and carefully looked over them. "Knympton is here," said Diarmid, placing a finger on the name, "and according to this chart we are now here," he finished moving his finger to where he thought the Abbeystery was located.

"Yes," said Krem thoughtfully, "but as you suspected, your charts are not quite accurate. That is a slight understatement, for, if you have relied on these charts to find us then truly a miracle has taken place." He fell silent for a few moments: "I have it now. I believe your boat is here," as he indicated a spot on the chart, "and we are here," he said indicating another spot, quite far from where Diarmid had indicated.

"Then that indeed is a miracle," said Everet.

"No miracle, Everet," said Anastasie. They all turned to look at her, silently questioning her statement. "The lad has talent," she explained.

"I agree that Diarmid has had a lot to do with our survival and arrival here," said Everet, "but from what Krem has just shown us, that doesn't explain how we found you so readily."

"Wrong lad, Everet," said the Sorella. "It has been through Aonghus that you were guided here." There were still puzzled looks on the faces that regarded Anastasie. "Was it not he who communicated with the fish and the dolphins?" she asked.

"Ah yes!" said Myrta beginning to understand what Anastasie was saying. "His nightmares have saved us."

"Not nightmares, Myrta," said the Sister, "spiritual experiences. They may have seemed like nightmares because of circumstances. This was also your first experience of such an event, and so you did not know how to interpret it."

"You mean I should not have been scared?" asked Aonghus.

"Not at all young man," said Anastasie. "Indeed I can understand that such an experience is very frightening when it first manifests. I can clearly remember my own first experience, and it terrified me alarmingly."

Krem gave a little cough to reclaim the attention: "What we need to do is retrieve your boat and fetch it to the River Pertyck which is not far from here. This river is navigable from here all the way to the River Kinouli down here at Trivias," he said using an index finger to draw over the flow of the river. "You could sail down quite easily."

"Ah," said Everet, "that sounds like a good idea, for the flow of the river would be in our favour, but we have no sail on our boat: it is a row boat."

"No matter," said Krem undeterred. "Perhaps we can make a few alterations, maybe build a small mast to which you can attach a sail. Would that help?"

"That would be excellent," agreed Everet, "for right now I have no heart to take up an oar again," he said, laughing.

"Tomorrow, then," said Krem, "we will take the horse and cart down to where you have beached the rowboat, and get you underway again."

"If that's what you really want," the Sorella added.

The Cranstouns looked at each other and, with smiling faces, in unison agreed that this was the case.

*****

After breakfast next morning it was agreed that Everet, Diarmid and Aonghus would accompany Krem and Edgar, one of the other residents, to fetch the rowboat: Myrta would remain at the Abbeystery, and carry out some work there.

The two acolytes sat up front, with the others accommodated on the platform of the cart. Krem gave the order and the horse moved off. The route was not the smoothest path they had ever travelled, and they were bounced about from time to time, sometimes quite unceremoniously, as yet another bump was negotiated. The boys found it fun to be thrown about in such fashion, and Everet too could see the funny side of the situation.

Krem directed the cart down the hill, trying his best to keep to the less steep slopes. The day was bright and the surrounding woods resounded with birdsong. Despite all the jolting it was a relaxing journey. Nonetheless, they reached sea level quite quickly, and the going became less bumpy. As they emerged from a little coppice of beech trees they arrived at the inlet where the rowboat had been left. Krem pulled the cart to a halt, and they all jumped down: the horse was tethered to a nearby tree before the men made their way to the rowboat.

"We will need to empty the boat of its contents first," said Krem, "then we can start worrying about how we will lift it onto the cart."

Diarmid was already undoing the tarpaulin, and the others joined in, organising themselves to unload what was, in effect, the Cranstouns only possessions. They took the boxes and bundles from the boat up to the cart, and laid them on the ground alongside: it didn't take them too long.

Next, they positioned themselves round the boat, Krem and Edgar on the same side and the other three on the opposite side. "Probably best if we can get a hold with both hands and walk sideways," said Diarmid. "It used to take eight sailors to carry one of these boats, but then again they used one hand to grip, enabling them to walk normally."

"Let's try Diarmid's way then," said Krem. "Everyone find a grip for both hands, and when I give the word, gently, and I mean gently, take the strain. When everyone is happy I will give the word to lift." They felt down into the rowboat, searching out secure hand holds, and, on finding them, took hold. "Take the strain," said Krem: they tightened their muscles, gauging the weight that had to be lifted. "Lift!" said Krem: they pulled on the weight, and inched the boat upwards from the beach. "Down!" said Krem, and they replaced the boat on the shingle.

Krem asked if everyone was comfortable with what was required of them. Aonghus indicated that he didn't feel able to lift and walk sideways so Diarmid suggested that Aonghus take up a position at the stern of the boat. "Let's try that, then," said Krem, so Aonghus repositioned himself then felt inside for something to grab on to.

"This feels better," he said.

"Here's the plan," said Krem. "We will lift and walk in small steps, taking five or six steps to begin with, and then we'll take a rest. The cart is not too far away and we will get there. What we mustn't do is be too optimistic about how far we can carry this load in one go." He looked round for agreement and got it. "Right," he continued, "take the strain: lift and walk."

They took the boat six paces up the beach and laid it down: they rested for a minute then repeated the exercise a few times. Krem checked that everyone was comfortable: they were. "Let's go again," he said.

Gradually the boat was moved up the strand towards the cart. Progress was not as slow as Everet first thought it might be. With everyone acting in unison to an agreed plan progress was smooth and evident. They had reached the point where the beach and the land met: now they needed to lift the boat up a small step onto the pathway.

They decided that Krem and Everet would lift the front of the boat high enough to get over the step whilst the other three would push from the stern: the idea was to get the bow onto the path. Having achieved that, it was easy then for them to push and haul the boat onto the pathway. Success!

They took a well earned rest whilst they discussed their next problem: how to get the boat onto the cart. After some discussion they came up with a strategy: they cleared away shingle from the beach close to where they had placed the boat, more than doubling the step down onto the beach. They had effectively created a shallow furrow just wide enough to take the cart. Krem then led the horse and cart down onto the shingle where he backed up the cart close to where the boat lay.

Diarmid and the three men were to lift the boat at the bow onto the cart whilst Aonghus tended to the horse. With a great deal of effort, endeavour and exertion, a lot of sweat, and the use of much muscle power, not to mention a few strong words said silently, they finally managed to achieve their goal.

"Make sure the horse does not move forward, Aonghus," Krem cautioned, "We need to ensure the cart does not move whilst we attempt to push the boat fully onto the cart."

"I will do my very best, Mister Krem," said the boy taking an even firmer grip on the horse's reins.

The men went round to the stern, and on Krem's command began to push, haul and shove the boat on to the cart. The bow of the boat slid this way and that, limiting their progress, so Krem called a halt. "We'll need to rethink this strategy," he said, "for plainly what we are attempting is not working efficiently. Anyone got any ideas?"

The men sat down to discuss their predicament, giving air to various views, and discussing each one's merits and demerits. They had been in conversation for some time without being able to decide on a solution.

"Can I suggest something?" asked Aonghus.

"Why, of course," said Krem. "We're not making much progress, so perhaps you can throw some simplicity into our discourse."

"Well," said Aonghus, "you may find this very strange, but I feel it worth considering."

"All ideas are worth discussion," said Krem, "but what makes you declare your idea to be strange?"

"It is strange because it is not my idea at all," said the boy. The men looked at him, puzzled.

"Aonghus," said his father, "if it is not your idea how can you contribute?"

The boy stood there for a few moments in silence, his eyes closed: he was obviously focussed on something else. At last he spoke. "I am merely the messenger. The idea is that of the horse."

Edgar's mouth opened wide in disbelief. "The horse's?" he said. "How can that be?"

"Edgar," said Krem, "it's not as crazy as it sounds. The Sorella has spoken of the boy's talent of being able to communicate with creatures. It was largely due to this ability that his family reached the Abbeystery." Turning to Aonghus he said, "Please go on, lad."

Aonghus confirmed that the horse's thoughts had come to life in his head as had the dolphins' words before. "The horse suggests that you uncouple her from the cart, and attach the rope from the boat to her harness," he explained. "If we use larger rocks to prevent the cart from moving, then the horse can pull the boat whilst the rest push as before."

"Now that is indeed a splendid way forward," said Krem. "Shame on us for not considering it."

"The horse has asked that I take her reins, and lead her down the shore," Aonghus said.

"Yes, of course," said Krem. "Let's find some suitable rocks to anchor the wheels of the cart then I will uncouple the horse."

It did not take them long to anchor the cart's wheels in the shingle, and for Krem to uncouple the horse. With Diarmid's help he tied the two ropes from the boat's bow to the horse's harness. They were all set to begin when Aonghus said, "As the horse pulls the boat those of you at the stern will need to lift it to make the angle of drag as low as possible."

The men considered this, and agreed that what he had suggested was indeed necessary. Krem had a mental picture of the boat's bow high in the air, and the poor horse struggling.

"Yes," said Krem, "that's what we'll do. When I give the word, Aonghus, lead the horse down the beach." The men took up their positions behind the boat, found suitable hand holds, and prepared themselves to lift when Krem gave the command. "Now, Aonghus," he shouted.

Aonghus gently pulled on the horse's reins, and she took a step forward, taking the strain on the ropes connecting her to the rowboat. She took another step forward, and the boat began to move. However, the men were not quite ready for this movement, and the boat dragged along the ground. "Hold, Aonghus," Krem cried out, and Aonghus asked the horse to halt.

"What we need to do is lift the boat before the horse's effort is engaged," said Krem to the others.

"Yes," Everet agreed, "I think we need to lift this boat as high as we can."

They repositioned their hand holds, and when they agreed they were ready for the effort Krem simply said, "Lift." With a struggle they manoeuvred the stern up to shoulder height, and then Krem called to Aonghus to take the horse forward.

This time they could feel the strain from the horse's efforts, and they took a very small step forward: this was just the movement required to overcome the friction, and the boat started to move forwards onto the cart. After several more steps the boat was loaded, and Krem again called out to Aonghus saying that they had succeeded.

Aonghus released the horse from its attachment to the boat, and thanked it for its idea and for its effort: he told the horse that she had made their job less onerous, and how much they all appreciated it. Krem, as he reharnessed the horse to the cart, thanked Aonghus for his intervention. "We could have struggled for some time yet," he said, "but thanks to you we have completed the task in a very efficient manner."

"Thanks to the horse you mean, Mister Krem," said Aonghus, smiling.

They cleared the rocks with which they had anchored the wheels, and Krem asked Aonghus to again lead the horse whilst the others pushed the cart from behind. "The shingle will try to cling on to us, that's why we need to put in one last big effort. You need to wheel us around, Aonghus, and head for that spot over there where there is no ridge between shore and pathway," he said pointing just along the beach.

Krem gave the word, and much effort was put into getting the cart rolling: it was difficult at first, but as they built up momentum they finally exerted enough force to set the wheels in motion. The men shoved, the horse pulled: gradually they made their way along the beach and up onto the pathway, where they stopped for rest and recuperation.

However, they were soon on their way again, retracing the pathways that had brought them to the shore. When the going started to get hilly and a bit rough they all dismounted, and Krem led the horse and cart up the slopes. It was heading for evening when they reached the Abbeystery, a most welcoming sight. "Tomorrow," said Krem, "we will look at ways of adding a sail to the boat, but for now what we need is some good food and a sound night's sleep."

Chapter 36: The Marshals' Station

Sefira had breakfast as usual, tidied up, then put on her coat before going out to the market place. As she closed the door behind her and turned the key in the lock she couldn't stop herself from taking a quick glance up the road to see if there was anyone from Ludley's gang watching her. She couldn't see anyone, but that did not mean there was nobody there.

She tried to put on an air of cheerful calmness as she wandered down the path and out onto the street. At the end of the street in which her house was situated, she turned into the main street, again taking the opportunity to steal a glance behind her. She couldn't be completely certain, but she could swear that there was someone watching her. Her heart skipped a beat, and she put a little urgency in her step.

Behind her Vangil emerged from the cover of some hedges to continue his stalking. As he carefully made his way along the street his mind was firmly on the success of this mission. Ludley had been apoplectic with rage when Vangil told him of his failure last time, but had fallen short of inflicting physical damage on the hapless gang member. For his troubles Vangil was now on permanent watch duties, and would receive no pay from Ludley for a month: a second failure could not be thought about.

He, too, quickened his pace, aware of what had happened previously. As he reached the corner he was somewhat relieved to see that Sefira was still within sight. He crossed over to the other side of the street, keeping up his quickened pace until he was more comfortable with the distance between him and his quarry.

Absolutely certain that she would not be harmed, Sefira relaxed and, knowing where she was ultimately headed, decided that she would try to find out for certain if she was indeed being followed.

She turned down this alleyway and that side road, crossing over as she felt the mood take her. At every available opportunity she would take a fleeting look to see if her intuition was true, but still could not be absolutely certain. She turned back onto the main thoroughfare, and stopped at the first shop to look in the window.

Hard on her heels Vangil came round the corner in a hurry, almost knocking her over. "Careful, young man!" Sefira shouted as she stumbled. Mumbling a few apologies the crook continued to walk down the road. He was annoyed with himself for his lack of care. At this rate Ludley's rage would surely turn to violence, and he too would disappear in mysterious circumstances, just like Mung. He crossed over and entered one of Knympton's many alehouses.

Now Sefira was satisfied that she was being followed. As calmly as she could muster she strolled down the road following after Vangil. By now he

196

was inside the alehouse, and had found a watching place beside a small window. Sefira passed by on the other side without giving him or the alehouse a second glance.

He watched her walk on by, down towards the town hall square. Satisfied that she had made nothing of the accidental encounter, he left the safety of the alehouse to continue his stalking brief.

However, his relief at not losing his target turned to apprehension when he saw her walk up the steps to the Marshals' Station, open the door and walk in. Frantically, he looked for a another suitable place in which to conceal himself. There was nothing apparent that would screen him from view so he had to believe that by sitting on one of the many benches dotted around the square he would dissolve into the general background.

Inside, Sefira was pleased to note that Sergeant Trine was on duty behind the desk. "Good day, Missus Mung," he said looking up from his writing. "How are you today?"

"I am very well, Sergeant," she replied. "I trust that you too are in good health."

"Indeed I am," agreed the policeman. "Now what brings you here today?"

"Two matters, Sergeant," Sefira said. "The first is to enquire into the progress in discovering what happened to my husband: where are we with that, please?"

"To be brutally frank with you, Missus Mung," said Trine quietly, "we have run out of leads and ideas. This case has baffled the entire force."

"That's very disappointing news indeed," said Sefira. "Which leads me on to the main reason I am here." Trine regarded her with a more focussed interest. "I do believe I am being watched and followed wherever I go."

Trine, who had been leaning on the desk, pulled himself up to his full height on hearing what Sefira had to say. "Have you seen this man?" he asked.

"Not clearly, until today," said Sefira. "In his rush not to lose sight of me he actually collided with me. I dare say he is somewhere close outside right now."

"Are you able to give me a description?" enquired the Marshal.

"Of course," said Sefira providing an ample portrayal of Vangil, as Trine made a note.

"Excuse me," he said heading for a door at the back of the office. He opened it, and summoned Constable Layford. "Layford," he said handing over the note, "read this and memorise."

"Right, Sarge," said Layford, "got it."

"Missus Mung here, says this man has been following her for some time now, and he may well be outside in the square waiting for her to emerge," Trine explained. "I want you to go out the rear door, and make your way to the far side of the square via the alleyways. Shouldn't take you more than five

197

minutes, at which point Missus Mung will leave by the front door. Watch her movements and look out for the man whose description should be firmly fixed in your head."

"Right, Sarge," said Layford making a move.

"Hold on, Layford," said Trine. "When you are certain that he is following her I want you to intercept him, and bring him back here. Restrain him if you have to."

"Right, Sarge," Layford said again as if repeating a mantra before heading for the rear door.

"Leave this with me, Missus Mung," said Trine, "Perhaps this man knows something about Yorlan."

"Or thinks that I do," said Sefira.

"Mmm," said Trine noncommittally.

They exchanged some small talk to pass the time whilst Layford got into position. "Thank you for taking care of this complaint," said Sefira. "Now I must get to the market before it is too late."

"Good day to you, Missus Mung," said Trine, "please take great care."

Vangil was alert to Sefira's exit from the Marshals' Station, and watched her as she headed in a direction that would take her to the main market area. He was perhaps too focussed on Sefira to notice Layford standing in the shadows surveying the square.

Layford's keen eyes had soon found Vangil sitting on the bench: there was something about Vangil that Layford didn't like. To the casual observer Vangil was bothering nobody, sitting idly watching the day go by, arms resting along the back of the bench and one leg perched atop the other. However, Layford could see that Vangil's intense gaze returned with great frequency to the door of the Marshals' Station.

Now the hunter would be hunted if he made a move in Sefira's direction. Hardly had the thought burst in Layford's head when Vangil sprung into action, obviously not as relaxed as he may have appeared. Just in time Layford moved further into the shadows, as Vangil took a good look round as if gathering his bearings, before setting off to follow Sefira.

Surreptitiously Layford trailed Vangil, keeping to the shadows and cover that the buildings round the square afforded him. It didn't take Vangil long to get back within close proximity of Sefira, and Layford now had both of them in view: both pursuers were happy with their actions.

Layford watched as Vangil tagged on to every change of direction and alteration of pace made by Sefira. He was convinced, and moved in on Vangil when they reached the market place. Sefira browsed down a row of stalls until finally reaching a greengrocer's stall. She picked up various items, and handed them to the stallholder for weighing and pricing.

Vangil stood several stalls distant, eyes still fixed on Sefira: it was too late when he noticed Layford, who had managed to dodge round to another avenue, and approach from the side.

"Afternoon, sir," said Layford to a surprised Vangil who tried to look beyond the policeman to where Sefira was completing her purchases. "Looking for something, are we sir?" probed the Marshal, "or maybe someone?" he continued.

Now that he had Vangil's full attention Layford could see the look of absolute horror on the crook's face.

"Not at all," said Vangil trying to keep his voice level. "I thought I saw an old friend over there," he said pointing.

"And did you, sir?" replied the Marshal refusing to follow the direction indicated by the outstretched arm.

Before he could react, Vangil found himself restrained by Layford: he struggled, or at least tried to, but the policeman's grip was tight and strong. "Best you come quietly, sir," he said, leading Vangil back towards the Main Square.

Layford marched Vangil back to the Station, keeping to the main streets: once before when in a similar situation he had taken his prisoner down an alleyway only for the wretch's confederates to lay an ambush. Once bitten, twice shy, Layford kept to where there were few opportunities for surprise attacks.

Back at the Station Layford effectively used Vangil as a door opening device, shoving him roughly through the stout wooden doors. Vangil stumbled into the Station, barely managing to keep his feet, coming to rest against the solid oak desk.

"Here he is, Sarge," said Layford. "Says his name is Dilmer."

"Thanks, Layford," said Trine. "Show Dilmer to the guest room. I'll be through presently to ask him a few questions."

Layford led Vangil through to a holding room, and told him to sit down. "Don't try anything stupid, Dilmer," said Layford. "As you can see there are no windows to escape through, and I'll be in the corridor just outside," he continued before exiting the room.

Presently turned into a little longer which was good for Vangil in some respects. He could quietly run through his story which he had had the good sense to concoct with Moldin. The two of them had agreed that each would give the other an alibi should they ever get caught watching Sefira Mung. Now the story would be put to the test.

Eventually the door opened, and Trine stepped in. "Right, Dilmer," he boomed, closing the door behind him. "Perhaps you can explain your actions to my satisfaction. I understand you thought you'd espied an old friend."

"That wasn't quite accurate, Sergeant," said Vangil, "but the truth is this is a delicate matter, and I did not want to broadcast it to all and sundry in the market place. You know what people are like: they nosey into things that are none of their business."

"So tell me," said Trine, "and perhaps we can clear this matter up quickly."

Vangil explained that a friend, an ex-colleague, had contacted him to ask for a favour. The friend, Moldin, had a friend who suspected his wife might be involved in a relationship of infidelity. The gentleman had no solid evidence on which to base any accusation, so he had asked Moldin to arrange for someone to watch his wife's movements: Vangil had been recruited, and his findings would help to resolve the matter.

"I see," said Trine, "and where might we find this Moldin so that we may verify your story?" Vangil gave him Moldin's address. "Excuse me," he said opening the door, and giving instructions to Layford to seek out Moldin and bring him in.

Returning to Vangil, he said "Is this your normal line of business, Dilmer? Spying on vulnerable ladies?"

"Not at all," said Vangil, "I sell high quality furniture in Trivias. As I explained, I am doing this as a favour to Moldin."

"Ah, you are from out of town. A person unlikely to be known to your target," said Trine stroking his chin. "Your occupation would certainly account for your lack of technique as a sleuth." Vangil smiled to himself, quite pleased that he seemed to be making progress. "Now, tell me the name of the woman you have been following."

"Name?" said Vangil, "I do not know her name. She was pointed out to me, discreetly by Moldin earlier today."

"So you have no idea who you have been following?" asked the policeman.

"No, I don't need to know her identity as such, just report on her to-ings and fro-ings," said the thief.

"Fine," said Trine. "We'll leave it there until your friend arrives. I won't be far away, so no funny business." Vangil's heart sank when he heard the key turn in the lock.

It didn't seem that long before Vangil heard voices and footsteps approaching: the key turned in the lock once again, and the door opened. Trine entered with Moldin and closed the door behind them.

"Well, Dilmer," he said, "your friend Moldin, here, has confirmed your story as far as it goes."

"What do you mean?" asked Vangil.

"Well, I have yet to ask him an important question, which I will now do," replied the big policeman. Turning to Moldin, he said, "What is the name of the lady that you asked Dilmer to follow?"

"Why, I pointed out Raddy's wife to him," said Moldin. "She was fetching some errands in the market. Why are you asking?"

"Your friend here claims he did not know her name, that's all," said Trine.

"I don't recall ever telling him," said Moldin. "I merely pointed out the woman to him this morning."

"Mmm," said Trine not knowing what to do next. "And if I tell you," he said to Moldin, "that your friend was following someone entirely different?"

"What!" said Vangil jumping up. "Are you saying I have devoted my energy to a worthless cause?"

"Looks like it," said Trine nodding his head.

"You idiot!" Moldin shouted. "I have paid you good coinage to come here from Trivias, and you follow the wrong woman. I will seek retribution from you," he yelled as he headed across the room to grab Vangil by his lapels.

Trine had to act quickly: he stepped between the two crooks, and pushed each backwards away from each other. "Calm down, Moldin," he ordered, "or you will find yourself locked up. As for you, Dilmer, I suggest you keep to selling furniture, and would suggest that if I ever see you around Knympton again you will incur my displeasure. Now get out of here both of you."

The crooks straightened their clothing and made a hasty exit, disappearing into the alleyways and shadows as quickly as they could. When they considered themselves out of harm's way they stopped, regarded each other, and burst into fits of laughter. However, their laughter was abruptly curtailed when they realised that Ludley would not see the funny side of it.

Vangil and Moldin took a good look around them to ensure nobody was watching them: satisfied that they had not been followed they approached *The Waggoner's*, and headed for the back room.

The rest of the gang had already assembled and the mood was light. There had been a good crowd in town today, and many a wallet, money belt and purse had been expertly separated from its owner.

"What ho!" shouted Moldin beginning to relax into the ambience of the atmosphere.

"Ah, Vangil," said Ludley, breaking off from his conversation with Boffe. "What news?"

"Not good in many respects," said Vangil solemnly.

"How so?" asked the chief thug growing suddenly serious.

Seeing the change in the gang leader's disposition caused a mild ripple of coldness to run through Vangil. "Well," he said, "I got picked up by the Marshals."

"Go on," Ludley encouraged.

"Somehow, and I don't know how," said Vangil, "I do believe that the Mung woman knew I was watching her. She would speed up, slow down, cross over the road, all for no good reason."

"And?" said the gang leader.

"She visited the Marshals' Station," said the erstwhile watcher. "I hung about and picked up her trail again when she came out: she headed for the market stalls. Next thing I know is I am in the clutches of a Marshal who marched me down to the station."

"She seems to have more wits about her than we ever gave her credit for," said Ludley. "Or perhaps, Vangil, your standard of work is slipping."

"My trailing techniques are first class," Vangil objected. "The woman must have some strange abilities."

"No matter," said Ludley. "What happened at the station?"

"Fortunately," said the crook, "Moldin, Raddy and I had devised an alibi in the unlikely event of one of us being caught."

"Unlikely? Hurrumph!" said the gang leader. "So?"

"Moldin and I were able to convince the stupid Sergeant that it was a case of mistaken identity, and he threw us out."

"Well, I suppose that's good news," said Ludley, "but where does that leave us?"

The gang members had ceased their chatter, and were listening intently to Vangil's story. As it unfolded there were times when they held their breaths in anticipation of an all too familiar outburst from their leader.

However, Ludley remained calm, maintaining control of his actions. After a rather long pause he finally informed them of his decision: that it was perhaps time to let this Mung thing go, and move on.

The gang looked at him in amazement and puzzlement. "Listen," he said, "we have devoted a lot of time and effort trying to find out what happened to Mung." They nodded in agreement. "We have been spectacularly unsuccessful in finding anything at all. Not one thing. The Marshals haven't a clue either from what we know. It's time to focus on our real work, and get back to dishonest endeavour."

"Wherever Mung may be," said Boffe, "he's not in this world. Take it from me," he finished, patting the handle of his knife.

"In some respects," said Ludley, "it's a pity for his wife who doesn't know the first thing about why her husband hasn't returned home. No word, no body to bury, nothing."

Ludley sat there for a few moments, somewhat subdued. Then he shook his head, and exhorted everyone to get back to nefarious activities.

Vangil, Moldin and Raddy could hardly believe their luck, having expected Ludley to have expressed his displeasure in a forceful way. The man had taken them by surprise: no harsh words, no raised voice, no violence or even a threat of it.

What had come over the man? Was he softening? Was he ill or had he lost his mind in some way? They just couldn't put their finger on why there had been such a turnabout in Ludley's attitude.

Even Boffe had been strangely quiet as well, certain that he had dispatched Mung to the next world. Then there was the unsolved mystery of why Mung's body had never been found.

Still, they had been ordered to get back to more familiar work: it would best to do that, and forget all about the Mung business.

Chapter 37: Rowboat Refurbishment

Next morning, after breakfast, Krem, Edgar, Everet and Diarmid set about drawing up plans to redesign the rowboat to incorporate a mast or some other device that would be capable of supporting a sail. Myrta and Aonghus joined the others of the community in doing whatever tasks were required.

Everet felt a bit out of his depth, so took little part in the discussion. Diarmid's input was invaluable, and after some time they came to a decision on the modifications required. Some lengths of sturdy timber would be required, plus much hard endeavour would be needed.

Krem indicated that there was sufficient wood of the kind needed stored in the workshop of the Abbeystery and he and Everet went to collect it: Edgar hurried off to gather what appropriate tools he could lay his hands on whilst Diarmid was asked to find suitable items to stabilise the cart: they had left the rowboat on the cart to avoid another heavy manoeuvre.

Soon the men were hard at work, consulting their drawing then implementing the design. They worked at a good pace, attested to by the noise of sawing and hammering, although they placed quality ahead of speed, and gradually the rowboat began to take on its new shape. By mid afternoon they felt they had reached a convenient place to stop work for the day. "Looks good," said Everet. "I'm sure this will prove sufficient to see us back to Knympton."

"I'd like to think so too, Everet," said Diarmid, "but please do not set your heart on this device delivering. Remember what we have is essentially a rowboat, and it may be that we have to end up rowing."

"The sail," said Krem.

"What about it?" asked Everet.

"Well, we haven't got one," said Krem. "As I understand it, and perhaps Diarmid can correct me if I am wrong, sails are made from a specially woven cloth." The sailor confirmed that this was so. "We do not have any here at the Abbeystery, and I doubt if any could be bought before you reach Trivias."

"Not to worry," Diarmid said, "we have the tarpaulin. It will have to do. So far it has acted as our shelter, now it must act as our propeller as well."

"Perhaps Myrta and some of the ladies may be able to make the alterations required to affix the tarpaulin to our mast," suggested Everet, looking at Krem.

"It would be good if your wife were able to do the work alone as we are very much committed to our work," said Krem, "but I can certainly find some materials for her to use."

"Perhaps so," said Everet slightly disappointed. "Let's seek her out and ask her."

Everet and Krem set off towards the Abbeystery, and quickly found Myrta, who was working alongside Anastasie and Gelsen. They put their proposal to

Myrta, and were delighted when she agreed that she could take on the task. However, Anastasie suggested that Gelsen might like to help out as the experience would benefit the community in due course.

"Where is the tarpaulin?" asked Myrta.

"It is with the rowboat," replied her husband. "I will bring it to you presently, along with our ideas of how it needs to be modified."

With that, the two men returned to the rowboat, whereupon Everet gathered up the tarpaulin, and asked Diarmid to accompany him to explain what needed to be done. Krem and Edgar looked over the work they had done, looking for any obvious errors in their reconstruction.

With the tarpaulin delivered, and Diarmid's instructions committed to memory, Myrta and Gelsen began their task of turning a tarpaulin into a sail. The job was not as onerous as Myrta first thought it might turn out, and the ladies had all but completed their task before the light faded, indicating it was time to prepare for Abendessen: they could finish the job in the morning.

*****

At sunrise the Abbeystery bell gently tolled, rousing the Cranstouns from their slumber. It was time to get up, get dressed, and head to the Main Hall for breakfast. Aonghus was still very tired, having slept very little the previous night. He had only just drifted off to sleep when the bell sounded. With a great effort he pushed himself from the bed, and slowly got himself dressed.

In the Main Hall the residents had already gathered, and had taken their places at the table. Guiltily, Everet, Myrta, Aonghus and Diarmid crept in, and, as quietly as possible, took their seats. Aonghus felt as if everyone's eyes were focussed on the family and on him in particular.

The meal was served with its customary efficiency and soon the murmur of conversation filled the air. Aonghus relaxed, almost quite forgetting his earlier experience: with some gusto he ate heartily, much to the approval of Myrta. "It's so nice to see you enjoying your food again, Aonghus," she said.

The Sorella pushed her seat backwards, the scraping of the chair legs against the flagstones making a high pitched noise that drew everyone's attention. "Sisters, Brothers, we give thanks for the meal just eaten," she said. "Now let us be about our business. Krem and Edgar will continue to help our guests prepare their rowboat for their long journey home, and Gelsen will help Myrta, otherwise you all know what your assignments are."

She opened her arms out to signal the end of the meal, indicating that the assembly were to get up from their chairs, and head out of the Main Hall in whatever direction was appropriate for them to reach their work place.

The men toiled hard all day, fetching wood, measuring, cutting and fitting. They rested little, putting their hearts and souls into the conversion of the rowboat. At last they reached the point when the last piece of alteration was complete, and they stepped back from their work to admire it from a practical angle. "It looks good," said Krem, "but then again I am no boatman."

"Nor I," said Everet. "Let's hope it will see us through our journey. What do you think, Diarmid?"

"I am but a sailor in the making, Everet," said the lad. "I have no boat designing skills. We have toiled hard and done as much as we can. Certainly it looks good enough, but it is untested. We will have to proceed with caution."

As they continued their conversation Myrta and Gelsen appeared, carrying the rowboat's tarpaulin. "My," said Myrta on seeing the converted boat, "you men have toiled greatly: it looks very good, but then, what do I know? Will it see us through?"

"Who knows?" said Everet. "As Diarmid has pointed out the structure has been designed by those with little knowledge of such things, and remains untested."

"We will have to trust then," said his wife. "We have been brought here without too many physical injuries. What we have been through has been terrible in its own way, but we have been helped by the unseen hand of Creation. Our experiences have taught each one of us much about ourselves, and I do believe we have all developed as individuals ever since we decided to leave Knympton behind us."

"That's for sure," agreed her husband, "and, in a strange sort of way, we must return to Knympton to complete our journey."

"Wise words, my friends," said Krem. "There are indeed lessons to learn for each of us from everything that happens to us. No matter how bad we may at first perceive a situation to be, there will be a message, a personal message, lying within it waiting to be unwrapped and implemented."

Everet and Myrta regarded Krem with a look of perplexed astonishment. "Please," said Everet, "do go on."

"It is my belief," said Krem, "that we are each here for a reason. That is to say we have something to fulfil during the course of our life. Let me also say that in my belief system this is not my first or only life at this physical level: neither is it my last."

"Krem," said Myrta, "I get the feeling that what you are about to say will require some deep thought on our part. Indeed you are already challenging some of our beliefs. Can I suggest that we postpone this conversation until later?"

"Of course," said the Frater. "I do apologise for going too deep at this point." Pointing to the tarpaulin, he said, "You have completed your work on the sail."

"Yes," said Myrta breaking into a giggle. "Gelsen has assisted me to adapt the tarpaulin to your measurements without destroying its normal functionality as a cover for us at night."

"Excellent," said Krem, "let us attach it to the mast and see if it's easily manipulable."

The men attached the tarpaulin to the fixtures they had created, and Krem gave the order to unfurl the sail. Diarmid and Everet pulled on the ropes, and the sail began to open out.

As if on cue a whisper of wind blew up and punched out the sail. The group looked on with a sense of pride that comes from a job well done. As they congratulated each other, a strong gust took hold of the sail, and the rowboat toppled over to the horror of the onlookers. Fortunately, the boat remained on the cart, although it hung perilously over one side. They rushed over to the boat, and were relieved to see that, on examination, no real damage had been inflicted. They righted the boat, and took down the sail.

"Can we expect the same result when the boat is in the water?" asked Myrta, alarmed.

"That's a possibility, I suppose," said Everet equally dismayed.

"Wait," said Diarmid pensively. They turned to regard him. "I have seen small sailing craft with strangely shaped keels," he went on, "and I have often wondered why. Now I am beginning to realise."

"Yes?" enquired Everet. "Please enlighten us."

Diarmid explained that the keel or mainstay at the bottom of the rowboat was shallow but heavy. This gave the rowboat balance, and helped to keep it upright in the water. The small sailing craft he had spoken of had keels that were deep and bladed. He drew a diagram in the dirt to illustrate.

"As I said," he went on, "I never really knew why it should be so, but now I think I do. When the wind blows and fills the sail, a boat with a shallow keel will simply topple over."

"Yes," agreed Everet, "we have seen that happen just now. How will your fancy keel be any different?"

"Because it is deep and bladed: when it sits in the water the blade acts as a resistance to the wind pushing the boat over. The boat may rock a little or list to one side, but it will not topple over."

The group considered Diarmid's explanation for a few moments, each trying to visualise what Diarmid had just said.

"Man," said Krem, "I can just about understand that. So we have some further work to do?"

"Looks like it," said Everet. "Diarmid, does this sail boat keel have a particular design?"

"I really don't know, Everet," the lad replied. "Perhaps there is some relationship between the shape and size of the boat and its keel."

"I think," said Krem, "that we just have to make do, and go with a deep and bladed arrangement."

"Perhaps," said Diarmid pointing to his drawing, "we can try to make one in roughly this shape."

"Well, yes," said Krem, "we can try."

Krem sent Edgar back to the wood store to look for suitable pieces from which to construct Diarmid's fancy keel. Whilst Edgar was looking in the store Everet, Krem and Diarmid examined the underside of the rowboat to determine how they might attach the new keel without major modifications.

By the time Edgar returned they had decided on a plan of action, and began its implementation. However, after a short time, the darkness of the late afternoon fell upon them, forcing them to stop work for the night. The Cranstoun's departure had suffered another delay.

Chapter 38: Sefira goes Out

Not aware of Ludley's decision, Sefira took particular care to survey up and down the road each time she left home.

Today was no different, although, in a way, it was a special day. Having satisfied herself that nobody was watching her, she closed the door behind her and turned the key in the lock. She made her way down the pathway and out onto the pavement. At a brisk pace she set off for town, her thoughts already about her next meeting with Yorlan.

At the first few corners she again checked that she wasn't being followed, then headed straight for Bruno's furniture shop. Without much ado she opened the door and walked in. "Mistress Mung," said Bruno, emerging from the back office, "how nice to see you again. I hope you are well."

"Indeed I am, Bruno," she replied. "I'm in rude health thank you very much. I trust all is well with you, too."

"Everything is fine, Mistress Mung," said Bruno, "just as it is meant to be."

"I'm glad to hear it," said Sefira. "Please, Bruno, call me Sefira."

"Thank you, Sefira," he said. "Now what you want to hear most of all, I imagine, is when your next visit might be."

"Oh yes," said Sefira, "are you able to tell me?"

Bruno confirmed that he did have news for her, and that the plan was for a visit on Saturnsday, two days hence. Sefira acknowledged that that would be more than fine, and told him how much she was looking forward to it. She also told Bruno of her encounter with Vangil, and how the Marshals had intercepted him. Since then she was reasonably certain that she was not being followed.

"Well done," said the drummer. "Your visit to the Marshals would appear to have had the desired effect."

"Now," she said, "Saturnsday. Shall I come here first?" she enquired

"No," said the shop owner. "Best to vary things, just in case." Sefira nodded her agreement. "Do you know the Church of the Apostles?" he asked.

"Vaguely," she replied. "It's towards the Eastern Gate is it not?"

"Exactly so, Sefira," said Bruno. "You will find it in the Square of the Holy Rood." Sefira nodded, slowly remembering how to locate it. "Please be at the campanile at midday," he went on. "Shamira will meet you and escort you to Brina's cottage."

"Thank you, Bruno," said Sefira. "That is wonderful news indeed. Now I must be on my way to collect my provisions."

"You are most welcome, Sefira," said Bruno walking to the door with her and opening it. "Have a good day, Sefira, and we'll meet again soon."

"Thank you, Bruno," said Mung's wife, "goodbye."

With an added spring in her step Sefira made her way to the market to purchase her needs for the day, smiling broadly to one and all. What a wonderful day to be alive!

Only two days to wait before she would see Yorlan again. Hopefully, she would hear more details of his double life, although she realised that there were still more tales of horror to hear. Her thoughts went out to all the people who had suffered, no matter how little, because of her husband's deceit and downright bad behaviour. She realised, too, that once the whole story emerged, Yorlan would have to face the consequences of his actions, no matter what the punishment might be. So far, he had indicated that he was willing to do so.

Chapter 39: Further Work

Next day the Cranstouns, Diarmid and Krem returned to the boat to attempt to redesign the keel, aiming to turn the rowboat into a sailboat. They drew their ideas on the ground so much that the area beside the boat looked as if it had been freshly hoed.

They talked much about how to make a new keel, and how to affix it to the current craft. In the end they decided that Diarmid's idea, although desirable, was not practical without a huge amount of deconstruction and repair. Instead, two rough and ready blades were crafted which would be affixed to the rowboat close to the rowlocks: it seemed to be the only practical solution.

After a great deal of sweat and labour they were satisfied that what they had produced would at least give them a chance of turning the rowboat into some sort of hybrid sailboat, although there were reservations about how strong a wind their new fangled attachments could actually bear. Nonetheless, they were happy with the outcome and returned to the Abbeystery to complete their arrangements for departure the next morning.

Having completed what they set out to do, Myrta approached the Sorella with a request that the guests be allowed to have their last evening meal alone: she explained that in better times before their current troubles erupted the family always ate the evening meal in silence, giving each one a chance to reflect on the day that had just passed, as was the practice at the Abbeystery. However, in the Cranstouns' practice, there was an encouragement to go deep into the stillness: this sometimes meant that the meal could last for quite some time.

The Sorella listened intently to Myrta's words before agreeing. "There is much to contemplate for you, Myrta," she said, "not just today, but all that has happened since you abandoned your home and safety. You will also have in your thoughts what you will find when you return."

"Indeed," agreed Myrta, "and I, we, appreciate your understanding."

"What you are doing is a brave choice, some might say it is a foolish choice, but I know that if you continue to trust the Universe you will find that the end result will justify your faith," said Anastasie. "I will arrange for your meal to be served in the Lesser Hall."

"Thank you," said Myrta, and she returned to tell the others.

"This is a fine idea," said Everet when Myrta had broken the news, "and it will give us time to send out our personal thanks to all who have helped us thus far."

"Diarmid," said Myrta, "I have included you without asking your consent, and for that I apologise. If this does not fit with your practice I can change the arrangements, but I do hope you will eat with us."

"There is no need to apologise," said Diarmid. "Of course I will eat with you. Together we have been through a great deal, and I consider myself extremely lucky to have survived such troubles relatively unscathed. I have seen many things I do not properly comprehend, and many words and theories I can scarcely begin to understand. Saying 'thank you' seems the least I can do in return."

"We appreciate that, Diarmid," said Myrta, "but you do not have to feel you have an obligation to join in if it's not what you really want."

"No, no," said the boy, "it's quite the opposite. I would like to explore further what it is I may find in the silence. The quiet was never a place I would have thought to venture to before. However, as I say, many strange things have happened since we embarked on this journey, and I now feel I must try these things for myself. I have found the practice here quite interesting in a superficial way. Now, I'd like to find out what the deeper stillness will bring."

"Excellent," said Myrta. "You do amaze me at times, Diarmid, with the wisdom that you speak."

"Really?" said Diarmid puzzled. "Can you give me some instruction or guidance on how I do this or what to expect?"

Myrta explained to Diarmid that, in normal circumstances, the evening meal in the Cranstoun household was eaten in silence. She told him that she and Everet had introduced the practice as they came to realise that the world, and its entire contents is as One: in short they believed that everything that exists is connected, one thing to another, and each thing to all.

She explained it was similar to what they had been doing at the Abbeystery, but, being on their own, they could take as much time as they needed. For them the evening meal was a meditation in which the food was the focus. Textures and tastes blended together, the diverse becoming the all. Without one part there would be no All.

She told Diarmid that Aonghus had at first found the concept difficult to understand, and it took much practice for him to be able to pass the meal time without a word being said. "An inward journey is like a pilgrimage, and is, first of all, the attitude of a mind firmly fixed within the heart," she said. "A periodic journey to the heart, particularly on a daily basis, is a good way of developing a mystical habit of mind."

"That sounds awfully complex," said Diarmid, "but I am willing to try it. Whilst we have been here I have obviously maintained the silence during the meals, but never put any meaning or purpose behind it. I can only gain benefit by doing so."

"Diarmid," said Myrta gently, laying a hand on the lad's shoulder, "you amaze me at times with your words of wisdom. In the mystical experience of inner silence words are distractions. It is in the inner silence that self appreciation manifests, so I would agree with you that there is benefit to be gained." She paused for a moment then continued, "Now let us go and prepare ourselves for dinner."

A short time later the bell sounded calling the occupants of the Abbeystery to Abendessen, and the Cranstouns made their way to the Lesser Hall where they found their meal already served for them. After they had taken their places at the table, Everet said a few words of grace, then invited the family to make their inner journey as they ate, thanking whoever and whatever each perceived had helped them during their traumatic journey.

To a great extent the silence of the Abendessen they had shared with the others in the community had prepared Diarmid for what Myrta and Everet were now outlining. It was one thing to sit in the silence, and be fully aware of what was going on round about: one could move, look around, and even make eye contact with others at the table. Now Diarmid had to concentrate his attention on quieting his thoughts and looking inward: it was a more focussed silence, and there could be no other ancillary activities.

Not quite sure what was expected of him, but being practical as ever, Diarmid concentrated hard on the words the Sorella had spoken of the Violet Flame and its uses. He tried hard to cut off from the Abbeystery, to see where his mind would take him.

Diarmid adjusted his posture so that he would be as comfortable as possible, trying to sit straight in the chair with his spine and head erect, legs and arms uncrossed, his feet flat on the floor. He sat like this for a few moments then reached forward to collect some food.

As he chewed it slowly he recalled the Sorella's instruction, and her words of the opening decree came flooding into his mind: "I AM a creature of Violet Fire! I AM the wholeness God desires!"

Almost startled at the ease with which the words came to him, the sailor took a few slow deep breaths aiming to calm the surprise. Soon he again felt centred and began giving out the decree with love, devotion and feeling. In his mind he heard the Sorella saying that repetition of the decree strengthens its power and draws down more light.

After a while Diarmid seemed to drift off to a kind of magical place where all was peace and light: he heard waves crash powerfully yet soothingly against a beautiful sandy beach. High in the sky seabirds hovered and circled, crying out the joys of life to all who would listen.

With this picture in his mind Diarmid began to concentrate on visualizing the Violet Flame. He created a large fire on the beach, and watched as the flames rose into the air, striving upwards to reach as far as they were able. As Diarmid watched the flames he saw their colour change from the vibrant yellows, oranges and reds into equally alive shades of violet, purple and even pink. He watched as the flames pulsated and undulated, dancing for his delight. Then, as he continued to watch, the Violet Flame cast its hypnotic spell: Diarmid was captivated, and he saw himself stepping into the flame. As he watched in fascination Diarmid saw the flames curling up from beneath his feet, passing through and around his body, and up over his head.

He was consumed, yet unharmed, and stood there completely enthralled. From where he knew not, words flooded into Diarmid's head: "In the name of the Power within me, I ask that this Violet Flame be multiplied, and used to assist all souls on this planet who are in need. I thank you, and accept it done according to the will of the Creator."

Diarmid felt a powerful feeling shudder through him, a feeling that exhilarated him to a level he never knew existed, and in that moment he realised that even a few minutes of Violet Flame was powerful, with the potential to produce positive results. In the same instant he realised also that persistence would be needed to penetrate age-old habits to their very core in order to change them permanently.

Gradually, Diarmid brought himself back into the Lesser Hall, and unhurriedly opened his eyes. He discovered that the others were sitting quietly looking at him, gently awaiting his "return". "Wow," he said, "that was sure powerful."

With some encouragement from Myrta, Diarmid related his experience to the others. "Before this adventure," said Diarmid, "I had no time for anything but sailing and seeing as many places as possible. However, after all our troubles, and this last adventure here at the table, I know that I have new realms to explore, and these are all inside my head."

"Yes, Diarmid," said Myrta, "all of Creation is wonderful, and what is equally wonderful is that you have discovered your inner self at an early age. Most people are not aware of their inner self, or choose to ignore it. Some discover it late in life, and sadly, some never see it at all."

At that point the door of the Hall opened, and Anastasie entered with two of the ladies. Whist the ladies cleared away the remnants of the meal and the dishes Anastasie sat down to chat.

She wanted to give Everet and Myrta as much encouragement as she could to see through their decision to return to Knympton to confront their adversaries. "You must trust that all will work out for the greater good of those involved," she said. "I'm sure you already know that the Universe works in strange and wonderful ways, and whatever emerges is always, always, the right answer. I know that from our perceptions we can disagree with that. However, when you look back and consider everything that has happened to you, and the way it has come about, you will understand the messages and lessons that have been given, enabling you to emerge stronger and better from whatever the situation was."

"You are right, Anastasie," said Everet, "it is hard to think that when something bad is happening to you that it is happening for a good reason.

Plenty has happened to us in the past months, more than I would really like to contemplate, but you have helped us to confront our miseries, whilst encouraging us to be bold enough to go for what we know is right for us."

"I am glad that you have found comfort and an inner strength to make the difficult decisions, Everet," said Anastasie, "and be assured, all of you, that we will continue to send out love and light to you as you make your way back to Knympton. The power of the Violet Flame added to the attributes of the Seventh Ray will win through."

"Thank you," said Everet. "I am sure we will benefit greatly from your intercessions."

"As with most things," said the Sorella, "different people feel different benefits. For example," she went on, "some people have reported that the life changes they desired had been made easier, some have felt an increased vitality and power to take control of their lives, whilst others still have felt a prolonged sense of wholeness and well-being, just about everyone who has said anything has commented on feeling a stronger connection to their spiritual source and soul purpose."

The group looked at each other and then at Anastasie. "Has anyone ever reported feeling nothing at all?" asked Myrta.

"Oh yes," said Anastasie, "but that's a valid reaction too. I might add that although you do not appear to feel any sensation it is not to say that nothing has happened."

"How so?" said Everet.

"Well, Everet," said the Sorella, "these energies work in subtle ways: we have yet much to learn about them, especially the Seventh Ray as it is the newest of the Rays and is only starting to manifest in a major way."

Everet still looked puzzled.

"Everet," said Anastasie, "Do you think you got here by accident or chance?"

"Possibly," he replied, "but then again our luck, if that's what it was, was very strong for such a long period of time, so I guess I have to answer your question with a 'no'."

"Exactly so," said the Sorella. "There were guiding forces working so far in the background that you didn't know they were there. They ensured your safety after the ship broke up, they sent the dolphins to guide and help you when you were in grave danger of being swept away, and they have done so much for you. It's the same with the Seventh Ray: it's one of these background forces. I know we haven't found the time for me to fully explain my understanding of the Seventh Ray to you. However, some of us recognise its power, and have resolved to do what we can to help it manifest in this world at this time."

"Yes, yes, I can see that now," said Everet. "I do believe each of us in this little group has had a deep experience during the course of our journey and we can all relate to what you are saying, indeed to what you are doing here. Once again I'd like to thank you for everything you have done for us, and I know that I am speaking for us all when I say that."

"It's nice to be appreciated," said Anastasie, "but we are here to serve. When we are of service to others we are at our happiest, knowing that we are sharing what we have and helping others. Now is there anything else you need to ask?"

There was a silence in the group. "Anything at all," said Anastasie. "If I can answer it I will."

Myrta looked up and said, "If I may, Anastasie, can I ask who I was mistaken for by Gelsen when we arrived? She got very excited."

"Ah yes, the Alban Eiler," said the Sorella with a laugh. "Undeniably the Novicia became very excited indeed. However, young Gelsen was mistaken, for although Alban Eiler means 'Light of the Earth', it is a concept, not a person."

"I am confused," said Myrta. "If the Alban Eiler is not a person why then did Gelsen mistake me for what you say is a concept?"

Anastasie explained that the time of year was drawing nigh when the balance of day and night would be equal, and that this balance point brought with it a magic for creating rebirth and regrowth. She explained that most people regard plants as vegetation with no feelings or life force, but there must surely be life in all living things, from rocks and stones, to rivers and springs, plants and trees: she said that all life is sacred. "How does a plant know when it is time to grow?" she asked them. They looked at her, baffled. "It cannot tell the time or see a calendar," she went on without waiting for an answer. "Yet it knows. If it has senses then it has awareness, if it has perception then it is more than an unresponsive life form. So it is the return of life to the Earth that is celebrated at Alban Eiler, the time of balance."

"But I still do not understand Gelsen's confusion," said Myrta.

"This time of year, Spring you most probably call it, is a holy time of transition for those who still follow Ancient Practices, and they call it Alban Eiler, Light of the Earth, as I have explained," said Anastasie. "This is what we do in the Dark Lands where both Gelsen and I have our origins. For us this is a time of renewal and new growth, when the natural world is re-born. It is said that on the day of the Vernal Equinox, the day of balance, the God of Light conquers the God of Darkness. However, the peoples of the Dark Lands are not the only ones who hold this day in reverence. It was celebrated long before them, by the Megali people who lived in the far east, and many other tribes between here and the far end of the world. The Ancient Darklanders, the Hohenvolk, called it Eostre, after their fertility goddess."

216

"Ah," said Myrta starting to understand, "and Gelsen thought I was a reincarnation of the Goddess."

"Yes," agreed Anastasie, "but you know, in some senses she wasn't entirely wrong."

"Now I am confused again," said Myrta, looking round the group for inspiration: nobody offered any.

"Well," began the Sorella, "the story of Eostre tells how this goddess found a bird with a life threatening injury. To save it, she used her powers to transform it into a hare. However, for reasons that have never been made clear, the alteration was not a complete success. Although the bird took the appearance of a hare, it retained the facility to lay eggs, so the hare would lay these eggs at this time of year, and leave them as gifts for Eostre." She let this sink in for a few moments before continuing. "This time of year is seen as a time when we, as humans, can transform ourselves in ways which we deem are necessary. Since Alban Eiler is the day of balance, we can use it to examine the stability or lack thereof in our own lives. We can have a clearout, a spring clean, either literally, by de-cluttering, getting rid of what objects or possessions we don't need, or figuratively, by cleansing our inner being. It is a day to seek equilibrium, to bring our energies back into alignment. It's a time for new hope, new beginnings, new relationships, a time to make life changes if we so desire."

"Yes, I'm beginning to get your drift, Anastasie," said Myrta.

"Me, too," said Everet. "We have been guided here to discover and learn the messages that we were either ignoring through non-awareness or failing to understand at a deeper level. Through your good ministrations, Anastasie, we have come to realise that things indeed have to change and here we now are on the brink of making these changes. It seems that we have chosen the right time for this journey."

"Or it has been chosen for us," said Myrta. "We must stay positive that the outcome, whatever it may be will be the right one."

"Excellent!" the Sorella praised them. "But please remember that you will never garner a harvest on any level of life unless you first plant the appropriate seeds. Taking a lesson from Nature, and doing so at Springtime, is the ideal opportunity for doing exactly this for your spiritual growth and personal development: consequently it will affect your future way of life so take good care of what you sow."

Chapter 40: The Church of the Apostles

The Church of the Apostles is a small, but impressive church which commands the northern side of the Square of the Holy Rood, itself an unimposing piazza close to Knympton's Eastern Gate. Though small in size it still adhered to the principles of the basilica form. It is shaped like a cross, the long nave intersected at one end by a transept, with the apse at the far end. Near the impressive high wooden doors, on the western side of the church is the campanile where the angelus was sounding as Sefira approached.

Sefira, hearing the bells, was suddenly reminded that today was indeed Lady Day, the day of the Feast of the Annunciation. As she sat down on a bench close by the bell tower, her mind wandered to a time when she was younger, and a regular church attender, she could almost see the priest entering the church, venerating the icons and putting on his vestments. In her mind she watched as the priest and the deacon prepared and blessed the bread and wine for the Eucharist.

The priest then walked to the Apse where he raised the Holy Bible over the Altar, making the sign of the cross with it and proclaiming, *"Blessed is the Kingdom of the Father and of the Son and of the Holy Ghost, now and ever and unto ages of ages."*

Turning to face the congregation he began the service. "Today we begin our transformation," he intoned. "Today begins our salvation through the revelation of the eternal mystery! Today the Son of God becomes the Son of the Virgin: today is the day the Archangel Gabriel heralds the coming of Grace. Together with Him let us cry aloud: *'Rejoice, Full of Grace, The Lord is with You!' Ave, gratia plena, Dominus tecum.*"

"Fiat mihi secundum verbum tuum," Sefira whispered softly, the response written indelibly in her head by years of childhood indoctrination. She was rudely disturbed from her mental church service by a gentle voice calling her name: it was Shamira. However, Sefira was still partially inside the church and didn't recognise the girl.

"Sefira, are you alright?" the girl asked, somewhat concerned. Sefira recovered sufficiently to identify Shamira as the girl who had taken her to Brina's cottage previously.

"Yes, yes," said Sefira, "just got caught up in something I shouldn't have and sort of lost focus for a few minutes."

"In that case then let's get going. The square is busy for some reason so we should use the hustle and bustle to quietly disappear and make our way to Brina's," said the girl. "Follow me." With that she headed for the eastern exit of the square, and it was all Sefira could do to keep up with the brisk pace that had been set.

They walked this way and that, and at one point Sefira was sure they had gone round in a circle: it was Shamira's way of making sure that they were not being spied on or followed. After what seemed an age they entered the woods and gradually made their way deeper into the undergrowth until at last they came upon Brina's cottage.

"I will leave you to make your own way to the door," said Shamira, "and I will see you again later to take you back to Knympton." With that, she was off, skipping down the path they had just travelled up.

"Thank you, and bye," said Sefira turning to watch the girl rapidly disappearing from view. Then she headed for the door of the cottage and gently knocked upon it.

The door opened and there stood Brina, large as life as always, beaming a great smile at Sefira. "How lovely to see you again, Sefira," she enthused. "Come in, come in," she continued, ushering Sefira into the hallway. "In you go, Yorlan is waiting for you."

As she stepped into the bedroom Sefira could have sworn that Yorlan leaped out of his chair, such was his hurry to greet her. Mung embraced his wife with such strength that she had to ask him to release her before he did her an injury. As he put her down he said, "Sorry, love, I'm just so glad to see you again. I know it has only been a few days, but it seems so terribly long."

"You haven't held me like that in many a long year," said his wife in mock admonishment. "I take it your health is increasing by the day."

Brina watched from the doorway for a short time as the couple exchanged small talk, then she entered, and asked Yorlan where his surge of strength had come from: it had even surprised her.

"Deep down I suppose," he said. "It is part of the healing, isn't it?"

"Very much so," said the Shaman. "Now sit yourself down and calm down. Here, Sefira," she continued, pulling up a chair, "sit here. I will go and make us an infusion of sage and monarda."

Whilst she was gone Yorlan told his wife about his ever improving health and his determination to right all the wrongs he had committed over the years, particularly the years just gone.

"And how are you going to accomplish that?" Sefira asked.

"Well, obviously I will need a plan, and I will need help. I would like you to be part of it all," he said.

"I will need to know more," said his wife. "I just can't get involved without some idea of what you have been up to all these years."

Mung agreed that there had been many indiscretions, all committed with the very best of intentions. However, each indiscretion only served to bind him more tightly to the dark side. He told Sefira in more detail how he had become involved with Ludley and his gang of thieves, thugs and blackmailers. Tears welled up in his eyes as he described some of the things he had been involved in, and some of the atrocious acts that had been carried out.

He was in full flight of pouring his heart out when Brina reappeared with the sage and monarda. She put down the tray on the dressing table, and proceeded to hand a cup of the liquid to Sefira, and then a cup to Yorlan. "Drink, Yorlan, this will help you overcome what must be defeated." She took the third cup from the tray, and sat down on the edge of the bed. "Now, what's happening?"

Mung explained that he needed Sefira's help, but before that was given she needed to know all about the past: he was trying his best to recite as honestly as he could what had taken place.

"This is good, Yorlan," said the Shaman. "It is part of your soul retrieval which will greatly help the healing process." Then she turned to Sefira and said, "This is hard for him, and I know it will be hard for you also. However, please try to understand what is going on in his body, in his mind, indeed right throughout his very being. The more you can ride with this the better and easier it will be on your future paths." She sipped from her cup, then looked at Sefira again. "Do what's comfortable with your inner senses, Sefira, nobody will force you to do anything that goes against your instincts. If you need to ask any questions please do so."

Mung continued with his tale of horror, some of which even shocked Brina, but she could see beyond the physical, knowing that here was a man desperate to make amends for his waywardness.

Sefira did not know what to say as her husband related tales of desperation and cruelty, merely punctuating Mung's account with Oh's, Ah's and other gasps of horror and astonishment. At the end of the story she put the cup down on the floor and reached out to her husband to embrace him. "That's a bad, bad life history, Yorlan," she whispered, "but the good thing is you have now admitted it and taken responsibility for setting matters aright. In your telling of those times I can see glimpses of the young handsome man I fell in love with, and I am certain that there is more of this charming man yet to emerge: the cloud does indeed have a silver lining."

"Does this mean that you will help me?" said Mung.

"Of course it does," said Sefira, "for it means I get back the man I married. Yorlan, riches are nothing but passing trinkets. Yes, it's nice to afford the odd treat, but so long as we have a roof over our heads and food in the larder then we have no cause for complaint." Mung looked at her, somewhat perplexed. "Tell me," she said, "can you take gold coins with you when you pass to the next world? No!" she answered her own question. "So all that ghastly business you got caught up in was for no real purpose, and think of all those poor souls whose lives you have sullied, tarnished or completely destroyed in the process. Yorlan Mung you have a lot of making up to do!"

Tears rolled down Mung's cheeks as he sat there totally bewildered. Some of the tears were outpourings of joy at Sefira's offer to help: the rest were for his victims and their families, and made him almost inconsolable. He shuddered, wracked with pain, his wife at his side, her arms around him, trying to bring comfort. Brina remained on the bed: "Let it all come out, Yorlan, let it flow, as long and as loud as it needs to be. Release it to the Universe, release it with love."

After some minutes of wailing and remorsing Mung began to recover, and soon was sufficiently restored to concentrate on his plans. "I really need to sort out this awful mess with the Marshals," he said. "Would it be wise to arrange a meeting with the Captain?"

"Well, you have to start somewhere," said Brina, "but I'm not sure what their enquiries have thrown up, after all you are a missing person."

"Yes, that's true," replied the patient, "and my being missing also brings into focus the fate of the Cranstouns: I assume they are still missing too."

"What I can tell you from my conversations with Captain Folgate," said Sefira, "is that they have run out of ideas. They found your badge and a suspicious blood stain, but nothing else. It's remarkable how Brina got you out of there without leaving any hints or clues. As for the Cranstouns, nobody has any idea where they went or why, although the speed with which they vanished has perplexed everyone. As I understand it, their landlord has been interviewed but could shed no light on matters either. Apparently they were model tenants and had caused no trouble to anyone."

"That's what attracted them to Ludley," said Mung. "They seemed to have a successful business, and Ludley decided that he wanted some of the profits." He pondered Ludley's decision for a few moments before continuing. "What you say, my dear, makes my reappearance a little more delicate than I had imagined. Do either of you ladies have any suggestions to make?"

"Meeting the Captain would be the place to start," said Brina, "but first he needs to be, how shall I put it, properly prepared. However we get you and him together the meeting will have to take place away from Knympton but still within an easy walk from here. Sefira, if you really want to help then I would suggest that it will have to be you who initiates the meeting. Let me consult with my guides and helpers and I will contact you in due course."

"You mean the cat?" said Sefira.

A surprised look came over Mung's face, and he stared first at Sefira, then at Brina.

"Probably," she said, "but don't rule out human contact," she finished with a laugh in which Sefira joined.

*****

Assured that her husband had recovered from his bout of guilt ridden grief, Sefira said that it was time for her to get back to Knympton. "You say your

221

goodbyes to each other," Brina said, "whilst I summon Shamira to guide you through the woods." With that she stood up, gathered the cups and went out of the room.

Mung and Sefira held each other closely for a few minutes, each enjoying the closeness of the other. Silently they held this pose until at last Yorlan gently kissed his wife full on the lips. "I cannot get through this without you," he said. "I know it hasn't been easy for you, and I know there are still many possible perils ahead. However, I want you to know how much I appreciate your being here, and also your willingness to help me."

"I am here for you, Yorlan," said Sefira, "and yes there have been difficult times. No," she said correcting herself, "absolutely awful times. However, I do believe that these are now behind us, and we can move on once amends have been made to clear up this whole nasty business. As I said earlier I want my charming husband back."

Outside, Brina took a few steps from the front door and stood in silence, eyes gently closed. "Archangel Chamuel," she said softly, "I ask you to find Shamira and request that she returns here to escort Sefira safely back home."

Chapter 41: Leaving the Abbeystery

As was the practice at the end of the meal, the Sorella stood up to address the assembly. "Sisters, Brothers," she began in her usual fashion, "today, although it has just begun, is already a happy and a sad one. This day our guests will take their leave from us. Whilst we will be sad to see them go, we are happy, too, for we know that, in our little sanctuary they have gained insight and guidance, and have taken a major decision which will affect all their lives. We wish them well, and we ask that they continue to receive guidance, strength and resolve to see their journey through to its end. We ask Archangel Zadkiel and the Angels to watch over them every step of the way."

Turning to face the group she said, "Dear guests, it has been our pleasure to meet and interact with you. We thank you for your contribution to Abbeystery life. Should you wish to return here at any time, you will be made most welcome. We wish you every success."

There was an initial ripple of applause that grew louder and was sustained for several minutes.

Everet looked at the Sorella: "May I say a few words?"

"Of course," she replied.

He stood up, facing the brothers and sisters a little hesitatingly. "I hardly know where to begin," he said, "but I would like to say that without your friendly welcome and generous support we would still be wandering this way and that, looking for we know not what. You have helped each of us enormously, and for that, and I know that I speak for all four of us when I say this, we would like to say a huge 'Thank You' for what you have given us. Now we take our leave of you knowing where we are headed, with a clear mission in mind. We know that we will become stronger in spirit as we strive to accomplish our goal. Hopefully one day, once our mission has been achieved, one, some or all of us can return to repay the love, kindness, generosity and inspiration we have received here. We wish each and every one of you the best. Thank you." As he sat down tears welled up in his eyes and slowly trickled down his cheeks.

The group lingered at the table whilst the rest of the assembly dispersed, then quietly returned to their rooms to collect what little personal items they still had. Afterwards they made their way outside to the courtyard where Krem and Edgar awaited. The horse and cart were at the ready: all that was required was to lift the boat onto the trailer and their return home could begin. After some struggles they managed to get the boat onto the cart, but it seemed to be sitting at a precarious angle. They looked, they discussed, and finally they set about rectifying the boat's position: now they were ready.

As Myrta climbed up beside Krem, Anastasie and Gelsen appeared: they were each carrying a small load. "We have had a search round the Abbeystery and we have decided that these items of clothing are excess to our immediate requirements," said the Sorella. "Please take them." She handed the bundle to Everet who thanked her and placed it on the back of the cart.

"In this box there are some preserved foods which we would like you to have also," said the Novicia. "It's a long journey, and whilst we trust that you will be successful, you will need to feed your bodies as well as your souls." They too were placed on the cart.

"And lastly," said Anastasie, "here are a few Crowns to help you buy what you cannot otherwise get. As Gelsen has said, it is a long and arduous journey that you are undertaking, and we need to ensure that it starts in the right manner so that it has a chance of finishing in the right way."

Everet accepted the coins gratefully and graciously. "Anastasie, we can never thank you enough for what you have done, but rest assured we will repay this in full. I give you my word. We are indebted to you."

"And with interest," said Myrta from her seat. "Thank you seems so sparse, so frugal, but be assured we will never forget what you have done, what you have sacrificed for us. Now we must go, but we will return."

They said their goodbyes, and Krem gave the horse the signal to move: the cart set off, with Edgar, Everet, Diarmid and Aonghus walking behind. Krem took them at an easy pace down to where the River Pertyck flowed. He brought the cart to a halt and waited whilst the walkers caught up with them. "Here we are," he said, "but it would be too much trouble to get the boat launched here. However, there is a fording point about a mile or so downstream. We can offload the boat then slide it into the river. Let's go!" he finished as he gave the horse the signal to move.

The path along the river bank was quite flat and wide, allowing them to make good progress: after a short time they came upon the ford. Krem brought the cart to a halt and Myrta got down from her seat.

After some to-ings, fro-ings and repositionings they finally managed to get the boat onto the river bank. They loaded it up with their possessions, little as they were, and the men proceeded to slide the boat down the pathway to the ford: soon the recently modified craft was floating gently in the river.

The group bade farewell to Krem and Edgar who climbed up onto the cart from where they watched the group get into the boat and set off downstream. "Goodbye," shouted Myrta from her position at the bow as she waved energetically. The two Fraters returned her wave then set off back towards the Abbeystery.

"You need to concentrate on where we are going, Myrta," Diarmid reminded her. "We are still sailing waters that are unknown to us. I know it's not the open sea, but there may be rocks or shallows that we need to avoid. The middle of the river should be our best course."

"That would indeed serve us best, Diarmid," said Everet, "and we can then gauge whether or not we have to row or use the sail."

The mid morning sun was peeking through the light cloud cover, and there was a slight breeze: all in all it was a pleasant experience to be on the boat under such conditions. After an hour or so Diarmid suggested they pull over to the bank so that he and Everet could change positions with Aonghus and Myrta, and let them rest for a while.

The time passed by almost aimlessly as the group watched their progress, mile after mile. The current was surprisingly quick for such a small river, although they were delighted that they hadn't had to work too hard to make this amount of distance. After another two hours or so they pulled in to have some lunch, during which they decided that they could travel even faster if Diarmid and Everet took to rowing.

Diarmid, seeing Everet's slightly pained expression, reassured his fellow traveller. "It's not like it was before," he explained. "The water is calm, the current is in our favour, and we will greatly increase the distance we can travel. We need to get as far as we can before we have to resort to wind power and all the unknowns that that will bring."

"Yes, Diarmid," said Everet, "your logic is impeccable. I can see that, and fully agree with what you are saying. It's just that, well, I'm not very good at rowing."

"You did remarkably well for someone who had never taken a blade before," said the lad, "and as I say, you will find this water much more to your liking."

"How far to Trivias did Krem indicate?" asked Myrta.

"Five days travel, maybe slightly more, he thought," said Everet, "but that was based on using his horse and cart."

"So perhaps we can cut the journey time significantly by rowing down the river," said his wife. "The sooner we get back to Knympton, the sooner we put this dark matter to rest."

They finished lunch and got underway once again, with Aonghus back at the helm, Myrta up front, and Diarmid and Everet in the middle with the oars. Aonghus, under Myrta's guidance, took the boat out into midstream. "Time to pick up the oar and lock it in the rowlock," said Diarmid: Everet complied with a sense of reluctance. "Just remember to take your time," said the sailor, "because we are not in a race. I will follow your rhythm as before. We will go slowly to begin with so that the action becomes familiar again. Remember not to dip too deeply, but don't worry if you do. Tell me when you are ready."

Everet pushed forward his oar and held the blade just above the surface of the water: then he let out a huge sigh and gave the word. The boat gave a judder as the effect of the stroke propelled it onwards. Another stroke: a third, fourth, fifth, and the boat had noticeably picked up speed.

"Good work," said Myrta. "That has certainly made a difference to our speed. If we keep to this rate we will do very well."

They rowed for a couple of hours, trying to keep to an even pace. There had been one or two hiccoughs along the way, but nothing too serious: whatever had occurred had not delayed them in any way. As the sun began to set and the darkness started to creep in Myrta suggested that they had travelled far enough for one day, and recommended that they stop for the night.

Chapter 42: Arrangements

It was two days after her latest visit to Brina's that Sefira heard the familiar scratching at her back door. Sure enough, when she peered from the kitchen window, Felina the cat was sitting patiently outside, waiting for Sefira to let her in. Sefira, as always, cast a glance in all directions as she allowed the cat ingress, carefully closing the door and securely fastening the bolts.

She followed Felina into the sitting room, and drew over the curtains discretely before sitting on the armchair opposite where the cat had taken up residence. Now aware of the drill Sefira let herself sink back into the easy comfort of the fireside chair. Closing her eyes she let her body relax until she felt she was part of the source of her comfort and then she heard the cat talking to her.

"That's it, just let go of everything and relax totally. Give into it; do not try to fight it. Imagine you are surrounded by a cocoon of golden white light through which negativity cannot pass. You are safe and you are protected."

Sefira took a few moments to follow Brina's instructions before indicating that she was ready.

"Excellent, you are very good at this Sefira, and it makes it much easier for me too."

"Thank you," said Sefira. "How is Yorlan?"

"He is doing well, Sefira. You have helped his recovery enormously by your positive actions."

"I'm pleased to hear he is progressing," said the Marshal's wife. "Now what do you have in store for me today?"

"Today, nothing, but tomorrow we will go to the Marshals' Station and speak to the head of the Constabulary."

"Shall I meet you there?" asked Sefira.

"No, I will meet you at noon at the campanile in the Square of the Holy Rood where you met Shamira. We will make our way to the Station from there."

"Very good," said Sefira, "I am very much looking forward to seeing how all this works out, and I trust that it will work out well."

"It's good to have trust. Send out your thoughts to the Universe or God if that's how you see things, and ask that what will emerge will be for the highest good of all concerned. However, please refrain from telling God how to do it, for he works in mysterious ways and sees much more than you or I."

"You have lost me with that," said Sefira. "Can you explain it more simply for a poor soul like me?"

"Too often, we call on Divine intervention when we are at our wits end and deeply caught up in a situation, usually one that is looking quite dire. We call for help but have a solution in mind: that solution is usually very specific and

selfish, so is not necessarily or usually the best one. So the Divine Creator does not grant the wish, and we say that our prayers have not been answered. If we explain the circumstances, ask for help to resolve it then step back from it all, that is detach ourselves, we are allowing the Creative Force to do what it does best, and we get a result that is in keeping with the best outcome for all involved. Very often these solutions take an unusual form, or the answer comes from an unexpected source."

"I think I see," said Sefira. "Thank you. Please give all my love to Yorlan, and I will see you tomorrow."

"I will pass on what you have said. Till tomorrow. Take care." And Brina was gone.

The cat was mewing as Sefira's attention returned to the sitting room. "Ah, Felina," she said, rising, "you will be wanting some milk for your troubles." The cat followed her through to the kitchen where Sefira presented her with a saucer of milk.

*****

Next day Sefira carefully made her way to the Square of the Holy Rood: occasionally she would stop and look about her, ensuring she was not being followed. At one point she sat down on a bench in the Market Square, and was suddenly alarmed when she noticed one of Ludley's men fairly close by. She shrunk down a bit on the bench focussing her attention on the man as he made his way between the stalls, until he finally headed up an alleyway.

At that point she quickly looked round about her immediate vicinity and, satisfied that all was well, quickly made off towards her appointed meeting place with Brina. Ever cautious, Sefira again checked her situation before finally entering the Square of the Holy Rood and making her way to the bench close by the campanile.

Sefira sat there, alert to the many people who were using the Square. Of course most of them were making their way into the Church of the Apostles to celebrate the noon Eucharist. She noticed the priest standing at the door, the Book of the Gospels held firmly to his chest.

As the campanile bells began to toll the noon, the priest gave a signal to one of the novices to open the inner doorway. He then raised the Book of the Gospels to shoulder level, its heavily decorated and intricately worked leather cover on full display, and proceeded to make his entry into the church. The acolyte followed him through, carefully closing the inner door behind them.

Sefira, on seeing this, let her mind wander once more to the days and times of her youth when she was a much more regular adherent. She knew that upon reaching the altar, the priest would bow in veneration of the altar, and then place the Book upon the altar, where it remained until the Alleluia. During the singing of the Alleluia, the priest removed the Book from the altar, proceeding with it to the ambo. Another acolyte brought the thurible, and handed it to the priest who censed the Book after which he handed back the censer to the acolyte to continue dispersing the incense whilst the priest gave the reading.

As before, Sefira failed to notice her intended rendezvous partner arrive. "Hello, Sefira," said Brina softly, recognising that Yorlan's wife was somewhat distracted.

Sefira jumped back to full awareness. "Oh not again!" she said: Brina looked puzzled. "Something similar happened last time when I met Shamira," she explained. "Sitting here in such close proximity to the church pulls my memories back to the times when I was in one almost every day."

"You can tell me more of this later," said Brina, "but right now we must make our way to the Marshals' station. However, before we proceed any further, let me arrange for us both to have the protection of the Archangels around us." The Shaman placed her hands on Sefira's shoulders and, in almost a whisper, called on Michael to guard them in their testing time. She also asked that whatever happened today would be in the best interests of all concerned. Finally, she asked that they be cocooned in a ball of golden white light through which evil could not pass. "Right," said Brina, "let's go." The two ladies made their way make towards the centre of town and soon arrived in the Market Square.

"Let's have a little wander round the stalls," said Brina, "just to make sure that we are quite alone and unnoticed. It's always good to browse. Who knows, we might even find a bargain!"

"Good idea," said Sefira. "It will help to calm me down a bit: I feel so tense."

They browsed the stalls, occasionally stopping to pick up items for closer inspection whilst checking that they were not being observed. Sefira was getting good at observation, and began to relish the chance to watch and look for the obscure. Brina soon noticed that Serifa was now much more relaxed, and suggested that it was now time to head for the Marshals' Station.

Chapter 43: Making Progress

The group woke up next day feeling fairly relaxed, although Everet's body had not fully readjusted to the rowing, and was still complaining. Nevertheless his spirits had been raised by the perceived distance they had travelled the previous day, and he was keen to get started again despite the aches.

Clearing up was done with ease, and the party were back on the boat soon after breakfast. The weather was still favourable as they set off. Diarmid reminded Everet in a gentle way to take his time and not to worry. "Right," said Myrta, "we are all ready so let's go!"

Everet's rowing had certainly improved from those first days of absolute necessity, and Diarmid praised him for the progress he had made. The river was widening with every mile they rowed so they took full advantage of the current whilst remaining in water that wasn't outrageously deep.

The hours and the miles passed unremarkably and seemingly very quickly: it was only by noting the sun's position high in the sky that they realised it was time to stop for a rest and something to eat.

As the afternoon wore on a breeze started to get up and it was Myrta who raised the idea of trying out the sail in order to give the rowers a rest. "We can try it whilst the breeze is gentle and the water reasonably shallow and flat," said Diarmid.

"Perhaps," said Everet, "when we pull in to make the adjustments to the boat's layout we can remove all our possessions at the same time."

"That's a good idea," said Myrta. "We don't want any accidents and lose what we have to the bottom of the river."

They headed for the riverbank where they unloaded their goods. Then they assembled the mast and affixed the tarpaulin sail to it. "We'll haul up the sail when we are out on the water," said Diarmid. "That is best practice. We will also have to insert our keel blades in midstream as well: the water is not deep enough here."

Diarmid and Everet got into the boat and they pushed off into the river. The boat drifted as the two men fiddled with the keel blades, the boat rocking to and fro whilst they cajoled and persuaded the blades into position. Occasionally Diarmid pulled on the tiller to adjust the boat's position. When they were happy that everything was in place Diarmid took the helm, and requested Everet to run up the sail. Slowly it was hauled into position, the breeze catching it and puffing it out. It wasn't the smoothest of rides, although it seemed to work, and Diarmid and Everet began to get the hang of manoeuvring the boom to work the wind in their favour.

Happy with their experiment, Diarmid steered the boat back up river to where Myrta and Aonghus were standing in rapt wonder at the apparent success of it all.

"Time to strike the sail, Everet," said Diarmid.

"Beg your pardon?" said Everet.

"Sorry, Everet," said the sailor. "Take the sail down please."

Everet undid the knot and the sail came clattering down. "Careful!" said Diarmid, but Everet had seen the danger, and took evasive action. "Now we must take the blades out as quickly as possible before we lose ground to the current." Having done all that they placed the oars in the rowlocks and pulled for shore.

"That looked wonderful," said Myrta. "Will the sail help us make a faster journey?"

"Maybe so," said Diarmid, "but we don't know what will happen to the boat's stability should the wind rise significantly."

"Indeed," said Everet, "the stability was just about manageable in this breeze. However, I think we should give it a try whilst the conditions are in our favour."

They loaded up the boat with Aonghus up front alongside Myrta. Everet pushed off with his oar and the boat began to drift lazily. Diarmid and Everet set about replacing the keel blades in their allotted positions, finding the job slightly easier this time round. "Right," said Diarmid, "let's unfurl the sail and get going." Everet duly hauled the sail back into place and sat down amidships to organise the boom.

The breeze again filled the sail and the boat jerked as it was propelled forwards: with the current and the wind supporting them, the boat settled down into a reasonably smooth passage.

Aonghus, now a little redundant, relaxed into the voyage and watched as the landscape alongside each riverbank subtly changed as their journey unravelled. To his right he could see the plains gradually rising into the foothills, which in turn gave way to the distant mountains. Even from this distance the mountains looked high, and he mused in his thoughts that they had come across perhaps those very peaks, although, he admitted to himself, they had not had to climb exceedingly high.

On the other bank it was mostly plains with the occasional range of hills, but nothing remotely as high as to the north. If he peered hard enough he thought he could make out the odd settlement in the far distance, but then again what he saw might well have been yet more forests.

Aonghus was shaken rather rudely out of his reverie as the boat began to shake and judder. "What's going on?" he asked in some alarm. "Why are we rocking so?"

"Just a minor disturbance in the current," shouted Diarmid. "Another river has joined with this one, thus we are sailing through the area where their energies mingle and enrich each other. Besides, the breeze has gained in strength."

"Will we be alright?" asked the boy.

"We'll get through it very soon," said Diarmid. "A little more patience and courage. Hold on tighter if it will give you more comfort."

"Perhaps we should pull in for the night after we get through this rough patch," said Myrta. "We have travelled farther today than yesterday and are making good time."

"A little longer, my dear," said Everet. "We must take full advantage of the circumstances, and the light is still good enough for us to see where we're going."

"I think Everet is right, Myrta," said Diarmid, and the party sailed further on before finally stopping for the night.

As they settled down for the night rain, began to fall, its pitter patter on the tarpaulin a slight annoyance for the party who were trying to get to sleep. Eventually their tiredness got the better of them, and they drifted into pleasant slumber. The rain persisted for a few hours more, and was gone by morning.

Chapter 44: News for the Marshals

Sefira and Brina casually walked up the steps to the Marshals' Station, pushed open the glass panelled oak doors, stepping inside and onward to the front desk. Sergeant Trine looked up from his paperwork, and, seeing Sefira, laid his pen down on the desk as he beamed a smile.

"Good day to you, Missus Mung," he said, "and who have you brought along with you today?"

"Good day to you, Sergeant," Sefira replied. "This is a friend of mine, Brina."

"You're welcome, Brina," said Trine. "How I can I help you today, Missus Mung?"

"You can ask Captain Folgate to see us, we have some information for him," said Mrs Mung, with a look that defied Trine to do other than what was requested.

"I'll see what I can do," he said as he made his way to the back office.

He returned some minutes later accompanied by the Captain. "Mistress Mung, and Brina," he said. "Please, come through," he continued as he indicated for the ladies to proceed to his office. "You know the way."

Brina followed Sefira and they entered the office with Folgate bringing up the rear: "Please, sit down," he said as he closed the door behind him then went round the desk to his worn, but no doubt comfortable, leather upholstered chair and sat down. "I understand you have information for me, and I assume it concerns Yorlan."

"We have some information," said Brina, "but can you please bring us up to date with what the Marshals have so far discovered about Yorlan's disappearance."

"I have nothing to add to what Mistress Mung has already been told," said Folgate. "Sadly, we have failed to find any clues save for Mung's Marshal Badge which we found at the Cranstoun premises."

"And what of the Cranstouns?" said Brina.

"Before I answer that," said Folgate, "may I ask who you are, and what your interest in this matter really is?"

"Brina is a friend," said Sefira. "As you will soon discover, she is deeply involved in this affair, Captain, but in a good way, not a criminal way. You have told me that this case baffles you: Brina has information that will solve most of this mystery for you."

"Indeed this case does have us baffled," Folgate agreed. "To answer your question, then, Brina, not a whisper has been heard of the Cranstouns," the Captain went on. "Even more strange how a family of three could disappear as suddenly and completely as they have done. Not a trace of them remains." He sat for a moment pondering, then added, "All we have is a possible very tenuous connection to a ship that sailed from Knympton at roughly the time they vacated their premises, but the ship is apparently reported as missing too!"

"How terribly frustrating," agreed Brina, making a mental note of the information. "Do you perchance know the name of this ship?"

"Yes, let me check our notes," said Folgate opening a drawer and retrieving a folder. Opening it, he scanned a few documents then looked at the women: "*The Venturer*," he said, "it was due to sail for Pender in the far south, calling in at the intermediate ports."

"Is there any reason why the Cranstouns would want to make a quick getaway to head as far from here as is possible?" asked Brina.

"None that we are aware of," said the Marshal. "We have even interviewed Cranstoun's landlord and he was as baffled as the rest of us."

"And is there any reason why Yorlan would have been at Cranstoun's premises?" Brina enquired. "I mean is there any record of a complaint being made by them or about them?"

"None recorded," said Folgate. "This whole case is fraught with strangeness, and try as we might, and we have devoted a lot of effort to it, we have come up with nothing. No reason, no motive, no bodies. Absolutely nothing to report and really I have no option but to leave the case open, although I cannot devote any further resources directly to it."

"Right," said Brina, "you have evidence that Yorlan was at the Cranstoun premises at or around the time that everyone disappeared."

"Yes," agreed Folgate, "that's about the sum and substance of it." He paused for a few moments then said, "There is another mysterious element to this as well."

"Which is?" prompted Brina.

"There was a fairly large bloodstain on the floor close to where we found Mung's badge. However, we cannot say whose blood it is. Indeed Cranstoun ran a butcher's shop, so it may even be an animal's blood, although my experience tells me otherwise."

"So your suspicions are that this was Yorlan's blood, and the amount would indicate a serious injury?" said Brina.

"Indeed," agreed the Captain, "and that only adds to the mystery: how someone with such a serious injury could get out of there without leaving a trail. For whatever reason Mung was at the Cranstoun place, we believe that there was a violent altercation leaving Mung seriously wounded. At this moment in time we believe that the Cranstouns, well Mister Cranstoun, has committed this act of violence, hidden the body somewhere, or otherwise disposed of it, then the family has made off in a hurry to avoid capture."

"Oh!" exclaimed Sefira. "You think Yorlan has been killed and his body disposed of."

"That's our current theory, Mistress Mung," said Folgate, "disturbing as it sounds. We have no other evidence to suggest this is not the case: unless you know something we don't."

Recovering, Sefira spoke up. "Well, yes, we do know something you don't, Captain, and that's why we are here. You will have to forgive us for not revealing this sooner, but when you hear what we have to say you will, I hope, understand why."

Folgate sat a little more erect in his chair. "I'm all ears," he said.

"Are you a religious man, Captain?" said Brina.

Puzzled by the question Folgate asked what was meant.

"Do you go to church? Do you pray? Do you believe in God?" said Brina.

"Yes," said the Captain, "three times yes, but why do you ask such a strange question?"

"Because you will need to call upon all your faith and belief as we gradually reveal to you what the situation is, and how it came about," said Brina.

"Try me," invited the Marshal.

What do you know of the Archangels?" she asked.

"Is this pertinent?" replied Folgate.

"It will help enormously, believe me," said Brina.

"Well, I know very little save their names," said Folgate. "There's Michael, Raphael, Gabriel and, er, oh yes, Uriel."

There was a pause before Brina responded. "That'll do for a start. What do you know of their functions and abilities?"

"This is getting crazy," said the Captain. "I'll play along a little further, but be aware that I do not have the time for much more of this tittle tattle."

"Oh it's not tittle tattle," said Sefira, "not when you hear what has happened. Brina is just trying to prepare you for what will seem a preposterous report."

"I will be the judge of that, Mistress Mung," said Folgate, beginning to show his impatience. "If you have anything to tell me please do so now."

"As you wish," said Brina. "I will also tell it as it happened. Yorlan Mung is neither dead nor missing."

The Captain's jaw dropped substantially and his eyes opened wide. "You have proof?"

"Oh yes," said Brina. "Indeed I helped in his rescue and subsequent improvement."

"Rescued from where and what?" demanded Folgate in his stentorious tone. "And how have you improved him?"

"As you rightly stated, Captain," said Brina gently, "Yorlan was involved in an altercation at the Cranstoun premises. Nevertheless, the Cranstouns were not involved: indeed they had long since fled from their home before this attack on your constable took place." The Captain's look indicated that Brina should proceed. "He was stabbed three times in the chest and stomach and left for dead. His Guardian Angel sought help from the Archangel Raphael, who, in turn, contacted me."

A look of complete and utter disbelief crossed Folgate's visage. "Now you understand why Brina was preparing you, Captain," said Sefira. "I have seen Yorlan, and although he was sorely afflicted he has improved considerably with Brina's tender and skilful ministrations. This is indeed no tittle tattle but is God's honest truth. My Yorlan is a much changed man after the experiences he has gone through. He is very much alive and can tell you much."

Folgate was flustered by this news and it showed. He stammered and stuttered before finally managing to sound coherent and once again in control. "So who did this to Mung? Does he know? Where is he now?"

"All in good time, Captain," said Brina. "Yorlan is still recovering, although he is greatly improved from the first moment I laid eyes on him. To answer your questions in the order you asked them. Some local thugs: he can identify them; and he is at my cottage."

"I don't think I know where that is," said the Marshal.

"You don't," Brina confirmed. "Also, it's best that it remains this way until Yorlan is finally ready to face you and tell you his story. I hope you will understand that this must proceed at Yorlan's pace and not yours. Please do not try to follow me home or to make enquiries concerning my whereabouts."

"Much as I would like to clear this up quickly and get hold of these ruffians I will accede to your requests knowing that you will ensure the safe return of Mung in due course," said the Marshal. "Can I ask that I be updated on his situation on a regular basis?"

"I will be happy to keep you posted," said Sefira, somewhat relieved at how well this meeting had turned out. "Even so, I will ask that when you do eventually visit Yorlan that you listen carefully to everything he has to say: there's more to this assault than meets the eye. It's a dreadful tale that will try your patience." She saw the questioning look in Folgate's eyes and added, "I am sorry to leave you somewhat in suspense, but forewarned is forearmed so you will know to expect the unexpected."

"We will carry on as normal here," said the Captain, "and until I know more, I will treat this information with the utmost sensitivity and confidentiality. Thank you for informing me." He stood up and indicated that the meeting was over.

"You are very welcome," said Sefira, rising. Folgate opened the office door and the ladies went out into the corridor, making their way back to the front desk where Trine was still busying himself in writing. "Goodbye, Sergeant," said Sefira as she and Brina left the building.

"Well that's certainly given the Captain something to think about," said Sefira as they walked through the Market Square. "I wonder what's going through his mind right now."

"Oh lots of things," said Brina. "Which ruffians, what else Yorlan is going to tell him, why did the Cranstouns disappear without trace or reason? There will be so many threads of ideas going through his head he will possibly not sleep well for a while."

"Not to mention Archangel Raphael," said Sefira laughing at the Captain's impatience when asked about the Heavenly Messengers and his disbelief when they were so implicit in her husband's survival.

"Oh yes," said the Shaman, joining in the mirth. "Luckily we left out the bit about our dear friend, Felina," and their laughter rose in pitch and volume. "Well, Sefira," said Brina, "we must part here. Go home, knowing that you are safe and have the protection of the Archangel Michael at all times: if in doubt just call out his name. I will contact you in due course. Just be yourself and do things as you would ordinarily: try not to bring suspicion on yourself. I am not yet certain that Ludley has called off his watchers, nor even that the Marshals will be keeping an extra watchful eye on you." She embraced Sefira. "Goodbye, my dear."

"Goodbye," said Sefira before turning to make her way home.

Chapter 45: Another Good Day

Myrta was first to waken, and as silently as she could, crept out of their makeshift shelter: the fire was barely alive so she quickly gathered as much dry grass as she could to help get it going again.

As she sat persuading the grass to catch fire Myrta felt a calmness within her that she had not felt for some considerable time. Not since the day before Everet had told her about those nasty people back in Knympton. The unease, or disease as Myrta was wont to call it, had set off a whole series of events that had turned their lives upside down and now inside out.

Fanning the flames of the dried grasses Myrta realised that Ludley's actions had fanned the flames of the intensity of their own mystical journey. Unknowingly, the man had set them off on the road to self discovery, and, to some extent, he deserved to be thanked for having done so. As she placed some thin branches on the fire Myrta let these thoughts swill round her head. She should be very angry and upset with this ruffian, but here she was giving out thoughts of almost forgiveness. Certainly a change had come over her, and she liked what was emerging.

"Is breakfast ready?" said Aonghus, pulling her back from her reverie.

"And good morning to you, too, my love," she said, a smile on her face.

Aonghus reddened in slight embarrassment. "Sorry, mother. Good morning. Is breakfast ready?"

"Not yet, but soon. Can you fetch me the package with the tea in it and I'll brew us a drink," said his mother.

The sound of the voices roused the other two, and they were soon out of their blankets, tidying up in preparation for another day's travel. As they sat they pondered on how far they had come, and how far they had still to travel. "I'll get the map," said Everet, "and we can have a jolly good guess at where we might be."

"I'm hoping that we can be a bit more accurate than having a jolly good guess," said his wife. "Diarmid will use his skills and pinpoint our location."

"I don't know about that," said the sailor, laughing, "but I will estimate our whereabouts."

Everet returned with the map and spread it out before them. "We entered this river somewhere around here," he said pointing with his finger. "Now, how far have we travelled along it?"

"I haven't a clue," said Myrta, "so I will leave it to you men to work out."

Everet and Diarmid concentrated on the map, looking for features in the landscape that they could relate to, but finding it difficult to do so. Much discussion took place and Myrta could see that these two were not making much progress. "Are we as lost as ever before?" she asked.

"Well, we're lost and we're not lost," said Everet.

"My dear," said his wife, "either we are or we are not: we cannot be both."

"Well, in the sense that Diarmid and I are unable to point to a location on the map and say categorically that is our location, we are lost," said the husband. "However, because we know where we are going, and that by travelling on the river we will get there, we are not lost."

It was then that Aonghus cast a glance over the map which he considered for a few minutes. He pointed to a spot. "We are there or very close to it," he said. The other three looked at him for an explanation. "Well," he said, "Diarmid has been steering us, Father has been tending to the sail on Diarmid's instructions and you, mother, have been concentrating on what lies in front of us. You have all been taken up with an important task that has required your entire concentration. I, on the other hand, have been somewhat at a loose end, and I have been watching the landscape change as our journey has progressed. Besides, we very recently passed by the point where another river joined ours. We are not far from where I indicated."

The others looked at each other, then at Aonghus, then at the map. "Absolutely right," said Myrta. "So your loose ends were not so unproductive as you thought. You are certainly developing some talents on this journey, young man."

"Just trying to help," said the boy.

"Well," said Everet, "it would seem that we are not too far from this settlement called Trivias. How long do you think it will take to reach there, Diarmid?"

Diarmid studied the map and opined that, with a fair wind propelling them and no mishaps along the way, they could possibly reach Trivias by the end of the day. This was good news and lifted their spirits. "However," Diarmid continued, "from Trivias towards Knympton the river bends and weaves rather seriously, and whilst that doesn't present any problems as far as boating is concerned, it does mean that we will be taking a rather circuitous route to our destination."

"But surely," said Everet, "to go by boat will be quicker than walking?"

"Possibly," said Diarmid.

"Let's not worry about that now," said Myrta, trying to take advantage of their upliftment, "We can send our thoughts out as we travel towards Trivias, and once we get there safely we can take some time to agree how best to proceed."

With that they finished off their breakfast, and packed their few belongings on the boat. Diarmid and Everet used the oars to push off from the bank and soon they were underway. Stowing the oars, the men set about slotting their keel blades into place, and running up the sail. The boat jolted as the wind caught in the tarpaulin and the speed began to gently pick up.

Aonghus continued to survey the landscape as it slipped by, and generally the journey proceeded in a calm and orderly fashion. It was in the early afternoon, just after they had pulled in for lunch, that they began to notice other boats on the river: small boats, some not as large as their own, being used to transport people and goods between the small hamlets that had sprung up on the river banks. As they passed these other boats they waved to the occupants and called out pleasantries which were returned with smiles.

The river, too, was changing, becoming wider, deeper, faster and more dangerous to the unaware. The countryside was more open too, and this allowed the wind to channel down onto the river, and so, later in the day the party found that keeping control of the boat became more difficult.

At long last they reached the outskirts of what seemed a largish town which they reckoned must be Trivias. Everet recommended that they sail through the settlement and pull in at the far extremity. He explained that moorings may come at a price, and they had to watch what little money they had very carefully. Added to which they didn't want to attract too much attention to themselves.

Myrta agreed that the few coins the Sorella had given them were to be used with awareness and prudence. "Besides," she said, "we are strangers here as Everet has pointed out, and we do not want to upset anyone by taking their mooring place, even if they are free from charge. We can always walk into town and see what fresh food we can buy: the markets still seem busy."

Diarmid suggested that they strike the sail, and finish the journey with the oars which meant that Aonghus had to scramble to the stern to take charge of the tiller. The boat rocked as he did so, causing Myrta to gently chide him.

With everyone in their new positions the men began rowing at a leisurely rate: the current was quite strong and assisted them greatly. Soon the buildings on the bank were beginning to thin out and Myrta noticed a point not far off where a stream was delivering its contents to the river.

"Head for it," Diarmid said. "That will make an ideal spot for us to put in to."

Presently, they reached the stream and drew up alongside its far bank. Diarmid jumped out onto the riverside and secured the boat: the others could disembark in a safer manner. Not a dozen paces from their mooring there were some low bushes which they all agreed would offer some protection from the elements.

"Aonghus and I will set up camp," said Everet to Diarmid, "whilst you and Myrta go into town and buy what you think we need to see us through the next few days."

Setting up their tent was fairly easy, so many times had they done it, and it was quickly ready to keep any overnight rain and wind off them, as it had done in the past. Everet sent Aonghus to look for some wood with which to start a fire whilst he went to fill up their containers with fresh water.

Diarmid and Myrta picked their way through the houses, aiming for the centre of what they assumed was Trivias. After a few wrong turns they finally stumbled across the market square where, to their relief, the traders were still doing a brisk business. They browsed around quite a few stalls just to check what was available and to compare prices before Myrta made the required purchases.

Satisfied that she had made sufficiently good purchases she indicated to Diarmid that they should try to find their way back to their mooring. Endeavouring to look as if they knew where they were going and what they were doing, Myrta and Diarmid strode purposefully towards the street that had led them to the market. However, somewhere they must have lost concentration and found themselves walking down a narrow lane.

"I don't remember this," said Myrta.

"Me neither," said Diarmid. "Let's turn and go back up to the road."

They retraced their footprints and quickly re-established their bearings. "I see where we went wrong," said Diarmid. "We took a sharp left when we should have just followed the road as it gently curved left."

With a sense of relief and renewed confidence in their steps they arrived back at camp soon after. "Mission accomplished," said Myrta. "We only got lost about three times," she went on, laughing. "Now let's get some cooking done, after which we can think about tomorrow's journey in the morning following a good night's sleep."

Chapter 46: Marshals and Villains

Back at the Marshals' Station Captain Norton Folgate was perplexed: he just could not seem to come to terms with the information Sefira and Brina had communicated to him. It was beyond his comprehension: he was a man of simple means and a regular church attender, but some of what he was told went way beyond anything the priest had indicated was possible. The priest should know: he was a dedicated man of God, and in the closest contact with the Almighty.

But as he pursued this train of thought he found himself getting dragged deeper and deeper into matters of the spiritual realm, and he was exceedingly out of his depth. Maybe he had to confide in the priest, or at least ask a few questions.

On the other hand the information given was a true revelation, and answered every nagging doubt he ever had about the whole affair. It was a baffling case which had eluded the combined brains of the force, and the matter remained uncomfortably unsolved. In the Marshals' world there was a place for everything, and everything had a place: except the Mung case.

They had expended a lot of time and effort on it, but had produced no results: only Mung's Marshal's badge had been found. Everyone and everything else associated with whatever went on between Mung and the Cranstouns had disappeared without the slightest trace. Frustrated by the lack of progress Folgate had to tell his force that the case was low priority: it hurt Folgate's professional pride that he had to virtually abandon a fellow officer.

Exasperated, all he could do was keep quiet and await further input from Sefira Mung and this Brina woman. It bothered him, too, that he didn't know her, didn't know of her, and his discreet enquiries since her visit had proved fruitless. He felt so disturbed by the lack of information about this woman that he was beginning to think she was a figment of his imagination, a ghostly companion of Sefira Mung.

Carefully he gathered up the papers strewn across his desk, placed them into the folder marked, "Constable Yorlan Mung: Disappearance", and put it into the top drawer in his desk. He then locked the drawer and tucked the key safely into his pocket.

He pushed his chair back from the desk, got up, went over to the coat stand where his greatcoat was hanging and put it on: he then put on his hat and went down the hallway to the front desk.

"Right, Trine," he boomed, "I'm off out to walk the manor and keep our lads on their toes. I don't know when I'll be back, and until I do return you're in charge."

"Yes, Sir," said the Sergeant, straightening up to his full height. "You can leave everything with me."

Folgate pulled the door shut behind him and headed off towards the Church of the Apostles: he needed spiritual assistance.

*****

Although the Black Crows had returned to profitable activities, and despite Ludley's instructions to them to forget all about the incident, Mung never seriously left their thoughts. Always there was that last, little, powerful nagging doubt about what had become of the Marshal. However, nobody said anything in public, nor did anyone confide in another privately: it became the great unspoken fear, and for this family of Crows fear was an excellent motivator.

As with everything that initially seemed bad, there was a good side to this for Ludley, for it served as a reminder to the gang what the price of failure could be, and indeed the quality of their work had noticeably improved since the day he had told them to forget Mung.

Ludley had noticed how more attentive the gang had become, and often, in quiet moments, discussed this with Boffe. "Do you think that despite everything Mung is still on their minds to an extent?" he asked his second in command.

"Hard to say because nobody mentions the man anymore," said the knifeman, "but it is doing us no harm if he is there in the background. We've raked in a small fortune lately."

"Yes," agreed Ludley, "and if Mung is embedded in their consciences then he is doing a better job for us now that he's dead than he ever did when he was amongst us." They laughed, then looked at each other in horror. "He is amongst us!" said Ludley.

"But in a good sort of way," said Boffe trying to lift their emotions, "There may be bad memories, but they're having a good effect."

"Let's hope so," said the leader. "Do you think Mung would come back and haunt us?"

"You mean as a ghost or spectre, I take it," said Boffe, "'cos it appears that he is haunting us in some kind of way."

"Yes, as something we can see or feel in a creepy sense. Right now that's not happening: he's just a bad memory," said Ludley still a little perturbed.

"Maybe Mung's as useless dead as he was alive, and doesn't know how to haunt properly!" Boffe laughed. "Can you imagine his bumbling attempts to find us?"

"I certainly can," said Ludley tersely, "and knowing the fool as I do, he will likely stumble upon the right method through no act of his own. Wait and see, he will appear in *The Waggoner's* before too long!"

"It's been quite a while since we dispatched him to the other side," said Boffe. "Nobody has found him, he's a lost soul wandering the dark realms unsure of which way to turn."

243

"That's exactly what bothers me," said the boss. "I'd be far happier knowing he was in the ground down the churchyard: it's not knowing anything that scares me rigid." He paused in thought for several minutes then went on. "You don't think he's still alive do you?"

"Now you're letting your imagination play stupid games with you," said the second in command. "He's dead. You were there. You saw me do him over. Three times I plunged my trusty blade into the man. We left him on the floor and the blood was pouring from him. Even if he had any strength left, which I doubt very much, he would have left a trail behind him, and he wouldn't have gotten very far considering the amount he was leaking."

"I know, Boffe," said Ludley. "I know that what you say is true. I've played the whole shebang over in my head a hundred times, and every time Mung comes out dead: there is no other conclusion. But where in Creation's name has his body gone? That's the bit I don't get, nor can I figure out how he could disappear so thoroughly."

"Perhaps the Devil reached up from down below and took him to help stoke the fires," said Boffe. "Ludley, you're becoming morose and in danger of becoming truly miserable. Turn your thoughts to our successes since Mung disappeared, and thank the man for paying back your long years of tolerance with his buffoonery."

"You're right, Boffe," said Ludley getting up out of his chair. "Let's get down to *The Waggoner's* for a well earned quaff of ale."

"Now you're talking sense again," said Boffe laughing.

Chapter 47: An Unexpected Visitor

Next morning, whilst they were eating breakfast and discussing their hopes for the day, they heard the rumble of a cart. Everet stopped talking, sat up straight, straining to take in the sound and where it might be coming from.

Diarmid, sensing what Everet was up to, said, "The road is not far from here. From the river it seems we are quite sheltered, but Myrta and I found the road to town not too far away on the other side of these bushes. Perhaps that's where the noise is coming from."

"No, Diarmid," said Everet, "it's closer than that and it's getting closer still."

"Yes," said Myrta. "Whatever or whoever it is, the noise is getting louder."

They all listened, and as they did so the noise stopped. The group looked at each other, in the hope that one of them had an explanation. There was a rustling of leaves which caused them to turn their heads in the direction of the sound. Diarmid was getting to his feet, ready to spring into whatever action was required, fight or flight.

A short, rather rotund middle aged man emerged from the greenery and was walking towards them: Diarmid considered his options and decided to stay and fight if necessary. "Good morning to yer," said the stranger, "I hope I'm not disturbing yer meal."

"Not at all," said Myrta. "Can we offer you a cup of tea?"

"That'd be lovely, ma'am," said the man continuing his approach. "My name's Darvel Snodgrass," he went on, offering his hand.

Everet stood up and shook the man's hand and introduced the group to him. "How can we help you?" he asked.

"Ah 'tis I who can perhaps help you," said Darvel sitting down and taking the cup of tea.

"How so?" asked Everet just a bit curtly. "How do you know we need help, and better still how did you know where to find us?"

Darvel explained that he was a boatbuilder with a yard at the other end of Trivias. He built simple, traditionally designed boats for the local merchants, and had seen the group sail by the previous evening. He said that he was particularly interested in the boat as it looked like a rowboat normally associated with sea going ships, yet had a mast and sail.

They told him of their adventure to date, culminating in how the rowboat had been modified in a bid to speed their journey back to Knympton. Darvel sipped his tea as the story unfolded, remaining quiet throughout. It wasn't until they started to describe what they had done to the boat that he perked his ears up.

"Amazing!" he said when Everet finally quietened. "So yers are heading for Knympton? Well, 'tis a long trip by river from here, and I fancy that yer little craft will suffer a trouble or two before long."

"What makes you say that, Darvel?" Everet said.

"Well, sur, the river takes more than a few meanders, mostly southward at first, then starts to wander its way north again," said Darvel. "It also widens and deepens considerably, and where it does, it does so suddenly, and yer will get some nasty eddies occurring."

"Right," said Diarmid, comprehending, "and of course we have no experience of the river so will not know where these points of danger are." Darvel nodded his agreement.

"So are you suggesting that you can guide us?" asked Myrta looking directly at the stranger. "We have no money to pay you."

"No, ma'am," said the boatbuilder. "What I want to suggest is that yers travel by road: it will be quicker and less fraught with danger."

"Sorry," said Everet, "but I don't see how abandoning our boat and going on foot is going to get us to Knympton faster than if we had used it. Besides it's still quite a way off, and the hike would leave us in a poor state of health."

"I'm not asking yer to do that, Everet," said Darvel. "I want to offer yer a trade. In exchange for yer's boat, in which I have already declared my interest, I will give yer a pony and cart. Yers can all travel on it, although yer will have to squeeze in a bit."

"Really?" asked Everet. "And do you have a map we can rely on?"

"Yes," said Darvel, "I do mean it, and yes, I can supply yer with a reliable map too."

They discussed various whys and wherefores then Everet said that the group needed time to discuss the offer, and suggested that Darvel return later that morning. The stranger agreed, offering to supply extra food as part of the bargain.

The group discussed the proposal which seemed too good to be true. Everet said that he was in favour of the deal, as he really had had enough of boats and the trouble that seemed all too closely associated with them. Myrta pointed out that there could well be more to the deal than met the eye: she could see dangers lurking. When questioned further she said that there may well be robbers and thieves lying in wait for them further down the road and, if set upon, then they would lose the pony and cart, not to mention their own lives.

"Yes," said Diarmid, "what if the food he is offering us is tainted or has been interfered with in some way? Maybe it's best just to throw everything in to the boat and get out of here before the man returns. He may even return with the scoundrels having seen how vulnerable we are."

The discussion took a very serious turn at these considerations, and the group was heading towards a decision that discretion may well be the better part of valour when Aonghus, who had been largely silent throughout, spoke. "May I say something?" he enquired.

"Of course," said his mother.

"It's all very strange to me, but as you are all aware, I seem to have this ability to converse with animals without actually saying something," said the boy.

"Yes, Aonghus," his mother agreed, "and it has been very helpful to us. Have you had another such instance?"

"Yes," said the youngster. "Whilst the man was telling us about the dangers of the river and suchlike I seemed to wander off into another place and saw myself standing in front of a pony and cart, no doubt similar to the one Mister Snodgrass was offering. Well, the pony spoke to me and was very friendly. He said he was going to take me home. I asked the pony what he meant, and he said that his master had become very excited when he saw us pass by in our boat. It seems animals can sense people's feelings, and the pony told me that Mr Snodgrass was particularly energised by it all."

"So, what are you saying, Aonghus?" asked his father.

"Well, we are all doubting Mr Snodgrass's intentions and getting ready to run away from possible trouble yet again. I don't think the pony is capable of telling lies, for it seems that Mr Snodgrass genuinely wants to discover what has been done to the boat, and to profit from it. The pony and cart he is offering is his genuine offer," said the boy.

"Aonghus has a point about running away," said Myrta. "It seems a bit ironic that in going back to face our demons in Knympton we are about to take flight from a similar set of demons here."

"You are right," said Everet. "We should also remember Anastasie's words about having trust in the greater nature of things. Shall we take a vote on our next course of action?"

Chapter 48: Folgate and the Priest

It was mid afternoon as Folgate entered the Square of the Holy Rood, making for the Church of the Apostles. It was quite breezy, so he pulled his tunic closer to his body to keep out the wind which had developed an edge during the course of the day. He pushed open the heavy door of the church and stepped inside into the vestibule.

From here he could see that the church was largely empty, with only one or two townsfolk inside: the church rarely closed its doors completely and was somewhere to go for comfort, consoling, confession or shelter from the weather. Folgate made his way to the far side of the congregational area, following the Stations of the Cross, until he reached the confessional box.

Looking around to see who may be watching, and satisfied that all heads were bowed, he opened the door, stepped in, and sat down. Composing himself he said, *"In the name of the Father and of the Son and of the Holy Ghost. Amen."*

"Bless you, my son," said the priest before reading a short passage of scripture.

"Padre," said Folgate, "I have not come to confess, but rather to ask your opinion on a matter that has been related to me, and of which I have no comprehension."

"I am intrigued, my son, please do continue," said the priest.

"Padre, is there somewhere even more private than the confessional where we can discuss this?" said the Marshal. "It's rather a delicate matter and involves the Marshals."

"Now I am truly intrigued," said the priest. "Follow me to the Sacristry."

In the Sacristry Folgate felt more at ease, and began to tell the priest the tale told to him by Brina and Sefira regarding Mung's angelic encounter: the priest listened in amazed silence as Folgate spoke. "That's an astounding tale, my son," said the priest. "Now, what is it you do not understand?"

"To be blunt about it, Padre," said Folgate, "my senses tell me that such a thing is not possible. Yet I have no reason to doubt the veracity of those who related it to me. Are we all being hoodwinked, do you think?"

"Tell me, my son," said the cleric, "what does your faith tell you?"

"Ah!" said the policeman. "My faith, such as it is, tells me that in God's world everything is possible."

"So where's your problem?" asked the pastor.

"If I relied on my faith, Padre," said Folgate, "I would believe every thief and ne'er do well I have to interview, and the safety of the community would be at high risk. I have to deal in real facts."

"I see," said the priest. "You now have a crisis of conscience. You'd like to believe the story as related to you, but something within you is rejecting this course of action. Let me tell you a little about Angels, and hopefully you can come to a decision."

The padre explained that Angels are not only messengers, but are also part of our consciousness, representing realms beyond thoughts and ideas. The human mind needs form, so the Light of Spirit takes on the physical form of an angel, to encourage direct communion with God. We create a vision that enables the Angels to appear in a form that we can accept.

The priest went on to explain that Angels take many forms, and get involved in many different types of activities, from nature angels to personal guardian angels. By way of further explanation he said that a nature angel is a protector of a particular area of the world such as a mountain. Archangels such as Michael with his sword of truth, serve as guardians for the entire world. A guardian angel, the priest told Folgate, is your personal protector who looks after you always. Your guardian is a very special kind of angel that is with you from the moment you are born to help you move towards the light.

"The Holy Scriptures," said the cleric, "tell us that Man was created a little lower than the Angels. Thus our faith states that these Divine Beings were produced to protect us when we are in spiritual or mortal danger.

"Remember that Angels are always present, but remember too that they only manifest themselves to us when God so wills it. The more we live our lives according to God's Word, in love and joy, in light and peace, and in service to others, the closer our angels will be to us, and the more we will sense their existence. I hope that helps you, my son."

"Indeed, Padre," said Folgate. "From what you have said I can see that such a scenario as is under discussion can truly have existed as described. But why would Angels intervene in such a fashion?"

"Captain," said the priest, "each and every one of us has a purpose to fulfil in this life. When we complete it we can give up our flesh and bones, enabling us to return to God knowing we have achieved our goal: then we can live our everlasting life in His glory. Sometimes there are occasions during the course of life down here in this earthly world when that purpose would not be filled by dying too soon, if you take my meaning: so the Angels, acting under God's Will, step in, as they have done with your colleague, to give him the chance to succeed in his mission."

"Now it's my turn to be intrigued," said Folgate.

"Have you seen your colleague since he was, er, rescued?" asked the Father.

"Not yet, but that time will come soon," said the Marshal.

"Expect to see a different man, Captain," said the priest. Folgate gave him a puzzled look as if to say he did not understand the priest's words. "Same physical body, Captain, but maybe a slightly different appearance of the features: however, that's not what I mean. Your colleague, having undergone this wonderful Angelic experience will be much changed on the inside for his soul will have been awakened. Now, if you will pardon and excuse me, I must return to the confessional."

"Of course, Padre," said Folgate, rising from chair. "Thank you for your time and your wisdom. I assume that the confidentiality of the confessional extends to the Sacristry?"

"Of course it does, Captain," the priest replied. "Your words are safe with me." Then, facing the Marshal he made the sign of the cross and said, *"May the peace of God, which passeth all understanding, keep your heart and mind in the knowledge and love of God, and of His Son, Jesus Christ our Lord. And the blessing of God Almighty, the Father, the Son, and the Holy Spirit be with you, and remain with you always. Amen."*

"Amen," said Folgate.

Chapter 49: Heading for Home

Darvel Snodgrass returned as requested to hear the outcome of the Cranstouns' deliberations: so confident that they would accept his offer, he came totally prepared with the necessary food, water and maps that he had agreed to provide. The deal was duly struck with the pony, cart and goods exchanged for the modified rowboat.

The Cranstouns transferred their goods from the boat to the cart and got ready to continue their journey. "I noticed that you were using the tarpaulin as a sail," said Snodgrass, "and I am interested to see how you have cut the sail, which I assume is part and parcel of the boat, so I have taken the precaution of also including a new tarpaulin in the goods I am exchanging. I hope you will agree to that."

Everet readily agreed, saying that he had not thought about that aspect of it, but now that a replacement tarpaulin had been provided the deal was certainly to be struck, and he and Snodgrass shook hands to complete the contract.

The group set off and, following the advice given by Darvel Snodgrass, they made good headway along the route, encouraged to see others travelling in both directions: so far so good. Darvel had indicated that it ought to take them no more than four more days travel to reach Knympton. Quite what they were going to do when they got there, they weren't sure.

It was as Snodgrass had indicated – a tight squeeze for all of them aboard the cart: even with the few possessions they had, space to spread out was at a premium. However, there was no good in complaining, as most of the work was being carried out by the pony in any case.

The pony wasn't complaining either as Aonghus was able to confirm. The poor thing was getting on in life, and had suffered more than its share of hard times along the way. It was only when he was bought by Snodgrass that life eased up a little, the boatbuilder having been the kindest master he had had by some way. Aonghus reassured the pony, whose name was Swale, that he would receive nothing but kindness from the group, and that his wishes would be carried out.

Fascinated with his latent talent, Aonghus passed the days in conversation with Swale who was a Hill Pony, originally from the southern regions of Valkanda, where the tin mining industry had flourished from very early times, and still goes on, albeit in a diminished function.

The tin mining industry was at the mercy of the geographical and environmental conditions of the area. The seams of lead were always situated on the high moors; the washing places had to be near a stream; the smelting houses were always on a hill to catch the wind and needed to be near a wood for fuel. The blocks of tin produced were transported over the moors to the ports on the South Coast and, if wood had run out, coal was taken back. The ore, fuel and tin were carried by strong, active pack ponies, working in gangs of 6 to 10, in the charge of one mounted man.

The Hill Pony was bred for the fast pack work and replacements were reared near the tin mines. The largest, strongest and most active ponies were chosen for pack work and were well fed to ensure fitness and speed. The Hill ponies became renowned for their great strength, iron constitution, endurance and the ability to get over rough country fast, and they travelled up to a hundred miles a week over some of the most difficult terrain in Valkanda.

These abilities were not lost on farmers, who found in them all that was required to work the small farms as the seasons came round. They could pull up to a ton in a cart; were sturdy shepherds' ponies, capable of covering great distances on the fells, and were able to carry burdens of hay up to 12 stones: often they also had to carry a rider and, when necessary, do so in deep snow.

This is what had happened to Swale: having worked hard for years in the mining industry he was sold to a passing merchant who mistreated him greatly before trading him for a crop of apples and other fruits to a hill farmer in the east. Swale's days on the farm were not particularly happy either, and it was when the farmer had come to Trivias to sell goods at the market that Darvel Snodgrass, recognising the poor animal's plight had paid more than a generous price to the farmer for him.

Of course, Aonghus related these stories to the rest of the group and they realised that Darvel had truly offered them a good price for their boat: he was certainly not the ogre they had initially thought him to be. Indeed, their initial judgment was what they most often talked about at rest times, and how they had got it so wrong. "If it hadn't been for your intervention, Aonghus," said Myrta, "who knows what sort of difficulties we might have found ourselves in by now."

"Yes," said Everet. "Although the river seemed busy, I am sure there are threats from some boat owners, never mind the dangers from the water itself. Also, Mister Snodgrass's map has been perfectly accurate thus far and his advice without fault. Truly is he a kind and generous man."

"Indeed," said Myrta, "and we must thank Aonghus for putting us to rights. It's easy to jump to the wrong conclusion when all the facts are not known. Added to that we let our fear direct us instead of trusting, as Anastasie and the others suggested we do."

"That small victory over fear and prejudice will help us to win another time," said Everet. "Let us take confidence from it, and act from within ourselves next time, for we may not have the benefit of an animal's wisdom."

"Yes," said Aonghus, "it was really Swale who provided the necessary information that enabled us to see where we had gone wrong in our thinking." Lifting his cup he said, "To Swale!"

"To Swale!" the others repeated, copying the gesture.

"Let's take a look at our map and determine how far we are from Knympton," said Everet, as he unfolded the parchment and spread it out.

The group studied the document for a while and then Diarmid, pointing to a location, said, "I think we are here, which is a little over halfway: maybe we can reach our destination in another two days."

"I can't argue with your assessment of where we are, Diarmid," said Everet, "nor with your estimation of how long it will take us to complete the journey."

"If that's the case," said Myrta, "then I would be concerned about arriving at Knympton at the day's end. The part of town we will encounter first is not a nice place to be once darkness comes down."

"Good point," said Everet. "So do we try to speed up and get there sooner, or do we travel at a more leisurely pace so as to try to arrive early in the day?"

"We could keep going as we are, but branch off here," said Diarmid pointing to a small pathway. "That would take us towards Berystede Wood where we could spend the night, and we could enter Knympton first thing in the morning."

"All of your points are possibilities," said Myrta. "Let us keep going as we are, and see what each day brings. We can make any necessary adjustments according to our progress."

"Yes," agreed Everet. "Let's continue at a pace that suits us: we can make adjustments as we travel on. After all, who knows what may be round the next corner?"

Chapter 50: More Arrangements

Two days after Folgate had consulted with Padre Pietro, Sefira Mung came into his office to tell him that arrangements had been made for him to see her husband. He was somewhat surprised to learn that he was to be met at the Church of the Apostles. This was surely a mistake, he thought, but Sefira was insistent: he was to be at the bench close to the campanile as the angelus bell struck at noon.

Folgate's thoughts took off inside his head. Was Mung receiving sanctuary and caring from Padre Pietro? Indeed the Padre had indicated that Mung's story was entirely possible, whilst also saying that Mung was a much changed man. What did the Padre know?

But then again, this Brina woman was involved in some mysterious way that he couldn't fathom out, and that bothered Folgate. This was certainly the more likely of the scenarios running rampant in the Marshal's mind. The Church was far too far from Cranstoun's shop for Mung to have reached it without leaving some sort of trail from his wounds, which, according to Sefira Mung, were deep stab wounds: the bloodstain on the floor of the Cranstoun workshop testified to that.

Mung must have been helped by Brina and person or persons unknown: that was certain as well. Mung was no lightweight and Brina could not have lifted him unaided. How Folgate hated this case: there were far too many unknowns and mysterious aspects to consider. Perhaps, he told himself, all will be revealed in due course.

The arrangements had been made by Brina, and didn't take Folgate's immediate plans into consideration, so he had had to rearrange the duty roster in order to make himself available. In some respects he understood that it was Mung's needs that were being primarily serviced, although there was much to be gained for the Marshals as well.

Folgate felt strangely conspicuous in his civilian clothes as he sat on the bench awaiting whoever was to conduct him to the meeting with Mung. Folgate was a man of uniform, and each day he wore it with great pride and respect: being out of uniform made him feel somewhat insecure. However, this is what had been specified and he had no doubts that his guide would make no contact had he come dressed as a Marshal.

The Captain had arrived early and had wandered round the Square of the Holy Rood several times, this way and that. He tried to mingle with the small crowds of people who came and went, always checking to see if he was being watched. His policeman's mind was very active, and he made several mental notes of items he deemed worthy of further investigation once this visit was over, thus permitting him to resume practical duty.

As the hands of the clock headed towards noon Folgate sat down on the bench and waited. He was the sole occupant and spread his himself comfortably on it: he didn't want anyone else to feel welcome to share it with him. As he turned to watch the faithful enter the church, it came to his mind that the Angelus was an old devotion whose history was nigh impossible to trace, but which was at least 700 years old. The Angelus originated with the monastic custom of reciting three Ave Marias during the evening bell. Now the Angelus was rung three times in the day, at 6am, noon and 6pm. It was said that it commemorated the resurrection of Christ in the morning, his suffering at noon and the annunciation in the evening.

Like Sefira before him, Folgate wandered in his mind inside the Church and could see Padre Pietro addressing the congregation ...

"The angel of the Lord announced unto Mary," said Pietro.

"And she conceived by the Holy Spirit," said the congregation, as one.

"Hail Mary, full of grace, the Lord is with you. Blessed are you among women, and blessed is the fruit of your womb, Jesus.

Holy Mary, Mother of God, pray for us sinners, now and at the hour of our death. Amen," everyone intoned together.

"Behold the handmaid of the Lord," said the priest.

"Be it unto me according to your Word," said the faithful, after which the second Hail Mary was intoned.

"And the Word was made flesh," Pietro declared.

"And dwelt among us," confirmed the worshippers, who then recited the third Hail Mary.

"Pray for us, O Holy Mother of God," pleaded the priest.

"That we may be made worthy of the promises of Christ," said the throng.

The Padre completed the devotion by praying, *"We implore you, O Lord our God, let your grace pour into our hearts, that as we have known the incarnation of your only begotten Son Jesus Christ by the message of an angel, so by His cross and passion we may be brought to the glory of His resurrection; through the same Christ our Lord. Amen."*

It was Sefira Mung's voice that aroused him from his daydream: "Watch where I go, Captain," she said, "then follow my footsteps, but do not get too close." The woman had slowed down to say this as she passed, but without stopping or looking at him.

Folgate tried to snap out of his reverie, but the image lingered on. In his usual fashion he tried to do several things at once, but only succeeded in slowing down his progress. By the time he came to full attention Sefira Mung had almost disappeared from his view.

Scrambling up from the bench, he then dithered before getting his feet to follow his brain impulses, and set off to follow the woman.

*****

The noon time appointment had been set in order to give Brina ample time to convey Mung to the meeting place. She did not want the Marshal to find out where she lived, knowing full well that her life would be under intense scrutiny thereafter if he ever found out.

She had asked her group of acolytes for ideas of a suitable location for the encounter, and the group had discussed the matter thoroughly before suggesting the Sanctuary of St Mary of the Angels, the home of some Brothers and Sisters who had become disaffected with the administration of the Church, and the over-elaborateness of its rituals.

What they had set up was a simplified, reformed liturgy, with a greater emphasis on service and pastoral care. Gone, too, were the myriad icons and statues, replaced by an austere, but simple, whitewashed interior.

The Sanctuary was a modest rectangular shaped building with a vaulted ceiling and simple decoration: there were plain seats instead of pews and kneeling posts. The altar was a table covered with a white cloth on which was embroidered the symbol of a fish.

On the wall behind the altar table hung a large unadorned cross of finest oak, and in front, slightly to one side, but yet very prominent was the oak pulpit, exquisitely carved with stylised roses. On either side of the central aisle the chairs were laid out in ten rows of five.

The Brothers and Sisters of the Sanctuary had been most willing to help out when Brina consulted them and told them of her need and the reasons why. There was no doubt in Brina's mind that the Brothers and Sisters could be relied upon to the maintain confidentiality, and Brina could sense that these people were sympathetic to her mission.

Ardvon had once again been asked to help transport Mung, this time from Brina's cottage to the Sanctuary. He had called in a few favours and now had the use of a horse and covered cart. However, it was not possible to get the vehicle all the way to Brina's and further assistance was required from Bruno to help Mung in the short walk from the cottage to the cart.

Mung was well wrapped up, not only to keep his identity close, but also to protect his wounds. Ardvon tried his very best to steer a route that was as smooth and even as possible, but even so, there were a few winces from the Marshal at the slightest jolt.

After what seemed an age, the cart came to a halt: Brina stuck her head out of the cover, and, satisfied that all was well, announced to Yorlan that they had arrived. Gently, Brina and Bruno helped Mung down from the cart and took him inside: Ardvon drove off to wait somewhere less conspicuous whilst the meeting took place.

The sun was out as they entered the Sanctuary and the effect of its light streaming in through the stained glass windows was stunningly beautiful.

Mung was helped up the central aisle, round past the pulpit and out through the door that led to the Vestry. As Mung sat down he let out a huge sigh of relief.

*****

Folgate initially had trouble keeping sight of Sefira as she walked into alleyways and back out onto the main thoroughfare. Now he was up with the pace, he could almost sense when the woman was going to sidetrack, so was able to devote more thinking time to wondering where she was leading him.

Almost on cue Sefira cut off from the main route into yet another alleyway. However, as Folgate rounded the corner to follow her, he found Sefira standing waiting for him: in his haste he almost knocked her flying.

"I do beg your pardon, Mistress Mung," said Folgate repositioning himself.

"Apology accepted," said Sefira rather tetchily. "Where we are going is just round the corner. We can walk the last few steps together."

Folgate racked his brain trying to visualise a map of this part of town in an effort to work out where Sefira was taking him. Sadly he couldn't find one although he made a mental note to walk the manor more often and familiarise himself to a greater extent with the back streets of his area.

They turned the corner and walked on for thirty or forty yards before coming to a halt outside the gates of the Sanctuary of St Mary of the Angels. "Here we are," said Sefira. "Let's go inside."

They turned the handle on the arched oak door, pushed it open then stepped into the church vestibule, closing the door behind them. Folgate and Sefira walked down the aisle and sat down in the front row: there were two others in the church, each bowed in prayer or contemplation. Neither had looked up when the strangers walked in. "We have to sit here and wait to be summoned," Sefira whispered. "I don't think we will have to wait too long."

"I hope not," said the policeman.

Folgate looked round this plainly adorned church: it was not at all like the Church of the Apostles, which seemed a veritable art gallery in comparison.

In the Vestry Brina was somewhat fussing over Mung, but she wanted to ensure that he was fit enough to keep the appointment with Folgate: the journey from her cottage to the church had been relatively smooth, but that notwithstanding, she had to take other factors into account. Sensing that he was indeed ready, she said, "Are you ready for this, Yorlan?"

"Yes," he said, "I need to do this to complete my healing. I have told myself that the outcome is unimportant as to my fate, but the process will bring me enormous benefit in more important ways."

Chapter 51: Sins and Transgressions

The wait seemed inordinate to Folgate as he began to fidget and move about on his chair. Sefira did her best to calm him down and pointed out that the less he moved around, the less attention he would draw to them. Just when he thought he could bear no more of the silent torture, the door beside the pulpit opened and a gentleman, soberly dressed, wearing what looked like an academic cloak appeared, carrying what Folgate assumed was a large Bible.

The man gracefully bowed as he made his entrance, and with equal poise climbed the half dozen steps into the pulpit where he placed the Bible on the lectern, opening it at a predetermined page. He then sat down and said a silent prayer. His duty over, the man stepped back down out of the pulpit and approached Folgate and Sefira.

"Sir, Madam," he whispered low, "please come with me."

He led them through the door, which he closed behind them and led them to the Vestry. He knocked on the door and, turning to return to the church, left them to await an answer.

Folgate was not surprised when Brina opened the door. "Good day to you, Mistress Brina," he said. "You sure know how to weave a web of intrigue."

"Thank you, Captain," said the Shaman, taking the remark as a compliment. "Please, come in."

Folgate and Sefira went in to the Vestry, and Brina closed the door behind them. "We are quite safe here. We are away from all prying eyes, and anything said will not pass beyond these four walls. Please," she said to the Captain, "be as gentle as you can, Yorlan is still very much recovering and is still very fragile."

"Yes, yes," he replied, "I understand. It's a very traumatic occasion for everyone, I guess." Then he approached Mung who was struggling to stand up to meet his Captain. "Yorlan, remain seated, there is no need for formality at this point," he said. "Please, I want you to remain as relaxed and as comfortable as you can."

"Thank you, Captain," said the Constable. "I never ever thought I'd say this, but it is good to see you."

The Captain said that he was relieved that Mung was still alive and could perhaps, in time, shed light on everything that had happened. The main thing for Mung, the Captain said, was for him to regain full health.

Mung, with Brina's help tried to explain that this meeting was part of that very process. "I sold my soul for silver," said Mung, "and I thought I was being a clever man. All the good intentions I had when I joined the force vanished into thin air the day I got involved with Ludley and his gang."

Mung went on to confess as many of his misdeeds as he could remember, and it was such a shocking revelation that, even on hearing some of them for the second time, Sefira Mung gasped in astonishment and disbelief on several occasions. Again tears poured from Mung's eyes as he told the grisly history of his damaged career as an upholder of the Law.

Folgate kept pretty quiet, letting Mung unload his guilt and grief, although sometimes he asked Mung for clarification of salient points in the account. The Captain's face twisted this way and that as the awfulness of Mung's story unfolded: sometimes there would be a knowing look as Mung's account gave insight into an unresolved or mystifying event.

Brina was monitoring the situation closely, and was looking for any tell tale signs of fatigue, stress, anger or anything else untoward. The more Mung confessed the more his self esteem seemed to rise, and this cheered her, but she was ready to step in and bring proceedings to a halt should that be required.

Folgate winced and frowned as Mung told his story, and although he sat quietly absorbing it, Brina could sense his rising anger and outrage. However, the Captain seemed to be in control of his emotions, and Brina let the retelling continue for a little longer.

Mung took sips of water as he related his tale of sorrow and underhand dealings, but this wasn't enough to prevent his emotions spilling out as he unloaded his guilt. He was beginning to reach the state where enough was enough, and Brina was ready to bring proceedings to a halt when Mung said, "And I think that's about everything."

"Well done, Yorlan," said Brina. "How do you feel?"

"Right now," he said, "exhausted, but relieved that the Captain has heard my tale. Now I await his response." Everyone turned to Folgate in anticipation.

Folgate cleared his throat, and looked a little uncomfortable. "Mung," he said, "I just do not know how to react. My emotions are all over the place, and I want to do so many things that I cannot bring myself to do one of them. Each thing I want to do is telling me it must be done first."

"Captain," said Brina, "that is quite understandable. You certainly seem calm enough on the outside, which is visible to us all. What we cannot see is what is happening inside to you, but some of us may have an idea as we have experienced similar feelings after hearing this almost unbelievable story. Perhaps you can give us an inkling of where your thoughts are taking you right now."

"My training and experience enable me to appear calm and in control," said Folgate, "but, believe me, my insides are all over the place like leaves in a storm. I am experiencing just about everything that is possible to feel. Certainly there is anger and disbelief that one of my constables has betrayed his oath of loyalty to such an extent, and my first instinct, Mung, is to clap you in irons and march you down to the station house."

Mung looked shocked and afraid: Sefira's mouth fell open wide and she raised her hands to her face to cover her horror.

"However," the Captain went on, "at this precise moment that would not be beneficial to you as you are plainly not fit enough to walk very far, and I plainly cannot carry you unaided. Then again, you still require ministrations on a daily basis, and that we cannot provide in the cells."

Relief overtook the Mungs on hearing this, but Folgate had not ruled out the idea completely.

"I am also conscious that what you have told me will help us to clear up many unsolved incidents, and may help us to prevent future crimes as well. Again, I need you in a healthy state to bear witness against those you have named in your treatise. I take it you are willing to aid the prosecution of these felons?"

"Most certainly, Captain," said Mung, "even if it means that I am implicated by association. I have to face the consequences of my actions, no matter how serious the outcome may be. To bear testimony against these people will complete my moral and spiritual healing. I have learned much whilst recovering from my wounds, and I am most indebted to Brina for everything she has done in saving me from a certain death, and offering me a new life."

"Oh Yorlan, you make me sound like the Messiah!" said the Shaman with a laugh.

"Perhaps not a Messiah," said Mung, "but certainly a Saviour," said her patient.

"Yes," agreed Folgate, "you have certainly carried out much good work Brina, no matter how far fetched and mystical the way it all happened. The whole community is going to benefit from your unassuming act of compassion. I need to leave here, and return to the station house where I have much to do in reviewing what I have learned here today against what is recorded in our paperwork. Also, I need to give a lot of thought to how I explain Mung's part in all this without my ever suspecting what was going on. I will want to speak to Mung again, perhaps more than once: how can we arrange this without raising any suspicion from anyone who may still be watching?"

"Of course," said Brina, "but only if Yorlan is up for it. His health, though vastly improved, still has a way to go. I know he is keen to do everything he can to try to right the wrongs he has committed, but his health comes first and foremost. If you need to interview him again then so be it, and I know it's not beyond your capabilities to find a way of making your desire known. When that happens we will look at the circumstances and act accordingly."

"Agreed," said Folgate getting out of his chair. He walked over to Mung and offered him his hand, which the constable accepted. "Mung, I cannot pretend to be anything other than outraged at this point in time by your declaration of guilt, but I am hoping that confession is good for the soul as the priest is wont to remind me. I will however pray that your health continues to improve, and I will also ask for guidance in resolving these matters in the best interests of all concerned."

"Bless you, Captain," said Sefira. "I detect that behind your hard exterior there lies a man with compassion and a strong moral fibre, a man who wants the best outcome whilst still upholding the Law."

"Hrrmpf," said Folgate a little embarrassed. "I will bid you all good day." On leaving the Vestry he returned along the passageway to the church, stopping at the door to listen in case there was a service being held, but he could hear no sound. Carefully, he opened the door and made his way down the central aisle towards the exit. However, something made him stop, and he sat down in one of the seats in the back row. Bowing his head, he offered up a prayer and remained in the quiet for some minutes before finally departing.

After Folgate had gone Brina suggested that Mung took some time in the Vestry to contemplate what had just happened, and to allow some of the weariness to drain from his body. Sefira bade him farewell in her new, more intimate fashion, and promised that she would be back to see him "soon".

Brina joined Mung in the silence and gave her thanks to the Beings of Light who had surrounded them all with love, light and protection. Having overseen Mung's transference to Ardvon's cart she thanked the Brothers and Sisters at the Sanctuary for their cooperation, hospitality and understanding. Then, with Archangel Michael's protective cloak thrown around her, and knowing that he walked beside her, she made her way back to her cottage.

Chapter 52: Good Progress

The Cranstouns journeyed according to the plan and map provided by Darvel Snodgrass, stopping for frequent rests at points close to where their benefactor had suggested they would find it welcoming and safe.

Sometimes other travellers would join them along the route and make pleasant small talk. Mostly they were traders wandering from place to place selling to the next location what they had purchased in the previous. This nomadic lifestyle took the traders from one end of Valkanda to the other and back again in a time honoured fashion.

Some of the traders even went beyond Valkanda's eastern boundary into virtually unknown lands, bringing back with them many luxury items which fetched good prices from the rich landowners. This was how the bigger towns of Valkanda had grown: as trade developed so the villages where markets were held grew in size, wealth and power. The growth in wealth and riches led to increased prosperity for the merchants, and also for the producers in the surrounding area, especially the farmers. Each town seemed to specialise in a particular commodity which was purchased by the incoming traveller and taken on to their next port of call.

The list of goods was almost inexhaustible: wool from the Crellaten Islands, furs from the Qaf Mountains, wood from the vast forests that grew south of Clyndor, salt and wine from Sala, horses and ponies from the foothills of the Khumbila Mountains, cloth and tapestries from Pender, glass from the many factories of Billington, and silks and spices from the lands beyond Valkanda.

However, there was a dark side to the merchants' lives. The trade that made them rich also brought wealth to the rulers and owners of the land in which the markets took place. Many of the rulers demanded a fee for allowing the nomads to trade on their land and towns, and when trade continued to grow, the rulers saw their chance to increase their revenue even further, and so a tax was introduced on all traded goods.

Gangs of thieves and robbers preyed on the travellers because of the amount of money being engendered. Amongst the merchants, too, there was great rivalry, and some of the entourages were more like private armies as the merchants sought to protect themselves by hiring mercenaries. Incidents were frequent, although many of the townsfolk never got to hear about them, while, steadily, the gangs, such as Ludley's, began to creep evermore into the towns where the pickings were deemed easier.

Another downside to the rise of the trading lifestyle was that many of the local shopkeepers were often run out of business because they could not compete with the selection of goods and cheaper prices offered by the travelling merchants. There were also those towns that became too dependent on the travellers and, over time, fell into ruin because of the wanderers. As the villages grew into towns, overcrowding became a problem, allowing disease to spread easily and quickly, killing thousands instead of the usual hundred or so in the smaller places.

The Cranstouns were fascinated by the tales the travellers told, but realised that this roving lifestyle was not really one they were likely to pursue. Although, as they reflected on the day's events each evening, they could see that their instinct to run from trouble was, in effect, a form of this travelling livelihood, even if it was being played on a vastly slower timescale.

The group had fast arrived at the conclusion that the pursuit of money and material goods was reducing society to an undignified level. Everyone's focus was on what they could gain without thought for anyone else's feelings or situation.

"It's a strange thing," said Myrta, "but people everywhere we have been seem to be out for their own gain. They want huge amounts of money and don't care much how they come by it."

"Yes," agreed Everet, "and they pile up the most awful collection of useless goods and chattels as if they were prize trophies for outstanding achievement. Makes you wonder what they think they will do with it all."

"Especially when something new comes to market," said Myrta.

"Not only that my dear," said her husband, "but it all gets left behind when they die, and those who survive most often fight amongst themselves to get their grubby little hands on the spoils!"

"So what should we do with the wealth that is obviously created?" asked Aonghus, intrigued.

"An interesting question, Aonghus," said his father who went on to explain that the wealth could be shared by all in the community, and that way more people would benefit. "Instead of having a few very rich people who own all the land and wield all the power," said Everet, plainly, "we would have facilities open to everyone, giving everyone an equal chance in life. Why, we might even have a ruling council that is elected annually by all residents and they could then make the big decisions so that the outcome would benefit the most people."

"But wouldn't that encourage people to be lazy, knowing that wealth is shared by everyone?" said the boy.

"Ah," said Everet, "following that line of enquiry is going to get you confused. There is a difference between the use of money and the love of money. Let me explain."

Everet tried his best to set out his description in simple words so that the boy, and the others too, would better understand. He told them that there had to be a basic education which brought forth what he called a work ethic. This work ethic, he told them, was based on the idea that the necessity for hard work is a promoter of a person's calling and worldly success, as well as being a sign of personal salvation. Everet stressed that worldly work was a duty which benefits both the individual and society as a whole, and therefore to work diligently was a sign of grace. "Do you understand, Aonghus?" he asked.

"I think so," said the boy. "You are saying that all work is a fine occupation, and that we should do it with a responsible attitude."

"Yes, Aonghus," said Myrta, "responsibility and commitment, those are the key words. Can you see what your father was getting at when he said not to confuse this with a love of money?" Aonghus' look told Myrta that he hadn't quite grasped the point, so she explained that a love of money led to greed and the desire to gain more, and this is what they were witnessing.

"Exactly so," said Everet. "What we must aim to do in this life is to build up a store of spiritual wealth, not to assemble a hoard of worldly treasure for it is but nothing, and only attracts thieves and robbers."

There was a long silence as Everet's words sunk in, sowing seeds of thoughts for the group. Each retreated into their own world to ponder the powerful lesson that Everet and Myrta had given. It was true that if everyone focussed on the worldly goods then chaos could be the only answer. Humans were creatures who preferred, in the main, to be congregated together: in families, in groups of friends, in towns and villages. Was it not right that they should share all things with all members?

"I think we should head for bed," said Everet. "We have travelled far these last few days, and I do believe that one more night after this on the road will be our last before we reach our destination. Who knows what waits for us there, but we will face it with courage and fortitude knowing that what we do is the right action."

Chapter 53: Folgate Wrestles with the Facts

Back at the Marshals' Station Folgate gave strict instructions to Trine that he was not to be disturbed by anything unless it was a matter of life or death. The Captain explained that he had very hard brain work to get on with, and needed no interruptions. "I am sure that you will be able to deflect anyone asking for me with your usual charm and diplomacy, Trine" he said, closing the outer office door behind him. It was a tone of voice that Trine recognised as the sound of absolute authority.

Once inside his own office Folgate removed his outer coat and hat which he hung on the coat stand in the corner then flopped down into his chair. He unlocked the drawer containing the Mung file and removed the paperwork, placing it on the desk in front of him.

Folgate looked at the folder for some minutes then sat back in his seat. He clasped his hands, closed his eyes and said a silent prayer, asking for help to resolve what was, to the Captain, one unholy mess. As he sat there in quiet contemplation a feeling of calmness pervaded his body to which he submitted more meekly than he would have anticipated.

The office seemed lighter and more airy than usual, and he had a feeling that he was being watched by unseen eyes from within the room. The Captain felt quite at ease and at peace with the world as he opened his eyes and sat forward, reaching out to open the folder, trying once again to fit the facts as recorded with what Mung himself had told him. The inner anger that the Captain had felt on hearing Mung's confession seemed to have evaporated in some strange way, and Folgate turned over leaf upon leaf of reports, measuring them against the new knowledge that he had obtained.

As time slipped by Folgate slowly began to see that Mung's confession sufficiently filled in the hugely gaping holes in the Marshals' scant information, allowing a bigger picture of the whole series of incidents to begin to form in his mind. However, there were still areas that needed further clarification: Sefira Mung would have to be contacted in order to arrange a further meeting with Yorlan. Discretion would be of the utmost importance, for the Captain had decided that none of this new information would be released to anyone: Mung had breached the confidence of the force, there could well be others, the very thought of which sent a very cold shudder down Folgate's spine.

The Captain sat at his desk in deep thought, trying to work out a way he could contact Mung's wife without alerting anyone else to the fact. Again he sat back in his chair and closed his eyes, hands gently clasped on his midriff. He tried to let his mind go blank, but found a myriad of thoughts coming and going. His brain was being pulled in a great many directions, and the more he tried to dismiss the questions that formed in his head, the more the questions multiplied.

Why had the Cranstouns not come again to the Marshals to ask for protection from Ludley? Had they really travelled on *The Venturer*? Where were they now? How many more undetected crimes had the crowd of Ludley's committed? Where did they gather? How did they get their information apart from that which Mung supplied? Where did they keep their ill gotten gains?

The questions were exploding in his head, but in amongst all them one thing became clear and could be eliminated from his mind – Padre Pietro knew nothing about Mung, his situation or his whereabouts. In the instant that Padre Pietro came into his mind Folgate realised that the priest could play a role in contacting Sefira. He snapped out of his repose, got out of his chair, marched over to the coat stand, grabbed his coat and hat, and proceeded out of the office as he struggled to get the garment on.

In the outer office Folgate told Trine that he now had urgent business elsewhere and doubted if he would return that day, so Trine would be held responsible for the Station until the change of shift at evening. That said, he rushed out of the door and into the hustle and bustle of the late afternoon.

Folgate strode purposefully down the main roads, taking the most direct route to the Square of the Holy Rood, hoping that Padre Pietro was going to be available for immediate consultation. However, the priest was not present at the church, and Folgate had to revise his plans. Still, this would give him more time to further reflect on what he now knew.

Having come this far, though, Folgate sought out the little Chapel of the Holy Mother within the Church. He stepped into it, lit a candle which he placed on the rack beside a few others already burning brightly, then sat down and bowed his head in prayer.

"Most Holy Mother," said Folgate ever so quietly, *"you were chosen to be the Mother of the Eternal Word made flesh. You are the advocate of sinners and I who am your most unworthy servant have recourse to you. I ask that you graciously be my guide and counsellor in this time of great trial and torture for me. Help me, I plead, to make contact with those who can help me out of this troubled situation."*

Folgate sat in his pew, eyes closed, head bowed, hands clasped before him, silently listening for any answer that might come his way. Time passed: the Captain had no idea how long he had been in the Chapel, but it had been long enough for his body to start to feel cold. This was what aroused him from his devotions: that and a need to move his body which was beginning to stiffen and go numb through lack of movement.

He made his way out of the Chapel and was heading for the Church doors when a voice called out, "Captain Folgate!" Folgate turned to find that he was looking at Sefira Mung.

Chapter 54: Knympton not so far away

The next day the Cranstouns made steady progress towards Knympton. They didn't want to go too fast for that would mean arriving at the town sometime in the early hours of the morning when there was still darkness, and they didn't want to encounter that scenario. There would be few Marshals patrolling, and Knympton could be a fearsome place if you turned up in the wrong location at the wrong time: it was fearsome enough even in the nicer parts.

Nobody said very much other than short snippets of small chat. Everyone was focussed on their own thoughts and feelings about going back to the source of their current misfortunes.

Diarmid's thoughts went back to that awful storm, and the breakup of *The Venturer*. He shuddered as those bad memories came flooding out of the recesses of his mind to play havoc with his inner feelings. He hoped and prayed that others had survived, but, if they had, where were they now? What hope had they of making a journey back to civilisation?

Diarmid had been very, very lucky indeed. Not only was he the only crew member who had managed to get to the row boat, he had ridden out the remains of the storm tucked inside it, and had found the Cranstouns. Together they had found a determination to find a way back to civilisation, wherever that journey would take them. They had fought off all that this world could throw at them, determined to find a way to battle through.

The boy was deep in thought at all these things that had turned out to be life changing and character building, and now they were back within touching distance of where it all began. They had to see it through, no matter what awaited them in the God forsaken, or so it seemed, town of Knympton.

Everet was no less lost in thought, and had to be reminded several times by Myrta to keep his concentration on the road ahead. "I am sure that Swale will take us safely along the way, my dear, but some guidance from you would be welcome," said his wife, as gently as she could. She realised what they were all going through. She too was not exempt from wondering about their reception in Knympton. It had all been going so well until that man Ludley made an appearance, and had threatened all sorts of nastiness. He was the cause of all the hardship and misery they had endured in the past months, and she was determined that he would be brought to justice. Myrta had acquired a new inner strength over her period of shipwreck which caused her to feel that nothing could stop her achieving whatever her wishes might be: as for that Marshal, well, words just failed her.

Aonghus passed the time in conversation with Swale. They talked about Swale's memories of the hard times he had suffered and the nasty people who had owned him. Aonghus winced at some of Swale's tales. How could anyone be so horrible to a beautiful creature like Swale? Aonghus couldn't understand it. "Look at it this way," Swale said, "all these experiences teach you something, so you should always be prepared to look for their meaning. Besides, I persevered through thick and thin until Darvel Snodgrass appeared on the scene, and I was, well, rescued I would say. My whole life turned about for the better from that moment onward."

"So you are suggesting that all our sufferings of late will come to an end, and we will enjoy a better life?" Aonghus asked.

"Everything is possible," replied the pony, "but it is what you make of each opportunity that counts. I understand from what has been said since I was traded to you, that your parents haven't always made the right choices for whatever reason, but not out of badness or a wish not to improve. However, this time they seem determined to do whatever it takes to ensure that their aspirations can be achieved."

"It would be nice not to go through something like this ever again, but I guess you are telling me that I cannot be certain that I won't?" Aonghus said somewhat resignedly.

"You will find that life always offers you many choices," said the pony, "so it is up to you to determine which ones you will accept, and which ones you will reject. Circumstances and experience play a huge part in determining your journey."

Just then Myrta suggested that they stop soon to have something to eat and drink. As they took their break Everet said that their progress was remarkably good, venturing that Knympton would come into view once they rounded a bend in the river not too far distant from where they were now.

"I thought we were not planning on going into Knympton in the dark," said Aonghus, concerned.

"That's right, my son," replied his father. "We're not. What we will do is go so far down the road then cut off into Berystede Wood for the night. You may remember that we had identified a little stream into which we were going to steer the boat. Well, we can still follow that plan, although we haven't got a boat, but I'm sure we will find a pathway that we can follow."

"Is there one showing on the map?" asked Diarmid.

Everet retrieved the map from the trailer, and they all had a good look at it, each one trying to find a suitable turn-off point from the highway. Having discussed the options quite thoroughly, they came to a decision about where they would leave the main road to head into the obscurity of the wood where, hopefully, they would spend a last night as refugees, before riding into town with a great determination to resolve their situation.

*****

Some hours later they reached the point on the road where they had identified that they must detour, and Everet pulled on the reins for Swale to bring the cart to a halt. "We must wait for some of this traffic to pass us by before we leave the road," said Everet. "I do not want too many people to see us leaving the relative safety of the highway for a minor road."

They waited until the road was as quiet as they thought it would get then moved across into the side road. Several hundred yards along the road they stopped again. "We'll wait here for a little while, just to make sure that nobody is following us," said Everet. "Can't be too careful."

Satisfied that they were quite alone, Everet set the cart back in motion at a slower pace: not only was the road of inferior quality, darkness was beginning to descend, and they needed to pick their way carefully forward. Eventually they stopped for the night in a clearing close to a small stream, and set about reconstructing their makeshift shelter for what they hoped was the last time. They lit a fire, prepared and ate their meal, then settled down to sleep. Tomorrow would test them to the full.

*****

Unbeknown to the Cranstouns they were being watched. Archangel Michael, always on guard at Brina's cottage became aware of the Cranstouns' presence and he was watching their every move as they unwittingly headed towards the Shaman's home. Michael, dutiful as always, reported to Brina that there were strangers in her vicinity.

"Do they seem aggressive?" asked Brina.

"They are not showing any signs of being so," said the Angel, "although there are a lot of emotional vibrations surrounding them."

"Tell me more, please," said Brina.

"There are four people. They have travelled in a little cart pulled by a pony. There are two adults and their child, plus an older lad. They seem a stable enough group but they are obviously concerned about some great matter which has troubled them for some time, and continues to do so," said Michael. "Other than that, you know I cannot take matters any further without a personal invitation."

"Of course," said Brina. "Please continue to monitor them, Michael." She got up from where she was seated and consulted her Book of Spells. Having found what she was seeking, she invoked the magic that would cast an invisible barrier around the strangers.

She returned to her chair and sat down. "Yorlan," she said quietly, "do you think you are fit enough to see some more visitors tomorrow?"

"Yes," said the Marshal, "I think I should be able to handle that. Who is it?"

"I am pleased that you feel able, Yorlan," said the Shaman, "but it may be exhausting and very emotive. If your visitors are who I believe them to be then another great step forward in your healing process will have been taken."

"You don't mean Ludley and Boffe, do you?" asked Mung suddenly on edge.

269

"No, Yorlan, you are not quite ready for them," said Brina, "but I do believe you are ready to face the Cranstouns."

Mung's face was a picture of amazement and astonishment. "The Cranstouns are here? In Knympton?"

"I believe so," said the Crone. "Camping in the wood not far from here."

"I would like to try to make peace with them," said Mung. "I imagine they will be more upset with me than I am with them. In truth I treated them like dirt, like nothing, and because of it they felt they had to flee. Goodness only knows what happened to them."

"Perhaps we will find out tomorrow," said Brina. "Try not to let this interfere with your sleep." Brina settled herself down to engage with Swale.

Chapter 55: Unexpected Encounters

Sefira Mung got up early and prepared her breakfast. As she ate it she pondered on the meeting she had had with Captain Folgate in the Church. How coincidental she had thought when it occurred, but now she was not so sure. One thing was certain; she didn't really understand why she was in Church: she hadn't attended for some long time, but then, last night, she had this urgent need to go to Church, without knowing why. The feeling was so powerful that she had to give in to it, and what a surprise it had been to find the Captain there too.

Folgate, for his part, had also seemed somewhat taken aback to find her there, but now, having had time to think about it all, she could see that indeed there had been invisible hands involved. At this point Sefira made the sign of the cross. "*In the name of the Father, Son and Holy Ghost,*" she murmured. Folgate had told her of his need to see Yorlan again, as soon as could be arranged. There were still some matters regarding this whole sorry mess that the Captain was unable to understand: the puzzle was still missing some pieces. Yorlan's confession had not answered all the questions. Sefira promised that she would make contact with Brina at the soonest opportunity and report back to him.

After breakfast Sefira cleared the table, washed and dried her dishes which she returned to their designated places in the cupboard, then went to get her coat and hat. She made a final check of the house before going out the front door and locking up. She looked up and down the street as she exited the gate, and, satisfied that she wasn't being watched, made her way towards town.

Every so often, as had become her habit, Sefira stopped at a stall or shop window just to double check that she was quite alone. For some time now it seemed as if Ludley had called off the watching brief, largely because, she liked to think, that no useful information was ever gathered. Still happy, she proceeded to Bruno's shop where she was greeted most courteously.

After exchanging pleasantries with Bruno, Sefira told him of Folgate's wish to meet up with Mung as soon as could be arranged in order to make progress, and hopefully bring the case to an end. Bruno said that he would pass the message on to Brina, and that she should go home and await contact.

*****

Brina also rose early that morning, and, satisfied that Mung was comfortably asleep, carefully gathered together those items that she would need in order to perform what she had to do. With her accoutrements loaded in her basket she left the cottage and proceeded to the little clearing she favoured when involved in her nature magic.

As was her ritual, Brina blessed the sacred space and entered into the circle she had drawn. She sat down at its centre, reaching into her bag from which

271

she extracted a white candle, some incense and her flint tool. She lit the incense, watching the smoke rise and disappear at the point where the visible Universe becomes one with the invisible. She took several deep breaths to compose herself: now she was ready for her special meditation.

She called on Archangel Michael to cast his cloak of protection around her and the Cranstouns, and to be on guard against any dark forces with his mighty sword: she felt Michael's cloak swathe round her, sensing also that his shield and sword were not far off either; protection was hers. To further assist her she called on Ariel and Sofiel, the Angels of Nature to oversee the needs of the animal with whom she was about to enter into contact; she called on Ambriel, the Angel of Communication to ensure that the message to be delivered was clear and understandable. There were shimmerings of light as the angels came to assist Brina.

She closed her eyes and after a few minutes was aware of her consciousness expanding outwards through the woods in the direction of the Cranstouns' camp. Gradually, she could feel the pony's spirit growing stronger and there with her in the circle. She felt the energy coursing throughout its body and its breathing escaping into the sounds of silence around them: Swale felt a similar awareness of Brina's spirit.

She felt the transformation beginning to happen. Slowly, she opened her eyes, and gazed unfocusedly out beyond the circle, seeing herself fully immersed into the pony. She welcomed it and allowed it to speak to her. She asked the pony if it would help to resolve the situation in which the Cranstouns had found themselves: Swale agreed.

Brina was somewhat surprised, pleasantly, that Aonghus Cranstoun had the ability to talk to animals and had had several conversations with Swale during their journey. "That indeed is a talent to have discovered," Brina said to the pony.

"Yes," agreed Swale, "and it has been very beneficial to them. Indeed it has led to their survival on at least one occasion."

"That is wonderful," said the Shaman, and she continued her conversation with Swale, outlining her plans for bringing the Cranstouns to her cottage to meet Mung. However, she asked Swale not to mention the Marshal, but to assure the Cranstouns that they would be perfectly safe: Swale assured her that he would do as she asked.

Brina then began to withdraw from the connection, telling Swale that she would see him very soon, and thanked Swale for his involvement. Brina slowly brought her senses back to the present, gathered up her items and returned to the cottage to prepare breakfast.

*****

The Cranstouns were awakened by a serious of snorts and neighs from Swale: Diarmid was first to react, emerging from the makeshift tent totally

272

alert and on his guard. Everet followed closely behind, looking all around for the source of whatever had caused Swale to react. They had a very good look round, but found nothing untoward, so could not understand what had caused the pony's actions.

By this time Aonghus was on the scene and he was stroking Swale's head, soothing him. "Are you alright?" Aonghus asked.

"Oh yes, just a strange pony dream. Everything is back to normal now, thank you. Please, have your breakfast then I will tell you some more. In fact I will tell you the whole of it."

Aonghus relayed the message to the others who looked at each other in mild puzzlement. "If that's all it was, then let's just get on with things," said Myrta. "This is going to be a challenging day for us all."

Aonghus was intrigued by Swale's offer to tell more: what did a pony dream about? He couldn't begin to imagine, and so he hurried down his breakfast, such was his excitement. The lad went over to where Swale was chewing on some nettles, sat down quietly beside his equine friend and gathered his thoughts. "Hello, my friend," he said. "Please tell me about your dream."

Swale began by apologising for not quite having told the whole truth about what had happened. He explained that he didn't want to cause alarm, and for the family to have their breakfast as normal. He then told Aonghus what really occurred. Aonghus was perturbed by a number of things Swale related and asked if there was anything further. Swale assured him that he had heard everything and that, despite the forebodings, everything would be alright.

Aonghus returned to the rest of the group looking rather dejected. "What's wrong, sweetheart?" asked Myrta, looking up.

"Swale's dream wasn't a dream after all," said Aonghus. "It was contact from a lady who lives in these woods."

Now he had everyone's attention: "Go on," said Everet. "We are all ears."

Aonghus sat down beside his mother and began to relate Swale's story. He told them that Swale had become aware of a lady's presence, but the lady, although close by, was a little distance away. This lady obviously could converse with Swale without being close enough to see him, and must therefore be some sort of strange woman indeed.

The lad reported that the woman not only knew of the party's arrival in the woods but also knew who they were. This caused consternation amongst the group who began to wonder what they had wandered into. They knew that their journey was going to have a difficult end, but this complication was totally unexpected. She had contacted Swale to get some background details, and she was soon to arrive at the camp in person. According to Swale there was nothing to fear: the lady, called Brina, had woven some magic spell of

273

protection around them to keep them from prying eyes and unwelcome enquiries.

"This doesn't sound very good," said Everet. "What can this woman want with us?"

"Who knows?" said his wife. "Perhaps we may not have long to wait to find out. Swale seems to think she has good intentions, therefore all we can do is keep an open mind about it. We have had enormous amounts of help from unexpected places, and this just may be another instance."

"You are right, my dear," said Everet. "However, let's take our attention away from it by getting our possessions, such as they are, back on the cart, then we will be ready to move into town after this woman's visit."

*****

Although they were expecting the visit and thought they were keeping a good lookout for her arrival, Brina turned up almost as if by magic, taking the Cranstouns by surprise. "Hello!" said the Shaman. "My name is Brina and I hope you were expecting me. I am sorry if my arrival has taken you by surprise."

"No, no," Everet replied. "Well, yes is what I really mean. Yes, we were expecting you, but you have caught us somewhat off guard. Anyway, welcome Brina, I am Everet Cranstoun, this is my wife Myrta and son Aonghus. This young man is Diarmid who has been an inspiration to us all, and without whom we would probably have perished in some remote spot."

Brina acknowledged each one as they were introduced. "You may be wondering all sorts of things," she said to them, "but I am here to help you resolve the situation you are in."

"How do you know about our situation?" Myrta enquired.

"From various sources which will become apparent," Brina replied, "but I would like to hear your account of things, if you would like to tell me it: that would allow me to see the whole picture. I appreciate that I am a complete stranger who has turned up unexpectedly and in a less than straightforward manner. However, I am trustworthy and I would not do anything that would put you in any danger."

"You have told us who you are," said Everet, "but not what you do. Also, it would be helpful to know how you fit into this bigger picture that you want to be able to see."

"I will happily do that," said Brina, "but let's all sit down and make ourselves comfortable." She began to tell them about what she did: she told them that there were many perceptions of her in Knympton. Some said she had occult powers: powers to gather up the past, powers to glimpse into the future, powers to bring about bad tidings, powers to heal.

She explained that sometimes she gave advice and magical gifts to visitors who were pure of heart, whilst some came searching for wisdom, knowledge and truth: to those who asked she always helped.

"Mostly, though," she said, "I get approached for healing, especially when all other attempts have failed: a kind of last resort. I have a very special gift for healing, just like you, Aonghus, have a very special gift for talking to the animals, and I have very good success rate. It has been said of me that I change everything I touch and that everything I touch changes."

"Is this why you live out here in Berystede Wood?" asked Myrta. "Because the townsfolk find you strange?"

"Partly," replied Brina, "but also because I am in communion with Nature, the Universe, and All there is. I have daily conversations with the Nature Spirits, the Angels, the Archangels and the other Beings of Light, and I need the quiet to maximise the experience."

"So how do we fit into your world?" asked Everet. "We lived in Knympton for some time, but have never been aware of your existence."

"Through a request for healing," said the Shaman. "My patient is the link and he is at a point in his recovery where he needs to meet you. But tell me this, Everet. Why have you returned?"

"We have returned to right a wrong," said Everet. "We need to do this for our own development. You have hinted that you know a lot about us, and I hope you will say more about that: for too long we have run away from confrontation, and it has done us no real good. Now we must face up to those who have threatened us, and declare who we really are. Now, as to your patient, someone we know?"

"You may recognise him when you see him, if seeing him is what you want to do," Brina said, "but you won't recognise his name."

"If he is one who had any part to play in what we have suffered, then we will most certainly want to see him," said Everet, "and I do believe I can say that on behalf of the whole party." The others nodded their agreement.

"So be it!" said the Shaman. "But first tell me your story."

Everet, Myrta, Aonghus and Diarmid proceeded to relate their version of events from Ludley's first appearance through their hurried departure, the awful storm, the post-shipwreck traumas, the Abbeystery, their trip down the Kinuli river and their arrival at Berystede Wood in preparation for the return to Knympton.

Brina sat in stunned silence at the story: she realised how little she knew of the Cranstouns' suffering, and her heart went out to them. Every twist and turn she shared with them through a deep empathy. "That is one amazing story," she said, "and soon it will end. It will end in satisfaction I can assure you, but there may well be a few more points where some pain must be endured." Brina explained that what the Cranstouns had told her of their situation up until their departure on *The Venturer* very much coincided with what she had already been told.

"There are several people that you need to confront face to face," she said. "Who do you think you need to face up to?"

"We had planned to go straight to the Marshal Station and begin there," said Everet. "That's where it all went wrong. We reported what Ludley was up to but we got no support from the Marshals. This time we are going to have it out with them, no matter what it takes."

"In that case," said the Crone, "you need to come and talk with my patient now. He is the one who set you on the road to misery and torment. He is the Marshal you spoke to when you tried to get help."

There were cries of disbelief and anger from the group at this news. "Are you harbouring a criminal?" Everet thundered incredulously. "Is there no honesty left in this world?"

Brina agreed that it could be construed in that way, and asked them to calm down. She explained that the Captain of the Marshals had been as angry as they when he first heard the news. She went on to say that the Captain was dealing with the matter because he now had much more information: now that the Cranstouns had arrived meant the case could be brought to justice.

"Come with me to my cottage now," she said softly, "try to remain calm and keep an open mind. The originator of your anguish is a different person today than he was then. Please listen to his story: he needs to confront you as much as you need to confront him. You can leave your belongings here; they will come to no harm: Archangel Michael will look after them for you and keep them safe until you return."

The group had a quick discussion and agreed to go to Brina's cottage.

Brina led the way through the wood to her cottage: it wasn't far after all. She asked the Cranstouns to wait outside whilst she checked that her patient was ready to meet them. As she opened the door she could see Mung sitting in the front room, but there was someone with him: how strange she thought. She scurried in to the room, and was a little surprised to see Bruno.

Bruno explained that he had been visited by Sefira who was passing on a request from the Captain to have further words with Yorlan. "How timely!" Brina exclaimed, "Yes, by all means let him come here. Can you bring the Captain here today? Use the scenic route to bring him." Bruno nodded his agreement. "Tell him it's today or not at all if he is in any doubt."

Bruno left by the kitchen door so that he would not encounter the Cranstouns, and made his way back to town. Brina confirmed that Mung was ready to receive his visitors before ushering the Cranstons into the front room.

Not knowing who or what to expect, the Cranstons entered hesitantly, and stood staring at Mung. The man sitting there bore a likeness to the Marshal who had betrayed them, but if this was the same man, then he had indeed gone through just as big an ordeal as they had. He was leaner, younger looking in some respects, but, rather, had an air of frailty about him.

Mung, for his part, stared back at the Cranstouns, recognising that they too had changed. Where had they been and why had they come back? Hopefully everyone's questions would be answered.

Brina suggested that the Cranstouns sit down and get comfortable: in that position they were less likely to resort to violence, although she did not think that things would get that bad. There would certainly be raised voices and angry words, but she did not expect anything more forceful.

"I recognise you," said Everet. "You were on the desk at the Marshal Station when I reported a threat. You may look a bit different today, but it was you, wasn't it?" Mung agreed that it was he who had taken the complaint. "So why did you do nothing about it?" demanded Everet in a voice that was rising in tone and volume with every word spoken. "Do you realise the grief, anguish and torture we have suffered because of that?"

"Yes," said Diarmid, "you are the Marshal that tried to intercept me when I was delivering a message to Mr Cranstoun. As I recall you came off second best."

"Indeed, indeed," replied Mung. "That also was me, and I came off second best in more ways than you can imagine at this point. I would like to tell you my story, to put matters, well, not right, I don't think I can do that, but maybe I can straighten them out a bit."

"We're all ears," said Everet still showing some anger.

"When I first joined the Marshals many years ago I was full of ambition and wanted to be the best that I could be," said Mung. "However, things started to go wrong when the promotions I expected never materialised." Mung then went on to explain how he started to indulge in beer as a comfort. He started to drink regularly in *The Waggoner's Inn* and that's where he came into contact with Ludley and his crowd, the Black Crows, and was rather quickly persuaded to walk on the wild side of the Law. The rewards were good in the early days of this deceit, but gradually they diminished in value. Mung wanted to step back to the right side of the Law, but he was too deeply embroiled in all the criminal acts that the Black Crows perpetrated.

He related his tale of woe up to the point where the Cranstouns had flown the nest much to Ludley's great displeasure. "Young man," he said looking at Diarmid, "you hurt me sorely when we had our little encounter, but it was nothing to what was to come."

He described his ordeal at having to explain why the Cranstouns had vanished without a trace, and of how Ludley and Boffe had taken him to the Cranstons' shop where he was savagely knifed then left to die with the hope that his death would be blamed on the Cranstouns.

"What!" exclaimed Everet, almost jumping out of his chair. "They wanted the Marshals to think I had killed a Marshal! I can hardly believe that." He was clearly outraged by the suggestion.

"It's true, Mr Cranstoun," said Mung softly, "no matter how unbelievable it sounds. This is the type of man Ludley is. He is cold, heartless and gives nothing for other peoples' feelings. All he wants is his way and he is not a pleasant man when he doesn't get it." Everet slowly sank back into his seat.

"I lost consciousness," Mung went on, "and the next thing I was knew I was here in Brina's cottage. She has explained to me how that happened, and maybe she can do the same for you as I still don't quite understand it all fully."

Brina explained about the higher connections that had been made which enabled her and Ardvon Gruvel to bring Mung to her cottage where she had ministered to him ever since, healing not only his physical wounds, but also attending to his spiritual needs. She also briefly explained what else had happened up to the point where the Cranstouns had arrived back in Berystede Wood.

"That's very interesting, Mr Mung," said Everet somewhat more calmly, "and it explains why you didn't help us. I can't say that I forgive you your sins, for you have caused us untold hardship and misery. Indeed, we too, came close to losing our lives in the aftermath of your disloyalty. Is this kind of treachery widespread within the Marshals? Would we again have been deceived had Brina not intervened?"

"As far as I am aware I was the only bad apple. That day you came into the Station was a stroke of good fortune for me, or so I thought," said Mung. "You picked the exact time I was covering for the Sergeant, and I believed that the information I gleaned would stand me in good stead with Ludley. Well, it did for a while, but then it all turned sour."

"It looks like it turned sour for us all, Mr Mung, although the brighter side has emerged for everyone," said Everet. "From your side of things it would appear that you have rediscovered your old self, and are willing to serve whatever punishment is placed upon you. From our side we too have learned a lot about ourselves to which Brina will bear witness, having heard our story, brief as it was in the telling."

"Yes," agreed Myrta, "it has been very painful, but once we can come face to face with that awful man and see justice done, we too will have come a long way forward in our lives. Hopefully, we can reopen the shop and get back to doing what we do best."

"What about you, Diarmid?" the Crone asked. "Where do you go from here?"

"Like my very good friends here I want to see that gang of crooks put out of harm's way," said the boy. "I don't really know for sure, but I believe I lost a lot of good friends and colleagues when the ship was ripped apart. I need to make contact with the shipping company to find out the exact situation. As for you, Mr Mung, I think that what you did was despicable beyond words. How a trusted member of the Marshals could resort to such a low level is beyond my comprehension, but I am sure you are as contrite as you have indicated. That being so, I wish you no further harm, and sincerely hope that you do indeed continue to walk on the side of right and good."

"That was a mighty fine speech, Diarmid," said Myrta approvingly. "I think you spoke for us all." Then she turned towards Mung and said, "Mr Mung, I don't think you really understand just exactly what we went through because of your skulduggery. We have lost everything we ever strived for, our business, our savings, our possessions and almost our lives, not once but several times. What we went through was almost soul destroying, and all because we had a successful business that attracted the attention of the lowlife of this town who wanted to live off us like leeches. To compound matters, when we needed help we were utterly, completely and absolutely let down by someone in a position of esteem, and supposedly trustworthy. Luckily we are a close family that supports each other, and with Diarmid's great help we have pulled through. Like you, we have gone through a transformation and hopefully we will be the better for it. I am sure that one day we will be able to forgive you your sins, but that day is not today, Mr Mung: I hope you can understand that. Now we need to see this Captain Folgate so that he might have all the evidence he needs to arrest and convict these criminals."

"You are right, my dear," said Everet getting out of his chair, "so we must be on our way. Thank you, Brina, for the intervention which has brought some peace to our troubled breasts. If you could lead us back to our cart we will be on our way."

"I have a better idea," said Brina. "Instead of you going to see Captain Folgate why don't you wait here and have lunch with us. The Captain has indicated that he wants to see Yorlan again, and I have told my go-between to bring him here this afternoon. He will be very surprised, and, I hope, delighted to find you here too."

"That is a good idea," agreed Everet. "We were a bit wary of travelling into the middle of town in case we were recognised and intercepted before we could reach the Marshal Station. Thank you." Everet sat down again.

"Excellent," said Brina. "I will go and prepare something to eat and leave you to chat further."

Chapter 57: A Surprise for the Captain.

Bruno made his way directly to the Marshals' Station where he told Sergeant Trine that his business was with the Captain. Since Bruno would not tell the Sergeant any details, Trine replied that direct access to the Captain was not permitted, so Bruno insisted strongly that the Captain be made available as this was a matter of great urgency, and close to the Captain's heart. Bruno stressed that failure to find Folgate quickly would result in a lost opportunity and cause a setback, the consequences of which were not to be contemplated.

"Wait here," said Trine gruffly, and disappeared through the office door. Within minutes he reappeared along with Folgate who enquired who Bruno might be. "I come with an answer to the request you recently made to a mutual friend," said Bruno, "but I do not discuss things of such importance openly."

"Of course," replied Folgate, "come through to my office." The two men headed for the Captain's office and closed the door behind them.

"You want to see Yorlan Mung again, Captain," Bruno stated, "and I have been sent to take you to that meeting. I am sorry that there is no notice: we need to go now."

Folgate unlocked his drawer and removed the Mung File then relocked the container. He tidied up the papers that were strewn across his desk before indicating that he was ready to depart. As they passed through the main office Folgate called out to Trine that he would not be available for the rest of the day. "This man has brought me important new evidence that I need to pursue urgently," he said.

Bruno led Folgate through the town by yet another route little known to the Captain, but Folgate could appreciate what was going on: neither of them wanted to draw any undue attention to themselves lest prying eyes tell tales. They wove this way and that, down alleys that had seen little traffic, along side streets with some strange looking shops, and occasionally they would venture out into the more public roadways.

Sooner than he expected, Folgate found that they were on the fringes of Berystede Wood, not a particularly pleasant place in the Captain's estimation, and he said as much to Bruno who reassured him that they were in no danger: in any case, they were close to their destination. They trundled up several paths, each one less worn than the last, until at last they came to a clearing. They crossed to the other side, ducked behind a large elm tree, picked up another small path, and soon Brina's cottage came into view.

"Here we are," said Bruno. "This is Brina's cottage. You are privileged Captain, for not many get an invitation to visit. I must leave you at this point and return to my employment. Go ahead and knock on the door, she knows you are here." With that Bruno turned and was gone so quickly that Folgate would have sworn he had disappeared into thin air.

Folgate stood in contemplation for some moments, gathering his thoughts. Mung had certainly contravened the Law and needed to be dealt with accordingly. But then again he had produced a whole load of evidence on which to arrest the band of brigands, which surely was worth some mitigation. His mind seemingly made up he proceeded to the door of the cottage and knocked.

"Ah, Captain Folgate," said Brina as she opened the door, "How nice to see you again: do come in. It's a busy little house today as you will see: some unexpected visitors, but I am sure you won't mind." She ushered the Captain into the front room where everyone else was gathered. "A surprise for you Captain," said Brina. "Can I introduce you to the Cranstoun family?"

Folgate stood there quite taken aback, his mouth opening and closing like a fish out of water. "Well I never!" he stammered. "Welcome back to Knympton. I for one am very glad to see you."

"It was our intention never to return," said Everet, "but events have overtaken that ambition and here we are. We would like to offer whatever assistance you require to put the criminals responsible for these reprehensible acts behind bars for a very long time."

"Yes," said his wife, "and we have heard Mr Mung's story, including his part in all of this. Now we'd like to hear what you have to say about the whole sorry mess."

Folgate sat down in the chair offered by Brina and began to undo his file. He quickly scanned some papers before asking the Cranstouns to relate their story to him which they did. Mung listened intently, giving some further insights into what the Cranstouns were telling, and Folgate, for his part, was asking questions at the points where he needed more clarification or did not fully understand.

It took some time and lots of revisiting before Folgate was finally in a position where he believed he had a cast iron case against Ludley and his crowd. "How many are in this gang?" he asked Mung. Yorlan thought for a moment then began counting them on his fingers, naming them as he went. "Eight," he said, "plus of course there is the Landlord at *The Waggoner's* and me; so ten in total."

"And is there a special time when all the gang can be guaranteed to be in one place?" asked the Captain.

"Yes," Mung replied, "Friday night in the two hours before closing time they will gather in the back room at *The Waggoner's* for a weekly report and a handing out of next week's assignments."

"And you, Mr Cranstoun," said Folgate, "would you be willing to face up to Ludley in *The Waggoner's*?"

"I most certainly would," said Everet indignantly. "It's the whole reason we have returned. You would be there too though, wouldn't you?"

Folgate assured Everet that he wouldn't be alone, that there would be Marshals in plain clothes in attendance, before turning to Brina to ask if Mung's health was up to the same task. Before Brina could answer, Mung replied that he most certainly was: it would be the final act in his purification, as he called it.

"We have three days to plan this operation," said Folgate. "I will work on it and get word to you people when I have sorted it out. Brina how do I get in contact because I cannot possibly go through what I did to get this meeting arranged?"

"I will send Bruno to fetch you here in two days time," said the Shaman. "You will need to work quickly."

"What are we to do?" asked Everet, "We have nowhere to go and I guess you don't want us to show up in Knympton until the trap is sprung."

Brina said that arrangements could be made for the Cranstouns to remain where they were in the wood, and she would see that they were cared for: that way everyone could be informed at the same time. "Now, Captain," she said, "I expect you are wondering how you are going to find your way back to Knympton." Folgate agreed that that was the case.

She told him to go back to the clearing where Bruno had left him, and to sit down in quiet contemplation for a short time. She told him to close his eyes and let the stillness overcome him. She advised him to silently affirm, "I am guided by the Light of God", whilst he sank into the tranquillity. Once he was at peace he was to call on the Angel Sariel and ask to be safely guided back to Knympton. When his short meditation was over she told him to be alert for the signs that Sariel was with him.

Folgate bade his goodbyes to the throng then went on his way. Brina watched until he had reached the clearing. She saw him go to the centre of the clearing and sit down. Satisfied that the Captain was alright she closed the door, and returned to her guests.

The Captain sat down and made himself as comfortable as he could. He closed his eyes and began to say the affirmation. Slowly calmness came over him as he relaxed into it. He asked for help from Angel Sariel for a safe journey back to town. "I do not know my way back from this spot," he confessed, "therefore I ask for a sign that will guide my pathway. I ask that the Light of God will shine upon me and be my guide and protector."

When he opened his eyes he sat there in the stillness, strangely enjoying what it offered him. He looked around seeking the sign that Brina said would be there. Patiently he surveyed all around him then became aware of a small twinkling dim light in front of him, at the edge of the clearing. As he focussed on it, it grew in brightness: he could see it was a pastel green colour and it was dancing, almost as if it was waiting for him to make a move.

Folgate stood up, dusted down his trousers and tunic, then walked across towards the light: at his positive movement the light split further into a dancing cascade of sparkles and began to lead him out of the wood, back to Knympton.

Back in the cottage Aonghus asked Brina why she had given the Captain these instructions. "The Captain has a basic faith, but he needs to strengthen it," she began to explain. "By making contact with the Angels he will realise that help is always available."

She further developed her answer by saying that it is best to compose yourself and wait. It wasn't easy to do, but being still helps you connect with the Angels to get guidance and support from them. "What we have to remember, Aonghus," she said to the boy, "is that we are all one at a spiritual level. Do you understand what I mean?"

Aonghus indicated that he sort of understood. "Focus on the fact that you and others are spiritual beings, and are always connected at that level: so too are the Angels spiritual beings. This assists in bringing harmony at all levels, right down to the physical level, where we mostly operate. If we spiritualise our thoughts, then we bring God's light into our consciousness, whereas, when we get caught up in material thinking, we block out any spiritual guidance which might be available to us."

Aonghus looked a little perplexed. "I know that's a very difficult answer for you to absorb at this time, Aonghus," said the Shaman, "but you know already that even the animals have a spiritual dimension. You know this because you can converse with them without actually speaking. Just extend that fact further and you will see that what I have told you is true."

Brina then said she would accompany the Cranstouns back to their cart, and help them set up their makeshift shelter for the night. "Tomorrow," she said, "we will bring you closer to the cottage so that we can get to know each other a little more."

Chapter 58: Preparations

The Cranstouns moved closer to Brina's cottage where life was a little more comfortable: Brina arranged for some fresh clothes to be brought for them to change into. Sefira Mung brought the stuff along, and had a long chat with them which both parties very much appreciated. There were conversations with Yorlan and Brina too, and altogether progress was most definitely made amongst all concerned.

Brina was also interested in Aonghus' new found ability to converse with animals, and she quizzed him about how he had discovered his gift. Aonghus told her all about the fish who, despite having been killed by him, came to his rescue when the family was greatly threatened in their boat. Brina listened intently, encouraging Aonghus to relive all these wonderful adventures. The boy seemed to grow in confidence as he told the stories.

"Perhaps you have other gifts that are yet to be discovered," said Brina. "Your ability with the animals is totally amazing in one so young."

"Perhaps you can help me to find out," replied the boy.

"Perhaps," Brina replied.

Later Myrta helped Brina to prepare the evening meal, enjoying being in a proper kitchen once again. She hadn't realised how much she enjoyed using her skills to prepare a meal, and her enforced absence from the appropriate facilities had brought it all home to her. She was the veritable queen of culinary creation, and even simple ingredients she could turn into a feast of great simplicity and value. Brina, recognising the pleasure that Myrta was getting from cooking, stepped back a little from the action, merely acting as go-for or indicating where implements might be found. Occasionally, she would make a suggestion about the preparation.

The meal, when served, was delicious, and compliments were paid to Myrta from one and all. The experience was such that there was little talk, but then again, that's how the Cranstouns preferred to eat their main meal.

Afterwards they cleared up and then Everet, Yorlan and Brina got themselves ready for the trip into Knympton, and the much hoped for witnessing of the downfall of the Black Crows. Before they left, the whole group gathered together and entered the silence. Brina asked for the help of various Archangels and asked the group members to send out positive thoughts about the events that were soon to take place. "Visualise the outcome," she softly intoned. "See it all unfold in your mind's eye."

Myrta, Aonghus and Diarmid wished them well, and urged them to be careful as they left for town, promising that they would return to the quiet to continue sending out positive thoughts. Brina led the two men down various pathways which just seemed to open up in front of their very eyes, and they made good progress.

Once they reached the fringes of town Brina let Yorlan lead the way to the Marshals' Station where they would be briefed on the details of the plan by Captain Folgate. He took them down streets that had some traffic, but not overly busy. The people they passed hardly gave them a second look as they made their way steadily towards the Marshals' Station. When they arrived they were ushered into the Briefing Hall by Sergeant Trine who shook Mung's hand. "Good to see you again, Constable," he said. They took their seats at the back of the room and awaited Folgate's entrance. As they waited a few of the Marshals turned round and nodded acknowledgement to Mung.

At last Folgate arrived, carrying a large sheaf of papers which he laid on the lectern at the front of the gathered assembly. "Gentlemen, and lady, tonight is an important night for the Force. At long last we have an opportunity to clear up a great many unsolved crimes in one fell swoop," said Folgate, his voice booming out. "We have this opportunity largely due to very valuable information gleaned by Constable Mung who was savagely beaten by these brigands in the process of gathering this evidence, and we also have tremendous witness from Mr Cranstoun and his family who were threatened by this foul bunch to the point where they felt they had to get out of town fast."

He explained what had happened with Mung, framing his account in such a way that Mung's treachery was not exposed to the rest of his comrades, and how Mung had been set upon by the gang who had left him for dead. "You will know that we found Mung's badge in Mr Cranstoun's workroom, and with no sign of Mr Cranstoun and his family our suspicions naturally fell upon them for whatever had happened to our colleague. Let me emphasise that Mr Cranstoun and his family are entirely innocent of any misdemeanour, and indeed have suffered much themselves. Here is what we are going to do to rectify matters and show the people of Knympton that we are a force to be reckoned with."

"Any questions?" he asked when he had finished his briefing. Nobody raised any, so Folgate told them to get going and get into position. Layford, who had been delegated to accompany Mung, Everet and Brina to *The Waggoner's*, joined them at the back of the Briefing Hall. "We'll give the lads a little head start to get into position. Are you ready for this?" he said.

"Oh yes," Mung replied.

"Most definitely," Everet affirmed.

Chapter 59: A Trip to The Waggoner's

After a little while they made their move, saying goodbye to Trine who was left to take charge at the Station. "Good luck!" the Sergeant called out as they closed the door behind them. The four of them made their way at a steady pace to *The Waggoner's*. Brina kept a watchful eye on Mung's walking ability, ready to bring things to a halt if she felt that he was losing energy. As they reached the final corner Layford asked them to stop and wait whilst he went on ahead to check if everyone else was in position.

He headed round the back of the Inn and met up with the Captain: the trap was indeed set, everyone was in position, nobody could escape from the back room of the Inn, no matter how hard they tried. Layford walked back to the others trying to remain calm and not let the excitement get to him.

"Everything's in place," he reported, "so let's go." They rounded the last corner and proceeded to the Inn, opened the door and entered the saloon. They stopped just inside the door and took a look around. It was very busy, as would be expected for a Friday night: also, it was late enough for the early drinkers to begin to feel the effects of the ale, and so the noise was a raucous, happy sort of noise, but so loud it was difficult to hear what anyone said. The barmaids were overworked trying to serve their thirsty clients, and there was much interaction between the servers and the served.

It was everything that Everet had no taste for, but he was here to awaken justice by facing those who had caused him near ruin, great mental anguish and severe physical discomfort. He was doing this for himself and for his family and nothing, not even this bawdy establishment was going to prevent him doing so.

Mung surveyed the scene which brought back memories of the times he had been in the back room with the rest of the Black Crows. Through there it was quieter, where many crimes had been planned over a tankard of *Moonraker*, a moderately strong fermented ale, imported from the south of Valkanda at considerable expense, only made available to Ludley's crowd, and not for sale to the general public. He would take pleasure in ordering the brew, and was keen to find out how George the landlord would react.

Brina, like Everet, was on edge on entering. Her senses told her this was not a nice place: not now, not when it was empty, not ever. She drew the cloak of protection ever closer round the group and waited for Layford's instructions. She tried not to notice the peering, leering eyes of the intoxicated as they fell upon her, but she knew what was in the minds of the viewers.

Layford surveyed the scene with the eye of a professional on a mission. He spotted several of the plain clothed Marshals seated together at a table close to the bar and nodded discretely to them: they acknowledged his presence. Litton was so well hidden close to the door they had just come through that Layford almost missed him, but again a tactful recognition was made. Satisfied that all was well for the springing of the trap he gave Mung the go ahead.

Mung, Everet and Brina squeezed through the crowd as best they could, trying hard not to disturb anyone's drink and inched their way to the end of the bar where Mung had spotted the landlord. Yorlan remembered that from where George was standing he could keep an eye on both the saloon and Ludley's back room. Finally, they found a space at the servery.

"Landlord!" Mung called out. "Some service if you will."

George looked at the three new arrivals and sauntered towards them, eyeing them up and down. "Yes, what would you like?"

"Two tankards of *Moonraker* please, and something a little less strong for the lady, please" Mung ordered.

"Ah, that's not a brew we serve in here, sir," said George. "Indeed I know of nowhere in Knympton where you can buy that."

"Don't be silly, George," said Mung. "You keep a barrel of the stuff just over there where you were standing. I know you don't normally serve it on this side of the house, but we'll have some for old time's sake."

The landlord looked a little perturbed and gave the group a quizzed look. "You look as if you are trying to remember something, landlord," said Everet, "Let me help you. You certainly don't know me, for normally I would never dream of entering a squalid drinking den like this, but my name is Everet Cranstoun and I used to run a very successful viander's business in town. Successful that was until your clients on the other side of that wall," said Everet pointing behind the landlord, "put paid to that with their criminal actions."

"I am not sure what you mean, sir," said George trying to keep his temper.

"Don't tell me you don't recognise me either, George," said Mung. "It's been a while but I am back. Constable Mung. Now get Ludley and Boffe round here now."

The colour drained from George's face and he reached out to cling to the bar for support, without which he would most likely have fallen to the ground in shock. "Mung?" he barely whispered, "but you're dead. Cranstoun killed you."

"Do I look dead?" asked Mung. "And would I go out drinking with my assailant? Will you tell Ludley or will I summon him?"

George, with a new found burst of energy, turned on his heels and headed for the back room. He burst in, all a fluster. "Ludley, come quick," he pleaded, "you're not going to believe this."

"Settle down, George," said Ludley. "What's rattled your cage?"

"Mung and Cranstoun," said the landlord. "They're out the front at the bar demanding to see you."

A silence fell over the gang: Ludley's faced flushed with anger. "Are you having me on, George?" he asked, his voice raised. "So help me, I will have your guts for garters if you are playing tricks," he went on, getting up from his chair. "Show me," he demanded. Boffe got up to accompany his leader, patting his waistband to make sure his knife was to hand.

By this time the plain clothed Marshals had moved into position close by Mung, Everet and Brina: they too were as ready for action as Boffe. Ludley was first to appear, closely followed by Boffe, and took a good look along the bar. "Hello, Mr Ludley," Everet called out. "How nice to see you again. Are you still running your little protection racket? I am here to see you get paid."

"It is you," said Ludley approaching, "and now I am in better light, I can see that you have brought that old has been, Mung, with you. Why don't you come round into the back room where we can better discuss business?"

Layford gave Litton a sign, and the latter rapidly left the saloon to signal to the others that the gang had been engaged. Layford then stepped forward with his colleagues and told Ludley and Boffe that they were under arrest. The crooks turned to make their escape via the back room, but found that the Marshals had already stormed it from the outside and that there was no escape.

Boffe reached for his waistband: however, Layford was quicker, and laid him out with a thunderous blow to his jaw, sending him crashing onto a table the legs of which gave way under the force. Ludley was about to try the same manoeuvre, but hesitated just long enough to feel the effect of Layford's other fist which sent him, too, sprawling backwards: Layford followed up and completed the job with another booming punch.

Seeing their two leaders laid out on the floor took the heart out of any fighting spirit the rest of the gang may have had, and they gave themselves up meekly to the Marshals. The Black Crows' wings had been well and truly clipped and they were clapped in hand irons before being led away to the waiting Marshal Wagon. Ludley and Boffe, after being cuffed, were unceremoniously thrown in the back of the wagon and lay on its floor, still unconscious.

Folgate, accompanied by the uniformed Marshals, entered the servery where he rang the bell loudly, demanding silence. "This establishment is now closed," he boomed, "Marshals, clear the place, and arrest anyone who gives any trouble. He turned to George and asked for the keys. "I will lock up," he said to George, "and you will be locked up."

"You should shew forth the praises of Him who hath called you out of darkness into his marvellous light." (1 Peter 2:9, King James Bible)

Bless them which persecute you: bless, and curse not. Be not overcome of evil, but overcome evil with good. (Romans 12:14, 21 King James Bible)

Epilogue

The court case lasted barely a week, played out in front of a packed courtroom: the public galleries were full to capacity each day. The recess for the jury's deliberation lasted less than an hour. The eight members of the Black Crows were found guilty of multiple instances of robbery, assault, fraud, extortion and actual bodily harm. For this they were each sentenced to fifteen years imprisonment at the notorious Saughtonhead prison, an establishment where compassion was unknown. In addition, Ludley and Boffe were found guilty of the attempted murder of a Marshal and trying to pervert the course of justice: a minimum sentence of thirty years imprisonment was ordered to be served consecutively with the previous sentence.

For providing a place of shelter for known criminals, and also for perverting the course of justice, George, the landlord, was given a custodial sentence of five years: his licence to sell alcohol was revoked with immediate effect.

Mung was found as guilty as the Black Crows and had the same sentence handed down. However, due to the evidence and information he had supplied this was mitigated to a three year suspended sentence, and he was ordered to give one hundred hours of his time to serve community projects. He was dismissed from the Marshals, but found employment in Bruno's Emporium.

The Cranstouns were awarded sufficient compensation by the Court for them to refurnish their accommodation, pay off what debts had accrued in their absence and to reopen the Viandery, which has flourished. Aonghus still continues to develop his spiritual gifts with Brina as his mentor and teacher.

Diarmid reported for duty at the local office of The Clerton Mercers where he told his story to the clerk. He was informed that, to date, nobody else was known to have survived the storm. He was thanked for the information, as nobody knew what had happened to *The Venturer*, only that it had been assumed lost in that freak storm. He was promoted to leading seaman and serves aboard *The Pride of Pender*. He still keeps in touch with the Cranstouns when he is in Knympton.